The German Suitcase

The German Suitcase

A Novel

Greg Dinallo

PREMIER
DIGITAL PUBLISHING

Premier Digital Publishing - Los Angeles

ISBN-13: 978-1-62467-026-8
ISBN-10: 1624670261

Premier Digital Publishing

www.PremierDigitalPublishing.com

Follow us on Twitter @PDigitalPub

Follow us on Facebook: Premier Digital Publishing

THE OATHS

"The physician must be able to tell the antecedents, know the present, and foretell the future - must mediate these things, and have two special objects in view with regard to disease, namely, to do good or to do no harm."

Hippocrates, *The Epidemics*

"I swear to thee Adolph Hitler, as Führer and Chancellor of the German Reich, loyalty and bravery. I vow to thee, and to the superiors whom thou shalt appoint, obedience unto death. So help me God."

Oath sworn by members of the SS

"I will neither treat any patient, nor carry out any research on any human being without the valid informed consent of the subject...While I continue to keep this Oath unviolated may it be granted to me to enjoy life and the practice of the art and science of medicine with the blessing of the Almighty and respected by my peers and society, but should I trespass and violate this Oath, may the reverse be my lot."

Hippocrates, Oath sworn by physicians

DEDICATION

For my grandchildren, Robert, age 12 and Amelia age 10, whose inherent goodness, sense of adventure, love of laughter, and tolerance for their fellow man have—despite their tender years—made the world a better place; and for their parents Eric Dinallo and Priscilla Almodovar whose altruism, personal integrity and commitment to public service have taught by example; and, especially, for my wife Gloria whose strength of character, grace under pressure, intellectual curiosity, willingness to take chances, creative depth, and unconditional love have given me the most wonderful life for more than fifty years.

ACKNOWLEDGEMENTS

For historical information, technical data, psychological analysis, and the testimony of those who survived, I am greatly indebted to the following authors and their scholarly works: Martin Gilbert, <u>The Second World War</u>; Heinz Hohne, <u>The Order of the Death's Head</u>, The Story of Hitler's SS; Dr. Robert Jay Lifton, <u>The Nazi Doctors</u>, Medical Killing and the Psychology of Genocide; and Michael Selzer <u>Deliverance Day</u>, The Last Hours at Dachau.

The anecdotes, observations and inner workings of the worlds of advertising, graphic design, photography, and fine art are from personal experience and a life-long immersion in the visual arts and creative expression.

PROLOGUE

Adolph Hitler's elite SS guard operated out of a fortress of deeply stained limestone in the center of Munich next to Nazi Party Headquarters. The Order of the Death's Head was ruled with ruthless precision by Reichsführer Heinrich Himmler and struck terror in the hearts of everyone who had contact with its black-uniformed henchmen as well as those lucky enough to avoid it. Indeed, in the more than two decades that the SS was in existence, many more German citizens went into No. 50 Schellingstrasse than ever came out. The concentration camps—invented by Himmler and operated by his SS—exterminated millions of Jews and other imagined threats to the National Socialist's obsession with racial purity, and incarcerated and/or killed many additional millions of political prisoners including Bolsheviks, Clergymen, Communists, Liberals and members of other groups, or individuals, judged to be an enemy of Hitler's plan for world domination.

"He's my Ignatius Loyola," Hitler once said of his Reichsführer. "Yes, faith! Faith in his Führer! That's what inspired him to transform the SS from a weak and ineffective organization into the one of bone-crushing power and iron-fisted discipline that we have now! And what was his stroke of genius? To infuse it with the principles of the Order of Jesuits! Who else but the Reichsführer would have thought of it? Can you imagine? An entire army of Nazi warriors who, just like Loyola's dedicated priests, swear eternal loyalty and blind obedience to their God and their Pope!" The Führer didn't feel the need to name the god and pope to whom he was referring. Indeed, his fervent approval of Himmler's choice of role models wasn't surprising; nor was their choice of staunchly Catholic Bavaria and its capitol city Munich—which means monk in German—as the springboard for their rise to power, since both men had been raised as devout Catholics.

Those were headier times. Now, more than six months after the Allied invasion of Normandy, Russian troops were advancing on Berlin from the East, and American and British forces were sweeping across France and Holland toward the Rhine from the West. However, one of the worst winters on record had slowed the ground offensive and kept the Allies from achieving their goal of ending the war by Christmas. The Führer, driven by ever-growing disillusionment and denial, had taken to his bunker clinging to the fantasy that his vaunted Schutz-Staffel would take advantage of the heavy snows and sub-freezing temperatures and, somehow miraculously, turn the tide of the war.

Under such extreme pressure, the control-obsessed Himmler had become all the more intent on keeping the troops in line. He had always mistrusted the German upper class and aristocracy from which the officer corps was traditionally drawn because their allegiance was, and always would be, to the military and the nation, not the Nazi party. The fact that, more than once, and as recently as last July, groups of officers born to privilege had attempted to assassinate the Führer, intensified Himmler's paranoia. In a desperate effort to tighten his grip—to insure the unquestioned and immediate execution of any order he issued—the Reichsführer had begun replacing Army officers with Party functionaries and political zealots, who had little military training, but would ruthlessly and brutally enforce National Socialist doctrine.

CHAPTER ONE

New York City, Monday, June 1, 2009

"Hey boss, it's me! —Yeah, yeah I got it! A stroke of genius," Stacey Dutton exclaimed into her cellphone, her spiky blond hair bristling with excitement. She had the Blackberry in her left hand, and the handle of an old suitcase that she had just found on the street clutched in her right. "Yeah, I wracked my brain all weekend and came up with nada. This morning, I'm leaving my building and damn near tripped over it. — Yeah, go figure — Nope. Nope, you're gonna have to wait til I get there. Ciao."

Stacey spotted the battered suitcase amidst the rolling hillside of trash bags, discarded furniture, household items, and miscellaneous building materials awaiting pick-up outside the West 79th Street service entrance of The Apthorp. Built by John Jacob Astor, the elegant pre-war apartment building had a barrel-arched entrance flanked by ornate iron gates that opened onto a courtyard with two marble fountains and limestone benches shaded by perfectly scaled trees…much like the Florentine palace after which it was modeled. Home to an eclectic group of the Upper West Side's wealthy elite, it had long been a source of high quality junk. Now, the once rent-controlled dowager was being turned into luxury condominiums; and the mass turnover of units and the emptying of storage rooms of belongings abandoned by long-departed tenants, had turned it into the mother lode. Far from unique to The Apthorp, this citywide scavenger hunt had been fueled by the real estate boom; and the stories of Manhattanites who had renovated and/or furnished entire apartments with what they'd found on the street were legendary.

Stacey Dutton was one of them. But this morning's find had nothing to do with her one bedroom, one bath with a view of The Apthorp's service entrance. As a copywriter for Gunther Global, a full service advertising agency, Stacey had been tapped to come up with a campaign idea for a client who was threatening to pull his account; and it was her quirky personality and nanosecond-fast cortex that had caused her boss to pull her off other assignments and have her work on this one, exclusively. Indeed, Stacey had one of those minds; the kind that when asked by a teacher to provide a synonym for friend, enabled her, without missing a beat, to reply: Tumor. And when the baffled fellow asked, Why? to answer: Because they both grow on you.

The hefty suitcase pre-dated roll-aboards, and lugging it around the city was a formidable task for its petite savior. So, instead of taking the subway, Stacey hailed a taxi. The driver swerved across two lanes cutting off a competitor and a city bus that almost rear-ended him. Stacey slithered between the bumpers and tossed the suitcase into the trunk. When she climbed into the back seat, the news crawl on the built-in TV screen read: OBAMA TO VISIT CAIRO. HOPES FOR MID-EAST PEACE RISE. The Pakistani cabbie stopped talking on his cellphone long enough to ask, "JFK? LaGuardia? Newark? Where you go?"

"No, no, Fifty-first and Park," Stacey replied.

"But you have suitcase!" the driver erupted. "Suitcase! With suitcase you go to airport! Forty-five dollars fare!" He capitulated with an angry groan and went careening down Broadway.

There were days Stacey wondered what she was doing in the advertising business. She'd long-ago given up trying to explain it to her family, all God-fearing, football-crazed Texans who drove pick-up trucks with gun racks and Sarah-cuda bumper stickers. It wasn't exactly where the editor of *Westerner World*, the Lubbock High newspaper, who had submitted short stories to The New Yorker as a teenager, and majored in creative writing and journalism at Columbia planned to end up. But Stacey was earning a living; and saddled with hefty student loans, she really needed to earn a living. Then again, Mad Men was the hottest show on TV, and she was Gunther Global's reincarnation of Peggy Olson, and then some…if fifty years after the fact.

Her quirky mind was fully engaged, accelerating like her boss' anthracite-black Porsche down the Long Island Expressway; and she knew from experience that once the creative fire started burning it wouldn't go out. She could already envision the print ads, the TV spots, and the internet pop-ups, along with the lines of snappy copy, and the lyrics for jingles. Indeed, she could see the entire ad campaign laid out in front of her. It was as if all the pieces of a puzzle had suddenly leapt out of the box onto the table and locked into place forming a complete picture; and as the cab snaked its way through rush hour traffic, Stacey's thumbs were dancing across the keys of her Blackberry, recording the ideas that kept coming.

CHAPTER TWO

Munich, Germany, Monday, January 8, 1945

Like all Nazi installations, the facade of SS Headquarters on Schellingstrasse was brashly identified by enormous flags. The white-circled swastikas, set against bright orange fields, shimmered ominously in the icy winter light. The massive steel door beneath them swung open, and a young captain strode through it into the snowy street at a hurried pace. Square-shouldered and trim, he had a strong profile and the military bearing prized by the leaders of the Third Reich. The distinctive all-black uniform of the SS—belted jacket, jodhpurs, jackboots, swastika armband, and cap with silver skull-and-crossbones perched above the peak—gave him an air of frightening authority. Though he had the panther-like stride of a Himmler acolyte, a closer look would reveal the serpent crest of the caduceus on his collar insignia, and the precise surgeon's hands that, protected from the cold by black leather gloves, were clenched into fists, one of which held a cigarette. The University District was at the opposite end of Schellingstrasse. Less than a fifteen minute walk from SS Headquarters. He wanted to run but didn't dare. He couldn't even chance being seen at the Medical School, now. Not after what had just happened. Not after the harrowing night he'd spent being interrogated by an SS major named Steig.

The streets were busy with pedestrians bundled against the cold, trailing streams of gray breath behind them. Edgy, exhausted, eyes sunken from fear and lack of sleep, Dr. Maximilian Kleist, Captain, Waffen-SS, moved swiftly between them, his woolen greatcoat, left unbuttoned in haste, flowing behind him. The workers and students who were trudging through the snow-blanketed city to offices, factories and schools that had survived the relentless Allied air

3

strikes, gave him wide berth as he came toward them, his jackboots clacking on the frozen pavement.

Yesterday, the industrial districts of Neuhausen and Schwabing had been heavily bombed; and the winter air was thick with the pungent smell of explosives, centuries old dust, and death. Rescue crews, hampered by the weather were still finding survivors in the collapsed buildings. The smoldering rubble was dotted with bits of brightly colored Christmas wrapping and the sparkle of shattered glass ornaments. The most seriously injured were taken either to the General Hospital in the Medical District southwest of the city, or to the Medical School and affiliated hospital in the nearby University District. At the latter, every member of the staff—doctors, nurses, professors and medical students—had been working round the clock treating casualties. Despite the chaos, things were gradually returning to what, during the war, had come to be considered normal, and classes had resumed.

Captain Kleist had almost reached the corner of Lentnerstrasse where he knew there was a public telephone. It was one of the few in the area that still worked and he had used it often, but never in such extreme circumstances. He was inhaling deeply on his cigarette when the roar of an engine rose behind him. He glanced back at SS Headquarters to see a staff car pulling out of the driveway. It came down the street toward him, SS flags fluttering above its headlights. He recognized the officer in the command seat next to the driver and shuddered. He knew all too well who he was; knew where he was going; knew what he would do!

Kleist turned the corner, dashed down the street and slipped inside the tiny phone booth. He set his cigarette amid the burn marks on the edge of the wooden shelf, pulled off a glove, and took a few coins from a pocket, setting them next to the cigarette. His hands were shaking as he lifted the mouthpiece and thumbed one of the coins into the slot. An electric hum. No dial tone. The line was dead. The young Captain jiggled the hook several times to no avail, then grimaced and left the earpiece dangling. He took his cigarette and hurried off, not wasting the time it would take to collect the coins.

Debris from a bombed-out building forced him to cross the street. As he reached the corner of Hiltenberg, a narrow road that ran north from Josephsplatz, he caught sight of a barman through the window of a small cafe. The crooked neon sign flickered Cafe Viktoria. What was he holding up to his mouth? A coffee mug? A beer stein? A telephone handset? Was he talking on a telephone?! Yes! Yes, despite the Christmas decorations in the window, and the reflections and condensation on the glass which obscured much of the interior, Captain Kleist was reasonably certain it was a telephone. He flicked his cigarette into the gutter and pushed through the door.

The cafe was nearly empty. A Christmas garland hung in loops above the bar. The air smelled of stale beer, cigarettes and wet wool. A layer of smoke drifted between the tables where a few customers sat hunched over glasses of schnapps and—due to the unavailability of coffee which could no longer be imported—steaming mugs of a bitter tasting substitute brewed from roasted barley seeds and acorns.

Captain Kleist strode between them with as much intimidating authority as he could muster. The barman stiffened at the sight of an onrushing SS officer and ended his call. "The phone," Captain Kleist said, sharply. "SS emergency."

The anxious fellow nodded and nervously wiped the mouthpiece with a bar rag. His eyes were locked on the Death's Head insignia on the young captain's cap, not the caduceus in his lapel. "Bitte…" He smiled faintly and pushed the phone across the scratched varnish with a subservient gesture.

Captain Kleist wanted the privacy of a telephone booth, but he had run out of time. Three of his closest friends and colleagues were in extreme danger, and he had no choice but to risk being overheard. He turned his back to the barman and those at the tables and began dialing a number with a University District prefix. He spun the rotary dial as fast as he could; but after each digit it circled back at a painfully slow pace that intensified his anxiety.

CHAPTER THREE

The taxi was still rolling to a stop in front of 375 Park Avenue, when Stacey popped the door. Built in 1958, the Seagram Building was the icon of modern post-war architecture, the supreme expression of Bauhaus International Style; or as Tom Wolfe wryly observed: Thirty-eight stories of worker housing used by capitalists as corporate headquarters. The bronze- tinted-glass facade was set back from the street amidst broad plazas and Olympic-size reflecting pools.

Stacey lugged the suitcase past the clusters of smokers gathered around an outdoor ash stand, getting their nicotine fix, then strode into the lobby, swiped her security pass through the reader, and headed for the elevators. Gunther Global's offices occupied the entire twentieth floor. The open-plan created a maze of workstations that was ringed by glass-walled offices. Isolated in these lushly furnished aquariums like fighting fish that would tear each other to pieces if forced to cohabitate, were account executives, creative directors, chief copy writers, and senior graphic designers.

Stacey hurried past the Industry Awards displayed in Reception, down a corridor lined with posters of notable print ads, and into her boss's office. Bart Tannen's aquarium had a putting green that ran along the windows, and a commanding view of the city. It also had his collection of international golf posters acquired during stints in GG offices around the world, during which he mastered his craft, became fluent in several languages, and worked at lowering his handicap; which is what he and his putter were doing when Stacey dropped the battered suitcase on his conference table.

As the agency's Chief Creative Officer, Tannen worked with clients who paid GG handsomely to create, develop, and deploy advertising strategies across national boundaries and diverse cultures. There was no more global a client than Steinbach & Company, a high quality trunk maker founded in Leipzig, Germany in 1847. Prices started at $4,500 and went into the stratosphere.

"That's it?" Tannen asked, peering at the suitcase through his tortoiseshell Oliver Peoples. His eyebrows were as thick as the rough that bordered the fairways at his country club; and his long hair, pulled straight back to cover a bald spot, was fastened in a puppytail above his collar. "You going to tell me what it is?" he went on, smoothly striking a putt that rolled into the cup. "Or do I have to guess?"

"Come on, boss. It's a vintage Steinbach," Stacey replied, surprised he had to ask. "The pebble-grain texture, the precise saddle-stitching, the machined fittings and latches; not to mention..." She angled it so he could see the bottom where a brass plate that proclaimed Steinbach was centered between the hinges. A serial number was engraved beneath the company name.

Tannen ran a fingertip across it. "If their records go back that far, chances are we can find out who the original owner was."

"Chances are we already know," Stacey said in her sassy way. She turned the suitcase, revealing white hand painted lettering on the other side. The large, characters were chipped, scratched and worn with age, but clearly read:

EPSTEIN, JACOB
GEB 1922 147
GRUPPE 12

"There's also this," Stacey went on, fingering a grimy luggage tag on which the same name, an address in Vienna, and several sets of numbers had been written.

The furrows in Tannen's brow deepened. "Where you going with this, Stace? I mean, we've got this filthy old piece of luggage with a name painted on it, probably by some rich-kid going off to boarding school or summer camp, and...and we're building an entire, multi-million dollar campaign around it?"

"Uh-huh, this one and others," Stacey replied becoming impassioned. "They've got character. The imperfections are like...like the lines in someone's face, footprints of our earliest ancestors in lava, hash marks in the military. I ever mention my daddy was a crew chief?" she prompted, lapsing into a West Texas drawl which, like so many who have ventured beyond the Longhorn state's borders, she could turn on and off at will. "Yup, F-111 Wing based in Clovis, New Mexico. Just a spit and holler over the border from Lubbock where I grew up." She smiled, faintly, and added. "Never was around much. He's into ranchin' now."

Tannen had become taken with her idea and managed a preoccupied nod. "In other words, each vintage Steinbach has a story to tell. The stickers plastered on the sides. The sweat-darkened leather on the handle. The dents, the bumps, the scrapes, the scars left behind by the vicissitudes of life..."

"There ya go! They're like people who—"

"Hold it! Hold that thought!" Tannen stabbed at his intercom and said, "Astrid, see if the boss can pop in here will you?" He hung up and, prompting Stacey to continue, said, "They're like people who…"

"…Who've lived interesting lives," she resumed without missing a beat. "Each one's got as many stories to tell as it has stitches. The places it's been, the people who sat on it in boarding lounges, waited for it in Baggage Claim, made love in hotel rooms while it watched from a luggage rack in the corner. Remember those fantastic Irving Penn shots of cigarette butts?"

"Yeah, sure," Tannen replied, baffled by what the connection could possibly be. "Large format camera. Poster-size, gritty, black-and-white platinum prints. Must've been like thirty-what years ago. Little before your time, wasn't it?"

"Yeah, well, I sort of acquired a copy of the coffee table book."

"Wait. Don't tell me…"

Stacey nodded sheepishly. "Yup, a dumpster dive. I'll bring it tomorrow. Each shot's like a…a portrait. Some crushed beneath a heel, others stubbed-out but standing tall. You can see every pore and fiber in the cigarette paper; count the strands of cellulite in the filters; see the texture of an ash that's straining to keep from falling off, the glistening moisture on a lipstick imprint. Each one has its own character and story to tell. Just like pieces of vintage Steinbach."

Tannen gestured to the suitcase. "I hasten to point out that our Mr. Epstein threw this one away."

"Yeah, just like Penn's cigarette butts," Stacey countered, unwilling to concede the point.

Tannen smiled in tribute. "Still, we've got nothing if we can't come up with a bunch of vintage Steinbachs whose owners agree to sign on, right?"

"Right," Stacey said, her mind racing for a way to keep him engaged. "You know those Louis Vee ads? The ones with the aging movie stars, the retired athletes, the deposed Russian leaders…"

"Cathy, Andre, Steffi and Gorby," Tannen said with a glance to the door where Mark Gunther, his boss and the agency's CEO had materialized. He had the physique and pulse rate of a marathoner, and a cool temperament that perfectly complemented his stable of hyperactive creative teams. There were those who attributed it to the fact that his father, who had founded the agency in the 1960s, left no doubt who would inherit the CEO's chair when he retired.

Stacey was on a roll and too charged-up to notice him. "Yeah, they're all so…so pretentious and staged. I mean does anybody who can spring for a Steinbach care about celebrity endorsements? I want to use real people who've lived fascinating lives with pieces of Steinbach that've lived it with them."

Tannen's eyes were wide with intrigue, now. "…that have accompanied them on life's journey," he chimed-in, with another glance to Gunther who was smiling broadly. "Not one that they've never seen before, that the product wrangler handed them just before the strobes flashed and the shutter fired."

"Exactly," Stacey said, delighted he'd become so engaged. "Our customers don't buy a piece of luggage, they choose it, like they'd choose a friend…a friend who'll always be there for them; and we're going to help them make that choice by introducing them to people who've already made it, people like—" She paused, having noticed Gunther, and spun the suitcase around so the hand painted name and data, were facing him. "—like Jacob Epstein! By telling their stories, by—"

"Excuse me for interrupting," Mark Gunther called out, crossing toward them. His tone was polite; but he had become stone-faced, his amused smile replaced by tight-lipped concern. "You may not want to tell his story once you hear it."

Tannen looked puzzled. "Why not? What're you talking about, Mark?"

"That," Gunther replied, indicating the hand painted lettering. "A couple of years ago, there was a story in the *Times* about a guy who went to a Holocaust exhibit and came upon a display of victims' suitcases. Most of them looked just like that one. The kicker was one of them belonged to his father who died in Auschwitz."

"I've got chills," Stacey said, hugging herself as if shivering. "This…this belonged to someone who died in the Holocaust…" she went on barely able to speak.

"Maybe they died; and maybe they didn't," Gunther replied. "Where'd you get it?"

"Pile of trash across from my building."

"Chances are it belonged to a survivor," Gunther concluded. "Someone who made it to America."

"Someone named Jacob Epstein," Tannen said.

"Who lives in The Apthorp," Stacey added, starting to brighten.

"Lived would be more like it," Gunther corrected. "That was a long time ago." He looked off for a moment, then asked, "Anything in it?"

Stacey nodded. "You can hear stuff moving around inside, but it's locked."

"Get a locksmith," Gunther ordered, softly. "I don't want it damaged. It's hallowed memorabilia."

"And we'll treat it as such," Tannen said in a respectful tone. "I think Stacey's got something solid, here, Mark. If you're on board, I'd like to run it up the flag pole and see if Sol salutes." The latter was a reference to Solomon Steinbach, great-great grandson of the company's founder and its current CEO.

"Tough old buzzard," Gunther said with an amused smile. "The only thing Sol salutes is the suitcase full of cash he takes to his bank at the end of every quarter. "Reminds me of the old timer who ran that Italian soup company."

"Alessandro Involta," Tannen said with perfect inflection, savoring the syllables. "The *capo di tutti cappi* of the minestrone mafia."

"My first campaign," Gunther said, reminiscing. "We put together an across-the-board program: logo, packaging, ad campaign. The works. We do the dog and pony show for the marketing guys, the product managers, the exec committee. Everybody loves it. The place is buzzing. We're all waiting for old man Involta to weigh-in. He sits there, arms folded, not a word. Finally he mumbles, 'I'm'a-no-like,' and heads for the door."

"I'm'a-no-like," Stacey blurted with a laugh.

"Yeah, that was thirty years ago; and to this day, nothing's changed, and— their sales and profits are off the charts."

"So the old buzzard was right," Tannen said.

Gunther nodded, his eyes darkening with concern. "We've still got our own old buzzard to deal with, Bart. I'm hearing ugly rumors…"

"Yeah, I know," Tannen said, sounding contrite.

"Be a shame to lose him," Gunther said, pointedly, heading for the door. "Concept's good. Really good. I'm counting on our dogs and ponies to take first prize."

Tanned nodded, then noticed Stacey staring at the suitcase. Despite Gunther's light-hearted story, the impact of its connection to the Holocaust hadn't diminished. "Cheer up kid."

Stacey frowned. "I'm trying."

Come on, the boss loved it. So will Sol. Besides, no way we're using the Holocaust to sell roll-aboards. You just acquired your first piece of vintage Steinbach."

Stacey nodded sadly and sighed. "I don't know if I could bear to live with it."

"Yeah, well, I guess Mr. Epstein felt the same way."

CHAPTER FOUR

The University of Munich consisted of two main complexes connected by a great domed hall. The multi-story Ludwig Maximilians block and the Amalien annex were built during the late 1830s and early 1900s, respectively, in the Italian Renaissance style. The urban campus spread across several square blocks and enclosed a number of treed courtyards. The Medical School fronted on Amalienstrasse, a broad boulevard that bordered the west side of the University District.

Christmas break was over and classes had resumed. Students bundled in winter coats, with wool watch caps pulled down over their ears and scarves wrapped about their necks and mouths, were streaming through the arched entrance arcades into the lobby. Many of them were young—almost too young to be attending Medical School; but the war had created an overwhelming demand for physicians; and the nation resorted to funneling students with high science aptitudes into accelerated Medical School programs. Specialization in Emergency Medicine and Orthopedic Surgery was encouraged.

Every morning, the vast lobby became a swirling crossroads as students with book bags and briefcases trudged up the staircases to classrooms and lecture halls in their clumsy galoshes. Others milled about chatting noisily. The marble walls and vaulted glass ceiling amplified the din into a deafening cacophony that rivaled the window-rattling thunder of yesterday's Allied bombing raids.

Professor Martin Gerhard strode swiftly down a corridor that connected the University Hospital to the lobby, lighting a cigarette. A surgeon's mask hung from his neck and a red-spattered gown billowed behind him as he made his way between students and up the stairs to his office on a mezzanine that ringed the lobby. The walls of the high-ceilinged room were lined with bookcases and covered with anatomical diagrams and step-by-step illustrations of surgical procedures. Skeletal structures wired to armatures stood against one wall. A Nazi flag hung against another.

The harried professor tossed the surgical mask on the desk, and was setting his cigarette in one of several Petri dishes that served as ashtrays when the phone rang. He slipped out of his gown, then returned to the door and closed it; but the cacophony that came from below easily penetrated its frosted glass window on which gold leaf lettering proclaimed: Department of Orthopedic Surgery Office of the Dean. A slight man in his mid-fifties, he wore bifocals that balanced on the bridge of his nose and lifted the phone with long delicate fingers that were pink from decades of pre-surgical scrubbing. "Professor Gerhard," he said, retrieving his cigarette from the Petri dish.

"Professor? It's Max, Max Kleist!" the young Captain said in an urgent whisper into the telephone. The far end of the bar in Cafe Viktoria angled into the wall, forming a corner. Max had tucked himself into it and cupped his hand over the mouthpiece so those at the tables couldn't hear him. "Thank God you're there."

"Yes, and I expected you would be too," the professor said with a slight edge, referring to his former student's habit of trading his uniform for a surgical gown when the number of bombing casualties became overwhelming. "We need every surgeon available, Max. Even SS surgeons."

Last Spring, Max was conscripted by the Waffen SS—as many doctors were—and ordered to report for duty upon completing medical school. His father, a wealthy Munich industrialist, saw little sense in his son dying for a lost cause, and used his connections to keep him from being assigned to the front where surgeons were in demand. Instead, the young Captain—who would have been a Lieutenant if not for his family's prominence—was put in charge of enforcing Nazi policy and programs at his alma mater.

The position was created in 1942 after Dr. Kurt Huber, a Medical School professor, and several of his students formed a resistance group known as the White Rose that distributed anti-Nazi leaflets denouncing Hitler and his regime. All its members were arrested, convicted of treason at show trials, sentenced to death and guillotined. Giving this assignment to a citizen of Munich, let alone a graduate of its medical school, violated a strict SS rule that prohibited members from being posted in their home town, city or district. The dictum was Himmler's way of insuring that the ruthless enforcement of Nazi policies wouldn't be compromised by personal considerations; and this rare exception was testimony to the elder Kleist's powerful influence with the Party hierarchy.

"I'm sorry, I couldn't be there," Max replied, sounding shaken. "I was on my way when I was picked-up and taken to SS Headquarters for a debriefing— or so they called it."

"You were interrogated?!" the professor asked, sounding alarmed.

"Yes, they kept me there all night. I'm being reassigned."

"Why?" the professor prompted with a nervous drag of his cigarette. "What happened? What's wrong?"

"They're cracking down. You're in danger. So are Eva and Jacob," Max replied, referring to two other students. "You have to warn them. When I left her yesterday, Eva said she was going to the E-R to—"

"I know," the professor interrupted. "They've both been at it all night; and as soon as—"

"The SS is on their way, now!" Max interrupted, through clenched teeth. He glanced over his shoulder, nervously, at those in the cafe and added, "You have to warn them. You have to get them out of there!"

"Now? My God, I—" Professor Gerhard paused, his eyes darting to the door in reaction to the sudden silence that came over the lobby below. The arrival of an SS staff car, always a black Mercedes sedan with the runic double-S insignia on pennants flying above the headlights, always had the same chilling effect. It was as if the students had been suddenly rendered mute and left to wonder who would be arrested for crimes against the Third Reich, this time. "I can't. It's too late," the Professor concluded.

"The SS is already there?" Max prompted, his voice breaking at the thought.

"Any second now," the Professor said, his eyes still on the door. "We'll come by the house as soon as we can. They wouldn't dare invade your family's privacy."

"I wouldn't be too sure of that after last night."

"We'll have to take that chance." The phone was still in the Professor's hand when someone rapped on the glass. The door swung open before he could respond. Three uniformed SS men strode through it.

CHAPTER FIVE

"Pretty damn good," Sol Steinbach said, sounding like he meant it after Stacey Dutton and Bart Tannen presented the concept for the ad campaign. He had quick eyes, a wiry physique, and a crusty familiarity that went with his hands-on management style. "It's classy and genuine. Good stuff. Real good. I like it a lot."

"Thought you might," Tannen said covering his sigh of relief with professional swagger.

Stacey's book of Irving Penn's photographs of cigarette butts was on the conference table next to the suitcase. It served as a prop during the presentation and, now, Steinbach was eagerly turning the pages of the exquisitely printed volume. "Amazing. I remember this show. I've belonged to MOMA for forty years. Haven't smoked in twenty; but I'm dying for a cigarette now." He laughed and closed the book with a thwack. "You think we could get Penn to do the print ads?"

Tannen shrugged. "I don't even know if he's still working. He's no kid. I can tell you that."

"Yeah," Stacey chimed-in, her thumbs dancing over the keys of her Blackberry. "Here we go. Born 1917. Makes him…ninety-two."

"Hey, I'll take twenty more years," Steinbach said with an infectious cackle. "I'm going to have 'em too. Know why? Competitive cycling. Now, that's a sport. Muscle tone. Cardio-vascular conditioning. Take it from me, Bart. Trade-in your golf cart for a racing saddle before it's too late."

"Yeah, I hear they do wonders for your prostate," Tannen said with a grin.

"Don't tell me," Steinbach said his eyes aglow with mischief. "You guys just landed the Flo-Max account."

"Can we count on you for an endorsement?"

"Lucky for you there's a lady present," Steinbach retorted with a wink to Stacey. "This little gal saved your ass, Bart. I should hire her and get rid of all

14

this overhead," he went on, gesturing to the posh office and astonishing view of the city.

"The suitcase was just waiting there for me, Mr. Steinbach," Stacey said, self-consciously. "I got lucky…"

"Makes three of us," Steinbach fired back. He stepped to the suitcase and examined it from different angles. "Dates to the thirties," he went on, zeroing-in on the serial number on the nameplate. He ran his fingertips over the pebble-grained leather, then the sweat-stained handle before going on to the precisely machined latches, pressing his thumbs against them. "It's locked. No keys, huh?"

"How I wish," Stacey replied.

"Mark suggested we get a locksmith," Tannen said.

"For what? I'll have one of my techs come over," Steinbach said. He grasped the handle and stood the suitcase upright. The sound of the contents moving about, got his attention; but the sight of the hand-painted data—that Stacey and Tannen had been careful to conceal during their presentation—was like going over the handlebars at high speed. Steinbach flinched, taken aback. He knew what it meant. He knew the ugly story this piece of vintage Steinbach could tell.

Tannen saw his reaction and winced. "Sorry, we were hoping you wouldn't see that, Sol."

Stacey nodded. "Yeah, we weren't planning on using this one, Mr. Steinbach."

Steinbach's busy eyes widened in an incredulous stare. "Why the hell not?"

"Well, we're…we're pretty sure it's from the Holocaust," Tannen replied, clearly surprised. "And we—"

"No shit, Sherlock. I know where the hell it's from." Steinbach pointed to the hand painted data. "That's his group number and prisoner reference number. They were assigned at the deportation center."

"Well, Sol, we felt it might be…be inappropriate to use the Holocaust to sell luggage. If you don't find it offensive, then, maybe, we could—"

"Offensive?" Steinbach interrupted again. "No, no, it's controversial. It'll get plenty of attention."

Tannen rolled his eyes. "Yeah like from the Jewish Defense League, the Wiesenthal Center, the W.J.C…" The latter was a reference to the World Jewish Congress.

"Hey, I give a lot of money to those guys," Steinbach protested. He removed his suit jacket, then unfastened the cufflink on his left sleeve and pushed it up to his elbow, revealing a tattoo on the outside of his forearm. The faded numerals read: A178362. "The 'A' is for Auschwitz," he explained bristling with anger. "On women, the number was followed by a tiny triangle because with our shaved heads and emaciated bodies the Nazis couldn't tell one sex from the other unless we were naked."

Stacey was visibly shaken. She'd learned what she knew about the Holocaust from living on the Upper West Side, her classes at Columbia, and the movies. When she was growing up in Lubbock, the state school board was more interested in the theory of Creationism than the fate of six million Jews in World War Two; and the only holocaust she heard about was the nuclear kind. The one 'them commies' were about to unleash. Stacey had never come face to face with a survivor, and gasped, softly, "Oh my God..."

"Exactly," Steinbach said. "We used to say that a thousand times a day. The Jews are God's chosen people? Chosen for what? Living hell?!" He shifted his look to Tannen. "So, we can dispense with the lectures on what's appropriate or offensive. Okay?"

"Sure. I'm really sorry, Sol," Tannen said like a chastised child. "In this business you learn to walk on eggs when it comes to these things."

"No way you could know unless you've lived it," Steinbach said, absolving him. "I was five years old when Auschwitz was liberated. I won't go into what I did to survive." He rolled down his sleeve and went about affixing the cufflink. "Father, mother, sisters all gone. And while they were being dehumanized, raped and exterminated, one of our biggest competitors—then and now—had a sign in the window of their store on the Champs-Elysees that said, No Dogs, No Jews."

"Louie Vee?" Tannen prompted with disbelief.

Steinbach nodded, grimly. "Hey, it's no secret. You can Google it. Then, they were collaborators. Now, they're a conglomerate."

"LVMH, right?" Stacey said, already thumbing the keys on her Blackberry.

"Louis Vuitton Moet Hennessy, SA," Steinbach said with exaggerated pretention. "Somebody wrote a book about the company and mentioned how they made money by playing ball with Petain and his pro-Nazi government."

"Found it," Stacey said, scrolling down the screen. "Louis Vuitton, A French Saga, by Stephanie Bonvicini." She scrolled again, and added, "In response to the charges the company worked with the Nazis, a spokesman said: 'This is ancient history. The book covers a period when it was family run and long before it became part of LVMH. We are diverse, tolerant and all the things a modern company should be.' That's a quote."

"They didn't deny it, did they?" Steinbach said.

"Yeah, well it's still going to stir up one hell of a hornet's nest, Sol," Tannen warned.

"It damn well better," Steinbach growled. "Like I said, controversy is good. Generates lots of free media. It'll make those Frenchmen squirm, too," he went on with a laugh. "More important than that, much more important, it'll keep the memory of the Holocaust alive."

"Gunther's been out front on that for decades," Tannen said, jumping at the chance to establish GG's Semitic bonafides. "The Never Forget campaign after the Seventy-Two Olympics was organized by this agency," he went on, referring to the kidnapping and murder of Israeli athletes by Palestinian terrorists.

"For all the fucking good it did," Steinbach fired-back. "Anti-Semitism is alive and well, Bart. We've got neo-Nazis in Paris abducting Jews off the street; Muslim wannabes in White Plains torching synagogues; bearded psychos in Tehran threatening to wipe Israel off the map." He took a moment to settle, and then said, "After the war, I came to this country with my Uncle Abe, the only other family member to survive. He rebuilt the business from scratch, and it killed him. I was twenty-two when I took over. For me, it's about profits. The more we generate, the more cash I have to support those causes that are close to my heart."

"You know boss," Stacey said, glancing to Tannen with a little grin, "Something tells me this piece of vintage Steinbach is going to be part of the campaign."

"You bet your Blackberry," Steinbach cracked. "That suitcase, and the guy who owned it, kick-off the campaign."

"Assuming he's still kicking," Tannen cautioned.

Steinbach responded with a preoccupied nod. He had slipped on his glasses and was bent over the suitcase, squinting at the area next to the handle. "Looks like this one was monogrammed."

"Hot-stamped in gold, as I recall," Tannen prompted.

"Eighteen carat," Steinbach replied, his voice ringing with pride. "Can't make 'em out. Fucking Nazis probably chipped 'em off for the gold." He removed his glasses, then smiled at a thought. "Come to think of it, I know a Jake Epstein. I know a handful of 'em. One belongs to my temple; another lives in the same condo in Florida; another's a surgeon. We served on a few boards together. Haven't seen him in years."

"Well, assuming we get lucky," Tannen said with as much optimism as he could muster, "Our Jacob Epstein would be damn near ninety if he's a day,"

Stacey's thumbs were flying over her Blackberry, again. "Two-hundred-forty-thousand hits," she said with a disappointed groan. "Jacob Epstein the Sculptor, the British financier, the rugby player..." She resumed thumbing the keyboard, using phone listings to narrow the search. "Okay, here we go. Lots of Epsteins in the Manhattan directory...not a single Jacob? A half-dozen or so J. Epsteins. Of those that list an address...not one lives in The Apthorp."

"The Apthorp?" Steinbach echoed. "Geezus, talk about hornets nests. I don't know who's in more trouble, those guys or the ones who bought the Plaza. Anyway, here's the drill: I'll have my people run this serial number. I'll also have 'em put together a list of clients most likely to have vintage Steinbachs. I want to focus on print. Find out if Penn is still working. If he isn't, look into Demarchalier and Meisel. I like Annie Leibovitz too; and I hear she needs the cash."

"She may need the cash, but she's doing Louie Vee," Tannen said, referring to Steinbach's competitor.

"Must be a mental block," Steinbach said with a laugh. "There's always Zach Bolden; but he's usually booked solid. I want to move on this fast."

"Me too," Tannen said, gesturing to the suitcase. "You're sending somebody to pick these locks, right?"

"Tomorrow. Won't take him a minute," Steinbach replied with a wily smile. "Who knows what we might learn about Jake Epstein once it's opened…"

CHAPTER SIX

Two of the black-clad SS men had remained in the doorway of Professor Gerhard's office. The third strode toward the desk, unbuttoning his winter greatcoat. His shoulder tabs sported the three-plaited silver threads of a Sturmbahnführer. "Professor Gerhard," he said, removing a glove and extending a hand. "I'm Major Steig, the new SS liaison. I thought I'd drop by and introduce myself."

"A pleasure," the professor said, forcing a smile. He hung up the phone and shook Steig's hand. Taut and sinewy, the Major had a malevolent edge and a self-conscious military bearing. There was nothing of the aristocrat in him, and Gerhard assumed he was one of the Nazi party functionaries with whom Himmler had been replacing members of the upper-class officer corps.

"You don't seem at all surprised," Steig said, with a glance to the phone.

Professor Gerhard shrugged, feigning indifference. "It happens all the time, now. People are here one day and gone the next. One gets used to it after a while." His mind raced to find a way to get rid of the Major and his henchmen, and warn the students who were in danger. He slipped his watch from a vest pocket as if he had a pressing matter, stubbed out his cigarette in the Petri dish, and said, "Forgive me, but we are overwhelmed with casualties, not to mention classes have resumed. I'm afraid I won't be able to give you as much time as I'd like."

"But you'll give me as much as I'd like, won't you?" Steig said, savoring the riposte. For years, he'd been a Nazi Party organizer in Munich. The exponential growth of local cells and ruthless purging of anti-Nazi infiltrators during his tenure had gotten Himmler's attention. An SS commission had been Steig's reward; and he relished exercising his new-found authority. He nodded to one of the SS men to close the door, then raised his chin as if challenging the professor. "It seems that Gleichschaltung isn't being enforced in your department," he said, referring to Hitler's program of Nazification designed to control every aspect of German life.

"Gleichschaltung..." the professor mused, taking a pack of Sturms from a pocket. "Cigarette?"

"An unhealthy habit. Frowned upon by the Führer," the Major replied with a dismissive wave. "We were discussing Gleichschaltung."

The professor put a cigarette between his lips and lit it, casually, as if he wasn't intimidated. "We've always done our best to integrate our programs with the goals and ideals of—"

"Then how is it that you've failed to carry out the most important order of all?! That the purity of the Aryan race be preserved and protected! That all Jews be purged from our institutions!"

"With all due respect, Major, my orders are to graduate as many surgeons as possible as quickly as possible without regard to ethnic background." He paused in search of a way to reinforce his position. "Surgeons who will bring glory to the Führer and the Third Reich by saving the lives and limbs of brave German soldiers wounded in battle."

"Who issued those orders? Captain Kleist?"

"Really, Major, you know as well as I he passed them on from higher ups. I can assure you he did his best to see they were carried out."

"Apparently, he failed to grasp the importance of racial purity. Perhaps, his involvement with one of the students in question clouded his judgment."

"Involvement? What are you referring to?"

"You expect me to believe you don't know Kleist and the Jewess Eva Rosenberg are lovers?! In direct violation of the Nuremberg Laws!" Steig exclaimed, referring to the anti-Semitic ordinances which, among other things, forbade sexual intercourse between Aryans and Jews. "I have it on good authority it began last year when he was still a student here."

"Major, I run the Orthopedic Surgery Department, not the Cardio-Vascular Lab. I have nothing to do with matters of the heart. Eva Rosenberg is a very talented doctor as is Jacob Epstein who I imagine is the other 'student in question'." The professor knew once the SS smelled blood nothing could keep them from the kill. He was certain all was lost when a bizarre coincidence occurred to him. It could be dangerous to mention it; but if it gave Steig pause, it was worth the risk. He dragged deeply on his cigarette, then added, "As I recall, the Führer's philosopher-in-residence just happens to be named Rosenberg as well."

He was referring to Alfred Rosenberg an Estonian who had been a Hitler confidant since the early twenties. His pseudo-scientific theories of Aryan racial superiority and virulent anti-Semitism had so captivated Hitler that he made Rosenberg editor of *Volkischer Beobachter*, the Nazi newspaper, and made his book, *Mythus*—an irrational work extolling the National Socialist ideology—the Nazi bible.

"Just because his name sounds Jewish doesn't mean he is Jewish. Even if he's *mischlinge*, he's been crucial to articulating the Führer's vision," the Major said, using the word for partial-Jew. "Some Jews with skills vital to the war effort have been exempted from Relocation. Some are even being allowed to serve in uniform. Several highly decorated. General Fritz Bayerlin, Commander of the Lehr Panzer Division for one. Admiral Bernhard Rogge for another. Both awarded the Knight's Cross with Oak Leaves and Swords by the Führer." Steig used a heel-click to emphasize the magnitude of their achievement. Indeed, the decoration he cited was equal to each man being awarded three U.S. Medals of Honor.

"My point exactly," the Professor said, thinking he had pulled it off. "You see both Doctors Rosenberg and Epstein excelled in our accelerated program as did Captain Kleist. All three are certified orthopedic surgeons; and make up the most creatively talented team of doctors I've ever taught. Their work in the development of prosthetics is nothing short of brilliant; and, despite Kleist's conscription, they continue to work together under my guidance. As you may know, Rosenberg and Epstein have Critical Skills Exemptions. I have their papers right here." He removed two documents from a drawer, and gave them to the Major.

Steig tore them in half and threw them on the floor. "All medical exemptions have been cancelled by order of the Reichsführer! Brave German soldiers don't need Jews to save their lives! Have you forgotten that all licenses to practice medicine issued to Jews have been nullified by the Nuremberg Laws?! That they are allowed to treat only their own kind to spare Aryan physicians from exposure to racial contamination?! Have you?"

"No I haven't, Major," the Professor replied evenly, exhaling a stream of smoke that filled the space between them. "It was Article Four as I recall; but under the circumstances, I thought—"

"The Führer does the thinking, Professor!" the Major exclaimed, slapping his glove on a corner of the desk. "You will see to it that the two Jewish students in question—and any others you know of—are purged from this institution! And their files sent to my office!" The Major tugged some paperwork from an inside pocket. "In keeping with the Führer's decree that every Jew add the name Sarah or Israel to his or her own, these warrants in the name of Eva Sarah Rosenberg and Jacob Israel Epstein call for their immediate arrest and deportation to a work camp!" He turned to the two SS men and nodded. "Find them. Search every classroom and lecture hall until you do."

"Wait!" the professor called out, causing the SS men to hesitate. "They're not here," he said in a bold lie. He took a clipboard from his desk and offered it to the Major. "You can check the schedule. Neither has class until later this afternoon."

"They'll be in custody by then!" the Major snapped. "The Reichsführer is outraged that this proliferation of Jewish doctors has gone unchecked; and that the high ethical and moral standards of Hippocrates which are essential to insuring the purity of German blood are being ignored!"

The professor suppressed his anger at how Himmler had twisted the meaning of the sacred Oath to coerce German doctors into diagnosing an imagined racial plague so its human carriers could be exterminated. "No doctor who trained at the University of Wittenberg Medical School needs to be reminded of his Oath," the Professor said, referring to the University in Northeastern Germany where Martin Luther taught theology and developed the theses that he nailed to the door of All Saints Church, initiating the Protestant Reformation.

"Evidently, the Reichsführer disagrees," Steig retorted. "I'm sure he'll be fascinated to know what makes Wittenberg so significant in that regard."

"Four hundred years of tradition," the Professor replied with pride. "Considering Herr Himmler's profound reverence for Hippocrates, I'm sure he knows Wittenberg was the first university to administer his Oath to medical students—in 1508."

"He also knows his orders will be obeyed! Don't disappoint him, again, Professor. Or I'll be back with a warrant that has your name on it!"

Gerhard nodded like a chastened schoolboy and toyed with his cigarette.

"You know, Professor," Steig went on with a smirk, "I've heard rumors you were involved with that traitor Huber and his White Rose troublemakers a few years ago."

"With all due respect, Major, the rumors were false then; and they are false, now," the Professor replied. "If I may, I'm quite concerned about Captain Kleist. As I said, he's one of the brightest students I've ever had. A fine surgeon, from a fine Munich family, and I was wondering if—"

"Captain Kleist will be dealt with," the Major interrupted. "If it wasn't for his 'fine Munich family' he'd have already been shot." He snapped off a Nazi salute, then spun on a heel and crossed toward the door, his greatcoat flowing behind him. One of the SS men opened it as he approached. "Search the classrooms and lecture halls anyway," he ordered as they followed him through it onto the mezzanine. "There's nothing in the Hippocratic Oath that prohibits lying to SS officers."

CHAPTER SEVEN

Mark Gunther's eyes were wide with disbelief. "The old buzzard wants to use it to kick-off the print campaign?!" he exclaimed, referring to the suitcase.

In contrast to the luxe style of Tannen's office, Gunther's reflected the flowery Provence palette of the Agency's Paris headquarters on Avenue Montaigne in the fashionable 8th Arrondissement. They had overlapped there when Gunther, who had been running it as part of his grooming process, handed the reins to Tannen prior to returning to the agency's New York office.

"I thought Sol would go ballistic. You made him aware of the downside, the potential for backlash?"

"He's counting on it," Tannen replied with an amused cackle. "By the way, he eighty-sixed the locksmith. One of his techs is coming over tomorrow at ten. I thought you might want to be there."

Gunther nodded half-heartedly. "Better put that on hold."

"Why? Sol's dying to find out what's in it."

"So am I. But that suitcase is hallowed memorabilia. The contents possibly even more so."

"I'm aware of that but…"

"No buts. It shouldn't be opened until we know if our Mr. Epstein is alive. If he is, we should get his permission, and invite him to be there."

"Why? He discarded it. Finder's keepers. No?"

"No. Granted the odds he's still kicking aren't much better than the Mets making the playoffs; but we should find out. Either way, it should be done by a professional, a Holocaust archivist."

"I wouldn't know where to start."

"Leave it to me," Gunther said, stealing a glance at his monitor. The spread sheet on the screen was titled European Profit & Loss. He saw the steeply descending trend line and winced.

"Problem?" Tannen wondered.

"Europe's not pulling its weight. Going to have to get my ass over there," Gunther replied, wincing again, this time at the news crawl below which read: PROMINENT IMAM CLAIMS JEWS HAVE INHERENTLY NEGATIVE CHARACTERISTICS. "Sol's right, you know. Anti-Semitism keeps rearing its ugly head."

"The global financial crisis…"

"Yeah, bad times always set it off. All of a sudden, Goldman Sachs, long revered for their incredible performance and ethical standards, are the bad guys."

"Envy. They made money when everyone else was losing their shirts."

"So did the Rothschilds," Gunther countered.

"I don't get it. I mean religion's just a crutch to cope with the cruelty of life. Why all the fuss over which one?"

"The Nazis didn't give a damn about religion. For them, it was about race. Racial purity." Gunther steepled his fingers in thought, making a decision. "How long we've been working together? Ten, twelve years?"

Tannen nodded, curiously.

"I've always been under the impression you were Jewish. I mean, it used to be Tannenbaum, right?"

"Uh-huh. I'm not a member of the tribe in good standing. My mother was a shiksa, my father loved shellfish, and we summered in Sag Harbor. Are *you*?"

"Am I what?"

"Jewish."

"No, but Grace is, you know that," Gunther said, referring to his wife. "Her family had a bookstore in Amsterdam. A rival turned them in for selling banned material. They lived like hunted animals."

Tannen nodded grimly. "So…" he said, sensing he'd been set-up, "where you going with this?"

"Well, for want of a better word, you seem sort of detached from an extremely sensitive issue."

Tannen looked stung. "If you're suggesting I'm not as outraged by Nazi atrocities as you are, you're wrong. Makes my skin crawl. So, I tuned-out— became detached if you prefer." He cocked his head and smiled at a thought. "There was one advantage to being Jewish…"

"Lox and bagels?" Gunther teased, deciding to lighten the mood. "Circumcision without anesthesia?"

"My bar mitzvah," Tannen replied, unable to keep from laughing. "Someone gave me a camera. Changed my life."

"Right you had a studio there for a while.

"Along with an endless supply of hot women, fast cars, international travel, shoots for *Vogue*, *Harper's*, *Vanity Fair*… It was one endless cocaine-driven bacchanal. But hey, I was young and foolish, then."

"Weren't we all, Gunther said, with a lascivious cackle and a glance to his watch. "Just enough time before my two o'clock to tell you a story. I had a social-psych prof once who got the class into this. Being a cocky Greenwich WASP, I got into it with this Jewish girl from Flatbush. Let's check some boxes, I challenged. Religion: I'd check Protestant, and you'd check Jewish. Ethnic Background: I'd check German, and you'd check Dutch. 'No,' she said, forcefully. 'No, I'd check Jewish.'" Gunther splayed his hands, implying it couldn't be clearer. "Get it, now?"

A thin smile tugged at the corners of Tannen's mouth. "Was she cute?"

"Very," Gunther replied with a mischievous twinkle. "We've been married for twenty-two years."

"Mazel tov," Tannen said with a chuckle. "Nice lady, Grace. The Hopper show at the Whitney a couple of years ago…that was hers wasn't it?"

Gunther nodded his eyes glowing with pride. "She's working on a Kandinsky retrospective at the Guggenheim now." He cocked his head in thought. "Come to think of it, Grace volunteers at the Wiesenthal Center in her spare time. She might have an angle on this archivist thing."

"I'm sure she would," Tannen said, his expression darkening at a recollection. "You know, when I was a kid, my Uncle Nat had a series of books on World War II. I start flipping pages, and before I know it, I'm staring at a mountain of emaciated corpses being bulldozed into a mass grave. It was sickeing. Paralyzing. My uncle, well, he was a kindly man who watched Meet the Press when Lawrence Spivak was the moderator, and subscribed to the *Kiplinger Letter* when it was a typewritten flyer. Pretty well-informed for a guy with a floor covering store in Brooklyn; but strictly old school. Kept his feelings to himself."

"So what happened?"

"He closed the book, looked at me with this sad smile, and said, 'One day, when you're older we'll talk about this.' But he died and we never had that conversation."

"You and I are having it now," Gunther said, softly.

CHAPTER EIGHT

A grime-blackened rescue worker in winter coveralls lumbered into the Emergency Room at the University of Munich Hospital carrying the limp body of a child. He made his way between the stretchers in the waiting area and past the queues of walking wounded slumped against the walls into the makeshift treatment center.

It had once been the Assembly Hall; but after the heavy bombings in April and July of last year, it had been taken over by the hospital to accommodate the ever-increasing number of casualties. The central core served as a processing area. The perimeter was lined with rows of curtained enclosures in which harried doctors and nurses, wearing sweaters and scarves beneath their gowns, treated the most critically injured victims. The air had an icy crispness and a medicinal scent that mixed with the odor of those who were still clinging to life, and of those who had lost their grip on it.

Dr. Eva Rosenberg had spent the last hour, trying to save the life of a young man whose broken body lay on a blood-drenched gurney. "We've lost him," she said with a defeated sigh to the nurse who'd been assisting her.

Despite the exhausting chaos, Eva still carried herself with the confidence of someone who had always been as smart as the boys in her class, and even smarter when it came to medical school. Her lynx-like eyes had the blue-green intensity of her Galician forebears who had also passed on their raven-black hair. Clasped at the nape of her neck, it swept across the back of her white smock which concealed her willowy figure.

During centuries of tumultuous history, Galicia had been controlled by warring Polish Kings, Austro-Hungarian potentates, vengeful Polish tyrants, and was, now, being overrun by brutal Russian troops. When the disorder that followed World War One gave rise to pogroms, Eva's father, an artisan who worked in gold, moved the family to Venice, in Northern Italy, where a more tolerant and wealthy clientele awaited.

Crushed by her failure to save the young man's life, Dr. Rosenberg gathered herself, then slipped between the curtains into the aisle. The rescue worker with the child was coming toward her. "Here! Over here!" she called out, fetching a gurney. The bone-weary doctor placed two fingers on the little girl's neck as two nurses joined her and rolled the gurney into one of the enclosures. "Her pulse is weak, her blood volume's low; and she's severely dehydrated."

The nurses knew what to do. They'd been doing it day and night for as long as they could remember. One affixed an oxygen mask over the child's face then slipped an IV needle into her arm. The other began cutting off her clothing that had stiffened with dried blood. "Piece of shrapnel here, doctor," she said, pointing to a shard of blackened metal protruding from the child's thigh.

"Might have punctured her femoral artery," Eva said, examining the festering wound. "If it did and we remove it…"

"Like a finger in a dike," the nurse said.

"Precisely. She could bleed to death before an O.R. becomes available." Eva traced the path of the artery with her stethoscope. "Evenly paced flow above and below the wound," she announced which meant it hadn't been pierced. "Let's get it out of there." She was grasping the shard with a pair of forceps when the curtain swept aside, revealing Professor Gerhard in a lodencoat and a hat that partially obscured his face.

"See you for a minute, Doctor?" Gerhard knew it would be unwise to make the reason public, and said it in as casual a tone as he could manage.

"Sure. As soon as I get—this nasty piece of shrapnel—out of here."

"I have an emergency that can't wait, Doctor," Gerhard said with more intensity, circling the gurney.

"So do I, professor. She could die if—"

The professor was next to her, now, and through clenched teeth, hissed, "So could you. The SS just paid me a visit. Your exemption's been revoked."

Eva stiffened, but maintained her concentration, and removed the piece of metal from the child's thigh. The fleshy crater filled with fluid but there was no spurting of arterial blood. "Dress the wound," she said smartly to the nurses. "And keep her warm. She's in shock."

"I'm sorry, Eva," Gerhard said, guiding her aside. "Max called to warn me but it was too late."

"No wonder he hasn't been here. Jake and I really missed him in Ortho last night," Eva said, referring to Captain Kleist's talent for orthopedic surgery; to the exceptional skills for setting broken bones, for screwing complex fractures back together, for reducing dislocated joints that all three of them shared, and that the Professor had cited to Major Steig to no avail. "Max," she said, her voice taut with concern. "Is he all right?"

"He's fine," the professor replied not wanting to take the time to explain. "You can't stay here. The SS have arrest warrants for you and Jacob."

The color drained from Eva's face.

"They're searching the building as we speak," the Professor went on. "You know where Jake is working?"

Eva shrugged, seeming as traumatized as the child she'd been treating. "He's here somewhere. Trying to put Humpty Dumpty back together again."

"Find him. Come out the morgue entrance. They won't be looking there. I'll be waiting in my car. Now. There's not a minute to spare."

CHAPTER NINE

Stacey was disappointed the suitcase couldn't be opened, and was determined to find the Jacob Epstein who, during the Holocaust, had painted his name on the, now, vintage Steinbach. She emerged from the subway on Broadway and 79th—as she did every day on the way home—and made a beeline for the Apthorp.

John O'Hara, one of several long-serving doormen, was on duty. From the standup desk in the lobby, he tracked visitors, workmen and deliveries on a computer that displayed the data on monitors above the banks of mailboxes and in the Resident Manager's office. He knew every resident in the building's 163 units by name, along with their friends and family, as well as old-timers from the neighborhood whom he allowed to sit and read in The Apthorp's 12,000 square foot garden—which was where he and Stacey were talking amidst the calming gurgle of its fountains.

"Naw, no Epsteins in the building," John said, his Jersey Boys pompadour undone by a breeze. He tapped a cigarette from a pack and lit it. "But I'm pretty sure there was one when I first started. Jake Epstein. He was a doctor. A pretty famous one, too."

Stacey's eyes widened with intrigue. "What do you mean famous?"

John shrugged, smoke streaming from his nose and mouth. "You know. You hear things, stuff in the papers, on TV…Dr. Epstein honored for this, made chairman of that. Had a lovely wife. She was a doctor too. Must be twenty years since they moved out."

"Moved out? As into another residence, or as into the family plot?"

"No, no," John replied with an amused chuckle. "Wherever he went, it wasn't in a body bag."

"You remember if he had an accent or anything?"

John flicked his ashes into a planter. "Yeah, New York-Jewish. You know, instead of Upper West Side, he'd say Upper Vest Side. With a V."

"Thanks," Stacey said, brightly, slipping him a ten. "Thanks a lot." Bound by the doorman's code of delayed gratification or disappointment, as the case may be, John pocketed the bill without looking at it.

Doctor. Doctor Jacob Epstein. This was a vital piece of information. Stacey had what she needed to narrow the search, and hurried across the street to her building. Its beige bricks and tacky aluminum windows were in marked contrast to her apartment that had a charming ambience. Indeed, furnished with an eclectic assemblage of found objects, it was the quintessential expression of her acquisitive personality.

She came through the door to find her boyfriend in the living room seated at her trestle table desk, the discarded one he had helped carry home and restore. Looking disheveled and sleep deprived, Adam Stevens was typing furiously on her computer while listening to the shimmering harmonies of a Phillip Glass Violin Concerto on his iPod. He had a pleasant face with sincere eyes and the two-day growth favored by male models and young leading men like Clive Owen, whom Stacey thought he resembled, which was why—when she wanted to get his attention or reinforce a point—she called him by the actor's name.

"Hey, surprise, surprise, didn't expect to find you here," Stacey said, dropping her shoulder bag to the floor and kicking off her pumps. "What's going on?"

"My computer crashed," Adam replied without looking up from his work, though he did stop typing just long enough to remove his ear buds. "I think the hard drive got fried. I hope you don't mind."

"No, but that's why God made cell phones, Clive. I mean, like, suppose I was getting it on with this *NYT* reporter and Columbia alum who just happened to be a guest lecturer in my Ethics In Journalism Class?" she teased, recalling the very circumstances which, several years earlier, had jump-started their relationship.

"You could've been getting it on with Clive himself, and I wouldn't have noticed," Adam said, fingers flying over the keyboard. "I'm sorry. I'm on deadline. I panicked."

"Which translates to what?" Stacey wondered rhetorically. "If you don't get that story filed, you'll join the long list of *NYT* casualties?"

"That's not funny," Adam said, his eyes riveted to the text-filled monitor. "They announced a hundred more layoffs, yesterday. Twenty-five in the newsroom."

"Unbelievable," Stacey exclaimed. "They can blow six hundred million on a new building but they can't pay the reporters who work in it."

"Yeah, along with the *Boston Globe*, the *L.A. Times*, the *Chicago Tribune*," Adam said, still typing away. "Hang in there. I won't be much longer."

"No problem, I just need to Google somebody when you're done."

"That's why God made Blackberries," Adam said, a little too matter-of-factly.

"Gee, Clive, how come I didn't think of that?"

"You want hard copy," Adam deduced.

"You're a rocket scientist, you know?" Stacey said with good-natured sarcasm; then in a conciliatory tone, added, "Yeah, I might want to print it out. Depends on what I find." She mussed his hair, affectionately, as she headed into the kitchen which had a pass-through countertop and was open to the living area. "Get you a beer or anything?" she called out.

"A beer would be great."

"Everybody keeps talking about the sorry state of the newspaper business," Stacey went on, pulling a couple of Coronas from the refrigerator. "Pretty soon there won't be any newspapers." She headed back into the living room with the beers, closing the door with a backward swipe of her foot.

"Story signed, sealed, and—" Adam mouse-clicked on Send before adding, "—filed! That'll teach those oil companies to contaminate groundwater in Queens!" Then, with the euphoria that always seems to accompany the completion of writing anything, he looked over his shoulder at Stacey and prompted, "Okay! So who are we Googling?!"

"We?" Stacey echoed, handing him the beer. "Who are you, my administrative assistant?"

"Among other things," Adam said with a salacious smile. She was standing right next to him, now, and he slipped his hand under her skirt, moving it slowly upward between her thighs.

Stacey emitted a little squeal as his fingertip found its mark, and twisted away from him. "Oh no. No way, Jose. Well, not until you Google Doctor Jacob Epstein for me."

Adam laughed and typed it in the search window.

"The word Doctor is key," Stacey warned as Adam clicked on Go. "Truth is, I actually did Google him on my Blackberry; but I didn't know he was a doc; and ended up with a coupl'a hundred thousand useless hits."

"Jacob Epstein the doctor," Adam announced as the screen came alive. Per standard Google format, the heading read: Results 1-10 of about 10,700 for Dr. Jacob Epstein. (0.35 seconds) "Let's see…He's an orthopedic surgeon… Inventor of prosthetic devices…Holder of dozens of patents. Not to mention Chairman Emeritus, Department of Orthopedic Surgery at Mount Sinai Medical Center. Has a Family Foundation dedicated to supporting Jewish charitable causes. Headquarters in NYC."

"Yessss! That's him. Has to be!" Stacey exclaimed, doing a little pirouette that positioned her over Adam's shoulder. "Born Vienna, 1920," she went on, reading from the screen. "University of Munich Medical School…surgical residency nineteen forty-four…Married to Dr. Hannah Epstein, nee Friedman." Her head tilted at a thought. "Is there an obit?"

Adam took a long sip of beer, then scrolled down the screen, and shook his head no. "Nope, no DOD."

"Which means he's still among the living. Yes!" Stacey exclaimed with delight. She held up her bottle of Corona to Adam's. "Way to go!"

"What's this all about anyway?" he wondered as they clinked in triumph.

"Campaign I'm working on," Stacey replied. "And he's the key to it."

Adam's eyes narrowed in confusion. "An eighty-what year-old retired orthopedic surgeon? What's he going to be pitching? Peg-legs for Somali pirates?"

"No, pull-levers for one armed bandits," Stacey retorted with an evasive cackle followed by a long swallow of beer. "Anything there about the Holocaust?"

Adam scrolled down the screen. "Yeah. Yeah, says he was at Auschwitz."

"Awesome!" Stacey said, envisioning the possibilities. "Bart is really going to go nuts when I tell him. This is fantastic!"

Adam looked baffled. "How could you say that?"

"I'm sworn to secrecy," Stacey said, mysteriously. "Agency-client privilege." She gestured to the computer, and added, commandingly, "Don't just sit there, Clive. Print that stuff out."

Adam recoiled, looking offended. "Pardon me?"

"That's what administrative assistants do, isn't it," she said in a sexy voice, undoing the buttons of her blouse; then, sensing his distance, she switched to a more sincere tone, and asked, "You're really worried about getting laid-off, aren't you, Adam?"

Adam nodded, glumly. "You know what reporters have in common with Cochran frogs and Indian pythons?"

"They're all cold blooded?"

"Thanks," Adam said, trying not to laugh. "They're all on the endangered species list."

"This isn't exactly the Golden Age of print journalism, is it?" Stacey said sadly; then brightening at a thought, she added, "But if Dr. Epstein works out, I've got an idea for a fantastic story that just might have your byline on it."

Adam looked up at her with an expression that ran the gamut from surprise, through hope, to curiosity.

Stacey nodded, reassuringly, then took his head in her hands, and kissed him. As their lips were parting, at that moment when the moist surfaces adhere for one last instant before releasing, she slipped a hand inside her open blouse and undid her bra, then gently hugged his face to her breasts.

"Got a little nervous energy you want to work off?" Adam mumbled, his voice lost in the soft folds of fabric and flesh.

"A lot," Stacey said in a breathy whisper.

"You're bad," Adam said as they slid down onto the rug in a passionate grapple.

"You have no idea," Stacey purred.

CHAPTER TEN

Snow was falling as Professor Gerhard's car pulled away from the morgue entrance at the rear of Munich University Hospital. The two-door Opel Olympia, first produced in 1935 in honor of the upcoming Olympic Games in Berlin, had more than 100,000 kilometers on it. After ten harsh winters, its heater was no match for the below freezing weather.

Just moments ago, Dr. Jacob Epstein was in an operating room trying to save the bomb-shattered arm of a young woman. He had repaired the torn musculature and circulatory vessels, and was reassembling the broken pieces of her humerus, prior to literally screwing them back together, when Dr. Eva Rosenberg entered with the shocking news that their exemptions had been revoked and SS warrants issued for their arrest.

Now, his head still filled with the medicinal odor of the O.R., the collar of his trench coat turned up against the cold, Jake slouched in the back seat of the professor's car, staring numbly out the frosty window. "Bastards," he grunted through clenched teeth. Despite his current distemper, he had an engaging smile, when he needed it, and dark, unruly hair that tumbled over his ears and forehead, softening his sharp features and eyes that sparkled with intelligence. "We should've known this was going to happen."

"We did know," Eva said. Bundled in winter clothing, she was sitting next to the Professor with her knees up against the dash, and her physician's bag nestled in her lap. "We just didn't want to believe it. We just wouldn't accept—"

"Enough," the Professor interrupted, squinting to see through the windshield where a single wiper was streaking across the frosty glass. "That's neither here nor there, now. You'll both have to go into hiding. You have no choice."

"Hiding?!" Jake erupted in frustration. "People are being blown to bits, torn to shreds, incinerated. We can help them. Why are we going into hiding?!"

"To stay alive long enough to help them later," the Professor answered gently. "I'm hoping you can spend a few nights at Max's. After that, we'll have to find a place where you'll be safe."

"What about our things?" Jake asked.

"Yes," Eva chimed-in. "Everything I own is in my room. Can we stop along the way?"

"I'd say it's up to the SS, wouldn't you?" the Professor replied.

Jake Epstein had a one room flat in a building on Augustenstrasse that catered to students. The non-descript structure was situated just off the corner of Ziebland in easy walking distance of the University. "I'm going to drive past," the Professor said as they approached. "If it's safe we'll come back around. Tell me what you see."

"I see trouble," Eva said, as the car rolled through the intersection.

"SS trouble," Jake added. "Two staff cars blocking the street and a personnel carrier. Which means all I've got are the clothes on my back and my briefcase." The latter doubled as a doctor's bag and, along with medical instruments, contained a worn copy of *All Quiet on the Western Front* which Jake had read as a teenager and was, now, rereading. Published in Germany in 1929, Erich Maria Remarque's anti-war novel was in Group 1 on the Führer's list of banned books: All Copies To Be Destroyed. This accounted for the *Mein Kampf* dust jacket with which Jake had shrewdly camouflaged his copy.

The professor detoured south in the direction of Eva's apartment, a third floor walkup on Koenigstrasse a few blocks from the Hauptbahnof, the main railway station. The working class neighborhood was across town from the Medical School; but rents were much lower than in the University District; and it was convenient whenever she wanted to take the train to Venice to visit her family. The street appeared to be clear of SS vehicles as they approached.

"Go around back," Eva said, removing her gloves. She tossed them atop the dash and fished her keys from her purse. "There's less chance of running into a neighbor."

Moments later, the car turned into a narrow alley. An icy veneer sheathed the cobblestones. The Professor drove through an obstacle course of parked vehicles, overflowing trash receptacles, and debris from air raids that had been bulldozed into mountainous piles. The rear of Eva's building was covered by black wrought iron staircases that zigzagged back and forth from landing to landing.

"As quickly as you can, Eva," the Professor said as the car lurched to a stop.

Eva was out the door before he finished and didn't stop to close it. She ran up the icy steps to the third floor landing, crept to the door, and wiped the frost from the small wire-glass window with a cuff. The corridor beyond appeared clear. The staircase was the building's emergency egress and the doors on the landings weren't locked. She slipped inside, then let herself into her room, and pulled a canvas rucksack from beneath the bed.

Minutes later, the bag was filled with clothing, toiletries, and a few treasured books. A framed snapshot of she and Max—arms around each other's waists, their faces alive with the enchanted glow that belongs to young lovers—stood on a table between the windows. She had just slipped it into the bag when the crunch of tires on snow got her attention. Two SS staff cars were approaching. One stopped in front of her building. Several SS men got out and trudged toward the entrance. The other vehicle circled a tenement that had collapsed during one of the bombings, and headed for the alley.

Eva slung the rucksack over her shoulder, took one last look around the room, scooped a bracelet from atop the dresser, and dashed into the corridor. Men's voices and the pounding of jackboots and clattering of military gear came from below, propelling her toward the exit. Once outside, she clambered down the icy staircases until she reached the alley and ran to the car. Without breaking stride, she threw the rucksack through the open door and jumped in after it. "They're here, Professor! They're here!"

Gerhard jammed the car into gear and floored the accelerator. The Opel rumbled off, skidding on the snow-slick cobblestones, and turned into the cross street just as the second SS car entered the opposite end of the alley. A short time later, they were heading east on Luitpoldstrasse toward the Prinzregentenbrucke, one of three bridges that arched with Neo-Romanesque grace across the Isar River. The latter—which flowed south through Munich to Upper Bavaria and the lake country north of Innsbruck at the foot of the Alps—was completely frozen over, its steep banks encrusted with crystalline splashes of ice that rose to the adjacent roadways.

The Professor's car came off the bridge into the ellipse that circles the Friedensengel, a grand monument to Germany's victory in the Franco-Prussian War. Atop its towering Corinthian column, a gilded statue of an angel with flared wings, soared high above the trees.

"The Angel of Peace," Jake said with bitter sarcasm. "Who do they think they're kidding?!"

"She's still standing," the Professor countered. "The way things are going for Hitler these days, she may yet prevail."

"If we ever live to see it," Eva said, curled up in her seat against the cold.

"I always thought cynicism was an affliction that came with age," the Professor said, attempting to lighten the mood. "How come I'm the optimist and you two are the gloom-and-doomers?"

"Because we are Jews," Eva retorted.

"We are the ones with targets on our backs," Jake chimed-in. "Bright, yellow, six-pointed ones."

"And I'm the one keeping you out of the crosshairs," the Professor said, "Jew or not, if I'm not careful, I'm next. Steig will stop at nothing," Gerhard went on, taking Moulstrasse that ran north to Bogenhausen, the city's most aristocratic residential district.

This was an area of stately mansions and imposing townhouses where royal barons mixed with the barons of industry and finance; where upper-class families—many untouched by the catastrophic collapse of the German economy, though not by the air raids that had destroyed a number of their grand dwellings—lived amid the very trappings of privilege against which Adolph Hitler railed. Indeed, the mentally and economically depressed working class --- having little connection to the cradle of culture that had produced the likes of Beethoven and Mozart; Schopenhauer and Nietzsche; Goethe, Brecht, and Mann; Durer, Holbein and Cranach --- found the Führer's fanaticism and policies of racial superiority compelling.

The Kleists lived on Possartplatz, a stately Square that enclosed an oasis of mature trees. Their bare branches, sheathed with ice, sent sparkling canopies arching above the streets. The art-filled townhouse had a quiet, neo-classic grandness befitting its owner's social standing and business prominence. It was one of several that still had Christmas decorations in the windows and on the door. Despite the constant threat of airstrikes the Kleists had decided against consigning their priceless collection to underground bunkers, preferring to live with it and, if need be, die with it. Indeed, despite Hitler's ban on modern art, many top-ranking Nazis, Hermann Goering among them, collected it with a passion, using the Führer's decree as an excuse to confiscate it from wealthy Jewish businessmen, bankers and art dealers, and keeping it for themselves.

From the moment the Opel left the alley behind Eva's flat, the Professor's eyes had been darting to the rearview mirror which was, now, blurred with condensation. "Jake. That car behind us," he said as they neared Possartplatz. "Can you tell if it's SS?"

Jake twisted around to the tiny window behind him. He wiped it with a glove and squinted to see through the streaked glass. "Looks like a black Mercedes…"

"That's what worries me," the Professor said, his suspicion all but confirmed.

"…but it isn't flying SS flags," Jake added.

The Professor winced. "Sometimes they take them off when they don't want to be spotted."

"Either that or Himmler sicced the Gestapo onto us," Eva said, referring to the Reichführer's iron-fisted control not only of the SS but also the state police. The Geheimes Staatspolizei, his plainclothes sociopaths who drove unmarked cars and operated without the constraints of a military code of ethics, were as inhumanely ruthless as their SS counterparts, only more so.

"We can't go anywhere near Max's place until we're certain it's neither of them," the Professor said. Instead of turning into Possartplatz, he continued along Holbstrasse for several blocks, then made a left into Muhlbaur, angling across the eastern-most section of Bogenhausen that had been turned to rubble by Allied warplanes. The snow had intensified making it even more difficult to see the car they feared was tailing them. If it was the SS or Gestapo, the snow might also make it more difficult for them to maintain contact with their prey; but when Jake peered out the window again, the black Mercedes was still behind them.

CHAPTER ELEVEN

Bart Tannen didn't go nuts as Stacey had predicted when she briefed him on her Google search, but he took immediate action. From the data she had downloaded, he knew that Dr. Jacob Epstein lived in a townhouse on East 78th Street off Fifth Avenue. He and his wife, Hannah, occupied the upper duplex while the lower three floors housed The Epstein Family Foundation. When his contact information turned out to be unlisted, Tannen called the Foundation and explained he was trying to reach Dr. Epstein about an extremely important personal matter.

"Well…" the receptionist mused. "The doctor's son is the Foundation's Director. He handles all family matters. Perhaps if you explained it to him…"

"Be glad to," Tannen said, prompting her to put him on hold and transfer the call.

"This is Dan Epstein," a polished voice said after a brief interval.

After identifying himself and his position at Gunther Global, Tannen explained that in the course of working on an assignment, the agency had come into possession of a discarded suitcase. It appeared to be Holocaust memorabilia. There were reasons to believe it had belonged to his father.

"You have my attention," Epstein, said, intrigued. "What's this about?"

"I'll be more than happy to explain; but it'd be a waste of time, if it isn't your father's suitcase. We just need him to take a look at it and say yea or nay."

"I couldn't get my father involved without meeting with you, first. I might even be able to make the determination myself."

"Fine," Tannen prompted smartly, seizing on the offer. "Where and when?"

Mid-morning the following day, Tannen and Stacey got out of a taxi in front of an imposing townhouse. A bronze plaque proclaimed: The Epstein Family Foundation. The limestone mansion—one of a dozen or so that lined East 78th Street between Fifth and Madison just off Central Park—would have sold for forty million at the height of the market. They checked in at the security desk in the reception hall where an exuberant spray of fresh flowers stood framed by tall windows that overlooked a garden. On one wall Dr. Jacob Epstein's many awards, honorary degrees, and memberships in professional societies were displayed; on another were brass plaques with photo-engraved diagrams of the many patents for prosthetic devices he had been awarded.

The Director's office had a quiet grandness due to its generous 19th Century proportions and fine period antiques. The historical illusion was broken only by the computer screens and Bloomberg terminals on the desk and the man who made the Foundation's investment decisions based on the data they provided. Dan Epstein always greeted his guests in shirtsleeves—the de facto, if misleading, symbol of Wall Street transparency—and looked resplendent in suspenders, striped shirt with solid collar and cuffs, and boldly patterned tie.

A competitive man in his mid-fifties, he played tennis on weekends, poker on Wednesday nights, and conducted investment seminars at the 92nd Street Y. Thirty years ago, he completed the combined JD/MBA program at New York University's Schools of Law and Business and joined Goldman Sachs. Two decades later, having become partner and General Counsel, he left to run the Family Foundation and had increased its endowment, substantially.

While Tannen made the introductory small talk, Stacey slipped a laptop from her shoulder bag and set it on the conference table. Now, she began stepping through a series of high-resolution images of the suitcase she had prepared with an agency photographer the previous day. Dan Epstein's eyes narrowed behind his frameless lenses as an image of the battered suitcase filled the screen. It was followed by close-ups of: the name Jacob Epstein crudely painted on the underside, its worn latches, and its sweat-darkened handle to which a makeshift luggage tag with handwritten data was affixed by a twisted wire. "You said it was found on the street?" he finally said, sounding incredulous and emotionally moved at the same time.

"Uh-huh..." Stacey replied in her brisk way. "I live on West Eightieth across from The Apthorp...the renaissance knock-off with the iron gates and garden? It was in the trash outside the service entrance."

"Oh, yes I know The Apthorp," Epstein replied with a wry smile. "I know it quite well. I grew up there."

"Oh-oh," Stacey said, flustered by her faux pas. "I'm really sorry. I didn't mean to be so flip."

"I couldn't have described it better myself," Epstein said, absolving her.

"Excuse me, would you mind if we cut to the chase, here?" Tannen said, his curiosity getting the better of him. "Is that your father's suitcase, or isn't it?"

Epstein nodded. "I recall seeing it as a child. The writing on the tag could be his; but handwriting changes over time so it's hard to be sure." He paused in reflection and prompted, "As I recall, it has something to do with an assignment you're working on."

Tannen nodded. "Steinbach, a high quality luggage manufacturer is the client; and now that we know the suitcase is your father's, we'd like to feature him and his suitcase in the ads that'll kick-off the campaign."

Epstein removed his glasses and rubbed the bridge of his nose. "Well, he either left the suitcase behind on purpose or just plain forgot about it, which leads me to believe he wanted to rid himself of the horrible memories it brings to mind." He slipped the glasses back on, and then concluded, "I'm not inclined to overrule that decision, subconscious though it may have been."

"If I may," Stacey said, her mind racing to find a counter argument. "Your theory doesn't seem to be in keeping with your father's commitment to Jewish causes…with the mission of this Foundation. Does it?"

"A valid point," Epstein conceded. "But one might also conclude establishing the Foundation was his way of depersonalizing the Holocaust, of making it about others instead of himself. If my father had his fill of it then, he certainly isn't up to dealing with it, now. No, as healthy as he may be, and he's quite spry for his age, thank God, I'm afraid the answer is no."

"But you haven't heard the idea yet," Stacey said, launching into a sales pitch. "The theme of the campaign is: Traveling Companions For Life, and will feature vintage Steinbachs and their owners who've shared meaningful experiences—like your father did with this one. You recall Irving—"

"Young lady," Epstein said, trying to interrupt.

"—Irving Penn's photographs of cigarette butts?" Stacey went on. "We're planning to use the same kind of character-enriched black-and-white photographs to evoke a sense of the past, of history, of people who have—"

"Young lady, please?" Epstein said, more sharply.

Stacey winced and shot an anxious glance in Tannen's direction.

"That slogan doesn't really reflect my father's experience, now, does it?" Epstein challenged. "Frankly, I'm not sure what you're proposing is appropriate or ethically acceptable. Furthermore, risk analysis is at the heart of my work, and I don't see the upside, here. Personally, I find it distasteful, disturbing…"

"We had similar concerns, Mr. Epstein…" Tannen said, deciding candor and a strategic pause would serve him best. "…until the company's CEO informed us he was a survivor of Auschwitz."

Epstein's brows went up, his indignation tempered by Tannen's reply. "I see…"

"And though Mr. Steinbach believes your father's endorsement will sell luggage," Tannen went on, sensing the tide had turned, "he even more fervently believes, that at a time when anti-Semitism is on the rise, it'll keep the memory of the Holocaust alive."

"He may very well be right," Epstein said, seeming to be reconsidering his decision. "As you know, my father has been in the forefront of that issue for decades." He paused and pursed his lips in thought. "You know, it hadn't even occurred to me to ask if the suitcase is empty. Is it? Is there anything in it?"

"Yes there is," Tannen replied, explaining that: the suitcase was locked; and the agency had decided to obtain permission from its owner, if possible, before having it opened by an archivist to insure the contents were properly handled and catalogued.

"That's very commendable, Mr. Tannen. They might have more sentimental value, even more historical value, than the suitcase itself." Epstein looked off for a moment. "Well, my decision may have been a bit hasty. I mean—" The intercom buzzed. He smiled in apology, circled his desk and lifted the phone. "Sure, put her on — Hi, what's up?" he said, his eyes drifting to a data-filled Bloomberg terminal. "Uh-huh, uh-huh — Honey, it's her day — Yes, from the minute she was born. So, why stop now? — Yes, yes it's fine with me — Love you too." He hung up, and with empathy, said, "My long suffering wife. Our daughter Melissa is getting married in two weeks. My father, who's a trustee at the Metropolitan Museum, has arranged for the reception to be held in the Temple of Dendur. His wedding gift to his granddaughter." Epstein laughed and added, "You'd think we were planning a presidential inaugural."

"I can imagine," Tannen said, laughing along with him. "Congratulations."

"Sounds fantastic," Stacey chimed-in.

Epstein nodded, enjoying the sense of fulfillment that accompanies such milestones. Even more enjoyable was the sense of relief that comes from suddenly seeing the key to making a difficult decision so clearly that it becomes easy. "I shared that with you because my wife's call reminded me these are very happy times for my family; and, seeing your proposal in that context... well, despite the potential for keeping the memory of the Holocaust alive, and fighting anti-Semitism that it offers, I've decided against my father's participation. I can't in good conscience ask him to relive it at this time in his life. I just can't. I hope you understand."

"Couldn't you at least mention it to him?' Stacey said, unwilling to concede defeat. "I mean it was his life. He lived it. Don't you think he has the right to decide whether or not he wants to participate?"

"No," Epstein said, sounding offended. "No one is more protective of my father's rights than I am, young lady." He paused, his eyes narrowing in suspicion; then, diagramming his thoughts with lawyerly precision, said, "Are you people suggesting—because the suitcase had been discarded—and is now in your possession—that my family's access to it and its contents—is predicated on my father's participation in this advertising campaign?"

"Absolutely not," Tannen said without hesitation.

"Good. Because I'd take legal action if you were. We have nothing more to discuss. I'll be in contact with your legal department to make arrangements to acquire the suitcase and its contents."

"Of course," Tannen said, having little choice but to accept defeat.

Stacey's posture stiffened, her characteristic tenacity driving her to try just one more time to get Dan Epstein to change his mind. Tannen's eyes were sending frantic signals to the contrary. A tension-filled moment passed before Stacey bit a lip, and shut-down the computer.

"Well, that went well," Tannen said as they left Tannen's office and hurried from the townhouse.

"Sorry if I screwed up, boss. Sometimes my mouth gets in the way of my mind."

"There's nothing either of us coulda, woulda, or shoulda said that would've made a difference."

"Thanks," Stacey replied. "I'm really glad you said that. Now what?"

"You remember the Sopranos?"

Stacey nodded. "Who doesn't?"

"Well, as Tony said before whacking Big Pussy, 'Never sit on bad news. Always deliver it in person."

They hailed a cab that was headed south on Fifth Avenue. Tannen called Steinbach's office and said they'd be there in ten minutes. The taxi was in a traffic snarl in front of the main branch of the New York Public Library on 42nd Street when Stacey's cellphone rang. The word Mom was blinking in the display. She thought about it, then slipped the Blackberry back into her handbag. The news line on the taxi's TV screen read: AHMADINEJAD REITERATES CALL FOR DESTRUCTION OF ISRAEL.

Steinbach & Company's offices were located on West 38th Street in what was left of Manhattan's Garment District. The building, clad in textured brown brick, was around the corner from the Garment Center Synagogue and the two-story tall Button-And-Needle sculpture on 7th Avenue. The outsourcing of manufacturing to countries with cheap labor had been the death knell of the needle trades; and for twenty years Sol had been running his operation out of what had once been a thriving coat factory. Leather samples were stacked on tables along with spools of waxed twine and plastic boxes filled with hardware. The only high-tech equipment in sight were computer monitors that displayed inventory-control and billing data, and the $12,000 Trek Equinox TTX SS1 Giro d'Italia racing bike in Steinbach's office. It was the same model Lance Armstrong used to win his seventh Tour De France. Sol used it to ride back and forth to work every day from his Upper East Side apartment.

"Excuse the outfit," Steinbach said, referring to the black polyurthene leggings and pullover slashed with bright yellow racing stripes that he was wearing. All hell broke loose soon as I got in, and I haven't had a minute to jump in the shower."

"No thanks to us," Tannen said.

Steinbach dismissed it with a wave of his hand, and settled behind a gray Steelcase desk that dated to the seventies. "Listen, before we get to your stuff, the serial number search hit a snag. In the old days, the company was based in Leipzig which ended up in East Germany. Getting out of there in one piece let alone with records was..." he let it trail off and splayed his hands in frustration.

"Yeah, the client database doesn't make the punch list when you're running for your life, does it?"

"Exactly. Fucking Communists were taking over everything. My uncle grabbed the patterns and records with one hand and me with the other, and got the hell out of there. It was amazing how many old world craftsmen ended up here. He hired every one he could find who had worked for a European trunk maker. It wasn't easy but—"

"Sol? Sol?" Tannen said, interrupting. "The records? The serial number?"

"Sorry, once I get started. Anyway, all the old records are in storage…somewhere in New Jersey. It's going to take a while."

"It's a moot point, anyway, Mr. Steinbach," Stacey said, getting into it gently.

Steinbach stiffened and kicked back in his chair. "Don't sugarcoat it. He's dead? He's dying? What?"

"No, we found him and he's fine," Stacey replied. "But we got turned down. He's not going to sign on."

Steinbach's shoulders sagged in disappointment. "The good doctor said no?"

"His son did," Tannen replied.

"Just like that?" Steinbach said, sounding incredulous. "Who the hell is this guy?"

Tannen gave him the data Stacey had printed-out from Google. As Steinbach scanned the pages, Tannen briefed him on Dan Epstein's refusal, mentioning his daughter's wedding, and his intention to acquire the suitcase and its contents.

"It's on me. I blew it," Steinbach said, shaking the pages in frustration. "This is the Jake Epstein I was on those charity boards with. Haven't seen him for years." He emitted a deflated sigh before his busy eyes came alive and he cocked his head at a thought. "Did you say his granddaughter's getting married?"

"Yeah. In a couple of weeks. Temple of Dendur yet."

Steinbach's expression brightened. His eyes took on a mischievous sparkle. "Don't let that suitcase out of your sight, Bart. This isn't over."

"It isn't?"

"Nope," Steinbach replied, stabbing a finger at his intercom. "Yeah, I need Bernice."

CHAPTER TWELVE

At about the same time Professor Gerhard was taking evasive measures on Munich's snowy streets, Dr. Maximilian Kleist, Captain, Waffen SS was with his parents in the library of the family's 19th Century townhouse. The walls, crafted of Bavarian black walnut, were inlaid with rosettes as were the coffers between the finely detailed ceiling beams. A circular staircase led to a cast iron balcony, making the upper tier of volumes accessible. Blackout drapes, drawn at night to ward off Allied airstrikes, and a book entitled German War Christmas—published by the Nazi Propaganda Office and distributed at home and at the front—were the only evidence of the War.

Konrad Kleist, a tall man with a strong profile and steel-gray hair that swept back in perfect waves, stood next to a marble fireplace. 'Concert,' a large canvas by the expatriate Russian, and one-time Munich resident, Wassily Kandinsky, who had recently died in Paris, hung above the mantle. Konrad's wife, Gisela, an elegant, fine-boned woman who favored Chanel suits, was seated on an Art Nouveau sofa. A black German Shepherd lay at her feet. Max, who had changed from his uniform into a tweed hunting jacket and corduroy trousers, leaned against the piano, smoking a cigarette. A cello that dated to the mid-18th Century stood nearby.

"What were you thinking, Max?" the elder Kleist demanded. "How could you have been so careless? For years I've been walking a tightrope. Not once have I teetered let alone fallen. And now…" He sighed and slipped a pack of North States from a pocket. Konrad favored the Finnish brand not only for their heady flavor, but also because the twelve-pack's slim profile didn't ruin the line of his bespoke suits. His gold lighter was engraved with a double-K monogram as were his cufflinks. He lit the cigarette and inhaled deeply, as if this would give him the strength to deal with the situation.

"I'm sorry, Dad," Max said, meeting his father's gaze. His tone was respectful, not remorseful, and made it clear he wouldn't be cowed. "I've done my best to live an exemplary life in the spirit of this family. I took every precaution, believe me."

"Yes, we're sure you did," his mother said softly admonishing her husband with a glance. "Perhaps, it would have been wise to share this with us before today."

"It wasn't an oversight, Mother," Max explained, exhaling a stream of smoke. "Eva and I thought it best to wait until the war was over and we knew what kind of a world we'd be living in before committing our hearts to it, or asking for your blessing."

Gisela Kleist's eyes were moist with empathy. "Of course, but with these...these sociopaths committing such unimaginable atrocities, it behooved you and this young lady to be more discrete."

"Believe me, Mother, we were. I'm not even sure Professor Gerhard knew."

"Then how?" his father asked.

"An informer," Max replied. "Someone must've gone to the SS."

"How many times have I said, trust no one but family," his father said, dragging on his cigarette to contain his anger. "You didn't see fit to take us into your confidence; but you shared this with someone else?"

Max nodded. "With Jake. Jake Epstein. But he would never..."

"You're sure of that?" his father challenged. "No jealousy? No anger at a German aristocrat romancing a lovely Jewish girl—one he secretly covets?"

"Jake's my best friend for God sake," Max protested. "He is family to me." He crossed to the fireplace, contemplating his father's words; then flicked his cigarette into the flames. "Eva's beautiful and smart. Every guy in school's interested in her. But would Jake sacrifice himself and Eva too? Does that make sense? He's got more personal integrity than anyone I know. It had to be someone else, someone at school, someone who saw us in a cafe, someone in Eva's building."

"Yes, I'm sure you're right," Konrad Kleist conceded, softly. "Someone who was in trouble with the SS; who traded you for themselves or a family member. The problem is, our support for the resistance has been possible only because it's been anonymous. We survived the White Rose tragedy, and so far so good with Red Orchestra; but this..." he paused, taking a moment to assess the consequences.

Red Orchestra was a network of anti-Nazi citizens from across Germany's social, political and religious spectrum who helped to rescue Jews and others marked for death; and sought ways to turn the depressed German populace against the Führer whose raging propaganda speeches had restored their self-esteem and convinced them Germany had reclaimed its rightful place in the hierarchy of nations.

"...but this—" the elder Kleist resumed, deciding brutal honesty would serve him best, "—this endangers everything!"

Max was visibly stung. "I'm sorry. As I said, I did everything possible to protect you, and this family; and I'll continue to do so."

"It's not that simple, Max. You see, I'm not one person. I'm three," his father said enigmatically. "Yes, there are three Konrad Kleists: A German patriot who was horrified when this evil fanatic came to power; a traitor who is doing all he can to destroy him; and a war profiteer whose company the Führer holds in high regard." He gestured to a wall of framed photographs. Among them were: Konrad Kleist with German business executives and industrialists. Kleist with European political leaders. The Kleists and their two young children at the Vatican with Pius XI and Munich's Cardinal von Faulhaber an ardent supporter of the Führer. The Pontiff—who abhorred the Nazis but thought Communism to be a greater evil—was presenting the Kleists with medals commemorating the martyrdom of St. Thomas More, the English statesman and humanist whom he had canonized four centuries after his beheading in 1535 by order of Henry VIII.

The photograph Max was staring at, now, was of two men shaking hands in front of a blast furnace from which molten steel was pouring. One of them was his father. The other was Adolph Hitler. "I've always been proud of you, Dad," Max said with an impish grin. "Almost every last one of you."

Konrad Kleist raised an amused brow. "You'd be wise to keep your pride in check. Though your ancestors began as humble blacksmiths, the company they founded manufactures armor plate, weapons-grade bar stock, and steel sheeting able to withstand crushing ocean depths, not to mention the finest barbed-wire made in Germany. You see the dichotomy here?"

Max nodded grimly, then broke into an amused smile. "Though I do vaguely recall rumors that the armor plate seems a little less impenetrable as of late; the bar stock not quite weapons grade; the steel sheeting not up to crush depth specifications…"

A Cheshire grin tugged at the corners of Konrad Kleist's mouth. "Really? And lo and behold the war will soon be lost; after which, all three of me plan to live a long and happy life with your mother, your sister and you…and your families, of course."

"I've no doubt of it," his wife said with heartfelt conviction. "Germany will once again become a humane and civilized nation where science, music, literature and art flourish." She stood and touched her son's cheek, tenderly. "You're in love with this girl, Eva?"

"Yes, Mother, I am. Deeply. She's a very special person, not to mention a bright and caring doctor."

"And what of her family?" his mother asked.

"They're Galician but they live in Venice, now. In the Jewish ghetto. Ever since Mussolini fell and our troops occupied Italy, many of their neighbors have been arrested and sent to concentration camps." Max paused, overcome by a sense of hopelessness. "We...We want to spend our lives together, raise a family, like you and dad."

"That's wonderful," his mother said. "We're very happy for you." She glanced to her husband and prompted, "Aren't we Konrad?"

"Of course we are," Konrad replied, dutifully. He knew his wife was doing more than eliciting his support, and knew exactly what she wanted. His eyes drifted for a moment then, with an anxious drag of his cigarette, he said, "What I'm about to say, Max, must stay in this room. Though the records seem to have 'somehow' been lost, according to family lore, my great-grandmother on my father's side was Jewish."

Max felt as if he couldn't catch his breath. He and his younger sister, Anika, were cared for by a Jewish nanny as children. Tovah Klausner was a nurturing woman who loved them as she would her own. By the time they had grown, she had become a member of the family and stayed on to run the household. Thanks to her, Max's Yiddish was more than passable—a fact that deepened his friendship with Jake beyond their interest in orthopedic surgery which had initiated it—but this—this was shocking news. He looked to his mother, gauging her reaction. Her composed smile left no doubt it was neither shocking nor news to her.

"Of course, being one-eighth Jewish is the secret to my success in business!" his father went on laughing at the absurdity of the stereotype. "And to my demise if that weasel Himmler found out."

"It's Eva's demise I'm worried about," Max said his voice hoarse with anxiety. "Eva's and Jake's. They need a place to stay. They need false papers. We have to help them."

"I don't see how we can get involved," his father said with finality. "Not directly. As you know, we do have certain connections that might be useful."

Max scowled. "The resistance? Headquarters has been giddy over reports it's been infiltrated. Besides, as a very bright person once said, trust no one but family," Max added, smartly. "What about the lake house?" he went on, referring to the family's chalet on Eibsee at the foot of the German Alps.

The lake country on the Austrian border north of Innsbruck was a year-round playground for the wealthy. Tennis, golf or water sports in the morning; skiing in Garmisch Partenkirchen, where the 1936 Winter Olympics were held, in the afternoon. Free of defense plants and military installations—other than border checkpoints and a contingent of mountain troops housed in what had been Olympic dormitories—the area wasn't on the Allies' target list.

"Eva and Jake could stay there," Max concluded. "Until new passports and travel passes can be—"

"No," his father said, sharply. "If they're found there we're all finished."

"We have to do something," Max protested. "We can't just allow the SS to cart them off to a death camp. There must be—"

"No, Max. No. I don't need any more phone calls in the middle of the night. You're lucky I was able to keep you from being arrested. Major Steig came this close to charging you with violating the Nuremberg Laws, racial defilement, and bringing disgrace on the SS! Charges for which you could face a firing squad."

Max shuddered visibly, then nodded. "Steig is an attack dog. A true believer. You can imagine my relief when he said I was being reassigned."

"Reassigned to what?" his father asked.

Max shrugged. "My orders are being cut. I have to report to headquarters early tomorrow."

"Some form of punishment," his father speculated, grimly. "The front most likely."

"The front..." his mother echoed with concern.

"Don't worry, the war will be over before I ever get there." Max hugged her, reassuringly, then smiled at a thought. "What about that cabin at the bottom of the gorge? It's miles from our place; and it's been abandoned for years."

The elder Kleist grimaced. "No. No, that's still too close for comfort."

"Konrad, please," Gisela Kleist implored. "Just for a short time, until my people can prepare their documents."

Her husband winced, then nodded. "All right, but I don't want to know which room they're sleeping in," he said with a self-deprecating chuckle. "I have to preserve some degree of plausible deniability."

Max was smiling at his father's joke when the doorbell rang. Anxious looks darted between them as the sound reverberated through the house. The dog got to its feet, and took up a position in the doorway that led to the corridor.

The housekeeper was replacing Christmas candles in the small chapel adjacent to the library. The perfectly scaled space with its straight-backed wooden pews and solemn stained glass windows was where Max and his sister Anika were baptized. A crucifixion by Cranach The Elder hung above the altar. A Madonna and child by Michael Pacher, and an Annunciation by Mathias Grunewald hung on the sidewalls. When the doorbell rang, Tovah left the chapel and hurried down the corridor toward the foyer.

The elder Kleist caught sight of her through the open doors of the library. "One moment, Tovah," he called out with a glance to his wife. "Are we expecting anyone, Gisela?"

"Not that I know of."

"Max?"

"It could be Eva and Jake. Professor Gerhard said he'd bring them here if he could."

"You told them to come here?"

"Of course," Max replied, angry at being chastised. "For obvious reasons, I've avoided inviting them to my home; but today I had no choice. They're lives are in danger! They've nowhere else to go!"

"What if they've been caught?" his father asked, suddenly unnerved. "What if they were caught coming here, and talked?"

You really think it's the Gestapo, his wife asked calmly.

"I've no idea," Konrad replied as the doorbell rang again. "Sometimes they ring. Sometimes they knock. Sometimes they knock the door down."

Gisela Kleist nodded resolutely, determining her strategy. If it was Himmler's henchmen, she would remind them of Germany's greatness, of its depth of character, of its soulful humanity; she would force them to acknowledge it; and dare them to destroy it. With quiet confidence, she went to the Bechstein, sat on the upholstered bench, and began to play. The room filled with the dream-like Adagio sostenuto of Beethoven's Sonata #14 in C sharp minor, the Mondschein Sonate.

Konrad Kleist took a deep breath and went to see who was at the door.

The German Shepherd followed.

CHAPTER THIRTEEN

Since the mid-1990s when the last wedding reception in the Temple of Dendur was held, private functions at The Metropolitan Museum of Art had been limited to corporate events. A fifty thousand dollar sponsorship entitled a company to one event, annually. Held in the evenings when the museum was closed, they had proved to be an effective fund raising tool. Now, in these difficult financial times, and in recognition of Dr. Epstein's generosity and longtime service as a trustee, the Museum agreed to make the Temple available for his granddaughter's reception; and on this sunny Sunday evening in June, the limousines and town cars were depositing guests at the Museum's rarely used north entrance that afforded them direct access to the Sackler Wing.

This magnificent extension to the Museum had been designed specifically to house the Temple which would have been lost beneath the rising waters of the Nile River when the Aswan Dam was completed in 1965. Commissioned by the Emperor Augustus the Temple deified two Nubian princes who, ironically, had suffered the same drowning fate it had been spared. Having been stored in crates for more than a decade, the massive sandstone blocks that comprised the Temple and its towering Gate were reassembled in this enormous pavilion beneath a slanted glass wall that ran its entire length, giving the space an ethereal glow.

The nearly four hundred wedding guests were seated alongside reflecting pools that formed a moat around the raised granite plain on which the Temple and its Gate stood. The dais, where the bride and groom, and members of the wedding party were seated, was situated between the two stone structures.

At this moment, Dr. Jacob Epstein, in a finely tailored tuxedo, was striding to a podium. Like many men, Jake had become more distinguished-looking with age; and other than a slight forward lean, he had the appearance and vitality of a man decades younger. His features had softened, and his once dark, unruly hair had settled into gentle off-white waves, but his eyes still had their intelligent sparkle. More than six decades after leaving his homeland, he still spoke with a slight accent which further enhanced his charm and his role as family patriarch.

"Hello, my name is Jake Epstein, proud grandpa of Melissa, our lovely bride," he began in a cheery voice. "On behalf of our son Dan and daughter-in-law Sarah my wife, Hannah and I welcome you to this special occasion. The other day, while drafting my remarks, I recalled that somebody famous once said: Irony is the art of becoming what we most detest. It brought to mind an incident in Israel, years ago, when half the audience walked out of a performance of Wagner's Ring in protest. Having made their point, they all went outside and got into their Mercedes Benz limousines and Mercedes Benz sports cars and Mercedes Benz taxis and went home."

A ripple of laughter spread though the guests.

"I mention that because some of you may be asking: Why would a devout Jewish family hold a wedding reception in an Egyptian temple? Weren't they the guys who conspired to have Moses and his scrappy tribe of Israelites slaughtered? Where would we all be today if Charlton Heston hadn't parted the Red Sea and saved their kosher *tuchas*?"

Those in attendance roared with laughter.

"Well, coward that I am," Jake went on in his endearing way, "I'm going to let my co-conspirator-for-life explain. Hannah?" he prompted, gesturing to the dais. Elegant in a silver-gray sheath, Dr. Hannah Friedman Epstein strode to the podium and embraced her husband. "Isn't she beautiful?" Jake said, beaming as applause rose.

Slender and secure with intense eyes beneath a cap of white hair, Hannah Epstein was, indeed, a striking woman. "Thank you, thank you so much," she said, as Jake stepped aside. "You know, for years people have said: Dr. Epstein has such a charming bedside manner; and I would ask: Which Dr. Epstein? And they'd always say: Dr. Jacob Epstein. Well, that's because, he always gets this Dr. Epstein to do the dirty work."

A wave of laughter broke across the room.

"So, why are we here in enemy territory?" Hannah asked rhetorically. "Well, Jake and I chose this Temple not only for its serene beauty; not only because of our respect for the Sackler brothers, distinguished physicians and philanthropists, for whom this magnificent wing is named, but most importantly because of the ecumenical spirit that being here symbolizes—the very same spirit that guided Jake and I when naming our Foundation. We didn't call it the Epstein Foundation. No, we named it the Epstein Family Foundation because we are really all one family on this earth; and we know that our extended family will Never Forget..." Hannah paused, letting the Holocaust slogan resonate. "...that though so many were lost in the Shoah, many were saved, as were my husband and I, by families who opened their hearts and homes when it would've been convenient to have kept them shuttered. We gather here in deep appreciation of all families who are committed to leaving the world a better place than they found it, not only for the Jewish people, but for all people. Thank you, and, now, please, enjoy!"

The vast space echoed with deafening applause.

Sol Steinbach, sitting at Table 23, couldn't believe his luck. The Epsteins'eloquent affirmation of their support for Jewish causes had more than paved the way for the sales pitch he would soon be making.

His wife, Bernice, sat next to him, networking, which for her was a subconscious act; more in the realm of exuding pheromones than, say, sending emails; and that's what made her the Upper East Side's networker extraordinaire. Indeed, she knew anyone worth knowing, because, for some inexplicable reason, anyone worth knowing wanted to know her; and, though Sol and Jake had been out of touch, and the Steinbachs weren't on the guest list, once given the task, Bernice had pulled it off as her husband knew she would.

Just an hour in the Museum's Trustees Dining Room with a few of the ladies-who-lunch from the Fifth Avenue Synagogue was all it took; that and the fact that the wedding happened to be mentioned in the same breath with certain charities the Epsteins and Steinbachs had in common. By the time the glasses of Pinot Grigio and salads Niçoise had been consumed, they all knew—without a word from Bernice—that the Steinbachs hadn't been invited to the wedding. A post office screw-up? A guest list computer glitch? Benign oversight? By the time dessert arrived, the word was spreading, via twitter and text, through the Synagogue's grapevine, to the, by then, burning ears of Dr. Hannah Epstein; and the next day an invitation, with a lovely note attached, appeared on the Steinbachs' doorstep.

Sol waited for a break between courses—when the exhibitionists were dancing, and the stock brokers and insurance agents were table hopping—before approaching Jake who had left the dais and was moving amongst the tables, chatting with guests.

"Sol! Sol Steinbach, of course I remember," Jake exclaimed, raising his voice above the music. "If it wasn't for you we'd have never caught that shyster embezzeling from The UJA's cancer fund."

"A minor leaguer compared to that son-of-a-bitch Madoff," Steinbach growled, guiding him aside. "Listen, Jake, I know you have to circulate, but if you can spare another minute, there's something I'd like to talk to you about."

"Your company's new ad campaign," Jake stated with a mischievous cackle. "You know, I can't believe I left that suitcase behind in The Apthorp."

Steinbach looked stunned. "How...how did you know? I mean, the people at my agency told me your boy was totally against the idea; swore that under no circumstances would he even raise it with you."

Jake nodded sagely. "Oh, I'm sure Daniel meant it when he said it," he explained with a proud glance to the dance floor where the father of the bride was dancing with his radiant daughter. "He's very protective of his parents; but, in good conscience, he knew he couldn't keep it from me."

"It must be some kind of role reversal thing that happens over time," Steinbach philosophized. "Children can't quite imagine their parents living the lives they've lived."

"They can't imagine them having sex, either," Jake said, with a lascivious chortle.

"Yeah," Steinbach said, laughing along with him, "I mean, all we asked him to imagine was you sitting on your long lost suitcase."

"Shocking!" Jake exclaimed. "Evidently Dan wasn't going to bring it up until after the wedding; but, when I showed him a draft of the remarks Hannah and I would be making today, he realized there was no point in waiting." He smiled at a thought, and added, "Not to mention he would have had to explain it to his mother."

"Well, we can all identify with that," Steinbach said with an amused chuckle. "So…where are we with this, Jake?" he prompted gently. "Are you going to sign on? Can I count on you for an endorsement?"

Jake's eyes sparkled with anticipation. "Of course. It sounds like fun!"

"Bet your *tuchas*! Two old Jews sticking it to those Nazi bastards!"

"Two old Jews?" Jake echoed. "Come on, Sol, how old are you?"

"Seventy, next month."

"Seventy? You're a kid. A little *pisher*."

"I'm old enough to have a number on my arm," Steinbach said, stone faced.

Jake nodded grimly. "That makes two of us. Dan mentioned you were in Auschwitz. I think that weighed heavily on his decision as well."

"Good, because we're going to help make sure the world Never Forgets…and maybe sell a little luggage at the same time."

Jake's eyes had hardened with commitment. He took a moment to process it, then brightening, said, "So, lights, camera, action! When do we start?"

"First things, first, Jake," Steinbach cautioned. "You happen to recall what's in the suitcase?"

Jake shrugged and splayed his hands. "Who knows. I mean, my neurons are still hooking-up on a regular basis; but it's been sixty years. A lot of old stuff, I guess. What else?"

"Well, at your earliest convenience," Steinbach said, smartly, "We're going to open it and find out ."

CHAPTER FOURTEEN

The doorbell rang again as Konrad Kleist crossed the foyer and approached the entrance of the townhouse. The sound was much more piercing, here, than in the distant library, and it made him shiver as if chilled. If it was the SS or Gestapo, he'd be the one to deal with them, not the housekeeper who was standing off to one side with the German Shepherd. Kleist took a moment to compose himself, then reached for the polished brass latch and forced an expansive smile.

The door opened to reveal the snow-dotted figures and reddened faces of Eva Rosenberg and Jacob Epstein—two faces Konrad Kleist had never seen before; but he had no doubt who they were; and was relieved they weren't henchmen from either of Himmler's dreaded organizations. Still, he was painfully aware that hiding two Jews from the SS and helping them get out of the country was extremely dangerous; and his apprehension hadn't eased.

"I'm Konrad Kleist, Max's father," he said, his cordial demeanor belied by an anxious glance to the street. "Please come in."

The two young doctors hesitated and looked back at the Opel that was parked at the curb, engine running. Professor Gerhard responded with a little wave, and drove off into the swirling snow as Eva and Jake stepped into the inviting warmth of the townhouse.

Konrad Kleist glanced once more to the street before closing the door. He wasn't looking for a black Mercedes with SS insignia and men in black military uniforms inside. No, he was in search of an unmarked car with men in leather trench coats and wide-brimmed hats that kept their faces in shadow—Gestapo men; but if they were there, neither he nor the Professor had seen them.

Tovah greeted Eva and Jake with a smile and took their coats along with Jake's briefcase and Eva's rucksack and physician's bag. The elder Kleist led the way down the corridor that was lined with canvases: Klimt, Kirchner, Schiele; Cezanne, Degas, Lautrec, Van Gogh; Kandinsky, Klee, Marc, Munter, among

54

them. The sound of the piano rose as they approached the library. Relieved her guests weren't vile men in trench coats, Gisela played the final passage of the Mondschien Sonate with joyful abandon, then got up from the piano, and said, "Welcome to our home."

Jake nodded awkwardly, rubbing his palms together to warm them before shaking her hand.

Eva broke into a shy smile, then sighed with exhilaration at the sight of Max, and ran into his arms. She held him tightly, with crushing force, as if this might somehow, miraculously, prevent the psychotic Jew-hunters from tearing them apart forever.

Indeed, the Reichsführer was right. How could it have gone on for so long? How?! How could they have lived in denial for so many months and years? How could they have allowed themselves to believe it would last when in their darkest moments they knew it would come to this unnerving end? It wasn't the Critical Skills Exemptions that had made them feel so falsely secure. No, it wasn't a few pages of bureaucratic boilerplate that they had taken to heart, but rather the exciting and deeply satisfying routine of life, of healing the sick, treating the wounded, comforting the dying, and doing so together, that had lulled the three of them into believing it would go on forever; that had caused them to believe that Himmler's bloodhounds wouldn't pick up their scent.

"Max has told us how proud he is to call you both his friends," Gisela said, as Max and Eva separated, the tips of their fingers lingering in contact. "And we were especially pleased when he told us of his strong feelings for you, Eva."

"We're very lucky to have found each other, Madam Kleist," Eva said her eyes aglow with the love and admiration she felt for her son.

"And we're both very fortunate to have you and your husband offer to help us," Jake said. "We're aware of the chance you're all taking."

"It won't be the first," the elder Kleist replied, his eyes brightening. "Perhaps it will be the last. Yes? Well, there's much to do and little time to do it. If you will excuse us, Max will get you settled and explain what happens next." The dog sensed he was about to leave and began drifting toward the door. "Kunst. Stay," Konrad commanded, guiding his wife from the Library.

The dog stopped in mid-stride, crossed the room and settled next to Eva, nuzzling her hand.

"Where's Professor Gerhard?" Max asked as his parents departed.

"He went back to school," Jake replied as the three of them gathered in front of the fireplace. "He can't be seen with us; let alone be seen here, now."

"You're right. He's taken enough chances," Max said, lighting a cigarette. "You'll spend the night. In the morning you'll be taken to an abandoned cabin in Partnach Gorge. I was hoping the professor could drive you; but we'll find someone else. You'll be safe there for a while."

"For a while?" Eva echoed incredulously. "No. No, I have to get out of here, now. Out of Germany. Back to Venice. I'd feel much safer there. Not to mention I'm worried sick about my family."

"I've stopped worrying about mine," Jake said, disconsolately. He didn't have to explain. Eva and Max knew he had gone home to Vienna on semester break only to learn that his family had been arrested by the Gestapo. The Leopoldstadt District, the city's Jewish quarter where Jacob Epstein grew up, was on a large island surrounded by the Danube River and its canal. Hebrew and Yiddish were the languages most often heard on its shop-lined streets. Jake's father operated a small apothecary on Grosse Schiffgasse just a few doors down from Schiff Shul, the main Orthodox synagogue; and Jake helped out in his spare time until he went off to medical school. "Eva's right," Jake concluded. "We should get out of Germany as quickly as possible."

"You should come with me," Eva said with her characteristic decisiveness. "Unlike the Austrians, and the French for that matter, few Italians have become collaborators, and many families, good people like Max's parents, are sheltering Jews."

Max nodded in agreement. "But you'll have to cross the Alps, all of Austria and half of northern Italy to get there. More than three hundred kilometers in the dead of winter. That would be challenging for the Wermacht's ski troops let alone two Jews on the run from the SS."

"We'll take the train," Eva said, undaunted. "That's what I always do. Six hours and we're there."

"Not without false documents," Max fired back, using a quick drag of his cigarette for emphasis. "The Gestapo board every train at every stop and check everyone's papers. You wouldn't stand a chance."

"We'll walk if we have to," Jake said resolutely.

"No, you'll take the train," Max said, smartly. "With new passports and travel passes. My parents have connections."

"Good," Jake said with a grin. "Because I don't even have a toothbrush."

"It comes with the room, powder too, and a square of chocolate on the pillow," Max said with a laugh. "I'll take care of the passport photos. Mom and Dad'll take care of the rest." He flicked his cigarette into the fireplace, then glanced to the dog, and said, "Come on, Kunst, we've got work to do." Max led the way to the entry hall where the elevator was located. The ornate cage-like car ran in an open shaft that was encircled by the four-story staircase.

Moments earlier, after leaving the library, Max's parents had gone directly to the chapel just across the corridor. Heads bowed, the Kleists crossed themselves and genuflected in front of the altar; then, as Gisela knelt in prayer, Konrad went up a few steps to the tabernacle.

Carved from a single block of marble, the small, mausoleum-like cabinet was centered atop the altar between two baroque candlesticks. Each seemed to be growing from within an exuberant spray of evergreen ferns and Christmas holly dotted with bright red berries.

Kleist slid the finely embroidered curtain, which cloaked the tabernacle's door, aside. Instead of the usual bronze casting with the Latin abbreviation IHS—Iesus Hominum Salvator, Jesus Savior of Men—and a keyed lock, this tabernacle had the case-hardened steel door and combination lock of a safe. He spun the dial several times, then grasped the handle and opened the door, revealing a chalice in which consecrated Hosts were kept. With deliberate reverence he set the vessel aside, reached deep into the tabernacle between banded packs of currency piled against the side walls, and removed a metal strongbox. It contained a supply of blank passports, identity cards and travel passes. He slipped two of each into a pocket, returned the strongbox and chalice to the tabernacle, and locked it; then, joined his wife at the foot of the altar. They genuflected together and hurried from the chapel to her office at the other end of the corridor.

The spacious room was filled with works of art. Racks of canvases ran along one wall. Shallow drawers beneath the worktable held reams of etchings, drawings, and lithographs. Rows of bookcases were crammed with oversized art volumes. The desk was piled with artists' profiles, provenance reports, transaction folders, and a ledger in which Gisela made meticulous annotations on the works she represented.

She went to the telephone, put a professionally manicured fingertip in the rotary, and dialed the number of a young graphic designer named Glazer who was one of her Red Orchestra operatives. After two rings, she hung up, waited a moment, and then dialed the same number again.

"D-K-G..." Glazer answered in a guarded voice. The initials stood for Druck-Knopfe-Grafik, the name of his studio. It was a wordplay on his clever idea to sew *druckknopfes*—literally, snap fasteners—on the sleeves of his shirts and coats and on his yellow star, so he could easily remove it on entering establishments that barred Jews, or when engaging in clandestine activities.

"This is the curator," Gisela Kleist said, cryptically. "We've just acquired two new pieces that need authenticating."

"You have everything I'll need to establish their provenance?" Glazer asked matter-of-factly.

"Yes, everything..." Gisela replied with a glance to her husband whose hand, in a subconscious gesture, was pressed against his jacket pocket. "...as always. All necessary documents and photographs. We can drop them off this evening if that's convenient—Excellent." She hung up and said, "The newsstand at the Hauptbahnhof after dark."

CHAPTER FIFTEEN

The first weeks of June in the Hamptons had been cool and wet, but Bart Tannen still managed to get in a few rounds of golf and spend time with Celine Sentier, whom he'd met a decade ago in Gunther Global's Paris office. Though Celine's flair for nouvelle cuisine had won his heart, on moving to New York, she traded-in her whisk and garlic press for a real estate license and a cellphone; and, with Tannen's backing, got into East End real estate—as in buy it, renovate it, flip it.

Last summer, after a day of scouting open houses, Celine returned to their East Hampton rental, and said, "I found a house…" She paused, eyeing him from beneath her Gunther Global baseball cap. "…for us."

Tannen was on the screened-in porch reviewing a proposal for a client. "You know the one I want," he said, without looking up from his work. "When it comes on the market, we'll—" he paused, struck by her inference. "Really?" Tannen asked, his overgrown brows twitching. "It's for sale?"

It, as Celine knew, was the cozy bungalow in Sag Harbor on Noyac Bay that Tannen's parents had rented every summer when he was growing up. "Uh-huh, just listed." She handed him the offering sheet and, forcing a huffy sigh, added, "You Americans are so sentimental."

"Unbelievable," Tannen said of the asking price. "Would've gone for thirty-K back then. What did we bid?"

"Well…" Celine said, squirming in discomfort, "I think maybe you want to—how you say—weigh-in, first?"

"What?!" Tannen grabbed her hand and lunged for the door. "If we don't get it, I'm kicking your little French derriere from here to Sag Harbor and back!"

"I did—I did! I put in a bid!" Celine squealed, bursting into laughter. "One-point- six. We may have to bump it, but we'll get it."

58

And they did; and Tannen had been working on it in his spare time ever since. After spending this balmy Sunday morning refinishing the back deck, he spent the afternoon cursing a little white ball that refused to Bite! Get up! Cut! or obey any of the other commands he gave it in flight. The days were longest in June, and it was twilight when he reached Shinnecock's closing hole. He was lining-up a putt when his cellphone rang. "Sol?" he growled, seeing the caller-ID.

"Get you at a bad time?"

"Naw, I was just getting it on in the shower with the Doublemint twins," Tannen replied with a cackle. "So?" he prompted, aware Steinbach was at the Epstein wedding. "That's fantastic!—Yeah, let me know. I'll have Gunther set up the archivist."

That same day, Stacey and Adam had ventured downtown to the Highline. Until about thirty years ago, the elevated tracks that cut through Chelsea and the West Village, carried railcars to the factories in meatpacking district below 14th Street. The abandoned right-of-way, with stunning views of the Hudson, had been turned into an urban park with seating areas amidst lacy trees and a variety of horticultural specimens. They had spent the afternoon strolling along the mile-long oasis and were exiting the glass-walled elevator at street level when Stacey's eyes darted to a swatch of boldly striped fabric amidst some curbside trash. It turned out to be the sling of a classic beach chair. Both the canvas and wooden frame were in good condition. "A scrub in the tub and it'll be like new!" she exclaimed, convincing Adam to haul it back uptown on the subway.

Dusk was falling as they returned to her apartment to freshen up; and unlike Tannen and the Doublemint twins, Stacey and Adam actually were getting it on in the shower when he called with the good news. Tannen's voicemail was more than enough to keep her pulse rate up. "I think we better do take-out," Stacey said, as she and Adam were dressing.

Adam frowned. "Why? I thought we were going to that sushi joint over on Columbus?"

"I can't. I've got to get back up to speed on Steinbach." Since the disappointing meeting with Dan Epstein, Stacey had been using her time to catch up on the assignments she had set aside to work on it, exclusively. "I haven't looked at it in weeks."

"Come on, it's an ad campaign for roll-aboards."

"It's a lot more than that, now," Stacey retorted. "Remember that story idea I mentioned?"

Adam nodded, his eyes widening with curiosity.

"Well, heat up your hard drive, Clive, because it's going to happen. Human interest. Nazis. World War Two. Holocaust survivors teaming up in an ad campaign."

"Your Dr. Epstein signed on?"

"Yup. He and the CEO of the luggage manufacturer."

"That's a helluva headline," Adam said, envisioning it: "Survivors use Holocaust to sell luggage."

"Real catchy, Clive. But the verb has to be more... more altruistic. Survivors Use Luggage To...To Memorialize Holocaust. How's that?"

"Terrific," Adam replied.

"Pretty damn good," Adam's editor at the Times said when he pitched the story the next morning.

"This is great," Tannen said when Stacey ran it by him. "Sol will be stoked."

"Fucking fantastic," Steinbach exclaimed when Tannen called. "That little girl is going to own prime time. You can't buy this kind of advertising and PR!"

"It's up to my father," Dan Epstein said, concerned the Foundation might be tarnished if the article was perceived as a public relations stunt.

"It's *The New York Times*," Jake said brushing off his son's concern. "All the news that's fit to print!"

"I have serious misgivings about that," Hannah Epstein said when Jake briefed her on his conversation with Sol Steinbach. Barely twenty-four hours had passed since the wedding reception; and they had spent the day at home recovering. Now, cocktails in hand, they sat on the plush sofa in the library of their art-filled triplex above the Foundation's offices. "I'm not so sure you should be doing this Steinbach thing at all."

"Why not?" Jake wondered. "Sol's one of us, one of the good people. Why shouldn't I help him out?"

"I didn't say you shouldn't. It's just that delving into the past has a way of...of stirring things up; things like suppressed emotions, forgotten events...even certain people for that matter."

"You sound just like, Dan," Jake said, wearily.

"I'm speaking of things Dan knows nothing about."

Jake's lips tightened. He nodded and took a long swallow of his martini; then he reached out and took her hand. "What would I do without you, Hannah? All these years...you take such good care of me."

"That's what I'm trying to do, now," Hannah said, ignoring his charm offensive. She held up her glass and exhorted, "*Vorsicht*, Jake. *Gehen sie mit vorsicht.*"

"Enough with the *vorsicht*," Jake said, unmoved. "I've been proceeding with caution all my life."

"Yes, and with good reason. Why stop now?"

Jake shrugged and drifted off in thought; then, he set his glass aside and, with renewed energy, said, "You're right. This is no time to be living in the past or the future for that matter. At our age, we should be living in the moment." He moved closer and began nuzzling her. "What's wrong with having a little fun with Sol, hmm..." he went on, kissing her neck. "...and raising funds for the Foundation at the same time?"

"You're incorrigible," Hannah said, with a girlish giggle, squirming in his embrace. "I'm sorry. I suppose you're right. I'll come along if you like."

"I thought you had a luncheon?"

"I can always beg-off and send a check."

"No. No, go. It's important. Besides, Dan insisted on coming. I'll be fine." He smiled and kissed her forehead, tenderly. *"Ich liebe dich..."*

"Oh, yes," Hannah said, burrowing into him. "I love you, too, Jake Epstein."

Mid-morning the next day, Dr. Jacob Epstein and his son arrived at Gunther Global's reception area. Tannen and Stacey, and Steinbach, accompanied by his technical consultant, had already assembled in the conference room along with Adam Stevens who was making notes while a *New York Times* photographer moved about quietly with her camera. The small talk had waned and an anxious silence had fallen by the time Jake and Dan Epstein were shown in by a receptionist.

Jake's eyes darted to the conference table. Wide in the middle, narrow at the ends, its forced perspective focused his attention on the suitcase that was perched atop the polished rosewood. Dramatically illuminated by a spotlight, the battered piece of luggage, with the worn, hand-painted lettering, could have been the featured work in an exhibition of found art. Jake stood there, transfixed, unable to take his eyes from it.

Stacey's heart was captured by the old fellow the moment she saw him. Despite her hardball lobbying, she suddenly felt almost maternally protective of him—and with good reason. She was responsible for reuniting him with his suitcase, for stirring up the horrific past it represented, for forcing him to relive it; and, now, she was concerned about how it might affect him. Watching this genial octogenarian staring at the suitcase with his slight forward lean, which made him appear almost childlike, was heart-wrenching. She was trying to imagine what was going through his mind, and was feeling like a parent who, having encouraged her child to partake in an activity, suddenly realized it contained an element of danger she hadn't anticipated.

The moment was broken when Mark Gunther arrived accompanied by two women. He introduced the fashionable, artistic-looking one with high cheekbones and observant eyes as his wife, Grace; and the tiny taut one with the earnest smile and black attaché as Ellen Rother, lead investigator and archivist for the Simon Wiesenthal Center's New York Office.

Adam slipped an audio recorder from his pocket and turned it on. The voice-activated, digital Sony PCM-D50 was favored by journalists for its long battery life, ease of operation and downloading to computers. It freed them to participate in interviews while insuring the accuracy of quotations. Like most of them, Adam used a spiral pad to record observations about people and places, and make research notes.

"Sorry to keep you waiting," Gunther said. "Grace and I took a few minutes to bring Ellen up to speed." He shook Dr. Epstein's hand and said, "Welcome to Gunther Global, Doctor. We're very pleased you're going to be working with us."

"Work? Sol promised it would be fun!" Jake said, providing a much needed moment of levity.

"Either way, it's a privilege to be part of this special moment, Dr. Epstein," Ellen said as if in the presence of royalty. "The Center is most appreciative of your generosity and many decades of support."

"The privilege has always been mine," Jake said with a benevolent smile.

Ellen returned it, then set her attaché on the table. It contained equipment to photograph, package, protect, and label the suitcase and its contents. She took several shots of it from various angles with her digital camera, then looked to Steinbach's tech, and said, "Can we open it, please?"

Everyone seemed to be holding their breath as the precise fellow came forward. He tried several keys from a set of masters, found the one he wanted, and jiggled it in the lock to awaken the pins from their decades of hibernation. The tumbler made a crisp, metallic sound when he turned it as did the second.

Ellen hesitated, feeling the weight of this solemn moment; then, as the others pressed-in around her, she thumbed the spring-loaded latches that popped open with startling German precision, and raised the lid. An odor of grime, sweat and death that had been festering for decades rose almost visibly into the air.

It wasn't pungent enough to stifle the gasp that came in reaction to what was inside the suitcase. Every pair of eyes was riveted to the bold gray and white stripes of a concentration camp uniform. The ragged garment obscured the other contents, but bits and pieces could be seen peeking from beneath it: A document stamped with a bright green seal of an Eagle clutching a swastika. The corner of a hardcover book. The cuff of a shirt. The tail of a necktie. A sheaf of snapshots—once bound by a now-disintegrated rubber band—in a side pocket of the silk lining.

The group surged closer, expecting Ellen to remove the striped uniform, revealing the items below. Instead, she began photographing the open suitcase from multiple angles, zooming-in on various details. "This is going to take a few minutes. So if you'll all please step back..."

Stacey had been sticking close to Dr. Epstein and, as the group moved aside, she noticed the old fellow's eyes were glistening with emotion. "Why don't you take a seat, Dr. Epstein?" she said, guiding him to a chair.

Dan noticed and joined them. "Dad? You okay?"

Jake nodded and wiped a tear from his eye.

Despite her act of kindness, Dan Epstein was glaring at Stacey whom he blamed, along with Tannen, for his father's distress. "This is what I meant," he said in a taut whisper to Tannen. "I knew it was a mistake to force him to relive it. I knew he'd be shaken."

Tannen nodded sadly. "We're all shaken."

"Enough of that talk," Jake called out, overhearing. "Don't worry. I'll be fine."

"I wish I could say the same," Steinbach chimed-in, his voice breaking as he turned away. He was trying to regain his composure when his cell phone rang. He pulled a sleeve over his watery eyes and flipped it open. A text message was crawling across the screen: Serial # match. Herr Konrad Kleist. Munich. Steinbach stared at it in confusion, then showed it to Tannen.

Tannen looked puzzled. "What?" he whispered, his overgrown brows arching like caterpillars. "The suitcase belongs to some guy named, Konrad Kleist?"

"Yeah, whoever he is," Steinbach replied clearly puzzled. "He bought it. Maybe as a gift? Who knows?"

"Maybe," Tannen said, unsatisfied. "I'd rather be safe than sorry, Sol. Soon as this is over we'll take the good doctor aside and ask him."

Stacey saw the whispered exchange and expressions of concern. She also saw Adam jotting in his notebook. "What's going on boss? I'm getting a bad feeling, here."

"I'm not sure. We'll get into it, later."

"Remember…there's a reporter in the room."

A few minutes later, Ellen put the camera in her attaché, and motioned the Gunthers aside. After a brief conversation, Ellen returned to the table, then closed the suitcase and snapped the latches. "Will you lock them, please?" she said to the tech. "This is much more involved than I expected," she explained, addressing the puzzled group. "It really should be done in a controlled environment. With Dr. Epstein's permission, I'd like to have the suitcase picked-up and taken to the Center's lab."

A disappointed groan rose in response.

"I hasten to point out we've got a photo session at the end of the week," Tannen said. Irving Penn was in long term retirement as he had thought; and though the search for other owners of vintage Steinbachs was ongoing, A-list photographer Zach Bolden had a rare cancellation; and Tannen had accelerated the schedule to take advantage of it. "We won't need the contents; but we're out of business without the suitcase."

"I understand," Ellen said, asking rhetorically, "Could it be done here? Yes. Could it be done in the subway in rush hour? Sure. But the lab is better. Much better. I guarantee you'll have the suitcase back in time. The contents, on the other hand, will take at least several weeks to process, properly.

"It's Dr. Epstein's call," Gunther said.

"As a man of science I'm always in favor of scientific methods," Jake said with a nod to Ellen.

"Good," Ellen said. "When I'm finished, each of you will receive a CD with a photographic record of every item, and written analysis that place each in historical context. Dr. Epstein will be given custody of the suitcase and its contents. It's my hope they'll be donated to one of the many worthy Holocaust museums. I'll arrange for it to be picked up. Make sure to give the key to the courier. In the meantime, the temptation to open the suitcase will be overwhelming. Please don't give in to it."

Grace Gunther leaned to her husband and whispered something. He nodded and, addressing the group, said, "Perhaps, it would be wise to give Ellen the key, now." It sounded like a suggestion but his eyes made it clear he wasn't offering them a choice. After a brief chat with Dr. Epstein, Ellen took the key, left the suitcase, and departed with the Gunthers.

"If you can spare another moment, Dr. Epstein," Tannen said, guiding father and son to a seating area where a pitcher of water and glasses stood atop a side table. "One thing I'd like to cover before we adjourn," he explained as the others gathered around them. "Does the name Konrad Kleist mean anything to you?"

Jake stiffened slightly, then seemed to brighten in reflection. "Konrad Kleist. My goodness. Of course. Why do you ask?"

"No big deal, Jake," Steinbach said, sensing the old fellow's discomfort. "According to company records, the serial number on the suitcase is registered to a Herr Konrad Kleist."

Jake nodded taking a moment to process it. "Yes, well, Herr Kleist's son was my best friend in medical school. A German Catholic who spoke fluent Yiddish," he said, savoring the irony. "His name was Max. If it wasn't for him, well…" He paused and bit a lip, shaken by the reverie. "Max Kleist and his family saved my life…and that of another student." He paused again, took a deep breath, and sighed.

Stacey poured some water into one of the glasses and handed it to him. After a few sips, Jake set it aside, and looked up with a mischievous twinkle. "So, I imagine you'd all like to know just how I came to be in possession of this suitcase."

His audience nodded in unison and leaned forward with rapt attention.

"Well, the other student and I, Eva Rosenberg was her name, were the only Jewish students remaining in the Medical School," Jake began in a low voice that made them lean in even more closely. "We had been granted special exemptions because surgeons were in such demand. When it became obvious the war was lost, the SS began cracking down, threatening everyone, even Max whom they had conscripted and thought was a loyal Nazi—until they found out he and Eva were lovers." He splayed his hands and shrugged. "Suddenly, Eva and I were being hunted. Two terrified students on the run in the dead of winter. Despite his own desperate straits, Max offered us refuge in his family's home. All we had to do was elude the Gestapo and get there. Don't ask me how, but we did. That afternoon I acquired the suitcase."

CHAPTER SIXTEEN

Max Kleist's living quarters were at one end of the third floor, his sister Anika's at the other. The German shepherd was the first one out of the elevator when the door opened. Kunst knew where Max, Eva and Jake were going. He bounded down the hallway and went straight to a windowed alcove, settling on the Persian rug beneath a drafting table. Drawing instruments were aligned on a sheet of vellum on which a prosthetic device had been rendered. Sketches of mechanical joints: elbows, ankles, shoulders, and hip structures, were tacked to a wall beneath shelves that held three-dimensional mock-ups. The living area of the bachelor-like suite was cluttered with tennis racquets, golf clubs, and ski equipment; and decorated with Bauhaus furniture and modern art.

"Make yourselves comfortable," Max said; then, feeling self-conscious about his palatial quarters, he joked, "It isn't much, but it's home." He was focused on Jake's need for clothing, and didn't notice that neither Jake nor Eva had laughed; nor that they had been stopped in their tracks by the sight of his SS uniform, hanging on a clothes rack between the closets. Their eyes, wide with the terror it always created, were sweeping over it from top to bottom: the silver Death's Head on the cap which was perched above the perfectly pressed jacket; the neatly bloused jodhpurs just below; and the jackboots, with their mirror-polished toe caps, standing on the floor. Eva and Jake had often seen Max in his uniform, but coming upon it like this was staggering.

Max was blithely rummaging in dresser drawers, sorting through armoires, and pulling things out of closets. He and Jake were both about the same height and build; and it didn't take Max very long to assemble a wardrobe for his friend. When finished, he went into a walk-in closet and came out with a suitcase.

The finely crafted piece of luggage was made of pebble-grained leather. A Steinbach hallmark. A secret tanning process, invented in 1846 by Israel Steinbach the company's founder, produced the unique texture. The company name and a serial number were engraved on a brass plate on the bottom. Based in Leipzig, Steinbach was one of four, high quality, European *malletiers*—literally trunk-makers—along with La Maison Goyard, Hermes, and Louis Vuitton. The leather had been saddle-stitched by hand with waxed linen twine and articulated with cast brass hinges and machined latches with keyed locks. Its corners were protected by brass fittings affixed with rivets. The interior, lined with paisley-patterned silk, had rows of neatly arranged pockets and compartments in the lid and on the sidewalls. This one was monogrammed with the initials KK which were hot-stamped in gold on the fascia above the handle.

"This ought to get you through a couple of days," Max joked, setting it on the bed next to the clothing. "The key should be in one of the inside pockets."

Jake almost whistled at the sight of it. "Are you sure you want to part with this?"

Max opened the door to the walk-in closet again, revealing several identical suitcases on a shelf with other equally well-crafted Steinbach pieces in various sizes. "I don't think it will be missed."

Eva had sought refuge from the SS uniform in a small Kandinsky on the wall next to the closet. The whimsical painting was alive with tumbling forms and vibrating colors from which the steeple of a red-roofed church thrust into a blue-coral sky. She had just moved into the drafting alcove, which had a view of the treed square and the surrounding streets, when Max joined her. "So, what do you think?"

"He's a genius. I've always loved Kandinsky. I've just decided that one's my favorite."

"Mine too. It's called Murnau With Church," Max said with a grin before pointing to the drawing on the drafting table. "I meant the prosthetic."

"I think you're a genius, too," Eva replied with an endearing smile that left no doubt she meant it.

"Thanks, but this is Jake's stroke of genius not mine," Max said humbly. "Combining metal and plastic was his idea. I just volunteered to refine the details."

"And whose idea was that one, and that one?" Eva prompted, pointing to the drawings on the wall. "Don't be so modest. We're a great team. Each of us has made valuable contributions to—" she paused, suddenly, her eyes darting to the windows.

"What is it?" Max asked. "You see something?"

"A black sedan. It looked like a Mercedes but I can't be sure. We thought we were being followed. We drove around for almost an hour." Eva sagged, defeatedly. Talk of paintings and prosthetics, which had been perfectly normal yesterday, were meaningless in the light of today's chilling reality. She brightened at a thought, and said, "Why don't you drive us tomorrow?"

Max shook his head no, sadly. "I wish I could; but I have to report first thing in the morning."

"And then?"

"Who knows? It's as if they gave me a day to get my affairs in order…" He let it trail-off, then took her into his arms. "We'll be together one day, Eva. We will. I've no doubt of it, but, for now…" His eyes drifted to the SS uniform hanging across the room.

Eva's filled with emotion. "Yes, yes we will. I should've known better than to ask. I recall how upset you were when your conscription notice came. I know how much you hate putting that—that—" She paused, the words sticking in her throat. "—that thing on every morning."

Max nodded grimly. "I didn't want to report then; and I don't want to report, now; but I've no choice. If I don't show up tomorrow—if I'm listed as a deserter—my family will pay the price; and I don't need to tell you what it will be."

Eva leaned her head on his shoulder and hugged him. They stood clinging to one another, wondering about the future, if there even was a future—for them, for Germany, for the world for that matter.

"Okay!" Jake exclaimed, startling them. He had been packing the suitcase and had no idea what was going on across the room. He closed the lid and swept it off the bed. "Are we ready to go on holiday?"

"Not so fast," Max said as he and Eva disengaged. "There's one thing you two have to do before you run off together."

"Get married?" Jake teased.

Max laughed and fetched a 35mm Leica from a drawer. The precision, pocket-sized camera had revolutionized photography when introduced in 1930. "By the power vested in me, I now pronounce you the handsomest man and most beautiful woman I have ever photographed."

"For the false papers," Eva said.

"Precisely. False papers with false names," Max said, pointedly. "Make sure you choose pseudonyms that are familiar, that you're comfortable with. The Gestapo has a knack for spotting people who haven't spent their entire lives answering to the name on their documents."

Jake set the suitcase in front of a blank wall, and sat on it, arms crossed, head turned sideways, chin raised slightly. "How's this?" he asked, making fun of his regal pose. "Do I look like an aristocratic German doctor or a low class Jewish one from Leopoldstadt?"

The precise click of the Leica's shutter came in response. Max advanced the film, taking several shots, then called out "Next!" Eva took Jake's place and glanced up at Max with a haunting sadness, as if the photograph he was about to take would soon be the only thing he'd have of her for the rest of his life.

The wistful moment was broken by the snap of the shutter and the arrival of a striking young woman who rapped on the open door as she strode swiftly through it. She set aside her schoolbag and a violin case and bent to the German shepherd who came from the alcove to greet her. "Hey boy," she said scruffing his ears. "How you doing?" At 22, Anika Kleist was three years younger than her brother; and, with her slender frame, long, blond hair, and sparkling cerulean eyes, was as classically attractive as he was handsome. "Hi, what's going on?"

"Plenty," Max replied, setting the camera aside. "I need to get this film processed before tonight."

"I can take care of it," Anika said; then, with the sassy bravado of someone who enjoyed taking risks, prompted, "I hear you're looking for a driver, too."

"They're not going sightseeing, Anika."

"Neither am I," Anika countered matching his tone. "Enough Mozart for one week. I'm going skiing with my friends." She whirled to Jake and Eva, and extended a hand. "Hi, I'm Anika. Max's little sister. He thinks I spend too much time worrying if my seams are straight. I'm afraid he isn't much for introductions."

"May I present the other half of the Kleist Choix du Roi," Max said, facetiously. The French phrase meant Choice of Kings, and referred to the royal preference for having both a male and female heir. "I shall one day rule the Kleist family empire; while Anika, playing romantic adagios on her violin, will win the heart of the dashing young ruler of another, thereby forming a strategic alliance." Max forced a smile, and added, "I've little time for social graces today, Anika."

"Well you should find some," Eva said, scolding him with a smile as she shook Anika's hand. "I'm Eva, this is Jake."

"Of course you are," Anika said with a perky flip of her hair, shifting her eyes back to Max. "Mom and Dad just briefed me. Since, I'm driving to the lake tomorrow, anyway, I could easily drop Eva and Jake at the Gorge."

Max winced. "No. No, it's too dangerous."

"What isn't these days?" Anika challenged. "I go almost every weekend, right? It's part of my routine. So there's less chance I'd attract attention. Besides, I know all the guards at the Starnberger checkpoint. They always wave me right through."

"Really?" Max said, smiling at what he was about to say. "I thought they threatened to arrest you if you didn't give them your phone number."

"That's why I always take, Kunst, along," Anika said, referring to the dog whose ears went up, his head tilting left then right. "He intimidates them. Right boy?! Right?"

Kunst responded with several crisp barks.

Max's head tilted from side to side as if he was considering something. He looked like he was mimicking the dog. "You know, I hate to admit it," he said, sheepishly. "But she's right."

"At last!" Anika exclaimed. "In front of two witnesses no less; and all I have to do to prove it, is drive them to Partnach Gorge without getting caught by the Gestapo or the SS."

The others all laughed nervously.

Jake picked up the camera. "Come on. You two are next!" he said spiritedly to Max and Anika. "Eva and I aren't going to be the only ones in your rogues' gallery."

CHAPTER SEVENTEEN

A pin drop silence had descended over Gunther Global's conference room by the time Mark Gunther returned from escorting his wife and the archivist to the reception area. Jake had covered the entire sequence of events that had brought him and Eva Rosenberg to the Kleist family's townhouse, ending with Max giving him the suitcase, taking the passport photographs, and agreeing to allow his sister, Anika, to drive them to a hiding place the next day.

Now, gathered around the old fellow, they were all trying to comprehend the enormity of it. Not to mention the absurd and evil stupidity of it. Jake didn't have to point out that the modern day equivalent would be two students at Mount Sinai Hospital Medical School being hunted by agents of the U.S. Government with warrants for their arrest and deportation to a death camp because they were Jews. The staggering incomprehensibility was soon replaced by breathless amazement that Jake was actually alive, there, with them; and, then, by burning curiosity to find out what happened next.

Jake sensed it and shifted in his chair, self-consciously. "You know, I couldn't have afforded that suitcase, then," he said with a laugh, nudging Steinbach with an elbow. "I'm not even sure I could afford it now!"

"You can have as many as you want. No charge!" Steinbach said, laughing along with him. "I couldn't buy the media coverage this is going to generate."

"Well, GG is still billing by the hour," Tannen teased; then caught up in the moment, he added, "Talk about traveling companions for life…"

"Let's keep our focus, people," Gunther cautioned with professional aplomb.

"The kick-off line is: Surviving Harrowing Journeys."

"Harrowing as hell," Steinbach chimed-in. "This is everything we hoped for and more!"

"Much more," Jake said pointedly. "This is the fuel that has kept my engine running all these years."

Stacey's eyes were aglow with quiet reverence. It was as if she was in the presence of royalty or the Pope. She didn't even know people like Jake Epstein existed when she was growing up in Lubbock, let alone could she have ever hoped to be privy to a first hand account of his struggle to survive such atrocities. "You've lived through some incredible times, haven't you, Dr. Epstein?" she prompted, her voice trembling. "I mean, like, my life's a total bore in comparison."

"Well, I had a psychopath named Adolph to thank for it," Jake replied in his soft accent. "You know, in 1920 when I was born, Germany was paralyzed by the psychological and economic impact of the War. The First World War. By the early thirties, things were improving. The motion picture business was thriving; a community of artists had formed: Kirchner in Berlin, Kandinsky in Munich; technical innovation had resumed; and the auto industry was expanding: Daimler Benz, BMW and...and..." He paused, feigning he couldn't recall. "...ah yes, a little company called Volkswagen started by a man named Porsche. Did you know, Josef Ganz, a Jew, came up with the original design and called it the Beetle? Yes, years before Hitler championed it and had him arrested on trumped-up charges. By the time I began medical school in the early forties, the Führer had been in power for a decade and had already invaded Poland, starting the Second World War..."

"Nothing like a World War to juice the economy," Gunther interjected, savoring the sarcasm.

"...which destroyed the nation," Jake resumed, pointedly, finishing his thought. "As I said, there's more. Much, much more."

"Well if you've got the time, we've got the time," Tannen said brightly. "It's your harrowing journey, Dr. Epstein; your story; and we need to hear it."

"Yeah, we're all ears," Stacey said, eager for more.

"We sure are," Adam chimed in. Until now, he had recorded it all, said little, and written a lot in his notebook. The more Jake talked the more enriched the piece he was writing became. "So, Dr. Epstein, did you and...and Eva, Eva Rosenberg, is it? Make it to Venice? I mean, what happened next?"

"Well, things didn't go quite according to plan. The Nazis saw to that; and, and we, well..." Jake emitted a weary sigh and took a sip of water from his glass. "As I said, there's so much more to tell..."

"I think maybe Dr. Epstein needs a break, boss," Stacey said, her maternal instincts, prevailing.

"A long one," Dan said, decisively. "I think we've had enough for one day. What do you say, Dad?"

Jake grimaced as if he wanted to continue, then nodded weakly. "I'm sorry, but I'm afraid, I've run out of gas. I hope you all understand."

"Of course," Gunther said. "We can always pick up where we left off. I'll have Bart schedule something at your convenience."

"I'll need to schedule some time too," Adam said, closing his pad and turning off his recorder.

Dan nodded and handed him one of his Foundation business cards. "Call me. We'll work something out as soon as my father feels up to it."

Several days later, the same group, minus Gunther, reconvened for the photo shoot at Zach Bolden's Chelsea studio. A brisk fellow with close-set eyes and shaved head, Bolden had an air of authority and thoughtful decisiveness that paid-off in a world overrun with massive egos and fragile psyches.

The cavernous space was painted a soft white and bathed in shadowless light that came from rows of saw-toothed skylights. The vintage suitcase, returned as promised, stood on a massive sheet of gray backdrop paper that rolled across the floor and up the wall to the ceiling. Bolden and several assistants—along with a white-haired stand-in who was sitting on the suitcase as Jake Epstein would soon be doing—were fine-tuning the lighting.

Despite her initial misgivings, Hannah Epstein had gotten caught-up in her husband's contagious enthusiasm for the project. She regretted not being with him when the suitcase was opened, and insisted on accompanying him this time. At the moment, they were sitting in lounge chairs in a corner of the studio where hair and make-up stylists were preparing Jake for the session.

"Do they do your Botox injections too?" Hannah teased as they hovered about her husband.

"You're just jealous because no one's fussing over you," Jake countered with a self-satisfied cackle.

"I'm crushed," Hannah said, hand over her heart. "I thought fussing over me was your reason for getting out of bed in the morning."

Adam overheard the charming banter and made a notation on his pad. He had been questioning Bolden, along with his assistants and stylists on technical matters, while the low-profile *Times* photographer worked with her camera. When the stand-in got up from the suitcase and went to retrieve Jake, Adam's eyes darted to the white, hand painted lettering that had been made almost luminescent by the high-key lighting. There was something curious about the data but he couldn't put his finger on it, and the thought evaporated as Jake arrived and Bolden tended to his camera signaling the session was about to begin.

The old fellow paused before taking his seat. The scene was powerfully reminiscent of that day in Munich when Max Kleist gave him the suitcase and photographed him and Eva sitting on it. Jake stared at it for a long moment; then, as he had done all those years ago, he sat on it and folded his arms across his chest.

Bolden worked with a Mamiya single-lens reflex digital camera. Favored by top professionals for its high-resolution and technical virtuosity, the RZ67 Pro IID, with its 6X7cm format, provided four times the pixel area of a 35mm camera. Over the next few hours, Bolden shot several sequences which required hair and make-up touch-ups, and many wardrobe changes: Jake in suit and tie; in a sport jacket; in a lab coat with a stethoscope draped around his neck; with a sampling of the prosthetics he had designed and patented arranged in the foreground; Jake standing next to the suitcase; holding it by the handle. For someone of his years, the process was wearying. The stress was intensified by the blinding strobe flashes that had him, and everyone else, blinking and seeing circles in front of their eyes. Despite the enthusiasm, advance planning and attention to detail, it was obvious that something wasn't right.

"I'm worried about Papa," Hannah said to Dan who had taken Jake's seat next to her. She shielded her eyes as the strobes fired yet again, then added, "I think he looks exhausted."

Dan splayed his hands in frustration. "I know, but there's no stopping him, Mom. God knows I tried."

"He seems to have lost that zest he always has," Hannah went on with a concerned frown.

Dan nodded, then caught Tannen's eye and waved him over. "I don't know about you, but it's obvious to us this isn't going very well."

"I'm aware of that," Tannen replied, playing down his concern which, for other reasons, exceeded theirs. "It's important to keep in mind that it takes—"

"Please, Mr. Tannen," Dan interrupted. "I warned you this could be emotionally draining for him. I think we should call it off."

"Let's not overreact. I was about to say, it takes time for photographer and subject to develop a rapport. To make the kind of connection that—"

"I'm not overreacting. They've been at it for hours. If it hasn't happened by now, it never will."

"Have faith," Tannen said; then, in an attempt to appeal to Dan's Wall Street mind-set, he added, "There's a lot of money on the line here. We can't come away from this with nothing. We've all made too big an investment."

Dan's eyes burned with disdain behind his frameless lenses. "You're worried about losing money?! I'm worried about my father losing his zest for life!"

"Dan, please," Hannah said, regretting her concern had stirred her son's antagonism. "Mr. Tannen is the expert here. Considering how excited daddy's been about this, the least we can do is give it a fair chance."

"We already have, Mom," Dan replied. "But if you feel that strongly about it…"

"I do," Hannah said with a crisp nod.

Dan locked his eyes onto Tannen's and, in a commanding voice, said, "The ball's in your court. Come up with a game plan, or the game is over."

Tannen had screwed up badly; and he knew it. The investment angle had backfired and allowed Dan Epstein to claim the moral high ground. Tannen wanted to cut him down to size and was on the verge of replying: *It's not your* call, kid, it's your mommy's! But embarrassing him in front of her might pressure Hannah into letting him pull the plug to save face, and Tannen didn't dare risk it. Instead, he held Dan's look and, in an equally authoritative tone, said, "Give me a few minutes."

CHAPTER EIGHTEEN

Konrad Kleist didn't have to wait long to make his clandestine delivery. Darkness fell early this time of year. As he always did on such missions, he dispensed with his chauffeured Mercedes and, accompanied by his daughter, used her Volkswagen instead. The black, beetle-shaped People's Car was a no-frills vehicle which didn't attract attention. Despite being championed by the Führer, few were manufactured during the war; and none of the more than 335,000 Germans who signed up to buy a KdF-Wagen, as they were called, ever got one. KdF stood for *Kraft durch Freude*—Strength through Joy; and those Strength through Joy cars that were built went to the Nazi elite, the Kleists among them.

Konrad didn't tell Kunst to "Stay" this time; and the dog, sitting behind them in front of the Volkswagen's split rear window, seemed fascinated by the falling snow as they drove along the Isar to the Ludwigsbrucke. The bridge arched across the river to a boulevard that—despite changing names several times and detouring around debris from buildings struck by Allied bombs—was the most direct route to the Hauptbahnhof.

Designed by Freidrich Bürklein, Maximilian II's court architect, Munich's main train station was constructed in the mid-1800s. Thanks to Allied air raids, it was under constant reconstruction, now. Despite them, the Deutsche Bundesbahn still managed to operate, more or less, daily, if not on the published schedule which had been further disrupted by the unusually harsh weather. Indeed, thanks to the latter, there hadn't been any air raid sirens wailing on this night, not yet anyway.

Traffic around the station was light, as it was throughout the city, due to the severe gasoline shortage. Kleist guided the Volkswagen into Bahnhofplatz the broad street that swept past the main entrance. The newsstand was just beyond the taxi line where passengers, stung by the biting cold, queued for the few available taxis. Its forest green kiosk was topped by a snow-covered cupola and festooned with copies of newspapers and magazines clipped beneath the overhanging roofline.

"Coast looks clear," Anika said.

"It always does until it's too late," her father cautioned. "Keep looking." He slowed his approach, then pulled to the curb before reaching the newsstand so he could keep it under surveillance.

Anika slipped a magazine from her handbag and opened it to a section from which a half dozen pages had been torn out. Her father took a business envelope from inside his jacket and placed it in the fold. In it were the two blank travel passes and blank passports—one Italian, the other Austrian—that he'd taken from the tabernacle, and the passport photos of Jake and Eva, that Max had taken, and which Anika had processed by one of her mother's operatives. The pseudonyms they had chosen had been written on the back of their respective photographs.

"Take no chances, Anika," her father warned as he secured the envelope to the pages of the magazine with two steel clips. "Remember, if the dealer doesn't say: 'Why do you ask?' just purchase a newspaper and leave."

Anika nodded, slipped the magazine in her handbag, and left the car. Her father watched as she walked toward the newsstand. Without taking his eyes from her, he tapped a North State from a pack and lit it.

The news dealer had an ink-smudged apron tied at the waist of his bulky mackinaw, and a wool watch cap pulled down over his ears. The fingertips of his gloves had been cut off enabling him to make change more easily while making small talk with customers.

"Excuse me?" Anika said brightly when he finished chatting with the woman ahead of her. "Do you have any copies of Gallery Arts Magazine left?"

The news dealer took a moment to slip some coins into a pocket in his apron, then glanced over at her and said, "Why do you ask?"

"Well, I bought this one from you this morning," she replied, removing it from her handbag. "But some pages seem to be missing. I'd like another."

"Sorry for the inconvenience," the news dealer said. He pulled a copy from the rack and gave it to her in exchange for the one that concealed the envelope.

"Thank you so much," Anika said, slipping it into her handbag as she started walking back to the car. She had gone a short distance when three men in black SS greatcoats confronted her.

"Fraulein Kleist, isn't it?" the officer said.

"Yes that's right," Anika replied, feeling the hair on the nape of her neck rising.

"Ah, I thought that was you. I'm Major Steig," he said with a bow that caused the silver death's head on his cap to catch the light of a masked street lamp, one of the few outside the station that were illuminated due to the nightly blackout.

"I'm sorry, Major," Anika replied, trying to stay calm. "If we've met somewhere, I'm embarrassed to say I can't recall having had the pleasure."

"No need to apologize. I'm taking over for your brother at the University, and it fell to me to review the Kleist family file." Steig let an insipid grin turn the corners of his mouth; then swept his eyes over her. "I'm afraid the photos don't do you justice."

"Thank you. I imagine you'll have reason to include others. Let's hope they're more flattering," she said, forcing a flirtatious giggle. "I really have to be getting along. So unless there's something else I can do for you, it's been—"

"On the contrary," Steig interrupted. "Perhaps I could be of service to you," he went on, trying to sound chivalrous. "I was passing by and couldn't help notice your problem with the news dealer."

"Oh, no, it's fine," Anika replied, searching for a way to delay him long enough to allow the news dealer to pass the envelope. "Just a few pages missing from a magazine I purchased this morning. He exchanged it for another without any fuss."

"I see. Which magazine was that?"

"Oh, I doubt it's one you'd be interested in."

"But you're wrong, fraulein. I'm very interested in it. You see, it's against the law to sell defective merchandise; and I intend to confiscate it before he sells it to another unsuspecting victim. The name of the magazine, please?"

"It's called Gallery Arts," she said, removing her copy from her handbag so he could see it.

"Of course," Steig replied, smugly. "Even I've heard of the Kleist Collection." He nodded smartly, and had just started walking toward the newsstand when a voice called out, "Major? Major Steig?!" He glanced over his shoulder to see Konrad Kleist, in a tailored lodencoat and fur hat, walking swiftly toward him with the dog.

The news dealer had been anxiously monitoring Anika's encounter with the SS men, and was relieved that Steig had been intercepted. Milton Glazer, Gisela Kleist's operative who would produce the forged papers, was due to pick up the envelope at any moment. It seemed an eternity passed before the bearded young man appeared. With the choreographed precision that comes from repetition, the news dealer removed the envelope from the magazine and slid it onto the corner of the counter just as Glaser strode past. He took it without breaking stride and soon vanished in a knot of darkened streets, nearby. There was no yellow star snap-fastened to the sleeve of his coat.

"I thought I recognized you," Kleist said, keeping the German Shepherd on a tight leash as he reached the Major and his SS entourage. "What's going on here?"

"Just having a friendly chat," Steig replied with a glance to the dog. "There was no need to bring reinforcements."

"I'll be the judge of that, Major," Kleist retorted. "My son may be under your command and subject to your harassment, but my daughter isn't."

"Daddy, it's okay," Anika said, warding him off with her eyes. "The Major was just being helpful."

"Thank you fraulein," Steig said, shifting his piercing eyes to her father. "With all due respect, Herr Kleist, your son is neither under my command nor subject to my harassment. But you Jew-lovers will wish he was when he gets his new orders. Heil Hitler!" He bent his elbow in a Nazi salute, then whirled, and marched toward the newsstand, the two SS men in tow.

The dog watched warily, straining at the leash, and growled after them.

The news dealer was still holding the magazine from which he had removed the envelope. He knew what would happen next, and slipped it into a trash basket as the Major shoved several customers aside to reach him.

"A young lady just returned a defective magazine," Steig said, holding out a hand. "Give it here."

"I discarded it," the news dealer said.

"I said, give it here!" Steig bellowed.

The news dealer responded with a compliant shrug, then fished the magazine out of the trash and held it in front of the Major's face. It was dripping with the greasy remains of a meal he had consumed earlier. Steig backhanded the magazine out of the fellow's hand and marched off. The two SS men followed.

Konrad and Anika Kleist stood stone faced as the trio went lumbering past in their black greatcoats. The dog was still growling and straining at the leash as father and daughter hurried to their car, bursting into laughter the instant they were inside. The moment of levity came to an abrupt end as the unnerving implications of what had just happened struck with sobering impact.

"What was he doing here?" Anika wondered with a shiver as her father pulled away from the curb. "He gives me the creeps."

"Psychopaths tend to have that effect on normal people," Kleist replied, his eyes narrowed in concern. "There are two possibilities: He was here because he followed us; or because someone tipped him off. Either way, this could be a big problem."

"Unless...unless, it was neither," Anika said.

"Neither? What do you mean by that?"

"Well, for what its worth, the Major said it was a coincidence. Maybe it was?"

"And maybe he's onto you. I'm not so sure you should be driving Max's friends to the Gorge tomorrow."

"Yes, but if he is onto me...why tip his hand?" Anika prompted, her eyes brightening with insight. "I mean, he could have caught all three of us red-handed tomorrow. Right?"

Her father's brows went up in tribute. "You know, Anika, you're a very smart young woman. Yes, you're very, very smart and you have guts."

"I can't imagine who I take after," she said, with a proud glance to her father.

"Your mother," Konrad said without missing a beat. "Whoever coined the phrase, grace under pressure, not to mention, strength of character, had her in mind, not me."

"That's what she says about you, papa."

"I rest my case," her father said. He shifted up a gear, and headed across the bomb-altered landscape in the direction of the Ludwigsbruke.

Anika stared into the darkened streets, hypnotized by the movement of the wipers as the jagged silhouettes of broken buildings paraded past. "I'm worried about Max, papa," she finally said, breaking the silence.

"So am I. The SS isn't in the habit of making hollow threats."

Anika nodded grimly. "Can't you do something? I know you've already interceded, once, but—"

"No, I can't," her father interrupted, bristling with frustration. "Thing's have changed. My influence has been blunted. Whatever Max's orders are, all we can do is pray the war ends before anything happens to him."

"Pray?" Anika challenged, her voice tinged with sarcasm. "You really think God gives a damn about us? About Germany? How could He have let this happen if He does? How could He have turned these monsters loose?"

"I don't know. I lay awake nights asking myself the same question, and keep coming up with the same answer."

"Which is?"

"He's testing our faith."

"Well, it's an unfair test. Our family has done enough to get a perfect grade. He can't ask us to give up Max too. He can't."

The dog barked as if it understood.

CHAPTER NINTEEN

Having resisted the impulse to cut Dan Epstein down to size, Tannen took Stacey and Steinbach aside to deal with his ultimatum. They were huddled in a corner of Zach Bolden's studio around a console that was outfitted with digital photo-editing and printing equipment. Indeed, the technical aspects of commercial photography had changed dramatically since Tannen had his studio twenty years ago. Developing negatives and making contact sheets from which the best shots were selected for enlargement had gone the way of carbon paper and typewriters—as had darkrooms with their macabre glow, tyrannosaurus-like enlargers, trays of pungent chemicals and tedious procedures. The results of a session could be evaluated immediately, now; and Bolden was sitting in front of two 40-inch flat-screen monitors, scrolling through the shots he had just taken. Like the cigarette butt photographs Stacey had extolled, these were gritty, textured, high-resolution black and white images that on first glance were exactly what she, and the others, had envisioned; but as Bolden mouse-clicked through them, they could all see that the key element was missing.

"Not what we were hoping for, are they, Zach?" Tannen prompted.

"Not even close," Bolden replied grimly. "They're flat, staged, without personality. It's as if we hired an actor to play the part…a bad actor."

"Yeah, Jake's the guy who lived it but you'd never know it," Steinbach said clearly distraught. "It's just not coming through."

Tannen nodded emphatically. "He's not engaged. His eyes don't have that—that Jake sparkle, that mischievous twinkle, do they Stace?"

Stacey responded with a preoccupied nod. She had been watching Jake from afar and, once again, felt responsible for the old fellow's plight. He sensed what was going on, but wasn't quite sure what it meant, and appeared bewildered. "I think he looks terribly lonely," Stacey said thinking out loud as she wracked her brain for a solution.

"Whatever, this is a disaster," Steinbach growled through clenched teeth. He fired a challenging look at Stacey. "Well, here's where the rubber meets the road, kid. Got any brilliant ideas?"

"Yup," Stacey replied without missing a beat. "You're the one who promised him it was going to be fun, right?"

"Yeah, so?" Steinbach fired-back.

"Well it's obvious it isn't. Look at him, all by himself out there. I think it's time you—"

"No shit Sherlock," Steinbach snapped. "Don't give me psychobabble. Give me an idea!"

Stacey's eyes flashed with anger then, resisting the temptation to retaliate, she said, "Hey, you're the client, Mr. Steinbach; and the client's always right, but…" She paused and held up her hands defensively, as if anticipating an onslaught of blows. "…with all due respect, you're wrong on this one, dead wrong."

"Me? Wrong? Why?" Steinbach challenged, rapid-fire.

"Because you didn't let me finish."

"I'm listening," Steinbach muttered grudgingly.

"Good. I was about to say, it's time to roll up your sleeves and make good on that promise. Your sleeves, Mr. S. Roll them up. You know what I mean?"

Steinbach's eyes narrowed in confusion. He was on the verge of unleashing another scathing rejoinder when they brightened with understanding. "Yeah, I do, I sure as hell do." His wiry frame sprang into action as he removed his jacket and tie, and rolled his sleeves up above his elbows, revealing the Auschwitz tattoo on his forearm. "Come on Jake, loosen up. It's time to have some fun," he said, striding across the backdrop paper to where the old fellow was sitting on the suitcase in a weary slouch. "You remember I said two old Jews sticking it to the Nazis? Well, that's exactly what this damn near seventy year-old Jew and this damn near ninety-year-old Jew are going to do! A hundred and sixty years of old Jews are going to roll up their sleeves and stick it to 'em! Don't just sit there, Jake. Come on! Roll 'em up!"

Jake looked a little uncertain at first; then, his eyes came to life. He got to his feet and, with Steinbach's assistance, removed his jacket and tie, and rolled up his sleeves, revealing that he, too, had a number, preceded by the letter A, tattooed on his forearm.

Steinbach caught Stacey's eye and nodded smartly in tribute, getting an affirming fist-pump in return. "We didn't just tour the continent on the fucking Orient Express, did we, Jake?!" he went on, rhetorically. "No, we just survived a harrowing journey; and that's how we should look! Like tough, proud, Holocaust survivors!" he exclaimed, mussing Jake's neatly combed hair into windblown thatches. "Are we having fun yet?"

"We sure as hell are!" Jake replied, erupting with laughter. He looked across the studio to where Hannah was seated with Dan and blew her a kiss; then he sat on the suitcase, folding his arms across his chest. The Auschwitz tattoo was clearly visible.

Steinbach had stepped behind him and, standing just off to one side, assumed a defiant, warrior-like posture with his arms folded across his chest in a way that displayed his tattoo. "How's this?!" he called out to Bolden who, anxious to capture this electrifying moment, had just affixed a fresh digital back to his camera. "Hope you've got some film left in that thing."

As the strobes began flashing again, Adam, who had been quietly observing it all, tilted his head as if trying to recall something. He squinted at the suitcase, staring at the white lettering that was visible between Jake's legs; and, as if cued by a strobe flash, made the connection that had eluded him earlier. His fingers began flipping the pages of his notepad. "Help me out here, will you?" he said, drifting to Stacey who was clearly delighted by what her exchange with Steinbach had instigated. "I'm confused."

"What about?"

"Dr. Epstein's age. I'm pretty sure Google had his DOB as 1920. I think that's what he said the other day, too, isn't it?"

"I guess. I don't know. I just heard Steinbach say he was damn-near ninety..."

"Yeah, me too," Adam said, still checking his notes. "Here it is: Born...1920."

"Well, that computes..."

"I know, but the DOB painted on the suitcase is nineteen twenty-two."

"Oh." Stacey shrugged. "So? What's the big deal?"

"It's called fact-checking, remember? You've spent too much time in the ad game making them up. I don't have that luxury."

"Come on, according to my daddy, Grandpa Dutton wasn't sure which side of the Rio Grande he was born on, let alone in what year. These old timers didn't pop out of the womb stamped with a bar code that got logged into a computer."

"Yeah, but you know the *Times*. Ever since Jason Blair..." Adam said, referring to the reporter who just a few years ago had fabricated dozens of news stories, "...they're back to fact-checking whether the earth orbits the sun or vice-versa."

Stacey laughed. "Hey it's a dirty job, Clive, but somebody's got to do it."

CHAPTER TWENTY

After passing the envelope to her mother's contact at the train station and returning to the townhouse in Bogenhausen with her father, Anika Kleist turned her attention to what Jake and Eva would need while in hiding at the abandoned cabin in Partnach Gorge. Giving Max and Eva as much time together as possible, Anika, Jake, and Tovah, the housekeeper, went about gathering blankets, quilts, canned foodstuffs, tins of biscuits, and bottles of water, along with a box of candles and a flashlight—all of which they carried down to the garage and began loading into Anika's Volkswagen.

"I've never gotten a flat," Anika said in her spirited way, as she removed the spare tire and hardboard liner from the car's forward trunk to maximize space. "And I've just decided I never will."

"Good," Jake said with a nervous laugh. "Because I've never changed one."

"And you won't have to...at least not tomorrow."

Tovah found a small electric heater in one of the storage lockers at the rear of the garage. It fit snugly in the foot well behind the driver's seat.

The next morning, Anika put the German Shepherd in the back seat and pulled the car out into the driveway where Eva, Jake, and Max—a jarring presence amidst the falling snow in his black SS uniform—were waiting. He would be leaving to report for duty as soon as the others departed, and had dressed accordingly. Jake shoe-horned his newly acquired suitcase into the trunk and got in the back seat next to the dog. The time Max and Eva had long dreaded had come, and they were standing aside, clinging to this last moment.

"This wasn't how I wanted you to remember me," Max said, referring to the uniform.

Eva set her rucksack on the ground and removed the framed snapshot of them that she had taken from her flat. "This is how I will remember you," she said handing it to him. "How I will remember us...always..."

"I…I can't believe it's come to this," Max said softly. "God how I wish we—"

"Enough…" Eva said, eyes welling with emotion. She hugged him tightly, then got in the car next to Anika. Max put the picture in the rucksack, then stuffed it into the trunk. He forced the lid closed and looked up at Eva who smiled wistfully as the wipers swept across the windshield in front of her. "Please go," she said to Anika, overcome by the sense of finality. "I can't bear it. I just can't. Please…"

Max watched them drive off, wondering if he would ever see Eva again. When the car was gone, he adopted a more erect, military posture and shook the snow from his greatcoat; then, Dr. Maximilian Kleist, Captain, Waffen-SS strode back into the house and went to the chapel where his parents were waiting. They spent a few moments, kneeling in prayer, then crossed themselves and went downstairs to the garage, joining Tovah and the chauffeur who was stowing Max's duffel bag in the trunk of the Mercedes.

"Let us know where you are," Gisela Kleist said, her voice quavering with emotion.

"Soon as I can," Max replied, forcing a smile. "I'll send you all postcards from the Riviera!"

"God be with you," Tovah said, softly in Yiddish.

"And with you, Tovah," Max replied in the language she had taught him as a child. "May He be with all of you and with Eva and Jake." He hugged his mother, shook his father's hand, and got into the car with the chauffeur. In less than fifteen minutes Max would be at SS Headquarters on Schellingstrasse where his orders awaited.

While Max was bidding farewell to his parents, Anika was driving across Munich to the Bundesstrasse No. 2, the roadway that cuts through the Alpine foothills to the town of Starnberg 30 kilometers to the south. The weather made driving hazardous, and it took an hour to reach the checkpoint at the northern tip of Lake Starnberger, a desolate area of iron-gray trees and drifting snow. The road narrowed and led to a bridge where a barricade marked with a swastika had been set up. A guardhouse stood nearby. Wisps of smoke curled from a stovepipe that pierced its snow-covered roof. A Nazi flag hung stiffly from a pole affixed to the facade. As the slush-spattered Volkswagen approached, a sergeant came from the guardhouse and walked toward the bridge. A sidearm hung from a belt that encircled his greatcoat. Anika slowed, expecting he would raise the barricade and wave her on as he always did. Instead, he held up a hand, forcing her to stop, and then stepped to the driver's window. Anika sighed and lowered it. The close-set eyes of a face she didn't recognize stared at her from beneath a Nazi helmet.

"You are going where, fraulein?" the sergeant asked, his breath coming in gray puffs as he spoke.

"Skiing," Anika replied, impatiently as the wipers chattered across the windshield. "Can we go now? We're losing all the warmth in here."

"Skiing where?"

"Garmisch-Partenkirchen, as I do most weekends in season. Ask Lieutenant Junger. He'll tell you."

"I don't see any skis," the sergeant went on, unmoved by her protestations.

"They're in our chalet on Eibsee."

"Eibsee," the sergeant echoed as if impressed. "A rich brat from Munich. A good-looking one too." He reached through the open window and started toying with Anika's hair. The dog growled and lunged from the back seat, snapping at his hand. The sergeant shrieked in pain. His eyes darted to the blood oozing from a gouge on one of his knuckles. He cursed and drew his sidearm, aiming it at the dog's head.

"No!" Anika shouted, shoving the Luger aside. It fired, wildly, sending Eva and Jake diving for cover.

A lieutenant came running from the guardhouse with his sidearm drawn. "What's going on, here?!"

"Her fucking dog bit me!"

"With good reason!" Anika retorted.

The lieutenant recognized her and holstered his pistol. "Lower your weapon," he commanded, glaring at the sergeant. "Holster it. Now!"

The sergeant seethed with anger, then complied.

"Fraulien Kleist," the lieutenant said, sounding embarrassed. "My sincere apologies."

"Accepted," Anika said, with a smile that could have melted the frost forming on his helmet. "It's always good to see you, Lieutenant Junger."

"The pleasure is all mine. Please excuse my sergeant's rudeness. He's newly posted and eager to prove himself. I hope you won't feel compelled to report this to your father."

"No, I don't think that will be necessary."

"Thank you for understanding." The lieutenant gestured to the barricade, prompting the sergeant to raise it. "You idiot!" he bellowed as Anika drove off across the bridge. "You know who her father is?! Herr Konrad Kleist. Head of Kleist Industries and close friend of the Führer!"

Inside the car, Anika glanced to the rearview mirror to see the checkpoint receding in the distance. "How'd I do?" she prompted stimulated by the encounter.

"You've got a lot of chutzpah," Eva replied.

"Yeah, enough for all of us," Jake chimed-in. "There's a little puddle on the seat back here…"

Kunst barked as if in protest.

"…and it wasn't the dog," Jake added with a self-deprecating cackle.

They still had almost 60 kilometers to go before they would reach Partnach Gorge and the abandoned cabin; and for the next several hours, Anika drove south through Traubing, and across the Hirschberg-Alm, continuing on to Weilheim and into the twisting, snow-blanketed hills of the Murnau district.

"Max and I spent summers here when we were growing up," she said, driving down Marktstrasse, Murnau's main street that was lined with shops. "My parents rented a villa on the lake every year before we bought the place on Eibsee. I learned to drive on these roads. See that building?" She went on, indicating an Art Nouveau facade draped in snow. "Kandinsky had a studio there. He and his artist buddies."

"The Blaue Reiter group," Eva said. "They were in the Biennale when I was in college," she went on, referring to the international exhibition held in Venice on odd numbered years. "Klee, Marc, Kandinsky, Gabrielle Munter...She was his girlfriend for a while, right?"

"Sure was," Anika said, impressed by the depth of Eva's knowledge. "My mother began buying their work when she opened her gallery after the war. The large Kandinsky in the library was painted when he was living here. It's called Concert."

"I really like the one in Max's room," Eva said. "Murnau With Church. The colors just resonate."

"I like it too," Anika chirped, brightly. "But Concert's my favorite. It was inspired by Schoenberg's violin concertos."

They had crossed the Eschenloher Mos, a plain of marshes splashed with blinding frost, and on through the two short tunnels between Oberau and Frachant. Soon, the Garmisch-Partenkirchen Basin flattened out revealing the spectacular Zugspitze towering above the Wetterstein Range and the ski areas beyond. The artistic chatter had given way to a somber silence and the breathtaking vista went unnoticed.

The towns of Garmisch and Partenkirchen—joined in 1936 when the Winter Olympics were held there—were on opposite banks of the Partnach River. A contingent of Wermacht mountain troops was billeted in the dormitories where Olympic athletes once lived. A Nazi flag hung above the post office that served as its headquarters.

Anika took the Mittenwald turnoff, bypassing the town, and headed east toward the Gorge. She crossed the railroad tracks near Kainzenbad Station, angling into a narrow side road. It bordered a rock-walled canyon sheathed with ice where the river gushed in a tumbling rage. At the bottom of the gorge, they came to a snow-blanketed cabin built amidst craggy rocks and towering trees. Before leaving the car, they looked for evidence of squatters, but saw neither tire tracks, nor footprints between the cabin and an outhouse, nearby.

Jake found an unlocked window and climbed through it, letting Eva and Anika in through the front door. The cabin was almost as cold inside as out, making their every exhale visible. The dog began sniffing the air and padding about as if conducting an inspection. A table with a snapped leg and an armchair with threadbare upholstery were the only furnishings. The power had been turned off which meant the space heater would be of no use though the candles would come in handy.

"That ought to take the chill out of the place," Jake said with a nod to the fireplace and cordwood stacked beside it.

"Which side of the bed do you want?" Eva joked, gesturing to the floor in front of the hearth.

Anika's eyes narrowed with concern. "I don't know about that. The smoke from the chimney could attract attention. I think it's going to be shared-bodily-warmth beneath a pile of quilts for you two." Then, trying to ease their anxiety, added, "Don't fret. I'll be back by the time you have the drapes hung."

Indeed, this would be home for Eva and Jake until Anika returned from Munich with their forged papers. They searched the cabin for a place to sleep and found a small, windowless storage room behind the kitchen. It had no exterior walls, was free of drafts, and would conserve their body heat. They knew that if something went wrong and Anika was captured with them, she and her family would pay with their lives. So, after helping to unload the car and arrange the bedding on the storage room floor, Anika wished them luck and, accompanied by the dog, headed for the chalet on Eibsee several miles west of the Gorge.

Eva and Jake looked about the tiny room trying to comprehend what had become of them: Highly accomplished, much admired, life-saving physicians in Munich, one day. Fugitive Jews being hunted like animals, hiding out in a frigid cabin, the next. Exhausted, Eva lit one of the candles and, still bundled in her outerwear, crawled beneath the bedding. "Come on," she said, gesturing Jake join her.

Jake hesitated, appearing to be uncomfortable at the prospect. "Maybe, I'll read for a while," he said, taking a book from his briefcase.

"My God," Eva gasped at the steely-eyed image of Hitler staring from the dust jacket and the Gothic typography of the title that slashed boldly across the bottom in a red band. "You're reading Mein Kampf?"

Jake smiled wearily. "Sorry. It's camouflage. Getting caught reading All Quiet On the Western Front can be dangerous to one's health."

"So can exhaustion. Come on…" Eva sensed his discomfort, and added. "It's okay. My brother and I used to sleep together all the time when we were little."

"I'm not your brother, Eva," Jake said with a sigh that hung in the cold air. He was sitting with his back against the wall, watching the light from the candle play across her face. His head was cocked to one side, his dark, unruly hair tumbling from beneath his cap. There was a look in his eyes Eva had never seen before. If she didn't know better she would have thought it had the intensity of longing, of lust. "It must be the hand-me-downs," she joked, suggesting that wearing Max's clothing had affected Jake's sense of identity.

"I'm not joking, Eva," Jake said, sounding hurt. "I'm not your brother and we're not little, and—"

"No, we're all grown up, and that's how we're going to act," Eva interrupted, her tone sharpening. "We're going to do whatever it takes to keep from freezing to death. If that means pressing our bodies together, our clothed bodies, that's what we'll do."

"Eva, listen, just for a moment," Jake pleaded, his voice quavering with emotion. "That first day in class... my God it's hard to believe it was almost three years ago...there you were, this spirited, intelligent, Jewish and, yes, incredibly beautiful, woman; and... and that's when I knew why I had risked coming to Munich for Medical School. I've had feelings for you from that moment; but you and...and Max became..."

"And I have feelings for you, Jacob..." Eva said, putting a fingertip to his lips to silence him "...as a fine man, brilliant doctor, and dear friend; but this is no time to talk about it."

"Of course it is. It may be the only time. We're living from day to day. Moment to moment. There's no future for us. We have only, now; and I've been waiting so long to tell you what's in my heart..."

"You're a sweet man, Jacob; but, you know mine belongs to Max. I'm in love with him, and want to be with him, and only him. There is no explanation for such things. They just are. I hope you understand."

Jake's posture slackened, his eyes glistening with remorse. "I'm sorry, Eva," he said, lowering them in shame. "I've acted childishly, improperly."

"No, you haven't. And you won't. I won't let you." She threw back the pile of bed covers and beckoned he join her. "Now get under here. We have to do everything we can to stay alive."

"Why? So the Nazis can capture and kill us?"

"Jacob," she said with a roll of her eyes, like a mother scolding a child. "It's time for bed. Now."

Jake sighed in concession and did as she ordered. Eva blew out the candle, then pulled the bedding up over them, and pressed her back against his. "Good night, Jacob. God bless."

"I hope so..." Jake said, feeling more vulnerable, now, than ashamed, "...but the desperate prayers of our people have gone unanswered for so long, I've little faith He'll hear ours."

While Eva and Jake huddled in the cabin's unfamiliar darkness, 60 kilometers to the north, a motorcycle came down the road toward the Starnberg Checkpoint. Its headlight, masked to a narrow slit, sliced through the blackness like an illuminated saber. The driver and an SS officer, riding in the side car, looked like snowmen in their white-splotched greatcoats. Both wore helmets and goggles and carried side arms. The motorcycle turned onto the snow-covered shoulder and slithered through the drifts toward the guardhouse.

The painted pine interior had a single bunk, several chairs, a desk with a phone and typewriter, a tack board on which bulletins and fugitive alerts were displayed, and a potbelly stove where a coffee pot hissed. The Sergeant, sporting a bandage on his dog-bitten knuckle, sat at the desk, two-finger typing a report. The Lieutenant stood at a window, smoking a cigarette while keeping an eye on the road. "We have visitors," he said as the SS officer climbed out of the sidecar and pulled a courier's bag from the foot well. He shouldered his way through the door, and pushed his snow-caked goggles up onto his helmet before pulling off a glove and taking an envelope from his bag. "Fugitive alert. SS Munich. Top priority," he said, handing it to the Sergeant.

The envelope contained two alerts. FUGITIVE JEW was printed in large letters across the top of each. The name Dr. Eva Sarah Rosenberg was beneath her photograph on one. Dr. Jacob Israel Epstein beneath his photograph on the other. The alerts stated that Major Heinrich Steig at SS Headquarters be notified immediately if they were sighted or captured; and that they be taken alive for purposes of interrogation. The photos had been obtained from Eva and Jake's student files which Steig had confiscated. Taken three years ago when they first came to the Medical School they depicted young, bright-eyed idealists eager to study medicine and the art of healing.

The sergeant's eyes widened at the sight of them. He waited until the courier, who had poured himself a mug of coffee, had finished it and departed before showing them to the lieutenant.

"Tack them up with the others," Junger said with a dismissive exhale of cigarette smoke after giving them a cursory glance. "We'll keep an eye out for them."

"It's a little late for that," the sergeant said with a self-satisfied smirk. "I think they were in the car, this morning, with your girlfriend."

"What?" the lieutenant said with a puzzled frown. "You mean with Fraulein Kleist?"

The sergeant nodded, smugly.

"You realize what you're suggesting? The Kleists? Harboring Jews? Are you positive it was them?"

"I'm not sure about the woman. She was so bundled up I could barely see her face. But him—" he stabbed an angry forefinger at Jake's picture. "—He was in the back with that fucking dog. I was staring right at him."

"That's...that's incredible. I can't believe it."

"Well, I'd hate to be the one who has to explain to SS Major—" The sergeant paused and glanced to the alert "—Steig, why we didn't report our sighting."

"You'd hate to be the one to wrongly accuse Herr Kleist of harboring Jews, either. Believe me," Lieutenant Junger retorted. He inhaled deeply on his cigarette, then turned to the window and stared at the blowing snow, wrestling with the dilemma.

CHAPTER TWENTY-ONE

During the week following the photo session in Zach Bolden's studio, Stacey and Tannen concentrated on developing other creative phases of the ad campaign; and contacting past Steinbach clients who possessed pieces of luggage that had attained vintage status. They had just wrapped up a meeting with several who had agreed to participate when the CD's from the Wiesenthal Center arrived. Tannen popped one into his computer and began reviewing the data with Stacey. As promised, archivist Ellen Rother had photo-documented, and annotated the historical significance of every item in Dr. Jacob Epstein's suitcase.

The visual and written data revealed that: The documents which had been partly visible when Ellen opened the suitcase were Jake Epstein's Displaced Persons Identity Card issued by a post war processing center and his Austrian passport. A photo, taken in his early twenties, was affixed to the latter by a metal rivet. The clothing had been manufactured in Europe during the period. Though of high quality, their total cost would have been about forty Reichmarks, or four U.S. Dollars at the 1945 exchange rate. Also among the items were: an empty Sturm cigarette package, a copy of *All Quiet on the Western Front* in a *Mein Kampf* dust jacket, a pillowcase, and a dog collar. Each of the snapshots found in one of the pockets was a close-up of a concentration camp prisoner's forearm. Each had a different number tattooed on it preceded by the letter A for Auschwitz. A few ended with a tiny triangle, designating a female prisoner. Though the prints were faded and crackled with age, the numbers could still be read. However, the shallow depth-of-field blurred everything beyond, making the prisoners' faces unrecognizable. The CD contained nothing more shocking than the concentration camp uniform that had brought gasps when the suitcase was opened. Regarding the latter, Ellen's report noted that a yellow triangle, which designated the wearer as a Jew, had been sewn above the left breast pocket as had a patch of white fabric with a prisoner number—A198841—stenciled on it.

That was yesterday.

This morning, Stacey, Tannen and Steinbach were selecting which of Zach Bolden's photos—the ones he'd taken of Jake and Steinbach together—would be used in ads that would soon be running, simultaneously, in *Vogue, Vanity Fair, Harper's, GQ, Esquire* and other fashionable magazines. The luminous, gritty, black-and-white enlargements had been tacked up on a wall in Tannen's office. Like the lined faces, gnarled fingers, fading tattoos, and depth of character of their two well-worn subjects, the nicks, scratches, gouges and stains in the suitcase's pebble-grained leather, along with the white, hand-painted personal data, were highly resolved, and rendered in extreme detail.

Steinbach's quick eyes darted from one to the other as he walked slowly past them. "They're perfect. Perfect. The client's always right…except when he's wrong. Mea culpa, kid," he said to Stacey. "I owe you one."

"Naw, we're even, Mr. S.," Stacey demurred with a glance to Tannen. "I had to do something to justify my billing rate."

"Why didn't I think of that?" Steinbach joked; then, he pointed to one of the prints, and said, "Don't like this one much. Not enough machismo. You agree?"

Stacey nodded.

Tannen cocked his head in thought and removed the print from the board. A short time later, they were on the verge of picking a winner when Stacey's Blackberry went off. She palmed it and glanced to the screen. The text message from Adam Stevens read: Plz call ASAP.

Adam had spent the time since the photo session working on his article—which would be published at the onset of the ad campaign—but hadn't yet finalized the draft. There was a good chance the Wiesenthal CD would contain information worthy of discussion with Jake Epstein; and the lack of deadline pressure had enabled Adam to hold-off the interview until after it had been issued. He began reviewing the data on his laptop the moment it was delivered to his cubicle in the Times Building, yesterday; and was puzzling over one of the snapshots of prisoner identification numbers when Stacey returned his call.

"Hi, I'm in a meeting. What's going on?"

"You check-out the Wiesenthal CD yet?" Adam asked.

"Yeah. Nothing earth-shattering. Why?"

"Well, it may not be earth-shattering, but what I'm looking at, here, is kind of weird."

"Sounds like Clive-the-fastidious-fact- checker's at it, again."

"Yeah. As a matter of fact…" Adam quipped.

"You're not still chewing on that date of birth thing, are you?"

"No, I ran that down. Turns out sometimes the prisoners painted the data themselves; sometimes the Nazis did it. I guess that could account for the discrepancy. I'll get it nailed down in the interview."

"Now, there's a thought," Stacey teased, good-naturedly. "So, what is it that's got you weirded out?"

"Not over the phone."

"Email me."

"No way. It's too sensitive. You should come over."

"I can't. I'm up to my ass."

"Take it from me, this could be your ass."

"Shit," Stacey muttered in capitulation. "It better be good, Clive."

The meeting with Steinbach and Tannen was winding down. Stacey explained the call was related to the *New York Times* story; then she hurried from the building and hailed a cab. "Forty-first and Eighth," she said to the driver.

It was less than a mile—a five minute zip in light traffic, but a frustrating, half-hour slog in midday gridlock. Stacey fidgeted with impatience as the taxi inched forward. She had just noticed the news crawl on the backseat TV screen—which she thought read: REPORT CLAIMS MICHAEL JACKSON FOUND DEAD—when her Blackberry rang. Mom was flashing in the display. She slipped the device from its pouch, and bit a lip while making a decision, then thumbed Talk. "Hi, Mommy…" she said in her West Texas drawl which had a way of surfacing whenever she spoke to folks back home.

"Hi, there pun'kin," her mother said, echoing her sugary accent. "Tried y'all a couple of times…"

"I'm sorry. It's been like twenty-four-seven at work," Stacey said, glancing to the news crawl which now read: IRANIAN GOVERNMENT CLAIMS NEDA SHOT BY ELECTION PROTESTERS NOT MILITIAMAN AS WITNESSES CLAIM. "You got the TV on? I think Michael Jackson died."

"Sure as hell did. OD'd in his own bed. That's what drug addict degenerates do. Probably had a coupl'a six year olds over for a slumber party," her mother replied with a snide cackle. "So, what'cha all workin' on?"

"An ad campaign, what else?"

"An-ad-campaign-what-else-for-what?" her mother said rapid-fire with a laugh, mimicking her.

"Luggage."

"Sounds real excitin'. Speakin' of roll-aboards, when's my little jet-setter comin' back home?"

"Christmas, I guess…"

"Book your flight yet?"

"Lighten up, Mom. It's only June."

"Be July in less than a week. Don't lollygag, Stacey. They're still lookin' for an English teacher down at the high school. I always said you shoulda—"

"Mom…" Stacey groaned, making it into two syllables. "How many times do we have to have this conversation? I live here. In New York City. I've got a great job, a guy who cares about me, lots of friends, an apartment I love…"

"Your daddy misses you."

"Maybe you should give him my number."

"Very funny."

"No it isn't. He never calls me."

"Hey, I live with the man; and he don't say but two words to me. I mean, he's just, I don't know…"

"Taciturn?" Stacey prompted.

"There you go with your words. If that means he's not much of a talker, then it's right on target."

The cab slowed and pulled to the curb next to the *Times* building. "Listen, I gotta go." Stacey stuffed a ten in the driver's hand. "Change is yours. I need a receipt. Sorry Mom, I'm dashin' to a meetin'."

"Who-all's it with?"

"A reporter for *The New York Times*."

"*The New York Times?* Y'all be careful, you hear? They think the gummint should be runnin' our lives."

"No one's runnin' mine but me, Mom."

"Like always," her mother retorted, unable to keep a hint of pride from softening her tone.

"Yep, like always. I gotta go."

"Okay. I love you pun'kin. We all do."

"I love y'all too, Mommy. Bye…" Stacey leapt from the cab, pocketing the Blackberry, then dashed into the lobby, unable to imagine just what Adam had discovered about Dr. Jacob Epstein's suitcase that had so unnerved him; that had provoked his secretive behavior and threatening remark.

CHAPTER TWENTY-TWO

Eva's wistful smile was all Max could think about during the drive to SS Headquarters. Even as he strode beneath the frozen Nazi flags and through the steel door, Eva's haunting image, framed by the wiper-streaked windshield of his sister's car, came to him. The bustling activity in the entry hall snapped him out of it. He quickened his pace and went to the Duty Office to pick up his orders. Like his father, he had no doubt that a combat unit would be his fate. The Eastern Front under siege by the Red Army? The West where Allied forces had taken Bastogne and were advancing on the Rhine? He tore open the envelope and stared at his new posting with disbelief. It was as pleasantly surprising as it was confusing; but he had no doubt his parents would be relieved. "I need to use your phone, sergeant," he said to the Duty Officer.

"All phones are restricted, Sir," the sergeant said. "Besides, they're holding transport for you." He directed Max down a corridor to a door labeled Motor Pool. It opened onto a courtyard where a military supply truck, vapor rising from its tail pipe, was waiting. A group of SS enlisted men, in winter gear sat shoulder-to-shoulder in the cargo bed. Max tossed his duffel into the cab, climbed up next to the driver and was soon headed down Dachauer Strasse, an arrow-straight highway that ran northwest from central Munich.

Less than half an hour later, Captain Kleist was at the main entrance of Dachau Concentration Camp. Wrought iron letters welded to the gate, proclaimed: *Arbeit Macht Frei*; literally, Work Makes Free. At sunset, the stark shadow of its message crept across the grounds. Set amidst peaceful glens of birch trees and towering poplars, through which the Wurm River meandered, Dachau had been established in 1933 to incarcerate and reeducate enemies of the state; and, early on, many had been declared rehabilitated and released, even Jews with the proviso they leave the country; but, over the years, Dachau had become yet another Nazi extermination factory.

The young captain was shown into the Commandant's Office in the Jourhaus, the camp's main administration building. "Dr. Maximilian Kleist, Captain Waffen-SS," reporting for duty, Sir," Max said, snapping off a Nazi salute with as much military bearing as he could muster. "Heil Hitler."

"Heil Hitler," the commandant said, raising his arm from the elbow without looking up from the file he was perusing. Despite his military polish, and the silver-plaited insignia of an Obersturmbannführer on his shoulder boards, Colonel Wilhelm Weiter, Waffen-SS, Kommandeur, Konzentrationslager Dachau, looked gaunt and weary. A Nazi flag behind him was flanked by stern photographs of the Führer and Reichsführer. Dreary, iron-gray light came from a window that framed a landscape of bare trees on the hillside beyond the train tracks that led to the main entrance. The colonel closed the file and looked up at Max. "Dr. Maximilian Kleist, Captain, Waffen-SS," he repeated. "Is that what you said?"

"Yes, Sir," Max replied, crisply.

"No!" the colonel snapped. "You are Captain Kleist, not Dr. Kleist. You are an SS officer first and a doctor second. Is that clear?"

"Yes, Sir."

"Good. Welcome to KZ-Dachau, Captain Kleist."

"Thank you, Sir."

"You know, it's against the rules for SS personnel to be posted in their home district?"

"Yes, Sir. I do," Max replied, trying to sound congenial. "It came as a surprise. I'm quite fortunate. My parents will be pleased."

"Really? According to your file—" Weiter said, slapping the folder on the desk, "—the reasons are disciplinary. Punishment for associating with Jews."

"They were my classmates, Sir. They were also fine doctors, I might add."

"One of them was also a fine lover, wasn't she?"

"Yes, Sir. She was."

"At least it was the Jewish woman," the colonel said, his tone making it clear he wasn't joking. "You know the Führer's views on homosexuals?"

Max nodded.

"You didn't impregnate her, did you?"

"No, Sir."

"Good. The only thing lower than homosexual Jews are heterosexual Jews. Do you know why?"

"No, Sir. I don't."

"They propagate."

Max's lips tightened. "As an officer and a physician I'm prepared to carry out my lawful duties, here, Sir, and conduct myself as a gentleman."

"I'm sure you will…" The colonel stood and circled the desk. "Having been assigned to the ramp, you will have many opportunities to do so."

"The ramp? I'm not familiar with it, Sir."

"It is the most important assignment in the entire camp. Given only to doctors…the finest doctors…from fine families like yourself."

"Thank you, Sir. Every member of the Kleist family strives to serve the Fatherland."

Weiter's eyes hardened. "Your oath is to the Führer, captain. The SS is sworn to serve him and only him. You will serve him by using your medical knowledge to prevent Jews and other degenerates from defiling the racial purity of the Aryan race."

"I'm not sure I understand, Sir."

"You will," the colonel retorted. "Speaking of your family, I've been informed your father, though a devout Catholic, a vital contributor to the war effort, and a confidant of the Führer, is also a lover of Jews. The disciplinary notice in your file states that SS Major Steig suspects your entire family of helping Jews avoid relocation to work camps."

Max locked his eyes onto the colonel's and, in a strong, steady voice, said, "With all due respect, Sir, Major Steig is mistaken."

Weiter studied him, then nodded, seeming to accept it. "Steig," he grunted, his lip curling with disdain. "He's a Party functionary. Not one of us. Not a true member of the officer corps which is why you've been given this chance to prove him wrong."

"I won't waste it, Sir."

"Don't!" the commandant exclaimed. "Be ruthless. Avoid ambiguity. Let nothing cloud your fealty to the Führer. Can you do that?"

"Yes, Sir. I can," Max replied.

"Let's hope so, for your family's sake." Weiter emphasized it with snap of his head, then circled back to his desk, and turned the pages of a binder. "We are expecting a trainload of prisoners in the next several days. Your first tour will be posted on the duty roster in your barracks. Check it often. A fellow officer and physician, who has served on the ramp with distinction, will conduct your orientation. Any questions?"

"Yes, Sir. I'd like to let my parents know I'm here. Is there phone I can use to—"

"No," the commandant fired back. "All telephones are for official use only. All calls are monitored. Even mine." He pushed a button on his intercom. "Send in Lieutenant Radek."

A man with slick, center-parted hair and a cruel turn to his mouth strode into the office, carrying his SS cap tucked under his arm. Lieutenant Klaus Radek snapped to attention with a heel-click and an energetic Nazi salute. "Heil Hitler, Herr Commandant."

Rabid. Attack dog. Dangerous…Max thought, taking notice of the medical caduceus on the collar of Radek's pristine uniform. No bedside manner.

"Good luck, captain," Weiter said, without acknowledging Radek. "Dismissed."

The air was biting cold as the two officers left the building. Their greatcoats snapped in the wind as they crossed the desolate grounds on frozen gravel that crunched beneath their jackboots. "KZ-Dachau was the ingenious creation of Reischführer Himmler. It's a privilege to be posted here," Radek said, leading the way down a broad street that bisected the compound. A group of prisoners were chipping ice from the pavement in front of a guard tower. Their striped denim uniforms provided little protection from the cold or from the truncheons being wielded by the SS guards to make them work faster. "Dachau is divided into two main sections: Military Garrison and Prison Compound," Radek resumed, unmoved by the display of cruelty. "The former includes housing for SS officers and enlisted personnel, the SS Training Center, and the Hygienic Institute where medical research is conducted. The prison is enclosed by electrified fences, a deep moat, and unscalable walls with seven guard towers. No one escapes from there. The prisoners work the gravel pits, build roads, drain marshes, and till fields. The skilled ones staff laboratories and workshops. We also supply workers to local armaments factories. Remember first and foremost Dachau is a work camp."

Max nodded. " I saw the sign in the entrance gate. Work Makes One Free."

"Another example of the Reichsführer's ingenuity," Radek said with an appreciative cackle. "A brilliant motivator. Don't you agree?"

"Yes," Max replied with a sly, sideways glance. "Second only to the truncheon as we've just seen. But none of the prisoners are ever freed, are they?"

Radek looked offended. "Death is their freedom. They work until they die of exhaustion, starvation, disease. In case you're wondering, we aren't able to house and feed everyone who is sent here. Your job will be to select the most robust and healthy."

"And the rest?"

"You mean, the elderly, the sickly, those who can't be productive workers?"

Max nodded.

"Exterminated on arrival," Radek said, with self-righteous aplomb. He pointed to an area between the prison and central kitchen facility. "In that courtyard over there."

Max stopped walking and locked his eyes onto Radek's. "So, I decide who lives and who dies." It was a statement not a question.

"No, Sir. They all die. You decide when."

"Children?"

"Children are parasites. They consume food, take up space and produce nothing. You won't find a kindergarten here."

Max shuddered, shaken to his core. Be ruthless. Avoid ambiguity. Let nothing cloud your fealty to the Führer. The commandant's advice had hit home in all its brutal honesty. He took a moment to settle, then lit a cigarette. He didn't offer one to Radek.

They were in the Prison Compound, now, striding down the Lagerstrasse that ran between two endless rows of beige stucco barracks. Each Block, as prisoner housing units were called, had a peaked roof, a few small windows, a single entrance, and a sign with large black numerals on a white field. Those aligned on the east side of the Lagerstrasse were numbered 1 through 17; those west 18 through 34.

"All prisoners are quartered here," Radek went on. "Each trainload pits the executioners who have orders to kill all Jews and undesirables, against the administrators who must provide as many slave laborers as possible. We doctors are caught in the crossfire: charged with selecting those who are to be exterminated; and, amist the poor hygiene of massive overcrowding, with maintaining the health of those selected for the work force. More than twenty thousand prisoners are housed in these barracks."

Max gasped. "Twenty thousand?"

"Yes, Sir. In thirty-four blocks. Maximum capacity two hundred per block; but we've stacked the bunks and assigned three prisoners to each. All but Block Thirty-One—that's the prisoner brothel."

"Prisoner brothel?" Max echoed, astonished.

Radek nodded smugly. "The whores are all Aryans of course. They service political prisoners, skilled sub-camp workers...*Juden Verboten.*" He emitted an ironic chortle. "Even with that, the Prisoners Committee complains the conditions are beneath human dignity."

"They are," Max said, forcefully. "This is a breeding ground for epidemics. "Tuberculosis, typhus, diphtheria..."

Radek nodded grimly. The situation too grave for even him to shrug off. "We've a massive outbreak of typhus we'll be lucky to contain. It's forced us to expand the Revier," he said, referring to the Prisoner Hospital. He pointed to the eastern row of barracks where another group of prisoners, supervised by SS guards, was constructing an exterior corridor that linked all but two of the seventeen housing Blocks. "It's staffed by prisoner doctors. Mostly Jews. None of us ever go in there."

Max looked aghast. "This isn't a work camp. It's a death camp...for us all."

Radek smiled slyly at what he was about to say. "The next time you see Reichsführer Himmler, why don't you suggest he change the nomenclature?"

Max glared at him in anger, decided the better of expressing it, and dragged deeply on his cigarette, picking up a pungent odor. "What do you do with the corpses?" he asked, emitting a lengthy exhale.

Radek nodded to the thin wisps rising on the wind. "Up in smoke," he replied, amused by his cleverness.

"There's a crematorium here?"

Radek nodded. "'Thou art dust and unto dust thou shalt return.' This is God's work. We're His little helpers." He gestured to some buildings in a cluster of trees. "It's next to the gas chamber. Neither is up to the task. The

Genickschuss has proved efficient," he said, referring to a point-blank pistol shot in the back of the neck. "Corpses are dumped in mass graves, doused with gasoline and burned...when we have gasoline."

Max had heard the rumors. Everyone had; but no one could believe such atrocities were taking place ten miles from Central Munich, in Catholic Bavaria, in Germany—a cradle of Western civilization where great literature, music and art were created and revered; where cutting edge advances in science were made; where the printing press was invented; where Guttenberg printed bibles!

On the face of it, being posted to Dachau was the next best thing to being posted to the Medical School. Max could easily go home on leave; and, of course, his parents would be relieved he wasn't in a combat unit; but Max wasn't relieved; because being posted to Dachau wasn't his punishment. No, as Major Steig's snide threat had implied, the Jew-lover's punishment would be more insidious than that. Indeed, being assigned to work the ramp—to make what were known as Selections—would force Max to engage in morally repugnant behavior and criminal acts.

At the completion of the orientation tour, Radek was leading the way down the Avenue of the SS, lined with the stately residences of the Commandant and the camp's upper echelon when, in a deceptively congenial tone, he said, "By the way, Max, I understand that you—" He winced as if catching himself. "My apologies, Sir. I shouldn't take such liberties without asking permission. May I use your Christian name, Sir?"

Max studied him warily. "No. No, lieutenant, you may not," he replied, asserting the privilege of rank; then deciding that, at this early juncture, it might be wise to be accommodating, he added, "Of course, it might be acceptable in certain situations. For example if we were off duty, having an informal chat, that sort of thing..."

"Ah, but we are off-duty and speaking informally, so it wasn't a breach of etiquette. Was it, Sir?" Radek prompted, pretending to be relieved. "All I was going to say was, I understand that you have a Jewish lover."

Max shuddered, his eyes burning with indignation, his fists clenching in preparation for combat.

"Just between us, Max," Radek went on with a jaunty tap on Max's shoulder, "you're not the only one with a taste for forbidden fruit. Despite those pesky Nuremberg Laws, I find Jewish women to be quite succulent. There's something about them that makes my mouth water." Then, with a sly lifting of his head that implied, 'Rank notwithstanding, I can do this and there's nothing you can do about it,' Radek added, "They are a disposable commodity, here. Feel free to have as many as you like. Just don't get caught."

CHAPTER TWENTY-THREE

The recently constructed *New York Times* Building was a modern, high-tech tower of shimmering ceramic rods and computer-controlled louvers. It took up the entire block between Fortieth and Forty-first streets opposite the Port Authority Bus Terminal, soaring 52-stories above the Eighth Avenue corridor.

Stacey dashed through the entrance past the glass-enclosed atrium where the spindly trunks and delicate foliage of silver birches climbed toward an overcast sky. The 560 vacuum fluorescent screens of Moveable Type, the art installation in the lobby, went by in a blur as she hurried to the security desk. Suspended on thin cables, the paperback-size screens displayed an ever-changing, replay of the day's stories and related material from the *Times*'s archives. The theme at the moment: ANTI-SEMITISM ON RISE IN EUROPE --- KOSHER WAREHOUSE FIREBOMBED IN PARIS — NEO-NAZIS DEFACE SYNAGOGUE IN DRESDEN — BERLIN HOLOCAUST MEMORIAL VANDALIZED WITH SWASTIKAS /WIESENTHAL CENTER ASKS EU TO INTERVENE — BENEDICT REINSTATES BISHOP WHO DENIED HOLOCAUST. Suddenly, all 560 screens reset. Now, the data tracing across them read: KING OF POP MICHAEL JACKSON FOUND DEAD — PERSONAL PHYSICIAN MAKES DISCOVERY — DRUG INDUCED CARDIAC ARREST SUSPECTED — GLOBAL OUTPOURING OF GRIEF OVER LOSS OF MUSIC ICON.

Stacey scrawled her name in the Visitor's Log; then, Security Pass pasted to her jacket, she popped into an elevator just as the door was closing. It took her to the fourth floor mezzanine, one of several overlooking the newsroom. Staircases, sheathed in red plastic panels, slashed through the open well like bolts of crimson lightning, connecting the work levels. She made her way between the paneled cubicles where reporters toiled in the glow of computer screens. Adam was kicked-back in his chair staring at an image from the Wiesenthal CD on his laptop when he saw her approaching. "Hey, there you are," he said, removing his iPod ear buds. "You hear about Michael Jackson?"

Stacey nodded sadly. "A drug-addicted degenerate, according to my mother."

"She's right…" Adam said, deadpan. "…a drug-addicted degenerate genius."

Stacey smiled. "So, what's the big secret?"

"Sensitive secret," Adam corrected in a low voice. "Not something I'd want overheard or hacked." He indicated the vast openness, and winced. "I love this place but it's like working in a fishbowl." He carried his laptop into one of the glass-enclosed side offices—that had been left unassigned to enable staffers to have private conversations—set it on the table and closed the door. The image on the screen was one of the black-and-white shots of Jake and Steinbach that would be used in the ad campaign; one of several Adam had acquired to use with his story and had scanned into his Photoshop program. "Our two heroes…" he said in his low voice.

Stacey nodded.

Adam touch-pad/clicked zooming-in to a close-up of Jake's forearm. "The prisoner ID number tattooed on Dr. Epstein's arm."

Stacey nodded again.

Adam touch-pad/clicked again, bringing up another window. Like the first it had an image of a forearm with a prisoner identification number tattooed on it. "I was poking around the Wiesenthal CD and came across this. It's from that packet of snapshots that were in the suitcase. They're all similar to this one."

"I know," Stacey replied, curiously. "The faces are all out of focus. The text suggests they were taken to make a record of the prisoner ID numbers."

"Taken by whom?" Adam prompted. "The Good Doctor? I don't think so. I mean, not too many prisoners were running around concentration camps with a camera."

"Not likely. I agree."

Adam touch-pad/clicked again, setting up a split-screen: Each image was a close-up of a prisoner identification number tattoo. The one on Jake's arm that Adam had zoomed into on the left; the snapshot from the packet found in the suitcase on the right. "Now, what's the first thing you notice?"

"They're both the same number," Stacey replied without hesitation. "A198841. They're identical."

"Good puppy," Adam said, patting her on the head. "Same number that's on the striped uniform by the way."

"So," Stacey said, evaluating the data. "You've got two pictures of Dr. Epstein's prisoner ID tattoo. A very old one, and a very new one."

"Exactly what I thought at first, too," Adam replied; then, trying not to sound too professorial, prompted, "Look more carefully."

Stacey leaned closer to the screen. Her eyes moved back and forth across the side-by-side images several times, then flickered with insight. "The numbers are the same but the handwriting's different!" She pointed to Jake's photo. "I mean, look at those eights they're like infinity symbols turned on end; and those sevens—I mean ones. Whatever. They're not even close."

Adam nodded smartly. "What are the chances the Nazis—fanatical record-keepers that they were—gave the same number to two different prisoners?"

"Slim and none."

"Yet we have the same number. In different handwriting. Therefore, we might conclude that..." Adam let it trail-off, suggesting Stacey finish the sentence.

"...they're not the same person."

"What a gal!" Adam exclaimed.

Stacey's eyes narrowed in thought. "Hold on. There were lots of concentration camps, right? Do we know for a fact that they didn't all identify their first prisoner as prisoner number one? And, thereby, were giving out the same prisoner numbers?"

"No we don't know that; but—" Adam tapped the screen. "—A is for Auschwitz, right? Both of them."

"Duh," Stacey groaned at her own denseness. "I knew that. So where we going with this, Clive?"

Adam shrugged. "Food for thought?" He zoomed-out the left image from the close-up of the tattoo to the wide shot of Jake and Steinbach, and pointed to Jake. "I mean, we know who this guy is. But who's this guy?" he asked, pointing to the image of the forearm on the right side. "No tiny triangle. So, we know it's a guy. Will the real Jake Epstein please stand up?"

Stacey rocked back in her chair, her spiky blonde hair bristling. "What are you getting at?"

"That I want to be damn sure before I write my story, that Dr. Jacob Epstein is...Dr. Jacob Epstein."

Stacey's jaw dropped. "You saying he's...he's some kind of imposter?"

Adam scratched at his carefully cultivated scraggle. "Maybe. Maybe not. I don't know."

Stacey pointed to the image of the snapshot next to the one of Jake and Steinbach. "Maybe he's the imposter? Whoever he is. If there even is one."

"Point taken."

"Yeah," Stacey said, sounding vindicated. "Either way, that's a quantum leap, Clive. I'm the one who's supposed to be writing fiction. Not you."

"Fiction?!" Adam exclaimed. "Hey, I've held-off my interview of Dr. Epstein until the CD was issued so I'd have as much information as possible before I—"

"Come on," Stacey interrupted, unwilling to let go of it. "You've had it less than a day. Barely enough time to scratch the surface."

"Yeah, and look what turned up."

"So? Why stop now? Dig deeper. I mean, there might even be some facts on it that'll clarify this."

Adam's shoulders sagged in weary capitulation. "Maybe we should continue this over lunch?"

"I can't. I have to get back," Stacey replied with finality. "As my boss says, never sit on bad news. Always deliver it in person. Maybe we could—"

Someone knocked on the glass, startling them. Adam's editor stuck his head in the door. Tall and rail-thin, due to an overactive thyroid that defied medical intervention, Paul Diamond had an easy-going demeanor that belied an incisive mind. In his mid-fifties, he had survived a downsizing in January when Metro lost its standalone status and was merged into National. "Saw you guys in here, thought I'd say, hi."

"Hey…" Adam said, weakly, closing the laptop.

"How goes it, Stace?" Diamond went on. "Ad game treating you okay?"

"Yup, same old, same old. You know how it goes: All human beings are flawed. Our clients have products that will make them perfect. We make the pitch. They fork over the cash and find Nirvana…" She smiled and splayed her hands. "Piece of cake."

"No thanks. I'm on a diet," Diamond quipped with a laugh. "Things looked kind of tense from out there. You guys okay? You sure you don't need anything?"

Stacey's jaw tightened. She fired a veiled look of apprehension at Adam.

"Naw," Adam replied, feigning nonchalance. "Fact-checking that suitcase piece."

"Evil Nazis. Holocaust survivors. Apthorp trash. Ad campaign," Diamond said rapid fire, enumerating the key story points.

Adam nodded. "That's the one."

"A good one. Keep me posted."

"Sure. Couple of iffy details I'm trying to run down."

"Just keep peeling that onion," Diamond advised as he sailed off across the mezzanine.

Stacey sighed with relief as Diamond descended one of the red-sheathed staircases to the newsroom; then, said, "You had my heart skipping beats, there, Clive; but you made the right call."

"For now," Adam said, unwilling to permanently concede the point. "There's no rush, Stace. I just want to get it right."

"You sure as hell had better," Stacey warned, her tone sharpening. "You could destroy this man, along with his family. Not to mention all the good he's done, and everything he's accomplished."

"I know. That's why I called you. Either way, I want to make sure I'm not writing fiction." Adam paused and locked his eyes onto hers. "Just make sure you aren't."

Stacey nodded, stung by, but appreciative of, his brutal frankness. She couldn't, wouldn't believe what Adam had implied; but was clearly unsettled by it. She had no doubt, this time, Tannen would go nuts.

CHAPTER TWENTY-FOUR

After leaving Jake and Eva at the cabin in Partnach Gorge, Anika spent the night at the chalet on Eibsee, and then drove back to Munich and her classes. By mid-week, the Kleists still hadn't heard from Max; and, after dinner, they retired to the library to commiserate. Gisela sought solace at her piano. Accompanied by Anika on violin, she was playing the andante from Mozart's Jupiter symphony when the room began vibrating with the drone of low-flying aircraft and the rumble of distant explosions. Her husband pulled the blackout drapes tighter across the windows. "They must be hitting the rail yards, again," Konrad said, sounding ambivalent. "The war is lost. It's just a matter of time. Pray that, wherever Max is, he manages to survive until it's over."

"You're right," Gisela said with steely resolve. "If Max were here, he'd be saying, don't worry about me, help my friends."

"We are, Momma," Anika said, reassuringly. "I'll have Eva and Jake on their way as soon as their papers are ready."

"My people tell me sometime tomorrow," Gisela said. "In the meantime, is there anything else we can do to make sure they're not caught by the Gestapo?"

"What about disguises?" Anika said, brightening. "Wigs, eyeglasses, a moustache, theatrical latex to age them. I could get them at school," she went on, referring to the Juilliard-like institution she attended where drama was taught along with music and dance.

"Too late," her mother said, decisively. "The photos on the forged passports won't match. Eva and Jake would have had to be in disguise when Max took them. Besides, the Gestapo checks papers on a whim. Keeping up disguises just isn't practical."

"Yes," her husband chuckled. "Just ask the British spy who limped about with a cane one day and was spotted by the Gestapo running to catch a train the next."

Anika nodded in concession. "As Max said, living with pseudonyms is going to be dangerous enough."

Mid-afternoon the next day, Anika headed back to Partnach Gorge with the forged papers. Her stomach was in a knot as she neared the Starnberg checkpoint. To her relief, her friend, Lieutenant Junger, not the dog-bitten Sergeant, came from the guardhouse as her car approached. He raised the barricade, waving her on across the bridge with a cheery smile; then, his eyes hardened and shifted back to the guardhouse as an unmarked, six-passenger, staff car came from behind it. Major Steig was in the command seat next to the driver. Four SS men in black greatcoats were behind them. The big Mercedes crunched through the snow onto the road and, keeping its distance, followed Anika's Volkswagen.

She was ten kilometers beyond the checkpoint when she first noticed the wide-spaced headlights and the distinctive grille in her mirror. Was it the Gestapo? The SS? Were they following her? Anika couldn't be sure. She stopped at a roadside cafe just outside of Murnau, had a cup of tea, used the bathroom, and was back on the road within twenty minutes. On this frigid day, there were few cars or shoppers on Marktstrasse when the Mercedes reappeared in her mirror. She had no doubt, now, that she was being followed; and knew that, whether Gestapo or SS, they would have already arrested her had she been their target. No, it was Eva and Jake they wanted; and they were counting on her to lead them to their hiding place.

Anika knew Murnau well from the summers she had spent there; and she led the SS car into the town's maze of twisting streets and back alleys, luring it down a narrow lane and through a blind curve where the road narrowed even further as it passed between two closely spaced buildings. The tips of the Volkswagen's bumpers scraped against the sidewalls, but the beetle-shaped car made it through as Anika knew it would. She also knew, the Mercedes with its much wider track wouldn't. As it came out of the turn, the driver hit the brakes hard at the sight of the narrow opening directly ahead, sending the massive vehicle skidding across the icy pavement. It came to a stop with its front fenders wedged between the two buildings. The last Anika saw of it, the driver was attempting to back up and extricate the vehicle. She was fairly certain the SS officer, shouting at him, was Major Steig.

Darkness had fallen by the time Anika turned onto the road that led to Partnach Gorge. Inside the snow-bound cabin, Eva and Jake had just finished a candle light dinner. He had made a splint for the table's broken leg from pieces of kindling and a length of rusty wire he'd found, and stacked-up cordwood for benches; and they'd been happily devouring their cans of cold soup and tins of biscuits in the 'Dining Hall' as they referred to it. Now, while Eva took stock of their supplies, Jake sat in the worn armchair with his *Mein Kampf*-camouflaged copy of *All Quiet on the Western Front*. He was reading Chapter Six in which 2nd Company, en route to the front, passes dozens of newly made coffins stacked in a schoolyard—coffins that the soldiers realize have been made for them; thus prompting the German soldier who narrates the story to conclude his emotions have been forever deadened, and his youth, and most likely his life, wasted. Jake had drifted off in somber reflection when Anika came bursting through the door.

"They're onto us," Anika said. She removed the forged papers from her handbag and put them on the table in front of her startled charges. "You have to sign these," she went on with unwavering focus.

The travel passes, student visas, and passports—Italian for Eva, Austrian for Jake—had been made out in the pseudonym each had selected. Their photos had been fastened with official steel rivets procured by a resistance member who worked for the manufacturer; each had been stamped with the Reichsadler—the Imperial eagle clutching a swastika in its claws—and boldly endorsed with forged signatures. Jake and Eva were keenly aware that the passports lacked the large red J, for Jew that had been stamped on their real ones by the Gestapo.

"What happened?" Jake asked as they went about signing the documents.

"Someone spotted us," Anika replied. "Probably at Starnberg. The SS must've gone to the chalet on Eibsee; and when you weren't there, they decided to let me lead them to you; but I lost them in Murnau," she said with a spirited laugh. "They may never get out of there!"

Eva's eyes darkened with concern. "Then you're in danger too."

Anika shrugged, unfazed. "My father will think of something. We have to go. Now. They're probably checking every hotel and ski lodge as we speak. Night trains are best, anyway. The Gestapo men are bored and groggy on schnapps." She snapped her fingers and winced. "Oh, I almost forgot," she went on, taking a glassine envelope from her handbag. Inside the long, narrow sleeve was a strip of 35mm film. Among the half-dozen negatives were the shots Max had taken of Eva and Jake for their passport photos. "This may come in handy."

"Yeah, the next time we need forged papers," Jake said with a laugh, taking it.

"It's not funny," Anika scolded. "Tuck it someplace safe. The Gestapo are always on the lookout for false papers. It could give you away."

"I've got just the place for it," Jake said, slipping it inside the pages of his book.

"That's not good enough," Anika said.

"It'll do for now," Jake said.

They gathered their belongings and packed the suitcase and rucksack, dividing up the foodstuffs they hadn't consumed, and then hurried from the cabin.

Anika knew the military presence in Garmisch-Partenkirchen and its status as a winter sports Mecca meant Zugspitze Station would be under strict

Gestapo surveillance; and decided to use Kainzenbad Station in nearby Mittenwald, instead. Once a teeming crossroads on medieval trade routes, it had since become a quiet hamlet of ski instructors and violin makers. Since it would be safer for Jake and Eva to appear to be traveling alone, Anika dropped them at different locations. After making their way through the town's darkened streets, they took up positions from where they could observe the station and the polished rails that split the white landscape in a sweeping arc.

The quaint structure had a dormered roof and arched colonnades with glass-paneled doors and transoms. The light that spilled through them revealed nothing alarming. No guards were posted along the tracks or on the platform; and there were no staff cars in sight. Despite this, Mittenwald was close to the German-Austrian border, and documents were routinely inspected by the Gestapo before passengers were allowed to board trains to Innsbruck, Vienna, Verona and points as far south as Venice.

The two Gestapo agents, posted here, passed the time between trains, playing cards and drinking schnapps in the station master's office. Due to the unpredictable schedules, they donned their trench coats and left its warmth to take-up their posts as each train arrived. This evening they had been joined by an SS major from Munich who declined their entreaties to join them and glowered at their undisciplined behavior.

Having lost Anika in Murnau, just hours ago, Steig still had no idea where Jake and Eva were hiding; but he had every reason to believe they were in this area. Furthermore, he knew Jake was from Vienna and Eva from Venice; and bet that if they were taking the train south, they would avoid Zugspitze Station and depart from Kainzenbad, instead. As Anika knew, it had a small Gestapo presence; and the major kept it that way, sequestering his entourage in the station's baggage room to avoid scaring-off his prey. Steig also knew that the Gestapo had a habit of horning-in on SS operations, and was determined to keep them out of this one. It was an SS operation, his operation; and he hadn't briefed them on it. For all the Gestapo knew, the SS major, cooling his heels in the station master's office, was catching the next train.

CHAPTER TWENTY-FIVE

"Dr. Jacob Epstein may not be Dr. Jacob Epstein?! What the hell does that mean?!" Tannen erupted after Stacey briefed him on her meeting with Adam. He was standing on the putting green that ran beneath the windows and struck the ball in anger. It skimmed across the AstroTurf and ricocheted off the baseboard.

"It's killing me too, boss," Stacey replied, eyes widening as the ball flew past her. "I've got a huge soft spot for the old guy; but I'm playing devil's advocate, now, okay? I mean, something isn't right, here. Like Adam said, it's weird."

"He's weird!" Tannen erupted again, tossing the putter aside. "He has no proof of anything. How do we know the other guy, with the same number tattooed on his arm, isn't the imposter? If there is one!"

"That's exactly what I said; but we can't just ignore this."

Tannen's eyes were popping behind his tortoiseshell frames. "Why not? We're on the verge of launching a hot ad campaign for an important client and your boyfriend's going to fuck it up!"

"Not if it turns out he's wrong. But if we launch, and it turns out he's right, we're screwed…big time." She picked up the golf ball that had rolled to a stop, nearby, and deftly placed it in Tannen's outstretched hand. "…Quadruple bogie for sure."

"Damn," Tannen mumbled, seething with frustration. "As much as I'm amazed by, and count on, every little twist and turn that quirky brain of yours takes, this is infuriating beyond words."

"I know. I'm sorry. If I hadn't spotted the suitcase in the—"

"Furthermore," Tannen charged on, "Your degree and boyfriend notwithstanding, you work for an ad agency not *The New York* fucking *Times!*"

"You're right; and I don't need to be reminded," Stacey replied contritely. "But it doesn't mean we aren't morally obligated to find out the truth."

"Morally obligated? Who do you think you are, Beate Klarsfeld?"

"Who?"

"She's a Nazi hunter. She and her husband. I'm pretty sure they're the one's who blew the whistle on Kurt Waldheim."

"The U.N. guy?"

"Yeah, not to mention former President of Austria," Tannen replied in condemnation. "The slightest hint of scandal—this kind of scandal—has the power to destroy not only Dr. Epstein, but Sol and his company, not to mention this one. The campaign is the least of it."

"That's why we need to get into it. We can't just blow it off."

Tannen conceded the point with a grudging nod. "Just remember, as the gang in legal would say, 'You can't put the toothpaste back in the tube.'"

"I know. Adam wants to get it right too. I know he does; but he smells a story, here—a hot one; and he's digging. He's not just going to roll over and—"

The intercom buzzed, interrupting her. Tannen stabbed at a button on his console. "What is it Astrid?" he asked, sounding annoyed. He groaned at the reply, then glanced to Stacey and, with a sarcastic cackle, said, "The devil's advocate and the devil…"

Stacey looked puzzled. "Adam? What's he doing here?"

"I've no doubt he'll tell us," Tannen retorted, pressing the intercom button again. "Send him in."

The door half-opened. Adam slipped through it into the office. "Sorry, but as Stacey knows, no phones, no emails, this story is mano-a-mano only."

Tannen nodded. "No problem. We were just into a little mano ourselves."

"Tell me about it," Stacey chimed-in. "What's up?"

"I took your advice. Soon as you left, I started digging deeper into that CD. Much deeper."

Stacey winced. "Why am I getting the feeling this is about to get worse instead of better?"

"Do I look like I'm delivering take-out?"

"Shit," Stacey groaned. "Now what?"

"The luggage tag," Adam said, sounding vindicated. "According to the archivist's report, it has an address in Vienna written on it, along with what seems to be a passport number, and Dr. Epstein's prisoner ID number."

"Yeah, I saw that," Stacey said, going to work on Tannen's keyboard. "Give me a minute…"

"I saved you the trouble." Adam handed her two printouts. One was a close-up of the prisoner ID number, A198841, tattooed on Dr. Epstein's forearm; the other was a close-up of the luggage tag. Creased, and darkened with age, it had a metal grommet at one end through which a twisted wire that secured it to the handle of the suitcase was threaded. "Look at how the numbers are written. They're the same on both."

Stacey swept her eyes over the printouts, then handed them to Tannen. "He's right, boss. Look at those sevens, they're exactly the same…"

"And the eights," Adam prompted. "Like you said, they're infinity symbols turned on end."

"Those aren't sevens, they're ones," Tannen said, unimpressed. He uncapped a pen and jotted the numeral seven on the printout. He used three strokes, not two, and emphasized the last one. "That's a seven. The Europeans make that little crossbar to differentiate between sevens and ones. Take it from me. I lived there for five years. The bottom line is there's nothing unique about that handwriting. Could be one person, then again it could be two or even three."

"Let me see if I have this right," Stacey said, assembling the pieces. "Not only do we have the same number tattooed in different handwriting on two Auschwitz prisoners, one of whom we're certain is Dr. Epstein; but, if Adam's right, we also have numbers written on Dr. E's luggage tag in the same handwriting as his tattoo. I get that right?"

Adam nodded. "Looks that way to me."

"Whoever wrote out the tag also tattooed Dr. E?" Tannen challenged.

Adam nodded again. "Yeah, I know it's weird, but it—"

"No it isn't," Stacey interrupted. "The Nazi freak at Auschwitz who tattooed the ID number probably had a pile of blank luggage tags on his desk and filled it out at the same time."

Tannen pondered it for a moment, then nodded in concession. "Not bad, smarty pants; but in fairness to Adam, and leaving no stone unturned now that he's set off this earthquake, didn't Dan Epstein say the writing on the tag looked like his father's?"

"Yeah, but he also said that he wasn't sure. That it changes over time, and…"

"Yeah, yeah he did, and it does," Tannen conceded.

"Going with it for a minute," Stacey went on, her eyes narrowed in thought. "If it is Dr. E's handwriting on the tag. We're saying…what? He tattooed himself?"

The furrows in Tannen's forehead deepened. "Why the hell would he do that?"

"I can think of a reason," Adam replied. "He did it because he wasn't Dr. Jacob Epstein…but wanted to be."

Adam's remark struck them all with surprising force. Even he hadn't realized the implication until he said it; and the three of them were stunned to silence, trying to come to grips with it.

"He's some kind of Holocaust wannabe?" Stacey finally said with a skeptical frown, snapping them out of the trance. "I don't get it, Clive. I mean—"

Tannen's cell phone rang, interrupting her. He plucked it from his desk and glanced at the display. "Hold that thought. It's the boss."

CHAPTER TWENTY-SIX

The Military Garrison at KZ-Dachau was staffed by more than twelve hundred SS officers and enlisted men. Four times the size of the prison camp, its acres of barracks also housed the troops who were constantly rotating through the SS Training Center. Its stately houses with fine lawns and picket fences—along with its shops, post office, movie theater, restaurants and community center—gave it the look of a quaint village. It even had its own, professionally run, highly discrete, and extremely active SS brothel.

Captain Max Kleist, M.D. knew of the large number of military personnel stationed at Dachau; and when he first saw his orders, he thought he was being assigned to its military hospital; but the commandant's ruthless briefing and Lieutenant Radek's horrific orientation made it clear that the Jew-lover's assignment would be—as Major Steig had threatened—cruel punishment; and Max knew, that he would soon be on the ramp making Selections.

Radek's tour had concluded in an Officers Housing Unit where Max's quarters were located. Officers were assigned to individual rooms with pictures of the Führer and Reichsführer above the desk that was opposite the bed and wardrobe. Max wasted no time emptying his duffel and storing his things. His 35mm Leica was among them. When finished, Max ignored the commandant's decree, and went in search of a telephone to call his parents and, perhaps, get some news of Eva and Jake; but camp personnel with access to phones refused to violate the restriction, warning him, sternly, against doing so.

Haunted by the inhumane prison conditions and cruelty he had witnessed, Max went to the camp's library and took out a book on medical ethics he had read as a student. It was written a hundred years earlier by Christoph Wilhelm Hufeland, one of Germany's great physician-humanists. Max spent the next few days immersed in its essays on the sanctity of life, and began writing a letter to his parents about his unnerving experience. His appetite had waned, and he went to the Mess Hall during off-hours, avoiding contact with Radek and other officers. As instructed, he checked the duty roster, often. Each time, the space next to Hauptmann M. Kleist had been blank; but this afternoon, written in a precise hand, Max saw: On The Ramp. 18:00.

The rest of the day was filled with gut-churning anxiety which was exacerbated by his concern for Eva and Jake. The image of Eva's face, there-and-gone between metronomic sweeps of the Volkswagen's wiper stayed with him as he donned his winter gear and left the barracks to take-up his post. The Luger he had been issued felt out of place on his hip as did the riding crop clutched in his gloved fist.

Searchlights atop the guard towers swept in wide arcs sending shadows across the grounds. The temperature had dropped and each bootstep ended with the crunch of frozen snow. Max exited the Main Gate and trudged up the ramp onto the platform that ran between the railroad tracks and the rear of the administration buildings. An incandescent glow came from their curtained windows warming the winter light. Max looked to the horizon where the streaks of polished steel converged, still thinking about Eva and Jake who, while Max was waiting in frigid darkness for a train to arrive at Dachau, were doing the same at Kaizenbad Station in Mittenwald.

Another SS officer came trudging up the ramp onto the platform, pulling Max from the reverie. Like Max's, his uniform had captain's insignia and a caduceus. He made no effort to acknowledge Max and, chin raised to the wind, stood at his selection station, waiting for the train. Soon, the shriek of a whistle broke the wintry silence. The two men turned, making eye contact. The other officer broke it off, quickly. Max thought he looked familiar; but his face had been masked in shadow, making it hard to be certain. Max hesitated for a moment, then crossed the platform. "Otto? Otto Kruger is that you?"

The officer turned to Max and glared at him.

"Otto!" Max exclaimed. He was so relieved to see a familiar face, that he was oblivious to the painful intensity in Kruger's eyes. "It's been a couple of years, hasn't it? The day after graduation, we were—"

"Max," Kruger hissed through clenched teeth. "You know what we do here?"

Max took a step back and nodded grimly.

"Then shut up and do it," Kruger said in a tense whisper as the headlight of a thundering locomotive, pulling a line of freight cars, sent shadows streaking the length of the platform. The massive engine came to a stop with the painful screech of grinding steel. It was still belching smoke and hissing steam when the spotlights began slicing the night in narrow, blue-edged shafts.

With drill team precision, a squad of SS guards, armed with rifles and truncheons, marched a group of prisoners onto the platform. The Sonderkommando as these groups were called—literally, special command—were made up of prisoners who knew how to wheel and deal within the camp system to survive, and were deemed trustworthy by their slave masters. During

Selections, the Kommando, in their striped prison uniforms, did the actual dirty-work under the direction of the guards who were loath to have physical contact with the arriving prisoners. On the Sergeant's order, two of them unlocked the door of the first freight car and rolled it back revealing the human cargo packed inside.

The prisoners burst forth in a frenzy. The frail and those who had died or passed out en route were trampled by those who surged into the frigid darkness, gasping for air. Blinded by the spotlights, the disoriented prisoners stumbled about, some bundled in heavy coats, others in shirtsleeves. Among them were elegantly dressed women in fine jewelry and furs, farmers in tattered mackinaws and bibbed coveralls, businessmen in suits and ties with natty fedoras. Some collapsed from exhaustion. A few protested their inhumane treatment. All were begging for water. Many clutched pieces of luggage on which personal data had been painted.

Loudspeakers atop the guard towers crackled to life. "There is no need to panic. Follow instructions. Go to the line to which you are assigned," a soothing voice instructed. "You will be given hot meals, soap and towels for showering, and assigned to heated barracks. If you are a doctor, a nurse, or have other medical training, raise your hand or make this known to your processing officer. There is no need to panic. Follow instructions and go to the line to which you are assigned…"

Max's eyes widened in horror as the SS guards, in mindless contradiction to the announcement, set upon the prisoners with their truncheons and rifle butts. *"Raus! Raus! Auf die Rampe! Form eine enzigen zeile!"* they shouted, beating them into silence and submission, and, in some cases, comas. *"Schnell! Schnell! Bilden eine linie!"* they went on, forcing the prisoners to form a line in front of Captain Kruger's station.

Members of the Kommando descended on their fellow prisoners and began stripping them of their belongings: prized articles of clothing were peeled from their backs, rings were pulled from their fingers, pockets were rifled, and suitcases were emptied and tossed aside onto a growing pile, their contents sorted into other growing piles. All personal belongings, jewelry, cash and other valuables—except for food, which Kommando members were allowed to keep—had been decreed property of the Third Reich by the Führer and were, therefore, confiscated.

With the dispassionate efficiency of a robot, Kruger went about making his selections, directing the confused and terrified prisoners to one of two lines which led to the camp's entrance gate: The elderly, the infirm, frail-looking women, and children to one that could have been labeled: Short-Lived Anxiety. Little Torture. Immediate Execution. The healthy-looking men, teenagers, and robust women to the other that could have been labeled: Delayed Execution. Be Tortured, Worked And/Or Starved To Death.

As Kruger went about his work, Max noticed that the prisoners who had responded to the call for doctors and medical professionals were treated more humanely than the others. They hadn't been beaten and stripped of their belongings, and were being escorted into the camp, suitcases in hand. Max's curiosity turned to concern when he realized that neither he nor Kruger, nor anyone else, had been issued clipboards. Names and ID numbers weren't being taken. Arrival records weren't being kept. Perhaps, those selected for work would be processed once inside. But what of the others? Would they be executed and disposed of as if they had never existed? Would there be no record of what had happened to them? Would they, as Radek had so crudely put it, just go up in smoke?

Any thought Max had of raising the issue vanished when the Kommando rolled back the door to the second freight car and the same violent scene was played out. This time, the prisoners were forced to queue in front of his station. Max was on the verge of retching as the clusters of frightened and confused people came toward him, clinging to each other, carrying infants and exhausted children, dragging pieces of luggage and bundles tied with rope, their faces wracked with fear, their eyes pleading for them to be spared, to be treated humanely.

Despite the soothing assurances being broadcast, humane treatment had nothing to do with it. Max's job was to make selections. To pick and choose and separate members of families, some of whom would soon be executed. Once again he could hear the commandant's voice: Be ruthless. Avoid ambiguity. Let nothing cloud your fealty to the Führer. Now Max really knew why the colonel, who seemed to despise him, had offered this almost fatherly advice. Max was trying to convince himself that if he didn't make Selections, Captain Kruger or the fanatic Radek or some other rabid Nazi would and these people would die anyway. Max was losing the argument, and on the verge of leaving his post, when he imagined the terrified faces and pleading eyes were those of his family: his father, his mother and his sister. Indeed, the commandant had left no doubt that Max would be signing their death warrants if he refused to carry out his orders.

And that was the moment Captain Maximilian Kleist, M.D. Waffen-SS made his first selection; and as he stood in the searchlight-slashed darkness, and the line of anxiety-ridden humanity kept coming toward him, Max made another selection, and then another. Individuals of every age, young couples, elderly couples, and entire families. Now, a strapping farmer, his robust wife, their lethargic teenage son and elderly grandparents came trudging toward him. Like all the others, their eyes pleading, their hands reaching out in supplication.

"How old is he?" Max asked of the boy.

"Fifteen," the father replied.

Max lifted the young man's face to the light and examined his eyes, then pulled gently at the skin on his neck that stretched like putty. "He's malnourished and severely dehydrated."

"We've had no food or water for days," the father explained. He had seen what happened to those who had preceded them; he knew what was being decided here, and quickly added, "He's a good, strong worker."

Max nodded and directed the parents and son to the workers line, but restrained the grandparents. Anguished by their separation, they all began calling out, and pressing forward, arms outstretched until their fingertips touched in one last desperate moment of contact. Max was devastated by their forlorn glances and, though the elderly couple's age dictated they be sent to the execution line, he was about to grant them a reprieve when two SS guards came running over.

"Zuruck in die linie!" they shouted at the younger three. *"Zuruck! Zuruck eine linie!"* One drove the butt of his rifle into the farmer's chest, knocking him to the ground where he lay writhing in pain. His wife and son screamed in fright, then rushed to his side. The SS guards set upon them with their truncheons, driving all three back toward the workers line; then, remaining at Max's station, they turned on the elderly couple and began driving them toward the execution line.

The painful scenario was tearing Max apart. Bile rose in the back of his throat. He was swallowing hard, trying to collect himself, when the door of the next freight car was rolled back. Scores of prisoners surged into the frigid darkness and blinding searchlights in an air-gasping frenzy. The commotion caused the SS guards to hurry from Max's station to Kruger's, at the other end of the platform. Max saw his chance and jerked his head toward the workers line, sending the terrified grandparents rushing into the arms of their overjoyed family; then, preempting any expressions of gratitude that might call attention to his act of kindness, Max threatened them with his riding crop, and began shouting, "Idiots! Stupid idiots! Back in line! Follow instructions! Remain in line!"

The deafening cacophony that prevailed was suddenly penetrated by the sharp crack of a pistol shot. It was followed by another and then another. Max winced at each of the evenly spaced reports that came from the courtyard Lieutenant Radek had pointed out during his orientation tour; and where Max knew many of the prisoners he had just selected, were being executed. And between each shot, the soothing voice kept coming from the loudspeakers in mocking reassurance: "There is no need to panic. Follow instructions. Go to the line to which you are assigned. You will be given hot meals, soap and towels for showering, and assigned to heated barracks. There is no need to panic. Follow instructions. Go to the..."

Once again, Max was on the verge of retching and leaving his post—on the verge of deserting; but the steady crack of pistol shots that were driving him to run were what ultimately stopped him. It wasn't the thought of them being fired into the back of his head—he didn't care about the consequences he would suffer should he refuse to carry out his orders—but the thought of them being fired into the back of his father's head, and that of his mother's and sister's; and, tormented by this unnerving vision, Captain Maximilian Kleist, M.D. Waffen-SS remained on the ramp, continuing to make selections; and by the time the fifteenth and the sixteenth and seventeenth freight cars had been unloaded, he, too, was making them like a dispassionate robot.

CHAPTER TWENTY-SEVEN

"Sounds like he's out of the country," Stacey said after Tannen finished the call with Gunther.

"Paris. His wife's running down acquisitions. Our European operation's awash in red ink. The boss decided to tag along and shake things up. Not a happy camper."

"His wife's with the Guggenheim, isn't she?"

"Uh-huh, working on a Kandinsky show."

"I was waiting for you to get into this with him," Adam said, referring to the questions he had just raised.

"No way. Bad timing. Besides, it's still too iffy. So, where're we at here?" Tannen prompted, rhetorically. "Two tattoos. Same number. Different handwriting. Ergo, different people—one of whom is Dr. Epstein. And, now, numbers on a luggage tag—possibly in his handwriting that seems to match his tattoo; which gets us back to Adam's idea that he tattooed himself because…"

"…he wasn't Dr. Jacob Epstein, but wanted to be," Adam said, finishing it.

"Yeah, I mean, what? He's a Holocaust wannabe?" Stacey prompted, picking-up where she had left off when Gunther called. "Why would he make believe he was in a concentration camp when he wasn't?"

"Survivor guilt?" Tannen ventured. "A lot of Holocaust survivors spent their lives feeling guilty about it; and/or about what they did to stay alive."

Adam nodded. "Like things they weren't proud of."

"Whatever," Tannen said, dismissing it; then his tone sharpening, he added, "The point is that Dr. E wanted to be a member of the club."

"That's one explanation," Adam conceded, implying he had another. "Let's not forget he's Doctor Epstein. And we all know about Nazi doctors."

"You mean Mengele and his ilk?" Tannen prompted.

"Mengele?" Stacey echoed with disdain. "I can't believe that's where you're at. It's ridiculous."

"Really?" Adam said, smugly, stepping to Tannen's computer. "May I?"

"Sure," Tannen grunted.

"If you think it's so ridiculous…" Adam said, accessing a story on the *Times* website that included a photo of a man with an aquiline profile, dimpled chin and arched eyebrows, "…check out this piece the paper did back in January on a Nazi doc named Heim. Ran some pretty ugly experiments on concentration camp victims. Never got caught. Matter of fact he practiced in Germany for a while after the war; but somebody blew the whistle on him and he fled to Cairo; lived there for thirty-what years before kicking the bucket in the early nineties. We know this because someone cleaning out a storage room in his building came across his briefcase. Sound familiar?"

Stacey's eyes flared with anger. "That's where all this is coming from, isn't it?! It's pure speculation, Clive. You don't know for a fact that Dr. Epstein's a Nazi. You have no reason to even suspect it, do you?!"

Adam was caught off guard and took a moment to collect himself. "No, no I don't," he replied, evenly. "I've just got this gnawing feeling in my gut that—"

"Then why even say it?!" Stacey challenged. "Are you that terrified of getting laid off? I can't believe you'd cook up something like this to save your ass."

Adam bristled with indignation. "Are you accusing me of fabricating a story?"

"It sure sounds like that's what you're doing!" Stacey replied, getting in his face. "For what? To sell newspapers?!"

"No! To sell luggage," Adam retorted. "It's my job that's on the line. Not yours."

"No, according to you, my ass is! You're the one making speeches about fact checking! It's on you to nail this down before deciding the man's a war criminal!"

"Hey, hey?! Knock it off!" Tannen said, stepping between them. "Neutral corners. Now," he commanded, directing them to opposite sides of the office. He gave them a few moments to settle; then, in the measured cadence of a mediator, said, "Okay. Now, Stacey, as I believe you pointed out earlier, we've no choice but to take this seriously. Right?" He waited until Stacey nodded grudgingly then, pursuing the logic, resumed. "And if what Adam suspects is true; if Dr. E is someone other than who he says he is; then the forearm in the snapshot from the suitcase that has the same prisoner number tattooed on it— belongs to the real Jake Epstein."

"Works for me," Adam said.

"Okay," Tannen said, taking a moment to collect his thoughts, "But why would he agree to do the campaign? Why would he even allow the suitcase to be opened? It was his call. We gave him every chance to say no."

"Yeah," Stacey chimed in. "Why would he risk getting caught?"

"Because he wants to get caught," Adam replied.

"Why?" Stacey challenged.

"Guilt," Adam replied. "Not survivor guilt. Plain old, normal, everyday subconscious guilt. He's damn-near ninety years old. Near the end of his life. He wants to fess up. Wants to make things right."

Stacey sighed. She looked crestfallen. "I hate to say it, boss," she said, her voice trembling. "I mean, the mere thought of it turns my stomach, but if Adam's right, it's a great fucking story."

"Yeah, it is," Adam said, sounding vindicated. "And, if I am right, the paper's going to run it."

"I applaud your parenthetical modifier," Tannen said, sensing he had regained some measure of control. "It suggests that as the responsible, ethical, truth-seeking journalist we know you to be, you'll be busting your ass to come up with the answers to a long list of questions, first. Won't you?"

"And those questions are?"

"Is he the real Dr. Jacob Epstein or not? If not, who is he? Is he a Nazi? Is he a war criminal? Not all Nazis were; and not all Germans were Nazis. Last but not least, whatever and whoever he is...why is he masquerading as a Holocaust survivor? If that's indeed what he's doing. At the moment, all you've got is a theory. Speculation."

Adam's jaw tightened. He felt exposed, like a student whose outline for a term paper had just been savaged by his advisor. "Yeah, I guess, you're right."

"*Voila!*" Tannen exclaimed, with a trace of sarcasm. "As Celine would say, ' *Il la vu la lumiere!'* In the meantime, we better give Sol a heads-up on this."

"Yeah, better he hear it from us..." Stacey paused and broke into a mischievous grin. "...than from some reporter for a tabloid."

"Not funny," Adam said, forcing a scowl. "On the other hand, she's right. If I spotted this stuff, it's only a matter of time before somebody else does. Which is another reason why I won't sit on it forever."

"Come on, Adam, you can't sit on a story you don't have—and you don't have it," Tannen said, pointedly. "We'll deal with it if and when you do." He held up the printouts Adam had brought with him. "I want Sol to see these? Okay?"

"Sure. They're yours."

"Thanks. Now, get your ass out of here. You've got a lot of work to do."

Adam nodded. He looked beaten as he headed for the door.

Tannen cocked his head struck by a thought. "Hold it," he called out. "Didn't Dr. E say his med-school buddy...a...Max...Max..." he paused, searching for the name.

"...Kleist," Stacey chimed-in, supplying it. "Max Kleist was the guy who gave him the suitcase."

"Right. Didn't Dr. E say he was in the SS?"

"Yeah, that's right, he did," Adam said, his eyes widening with intrigue as he drifted back toward them. "I forgot about that."

Stacey nodded. "He also said he was an anti-Nazi who was conscripted and forced to serve."

Adam groaned. "That's what they all said."

"Enough," Tannen said, his tone sharpening. "I was about to say, maybe you should find out whatever you can about Max Kleist, too, while you're at it."

"Maybe I should," Adam said, suddenly re-energized.

"Okay, but from here on, there's something all of us need to remember. Something really important—" Tannen said, with a strategic pause. "—the tar goes on a lot easier than it comes off." He made eye contact with Adam and prompted, "Got it?"

"Yes, I do," Adam replied as if he meant it; then glancing to Stacey, he added, "Despite what some people think, not all journalists are cold-blooded."

Tannen waited until Adam had left the office, then turned to Stacey and prompted, "You okay?"

Stacey nodded and broke into a coy smile. "He's not always cold blooded."

CHAPTER TWENTY-EIGHT

Eva and Jake had spent several hours hiding in Mittenwald's frigid darkness before the rumble of a locomotive and the flicker of a headlight got their attention. Each waited until the train came thundering into view before entering the station.

Eva went directly to the ticket window. She couldn't see Major Steig observing from his vantage point in the station master's office. Neither she nor Jake had any idea what he looked like; though the sight of an SS uniform would have caught their eye. Steig had never seen them in person, either, and was relying on the fugitive alerts to identify them—on photographs taken three years ago when, as bright-eyed altruists, they first came to medical school. They appeared different, now. Hardened by the horrors of war, having treated so many of its casualties, and by their current status as fugitives, they had taken on the distant stare and weary posture of combat soldiers. So, when Eva bought her ticket, the major—like the sergeant at the Starnberg checkpoint—didn't recognize the lone, young woman whose turned-up collar was encircled by a scarf, and whose tumbling, raven-black hair was concealed beneath a knitted wool hat pulled down over her ears. Eva left the window and made her way between the barricades that funneled passengers to a stand-up desk where a Gestapo agent was checking documents.

Across the station, Jake was sitting on a bench, pretending to be reading a discarded newspaper. The headline read: FÜHRER VOWS VICTORY. PREDICTS ALLIES WILL SURRENDER BY EASTER. Jake waited until Eva had left the ticket window before joining the short queue.

At the security desk, the leather-jacketed Gestapo man glanced at Eva's ticket and smirked. "Venice? All of northern Italy is under the Führer's rule, now," he bragged, going on to review her travel pass, and visa. "You'll feel right at home."

"It is my home," Eva said, wishing she hadn't.

"Passport," he said, staring at her icily.

Eva took it from her purse, reflecting on Max's warning about the Gestapo's uncanny skill at detecting pseudonyms, and handed it to him. Would the agent ask her name? Or use it in some way to test her? He glanced from her passport to her face and back, then stamped her documents with a bright green Reichsadler, and returned them. Eva forced a smile, shouldered her rucksack and began walking from the desk.

"Fraulein Haussmann?" the Gestapo agent called out.

Eva froze and turned back toward him, trying not to seem intimidated. Lisl Haussmann, the pseudonym she had chosen, was the name of a high school teacher in Venice who had been her mentor. It had a comfortable familiarity and recalled pleasant times which she hoped would be reflected in her demeanor.

"Is that one N or two?" the Gestapo agent asked.

"Two," Eva replied, calmly.

"I just wanted to be sure I had it right." His sly smile left no doubt he'd been testing her.

As the Gestapo agent turned his attention to the next traveler, Eva hurried through the door that led outside to the platform. Another line of barricades funneled passengers to a door in the middle coach of the train through which everyone boarded; and where the other Gestapo agent was checking documents for the Imperial Eagle stamp to make certain no one had managed to skirt the security check inside. The locomotive was building up steam for departure when Eva joined the queue.

Inside, Jake had purchased his ticket and was at the security desk. The Gestapo agent reviewed his papers and stamped his passport. "Thank you Herr Dietrich." Like Eva, Jake had chosen a familiar name as a pseudonym, that of Erich Dietrich, a childhood friend with a quirky sense of humor who made him laugh. He picked up his suitcase, and walked away, suppressing a sigh of relief. They had made it. By morning, he and Eva would be in Venice. Dare he even allow himself to think it?! All he had to do was cross the station, go through the door to the platform, and board the train.

Major Steig may not have spotted Eva, but he had an immediate flicker of recognition when Jake stepped to the ticket window, moments ago. The major's eyes had darted from the fugitive alert to Jake's face several times. The three-year-old photo, now a poor match for Jake's hardened countenance and the cap that kept his face in shadow, made it hard for Steig to be certain; but he had nothing to lose; and, now, having deployed his SS henchmen, he moved swiftly from the station master's office in pursuit of his prey. "Dr. Epstein?" he called out. "Dr. Jacob Epstein?"

"Yes?" Jake said, glancing back over his shoulder. It was instinct, pure reflex, an unthinking reaction from a lifetime of conditioning as Max had warned. He gasped at the sight of an SS major striding toward him in his black greatcoat and silver death's head gleaming atop his cap, then dropped his suitcase and ran.

"Halt!" Steig shouted, pulling his sidearm from its holster. "Stop him! Stop him!"

Three uniformed SS men emerged from concealment in pursuit. Despite his desperation, Jake had the presence of mind to run toward an exit opposite the one that led outside to the platform and waiting train, leading them away from Eva.

"Halt!" Steig shouted again, firing several shots overhead as Jake sprinted toward the door. The transom shattered, showering him with glass as another SS man burst through it from outside blocking his way. Jake froze and raised his hands. The SS man drove the butt of his rifle into his stomach, sending him to the floor, then raised it, preparing to deliver another blow to his skull.

"No! I want him alive!" Steig shouted. "He has information that—" The piercing shriek of the train whistle interrupted him. "The train! Stop the train and search for this woman!" he shouted, waving the alert with Eva's picture; but by the time the Major and several of the SS men had run through the station and onto the platform, the train had already departed and was a distance down the tracks, gaining speed.

It didn't matter if Dr. Eva Sarah Rosenberg was on the train or not, the major thought as he watched the light from the last car receding in the darkness. He had no doubt he'd get her, eventually. It was the Kleists' blood that Steig smelled, now. They were the prize. And Dr. Jacob Israel Epstein was the key to winning it. The major went back into the station, picked up Jake's suitcase, and joined the SS men who were holding him. "I believe this is yours, Doctor. Perhaps you'd like to scrub-up before we question you. I'm a stickler for hygiene when it comes to exploratory surgery."

Jake was taken to an interrogation chamber in the basement of the SS Station in Garmisch. The major put the suitcase on a table in the dank, stone cavern, and began rifling the contents. *Mein Kampf?!*" he exclaimed, coming upon the book amidst the clothing he'd disrupted. He made the obvious assumption, and flipped the pages without really looking at them or, as Jake feared, noticing the dust jacket didn't match. Steig turned it over, shook it several times, then threw it back into the suitcase. "Judging by your reading matter, Epstein, there may be hope for you yet," he said facetiously, his breath visible in the cold air. At the jerk of the major's head, one of the SS men closed the suitcase, opened the door to an anteroom, and tossed it atop other pieces of luggage and duffel bags piled on the floor.

Jake spent the night in the freezing chamber being threatened and beaten by the major and his SS thugs. He'd been relieved that Steig hadn't noticed the KK monogram on the suitcase and refused to even recognize the name Kleist let alone implicate them as enablers of his escape attempt. He knew the major needed his signed testimony to accuse citizens as prominent as the Kleists of harboring Jews; and the sheer pleasure of frustrating him reinforced his resolve not to cooperate. By the time the sun was rising over Zugspitze, his face bloodied, his body aching, Jake had taken all the punishment they had dished out with courage and silent dignity.

Steig looked bleary-eyed and exasperated. He drained a mug of cold coffee, then put a sheet of paper and a pen on the table in front of Jake. "Simply write that the Kleist family helped you to avoid being arrested by the SS. Sign it. And you're a free man."

Jake glared at him with contempt. "Sure…"

"You hear what I said? A free man!" Steig screeched; then, in a friendlier tone, said, "Your exemption will be restored. You will be able to practice medicine; and you will be free to travel anywhere you wish."

"I give you the Kleists' heads, and you let me keep mine?" Jake said in mocking paraphrase. "Is that it?"

Steig nodded. "Precisely. You have my word as an officer and a gentleman."

"Four Germans for one Jew? Our stock is on the rise." Jake swept the paper and pen onto the floor, then locked his eyes onto Steig's and said, "Go to hell!"

Steig backhanded him across the face, knocking him from the chair. Jake moaned in pain and tried to get to his feet. One of the SS thugs stomped a heel into his back, then pulled his sidearm and pressed the muzzle against Jake's head.

"No," Steig said, seething at having failed to break him. "Take him to Munich with the others. The Reichsführer has uses for doctors. Even Jewish ones."

Jake was taken from the interrogation chamber and loaded into the rear of a canvas-backed military truck with a group of local residents who had been identified as Jews and arrested. The vehicle had just started to pull away when an SS guard shouted after it. The truck lurched to a stop and backed up a short distance. A moment later, a valise came sailing over the tailgate into the rear of the truck, landing amidst the huddled prisoners. It was followed by a suitcase, and then another and another; several duffel bags came next, then more suitcases. Jake's Steinbach was one of them.

Six hours later, literally freezing to death, they arrived at the main deportation center in Munich which was adjacent to the rail yards on the city's perimeter. Lugging their suitcases, the prisoners were herded into a corral with hundreds of other Jewish deportees who had been given brushes and buckets of white paint, and were writing personal data on their luggage.

"Name, year of birth, and the prisoner reference number and group number that you were assigned when you got here," the SS man kept repeating as if to children. "In case you've forgotten, this is group number twelve. You people are always getting your bags mixed up. It will be much easier to identify them later if you do as I instruct. Name, year of birth, and your prisoner reference number and group number that…"

"My valise has a luggage tag," one of the prisoners said. "May I omit the information that—"

"No!" the SS guard shouted, striking him with his truncheon. "Tags get ripped off. Paint is forever. No questions. Do as instructed!"

Though it pained Jake to deface such a fine piece of luggage, he wisely complied. When finished, he and the others were herded into a freight car by SS men who used truncheons to pummel resisters and stragglers and those who went in search of a child or loved one from whom they had become separated. The door rolled shut with the chilling screech of steel on steel and the harsh clank of wrought iron hasps, plunging the interior of the freight car and its human cargo into darkness. Some were moaning in pain. Many were weeping. Others were shouting and pounding on the wooden sidewalls in protest. They were packed-in so tightly there was barely enough room for everyone to stand, let alone breathe. Perhaps, Jake thought, their combined body heat would keep them from freezing to death en route to their destination.

The train lurched forward with several sharp jerks, then started to roll, heading out of the yard on rails that glistened from constant use. Every train departing the Munich freight yards on that spur had the same destination. Indeed this one—and all others that had preceded it, and all those that would follow—went to one place and one place only, making no stops in its 500 kilometer journey through Czechoslovakia to the town of Oswiecim in southeastern Poland and a concentration camp of the same name that in German was called Auschwitz.

CHAPTER TWENTY-NINE

"For the love of Jesus!" Steinbach exclaimed after Tannen and Stacey briefed him on Adam's suspicions and the threat they posed. "You two really are the Bad News Bears, aren't you? It's the only time you ever come over here."

Stacey shrugged and shot a helpless look to Tannen.

Tannen splayed his hands.

The smell of leather and machined brass hung in the silence, intensified by samples of the new line that were neatly stacked in every corner. Steinbach had papered the office with Zach Bolden's black-and-white photo blow-ups of him and Jake. The powerful images with their proudly displayed Auschwitz tattoos—*Two old Jews sticking it to the Nazis!* as Steinbach had put it—looked down, mockingly, from every wall.

"So now what?!" Steinbach went on, still charged-up. "Instead of a story about Holocaust survivors and a vintage Steinbach, it's going to be about a Nazi war criminal?! This is a fucking disaster!"

"You said you wanted controversy, Sol…"

"Well, I'm getting more than I bargained for!"

"Maybe we can spin it so Steinbach and Co. get the credit for unmasking him," Tannen offered unconvincingly, "…if it turns out that's the case."

"I mean, like…" Stacey ventured with an uncertain pause, "…like there's no way *The Times*'ll run the story without resolving this first, right?"

Tannen grunted in the affirmative.

"That's the upside?!" Steinbach challenged. "We sure as hell can't postpone the launch til then! I've got a factory going twenty-four/seven. A warehouse busting with inventory. Sales reps priming the pump. Retailers screaming for merchandise! I've got to start selling luggage or I'm screwed."

"Then start selling," Tannen counseled, his voice reclaiming its authority. "Get ahead of the story. Either way, it'll minimize negative impact and boost sales."

"Negative impact? This is a catastrophe!" Steinbach roared, gesturing to the photo blowups that surrounded them. "How the hell can I run these ads?!"

"Stay the course, Sol," Tannen said, forcefully. "Not much else you can do until *The Times* sorts it out."

"Are you nuts?" Steinbach erupted. "I'm not leaving it to them. No fucking way!"

"Then who?"

"I don't know," Steinbach replied, bristling. "I need a ride." He sprung to his feet and strode toward the private bathroom where he showered and changed after biking to work each morning. He paused and, loosening his tie, locked his eyes onto Stacey's. "You've saved my ass more than once, kid. I'll be in here changing. When I come out, I'm expecting you to knock my socks off."

"Knock my socks off?" Stacey mouthed, stifling a giggle as Steinbach retreated into the bathroom. "Do people still say that?"

"My father does," Tannen replied with a little smile. "It's an elder thing."

Stacey's eyes sparkled with mischief. "So, as the elder statesman on this team, any bright ideas?"

"Yeah. You're going to knock his socks off."

Stacey rolled her eyes. "Way I see it, we're at the tipping point, here," she said reflecting on a book she'd read recently. She crouched to one of the sample suitcases and opened the latches, then snapped them closed, then did it again and again—snap-click, snap-click, snap-click, her mind racing in search of an answer. "By the way, the tipping point is that moment when all factors and forces in a given situation are at critical mass and everything is about to change simultaneously."

Tannen's eyes twinkled with insight. "The shit's about to hit the fan."

Stacey groaned. "Well, that is another way of putting it." She was still snapping latches when Steinbach reappeared in his yellow-and-black cycling outfit and no-heel shoes. He came toward her in an awkward gait and arched his brows expectantly.

"Go back to the experts," Stacey said, smartly, before he could ask. "The Wiesenthal Center. Nobody knows more about war criminals, right? If anybody can sort this out, it's—"

"You're right," Steinbach growled. "Why didn't I think of that?"

"Not much point in knocking your own socks off."

Steinbach laughed. "What was that gal's name?"

"Rother. Ellen Rother," Tannen replied.

"Right. Set a meeting, ASAP." Steinbach went to his Giro d'Italia leaning against the wall and rolled it toward the door, setting its titanium derailleur to clicking. "Oh…" he said, glancing back at Stacey, "…in case you're wondering, your boyfriend isn't invited." He rolled the bike into the corridor, leaving Stacey and Tannen in the office, mouths agape.

"Hell of a character, isn't he?" Tannen prompted.

"A comic book character," Stacey replied with an appreciative chuckle. "Kind of like Clark Kent going into the phone both and coming out as Superman."

Tannen's brow furrowed . "We could use the man of steel about now."

"You thinking it's time we get Gunther into it?"

Tannen winced. "Naw, it's still too…too dicey. Besides, he won't be back til next week. We can't wait that long." He plucked his cell phone from its holster. "I better get this thing set up."

"I've got a call to make too," Stacey said with trepidation, slipping her Blackberry from her handbag.

Tannen smiled, knowingly. "Good luck."

"You think it's the right move? Calling him…"

Tannen waggled a hand. "It's always better when Celine just comes up behind my chair and hugs me. Doesn't say a word. Doesn't have to. Know what I mean?"

"A little tenderness…"

Tannen nodded.

Stacey thanked him with a smile and put the Blackberry away.

Tannen set-up the meeting with Ellen Rother for the following morning, then he and Stacey headed back to the office. The city was steeped in sweltering humidity which had a way of intensifying the pressure. Stacey focused on developing ads that would feature other owners of vintage Steinbachs. Tannen worked on contingency plans and damage control in case the ads featuring Jake Epstein had to be pulled, and on scheduling photo shoots with Zach Bolden. When they finally called it a night, Tannen headed to the driving range at Chelsea Piers. It was a short walk from his West Village condo in one of the austere, glass boxes that had been built recently along the Hudson. Stacey headed south on Park Avenue, calling Adam's editor at The Times en route.

"Paul? Yeah, hi, it's Stacey. Any chance he's still there? Oh, okay," she sighed, disappointed. "I was going to have you call down a pass so I could surprise him. Yeah, probably is. Thanks." She pocketed the Blackberry and headed into Grand Central, taking the shuttle to Times Square where she caught the subway that ran up the west side from the Battery to Van Cortlandt Park in the Bronx.

Along with its swirling litter, thundering racket, and nauseating olfactory offenses, for $2.25, the Metropolitan Transit Authority also provided its subway riders with a cellular dead zone. Nary a catchy personal ringtone had ever been heard in these tunnels cut through the bedrock from which skyscrapers soared. Indeed, New Yorkers were free to think, reflect, zone-out, read a book, blast their iPods, decide whether to cook or get takeout, replay the day's events, sleep, or as Stacey Dutton was doing now, indulge in self recrimination.

In unnervingly close, if not intimate, contact with dozens of strangers, she was holding onto a pole with one hand, and a paperback of Malcolm Gladwell's

Outliers—a quirky analysis of why some people succeed --- with the other. The words became a blur as her mind kept replaying her spat with Adam. Stacey knew she was wrong, knew she had unjustly accused him of something unethical, something she believed him incapable of doing. Heartened by Tannen's advice, she was anxious to apologize and make amends. When the No. 1 train pulled into the 79th Street station, she bolted from the car and sprinted up the stairs, making a beeline for the Crunch Gym on 83rd and Amsterdam. She often took this circuitous route to her apartment, pressing her nose to the glass if Adam was there, making him laugh; but he wasn't on one of the window-facing treadmills he favored. The news crawl on the ubiquitous TV monitors read: HANNAH MONTANA GETS NAKED. SEXY PICS FOUND ON MILEY'S IPHONE. DAD BILLY RAY FAULTED OVER *VANITY FAIR* PHOTO SPREAD.

Adam wasn't at the Starbucks on 81st and Columbus either; but, Stacey brightened at the soft click of a keyboard on entering her apartment. Adam glanced over his shoulder then back to the monitor without acknowledging her. After setting her things aside, Stacey slipped up behind him, wrapped her arms around his shoulders, and kissed the top of his head. A long moment passed before he swiveled to face her. "How're you doing, babe?" he asked, looking up at her with concern. "You okay?"

Stacey nodded, clearly relieved, and despite Tannen's advice, said, "I'm sorry, I was way out of…"

"Shussh…" Adam whispered, his face against her breast, his arms squeezing her torso, tightly.

"How're you doing?" Stacey prompted, softly, surprised by the intensity of his embrace. "You okay?"

"Yeah…yeah, I guess," Adam replied as he released her and leaned back slightly.

Stacey's eyes glistened with remorse. "The old guy just speaks to me, you know. I mean, I feel kind of protective toward him, almost maternal…"

Adam nodded, knowingly. "Very admirable traits. Not terribly useful for an investigative journalist, but admirable."

"I know. I don't have your certainty…your… your…" Stacey paused, unable to find the word she wanted which didn't happen very often.

"Detachment," Adam said, supplying it.

Stacey nodded as if conceding a flaw.

"Then you made the right choice, didn't you?"

"Yeah, yeah I guess," Stacey said, awkwardly. Then, pushing past it, she gestured to the data on the monitor and asked, "So, what're you up to?"

"Maximilian Kleist," Adam replied with a sigh. "Over six million hits. M.D.—Nazi—SS—Auschwitz narrowed it to a couple of thousand. Lots of Maxes. Lots of Kleists and von Kleists; but Max Kleists?" He held up three fingers. "A guy in Berlin on Facebook; a guy in New York suing his father-in-law for busting-up his marriage; and a guy with restricted access. I'm still waiting on the German Military Archives; but the word is they're notoriously slow. I've got nothing. It's a total wipe out."

"Well..." Stacey said, coyly. "I'd say, total sounds a little extreme..."

"What?" Adam prompted, sensing her inference. "What's going on?"

"I shouldn't tell you..."

"As I recall," Adam said softly, nuzzling her. "That's what you said the last time."

"As I recall, this is what you did the last time." Stacey emitted a squeal and spun from his grasp. "We're getting the Wiesenthal Center into it. Tannen set up a meeting."

Adam raised a brow. "When?"

"Tomorrow morning," Stacey replied; then, sounding apprehensive, she added, "You're not invited. I mean, you were specifically not invited."

Adam sagged in disappointment, then brightened at an idea. He reached to his backpack beneath the desk and removed his recorder. "Do me a favor," he said, getting to his feet and offering it to her. "Take this with you?"

Stacey's eyes narrowed with uncertainty. "You mean, like...like wear a wire?"

"Well..." Adam mused. "I guess that's one way of putting it. Actually, it has amazing range. Just leave it in your bag and press Record."

"Come on, Clive, you know I can't do that."

"Hey...it's not Clive who's asking," Adam said, taking her face in his hands. "It's me. Adam. The guy who's in love with you. The crass tabloid reporter who's still smiling over that sweet moment before..."

Stacey's resistance crumbled with a sigh as she embraced him and, cheek pressing against his stubble, lips grazing his ear, whispered, "I'll always be your little undercover girl...under the covers...on top of the covers...between the covers...always...but not tomorrow. Not at that meeting. I can't."

Adam leaned away from her with a puzzled frown. "You're not serious..."

Stacey nodded. "It'd be wrong. You know it."

"Come on, babe. I've got a lot riding on this."

"Don't do this," Stacey pleaded, running her fingers through her spiky hair, nervously. "You're confusing me."

"Why? I'm just asking for your help."

"No, you're asking me to be disloyal. To do something underhanded. I'm confused because...I mean... Well, you're...you're Adam: the ethics guy; the guy who lectures at Columbia on moral ambiguity; who doesn't cut corners, plays it straight; who said it's a search for the truth..."

"Look, I really need to break this story," Adam pleaded, his eyes widening.

Stacey backed away a few steps and, holding his look, said, "You know, I felt really bad for what I said in Tannen's office; it was a low blow; but—"

"Really low," Adam interrupted, pressing his advantage. "Now's your chance to make up for it."

"—but now…" Stacey continued, ignoring his retort. "Now, I'm starting to think, maybe, I was right. I'm getting the feeling you'll do anything to make this story into something it isn't."

"Well, listening to your bullshit isn't one of them!" Adam exclaimed, eyes flaring. He sent the desk chair rolling with an angry shove, scooped up his backpack, tossed the recorder into it, and charged out of the apartment, slamming the door after him.

Stacey shuddered, trying to come to grips with what had just happened. Her eyes welled with emotion, sending tears streaming down her cheeks. She took a deep breath, then stepped to the computer where the results of the Google search were displayed. She grasped the mouse and after several clicks, the screen went black.

CHAPTER THIRTY

Max hurried down the corridor in the Officers' Housing Unit, pulling off his greatcoat. He fumbled with the key to his room, got the door open, and charged through it, tossing the coat on his bunk en route to the lavatory. He bent over the toilet and vomited, then vomited again. He took a few moments to recover, then flushed it and, with his mouth and nostrils aflame with the sting of bile, went to the sink to wash up.

This wasn't the first time this had happened.

The trainloads of prisoners had been arriving at ever shorter intervals. Max had done several more tours since his shocking initiation with Kruger. As with the first, anxiety and tormenting guilt gave way to dispassionate decision-making. After each, Max retched violently, slept poorly, and wrestled with his conscience fearing he was becoming not only desensitized but dehumanized. He continued to avoid his colleagues and spent off-duty hours in his quarters, working on designs for prosthetics, listening to music on the radio, and reading Hufeland's book on medical ethics.

Max shut off the spigot and was reaching for a towel when he caught sight of himself in the mirror above the sink. He was stunned by the image that stared back at him. His face had lost its freshness, his eyes their aura of hope. He seemed to have aged ten years in not even as many days. Who is that person? he wondered. What is he doing here? How could he be involved in this—this evilness. It was as if he had created another person to cope with the discord the way abused children create another self who deserves the abuse. The inhumane nature of his assignment had been so disturbing that he retained the letter he had written to his parents, adding page after page on which he documented it.

A gusty wind was rattling the windows as Max addressed the envelope. He had just set it aside, intending to mail it at the camp post office in the morning, when someone knocked on the door.

"Hello, Max," Captain Kruger said with a friendly smile when Max opened it. "Can I come in for a moment?"

"Of course," Max replied, relieved after the way Kruger had acted on the ramp.

"I'm sorry about the other night," Kruger said as Max closed the door. "But the ramp is no place for collegial chatter."

"I know, Otto. At least I do, now. I'm the one who should be apologizing. I had no idea what was—"

Kruger put a finger to his lips and turned on the radio. The inexpensive Deutscher Kleinempfanger—German small receiver—had been distributed at the Führer's order to German households and military installations by the millions. Its Bakelite cabinet had two knobs, and a speaker covered with coarse cloth. An Imperial Eagle, clutching a swastika in its claws, was perched above the dial. Kruger thumbed it and found Die Walküre from Wagner's Ring, ever-present on Third Reich broadcasts as were the Führer's rantings and those of his Propaganda Minister Josef Goebbels. "That should convince any eavesdroppers we're good Nazis," Kruger said with a wily smile. He produced a pack of Sturms, gave one to Max and took one himself. "When I'm on the ramp, I block out all thoughts of people, places, family, everything." He struck a match and lit Max's cigarette, then his own. "It's the only way I can get through it. Coming upon you so unexpectedly, well..."

Max nodded. "You're not alone, Otto."

"Yes, I watched you out there. I knew you'd understand." Kruger took a deep drag of his cigarette. "You still keep in touch with Professor Gerhard?"

"Of course. I was the SS liaison to the Med School. Being reassigned so close to home, again, was a big surprise. I expected a combat unit."

"So did I. It's been almost a year. Home is a distant memory." He exhaled wistfully, then noticed the envelope on the desk. "What's that?"

"Oh, just a letter to my parents."

Kruger winced. "I wouldn't post it if I were you. Nothing leaves here. Not since the war started going badly. No phone, no mail, no passes and no visitors."

Max took a thoughtful drag of his cigarette. "It sounds like we're prisoners too, Otto."

"Precisely. They don't want anyone to know what's going on. They're terrified of the consequences if the Allies win." He finished it with a look that said: And let's hope they do! A thought neither dared say aloud despite the thunderous music from the radio. "The mail is confiscated to catch dissenters," Kruger went on. "If you've written the truth, you'll be accused of treason."

Max slipped the envelope into a drawer. "I've come too close to chance it, again."

"A problem with your friends?" Kruger prompted in a veiled reference to Jake and Eva.

Max nodded. "They're on the run. I got Professor Gerhard and my family involved. They're all in danger, now, thanks to me."

Kruger sighed in commiseration. "Speaking of families. I'm afraid those old folks you spared on the ramp the other night were culled out during processing."

Max felt as if he'd been gutted. His eyes hardened with insight. "It was Radek, wasn't it?"

Kruger nodded, grimly. "I'm told he executed them. Personally. Be careful, Max. You've made an enemy. I wouldn't have told you such upsetting news, otherwise."

"Thanks, Otto. Thanks a lot."

"You'd do the same for me, Max," Kruger said, stubbing out his cigarette. "I was on my way to the Officer's Club. I'd been hoping to see you there."

Max shrugged in apology.

"You should come, Max. It'll do you good. We're all doctors…good men. We blow off steam, get drunk and laugh. God knows you need it. Come on. I insist."

Max was considering it when the musical broadcast was interrupted by a shrill voice: "Our beloved Führer has. designated Berlin a fortress city!" Josef Goebbels exclaimed, launching into one of his tirades. "And has denounced claims that it will soon fall as vicious lies! The great German people are not demoralized by such mendacity! The destiny of the Aryan race is…" Max turned off the radio and led the way from the room, sharing a knowing smile with Kruger.

The Officer's Club at Dachau was richly furnished, dimly illuminated and alive with the clack of billiards and repartee like a British men's club; but instead of balding butlers in cutaways, attractive Jewish prisoners—from the wives and daughters of farmers to those of wealthy bankers and aristocrats—were forced to serve food and drinks and, despite the Nuremberg Laws that forbade sexual intercourse between Jews and Aryans, often themselves. Officers in black tunics, jodhpurs and gleaming boots gathered around tables, preened in club chairs, and slouched on sofas. The room sparkled with badges of rank, silver buttons, gleaming buckles and braided lanyards. A wall of shelves held rows of black caps with silver Death's Heads above the peaks, their hollow eye sockets bearing blind witness to the goings-on.

Kruger introduced Max to a group of officers at a table covered with steins, tumblers, and stemware. The alcohol worked, quickly; and, soon, they were rocking with laughter and reminiscing about hometowns, families, and women they had left behind. Max reflected on his love for Eva, but didn't dare mention he pined for a Jewess. His concern that Kruger might make a slip, was alleviated by a wink that signaled Max had nothing to worry about. Otto was right. In the company of these men, family men, educated men, physicians, Max felt almost human, again. After a while, Major Karl Heiden, an older fellow, holding court at the head of the table, leaned to Max and asked, "So, how are you doing? Have you been coping?"

"No, not very well, I'm afraid."

"Well, we've all been through it, son," Major Heiden said with the bedside manner of a small town doctor. "It takes time. You'll get used to it."

"I am getting used to it, Sir. That's what worries me. It gets easier and easier. Though I can't imagine ever getting used to playing God."

"That's not the way to look at it, my boy," the older fellow counseled. "You're a surgeon, aren't you?"

"Yes, yes I am. Orthopedics is my specialty."

"Well, there you have it," the Major concluded, signaling a waitress for a refill. "Making selections is no different than amputating a gangrenous limb or cutting out a bone cancer. By excising these threats to the nation's health we're saving lives as our oath mandates."

Max looked confused. "You make it sound as if we're practicing preventive medicine."

"We are," a young lieutenant with thick-lensed glasses chimed-in. "Working on the ramp is analogous to using a microscope in the lab to detect cancer cells or replicating viruses so they can be dealt with before they destroy the host body."

"A convenient metaphor," a middle-aged fellow, sporting captain's insignia, said. "Fine, if it helps you sleep nights. I much prefer this." He held up his glass of whiskey and grinned widely.

"I'll drink to that!" an officer with a cocky air and a waxed moustache, exclaimed, before draining his glass. "What appears benign at first all too often turns out to be pernicious under higher magnification. The lieutenant's analogy is no exception."

"Yes, but it helps when the anesthesia wears off," the young officer retorted, raising his glass. "Prost!"

"Gentlemen, please?" Kruger said, tired of their jousting. "It's time we stopped treating our oath as something to be..." He wanted to say manipulated and subverted; but thought the better of it. "...to be redefined, so we can claim we're living up to it."

"But we're not redefining it, are we?" the cocky officer prompted, blotting droplets of foam from his mustache. "Others are doing it for us."

"Each of us still has to live within the dictates of his conscience," Kruger said, pressing the point. "It's a personal, individual choice."

"Not anymore," the young officer protested, fueled by the martinis he had consumed. "Have you read *Mein Kampf?*"

"Of course. Who hasn't?"

"Well, the Führer makes it very clear," the young officer lectured. "Those with social and genetic disorders that threaten Aryan survivaal must be identified by medical analysis. As Major Heiden said, when we make selections we're using science to eliminate racial impurities and ensure the nation's health."

"Thank you," the major said, reasserting his authority. Numbed by the alcohol, he had drifted off, seeming disengaged. "I'm afraid we're forced to revisit this matter every time a new fellow joins the team. You seem like a nice young man and, I'm sure, a fine surgeon" he went on, absolving Max with a smile. "But, none of us were happy to see you. Why? Because we're tired of all this soul-searching. Who is most qualified to root out these racial cancers? Doctors. It's as simple as that."

Max had been sitting quietly, sipping his beer, taking it all in without taking part. Now, he heard himself saying, "Yes, assuming one accepts the premise; but it's a false premise, and—"

"It's the Führer's premise," Major Heiden snapped, his voice taking on an edge. "He has declared that Jews, gypsies, Bolsheviks and other degenerate species must be excised; and I've seen first hand what happens to those who disagree."

"So have I, major; but how do you explain this to an outsider who claims it's mass murder…the extermination of an entire race of people?" Max asked, being careful to attribute the question to a third party.

"Gentlemen!" someone called out before the old fellow could reply. "Am I mistaken or has Captain Kleist just accused the Führer of mass murder?"

Max knew the voice. He turned to see Radek standing behind him with an entourage of SS men. Kruger signaled him to ignore the provocation; but Max sprung to his feet as if welcoming it. "Quite mistaken. I never mentioned the Führer, lieutenant. You did. And I have witnesses."

"I'll be sure he gets their names," Radek said with an insidious smirk. "I hasten to remind you—and your witnesses—that such remarks are grounds for disciplinary action, if not the firing squad."

"So is insubordination," Max retorted. "In case you've forgotten, lieutenant, I outrank you."

"Not for long. Not after the commandant learns of your disloyalty on the ramp," Radek countered, poking a finger into Max's chest. Max brushed it aside. "Keep your hands to yourself, lieutenant." Radek stiffened, threateningly, bristling within the knife-edged creases of his uniform. Max stood his ground glaring at him. They were on the verge of blows when Kruger lunged between them. "Gentlemen?! Gentlemen, stand down! Stand down or you'll both face disciplinary action!" The two men's eyes remained locked as other officers, responding to the commotion, gathered around them. Finally, they each took several steps back.

"Good," Kruger said, forcing a smile. "Now let's return to our seats and enjoy the rest of the evening."

Max managed a contrite nod.

Radek smirked, then snapped his fingers at a young waitress passing with a tray of drinks. His entourage pounced like a pack of retrievers, delivering her to him, swiftly. Despite her physical maturity, she was still in her teens and self-conscious about her low-cut costume. Radek swept his eyes across the frightened girl's creamy bosom as he plucked a glass of whiskey from her tray and toasted, "To Captain Maximilian Kleist who seems to have forgotten that he has taken two oaths: One as a doctor and one as an SS officer."

Max took his stein from the table and, without missing a beat, said, "To Dr. Klaus Radek who suffers from the same malady!" He cocked his head, feigning uncertainty. "Did I just call you Doctor Radek? No offense intended, lieutenant. I take it back."

"Along with your oath to the Führer to prevent these vermin from soiling the Aryan race!" Radek swept his glass in an arc past the assembled officers. "Prost!"

Some of them forced smiles. Others raised their glasses halfheartedly. A few thrust them into the air.

"What are you waiting for?!" Radek exhorted the laggards. "Toast the Jew-lover!" He drained the glass and slammed it atop the table. "Keep in mind the alternative to Selections is typhus duty in the prison hospital!"

"That's right," one of the officers said. "Goetz lasted less than three months, remember?"

"You mean, he died of typhus," Max said.

"Yes! Painfully! Horribly!" Radek exclaimed with glee. "Served him right as it will you, captain, should your disloyalty continue. Heil Hitler!" He snapped-off a Nazi salute. "Bring the Jewess," he ordered, striding off. The SS men who, still had the young waitress in tow, knew what that meant; and, from the look in her eyes as they escorted her from the club, so did she.

"He's going to rape that girl, isn't he?" Max said unable to contain his disgust.

"Don't," Kruger said sharply, sensing Max was about to intercede. "Ignore him. He'll keep baiting you until you're hooked, boated and gutted, if you don't."

"Where do you think he takes them?"

Kruger shrugged. "I've no idea. He'd be a fool to risk violating the Nuremberg Laws in his quarters or the SS brothel."

Max nodded, bristling in silence.

As the group around them dispersed, Kruger noticed a neatly groomed officer, taking a seat at a distant table. "See that fellow with the glasses?"

"The one in the corner by himself?"

Kruger nodded. "Major Ernst Bruckmann, M.D. He was transferred here from Auschwitz. He refused to do Selections…and got away with it."

"Are you suggesting I talk to him?"

"Couldn't hurt. He gave me some good advice."

Max cocked his head in thought, then crossed to where Bruckmann was sitting, and introduced himself. The major nodded formally, but declined to shake Max's hand. "I've been expecting you. Most doctors assigned to the ramp find their way to my table sooner or later."

"And what do you tell them, Sir?"

"Stay away from the typhus ward. There's a reason why I sit alone and don't shake hands."

"Are you saying you were assigned there for refusing to do Selections?"

"No, but I visit it regularly," Bruckmann replied, matter-of-factly. "It seems like the right thing to do."

"Of course it is, we're doctors, aren't we?"

"It's not easy to be one here."

"As I'm learning. If I may, Sir, it sounds like you're able to set your own terms. How do you manage it?"

"Luck. I have friends in high places who protect me. The head of the Hygienic Institutes for one."

"Dr. Mrugowsky?" Max prompted, brightening.

Bruckmann nodded.

"I'm reading Hufeland," Max said, referring to the essays on medical ethics which had been reprinted many times since its initial publication. "Dr. Mrugowsky wrote the introduction to the copy I got from the library."

"'Only in the art of healing does the physician find the myth of life'," Bruckmann said, quoting from it. "I'm sure Joachim meant it when he wrote it; but he seems to have lost his way as of late." He paused and took a thoughtful sip of his drink. "Is it true you were reassigned here as a matter of discipline?"

Max nodded. "They've threatened my family, too."

Bruckmann looked baffled. "Your surname is Kleist, isn't it? Your father is…"

Max nodded emphatically, stopping him.

"My God," Bruckmann gasped. "Why?"

"I've some friends…Jewish friends."

"From medical school," Bruckmann said knowingly. "I'm surprised you weren't assigned to the Typhus Ward. The outbreak is massive. The prisoner doctors are sick and overwhelmed. I do what I can." He looked off, then chuckled softly in reflection. "Two years ago when I reported to Auschwitz, I was so naive, I brought my wife along. Can you imagine? I sent her home soon after."

Max smiled in empathy. "I'm sure I'd have done the same, were I married, Sir."

"Well, focus on the things that matter in life," Bruckmann advised in a paternal tone. "Do whatever it takes to get through this with your sanity intact. Rumor has it the Russians are in Warsaw. If it's true, you won't have to do it for long. Good luck."

"To you too, Sir," Max said, before taking his leave and joining Kruger and the others at their table.

"He was recruiting you for the typhus ward, wasn't he?" the young lieutenant asked, slyly, peering at Max over the top of his thick lenses.

"No, we were just getting acquainted."

"Stay away from him and from the Revier," the officer with the waxed mustache advised. "None of us go near the place."

Max looked baffled. "But we're facing an epidemic. It needs to be contained."

"Easier said than done, Max," Kruger cautioned. "Unless you're willing to risk a death sentence."

"Let's not overreact," Major Heiden counseled in his gentle way. "I've heard talk of bringing in prisoner doctors from other camps to deal with it."

"What's the point?" the young lieutenant asked, rhetorically. One way or the other, they're all going to die, anyway."

Max was the one who was dying. Dying inside. He wanted to say: But we're all going to die! And he desperately wanted to ask: How could the philosophy of Hippocrates have been so subverted? How could medical professionals become enablers of the Führer's evil obsession with racial purity? How could decent family men go about excising entire ethnic groups from the family of man because they had been labeled social cancers by a madman?! How could we doctors, trained as healers and sworn to protect life, allow ourselves to become ruthless executioners?! He was on the verge of making the challenge when, as he had on the ramp, he imagined his father, mother and sister driven to their knees by truncheons; imagined the muzzle of Radek's Luger pressed to the back of their heads, imagined the sharp crack of gunshots and the grotesque explosion of brain matter; then, reflecting on the advice he'd been given, Max bit the inside of his lip until he could taste his own blood, and remained silent.

CHAPTER THIRTY-ONE

Tannen was the first to arrive at 50 East 42nd Street a nondescript building on the corner of Madison Avenue where the Simon Wiesenthal Center's Eastern Headquarters were located. The entrance, between Cohen's Fashion Optical and a RadioShack—where the Breaking News headline on TV monitors in the window read: LAPD SEEKS TO QUESTION MICHAEL JACKSON'S DOCTOR—was flanked by two American flags. It led to a narrow lobby with a vaulted ceiling where a security guard in a red blazer stood at a small desk. There were no plaques heralding the Center's presence whose offices were on the sixteenth floor. Tannen was securing a visitor's pass when Stacey blew through the door, clutching a Starbuck's latte.

"Sorry, the subway was a disaster."

"Relax. We have to wait for Sol." Tannen splayed his hands and prompted, "So?"

Stacey looked baffled. "Sorry, the caffeine hasn't kicked in yet."

"The hug…" Tannen prompted.

Stacey sighed. Her posture slackened. "I screwed it up. Then, he really screwed it up." She shook her head in dismay and took a sip of coffee. "Don't ask."

Tannen's head was bobbing in commiseration when Steinbach came striding into the lobby.

Unlike its occupant, Ellen Rother's office was threadbare and rumpled. Stacks of files teetered on windowsills and marched across the desk, framing the tiny figure behind it. Images of the fugitive Nazis that Simon Wiesenthal had spent a lifetime pursuing were displayed on one wall. Among them: Adolph Eichmann, architect of the Holocaust; Franz Stengl, commandant of Treblinka; Karl Silberbauer who arrested Anne Frank; and Josef Mengele, the angel of death at Auschwitz who, to Wiesenthal's frustration, drowned, accidentally, before he could be captured and tried for war crimes.

Dr. Epstein's suitcase was in the center of a long table, its contents arranged neatly around it. A descriptive label or tag had been affixed to each. A supply of archival packing materials was nearby. "I have good news," Ellen said brightly. "Dr. Epstein has decided to donate his memorabilia to the Holocaust Museum in Washington D.C."

"That's great," Tannen said, forcing a smile. "I'm afraid our news isn't as good." He brought Ellen up to speed on the problem, giving her the printouts Adam had made: the first two depicted prisoner ID number A198841 tattooed in different handwriting, one of which was on Dr. Epstein's forearm. The third depicted the numerals on the luggage tag that appeared to be in the same handwriting as his tattoo.

Ellen took a few moments to study them; then, her eyes saddened, and she said, "This is very troubling."

Tannen nodded, glumly. "If the implications are true, we've probably exposed a war criminal. If they aren't, and word of this gets out, a decent man with a lifetime of good works and professional achievement will be ruined. Either way, as they say, the tar goes on a lot easier than it comes off."

Ellen's lips tightened into a thin line. "It certainly does. Perception is everything."

"And if it gets on the Internet, it's the only thing," Stacey added. "There'll be no stopping it."

"That's our dilemma," Tannen concluded. "We need guidance. We need to determine the truth."

"And we need discretion." Steinbach added.

"So do we," Ellen responded, forcefully. "We also require proof beyond any doubt, not just reasonable doubt; and we don't leak to the press. These matters become public through the legal process."

"Unfortunately, the press is already involved," Tannen said. "Adam Stevens from *The Times* brought this…this matter to our attention."

"The reporter doing the human interest story…"

Tannen nodded.

Ellen winced. "A very astute young man. Is he a reasonable one as well?"

"Stace? You know him better than anyone," Tannen prompted, then in explanation added, "They have a…a personal relationship."

"Had," Stacey corrected. "Without getting into details, he asked me to help him get this story. It made me uncomfortable. We argued about it and he freaked out. There was no reasoning with him."

Ellen nodded, resignedly.

Steinbach was fidgeting with impatience. "Let's cut to the chase. Is our guy a war criminal or not?"

"It's not that simple, Mr. Steinbach," Ellen replied. "Many professionals and intellectuals of the day weren't rabid Nazis. Doctors faced the additional dilemma of being true to their Hippocratic Oath without being labeled traitors."

"Change the spelling..." Stacy quipped in her sassy, shoot-from-the-hip way.

"Change the spelling?" Ellen echoed, mystified, as were Tannen and Steinbach.

"Uh-huh, from crat to crit," Stacey explained with a nervous giggle. "Hippocrats? Hypocrites? They could blame it all on a typo."

"How wonderfully clever and glib," Ellen said with a thin smile. "I can see why you're so good at what you do. I can also see you find this subject disturbing and are relying on your sense of humor to cope with it."

Stacey looked chastened and nodded. "It gives me chills...really weirds me out."

"I know," Ellen said with heartfelt empathy. "But it's important to remember the Nazi vision was a biomedical one. Doctors were drafted into the SS early on. Hitler was a psychopath but he wasn't stupid. His plan to purify the Aryan race was insane but finely crafted. Who better to legitimize it, to diagnose and remove the racial cancers he imagined, than physicians? Many were coerced into carrying out his vision."

"Nobody coerced that bastard Mengele," Steinbach said, trembling. "He loved every minute of it."

"A monster, as my grandparents can testify."

"But they survived..." Steinbach prompted.

Ellen nodded. "God knows how."

"Mine didn't."

"I'm very sorry," Ellen said, clearly moved. "But we've learned not all Nazi doctors were Mengele. Some were conflicted by what they were ordered to do. They drank heavily and were tormented by nightmares. As a matter of fact, a distinguished professor of psychology wrote a book about how Germany's doctors were turned into mass murderers." She went to a wall of bookcases, scanned the titles, and removed a hardback which she handed to Steinbach.

Discrete gray lettering at the top of the black dust jacket spelled out: Robert Jay Lifton. Below, dynamic uppercase lettering, with an incised black borderline, that made the white characters vibrate, proclaimed *The Nazi Doctors*; and at the bottom, in more lyrical red lettering, the book's subtitle: *Medical Killing and the Psychology of Genocide*.

"Robert Jay Lifton," Steinbach mused, examining the hefty volume. "Sounds familiar..."

"Not surprising. He's the leading authority," Ellen said. "One of the many doctors he interviewed was an SS officer who was on the ramp at Auschwitz. Ernst B., as Dr. Lifton called him, found it so unnerving that he refused to do any more selections. Fortunately, he was supported by a mentor who had him transferred to Dachau."

"But he was on the ramp at Auschwitz," Steinbach said in condemnation. "He did selections, right?"

Ellen nodded.

"That makes him a war criminal," Steinbach stated. "That was the deciding factor at Nuremberg, wasn't it? You were either on the ramp or you weren't."

"Yes, in most cases," Ellen replied. "People were hung for it; and Dr. Ernst B. was eventually arrested and brought to trial; but he was acquitted of all—"

"Acquitted?!" Steinbach interrupted, outraged.

"Yes, of all charges," Ellen resumed, gently. "The prisoner doctors he worked with at Dachau testified on his behalf. All of them—most were Jews, by the way—said he was humane and caring toward the prisoners and put himself at risk to help them."

Steinbach was stunned and muttered, "I had no idea..."

"If it helps..." Ellen went on, "...his mentor, a Dr. Mrugowsky, who was head of the Hygienic Institutes, was executed for conducting fatal medical experiments."

"That's an amazing story," Tannen said, clearly moved. "But, can we get back to our doctor?"

Ellen sighed in dismay. "As I said, this is very troubling. For two reasons: Money is one. Dr. Jacob Epstein is the other. Not necessarily in that order."

Steinbach looked puzzled. "Money? I don't get it."

Ellen nodded glumly. "Despite your generosity and that of many others, Dr. Epstein among them, the Center is on the verge of bankruptcy."

Ellen's three visitors emitted a collective gasp.

"That's how everyone reacts. Well, almost everyone. Racist web-sites and publications are cheering openly. We've cut our staff to the bone. What resources we do have are being used to press active cases. It takes decades to track these monsters down."

Stacey nodded. "Adam was telling us about this Nazi doc who'd been living in Cairo for thirty years. I think his name was Heil or Heinz...something like that."

"Heim," Ellen said smartly. "He was a monster in the Mengele mold. But Dr. Jacob Epstein? A Jewish-American aristocrat? Who would donate to investigate him? For Mengele, yes; for Eichmann, yes; for Heim, Entress, Vetter, yes. All human scum."

"People would mortgage their condos in Palm Beach to nail those bastards," Tannen joked, in an attempt to lighten the mood.

"People did mortgage their condos," Ellen retorted without cracking a smile. "Dr. Epstein is a Jewish icon. A lion. A former chairman of the WJC who has donated more money to, as you put it, nail these monsters than anyone. Furthermore our---"

"Playing devil's advocate," Tanned interjected, "Can you think of a better cover?"

"That's rank speculation Mr. Tannen. I was about to say our donor base has been decimated by the global financial crisis and the likes of Bernie Madoff."

"Cancelling this year's fund-raiser didn't help," Steinbach said. "My wife was on the verge of melting her Platinum Card on a Versace when you pulled the plug. We still ponied up by the way."

"And it's much appreciated; but when we ran the numbers, we realized the gala would've cost more to put on than it would've raised. By the way, Dr. Epstein's Foundation is one of the few that hasn't cut back or eliminated its contribution. You want the Center to use *their* donation to prove he's a war criminal?"

"I love the old guy," Stacey said with a tremor in her voice. "But if he is guilty, there'd be something Shakespearean about that, wouldn't there? A sort of poetic justice?"

"Justice is our focus. If it comes with a little poetry, fine," Ellen replied, matter-of-factly. "Nobody wants to get these monsters more than we do."

"Adam's a close second," Stacey warned. "And his motives aren't as altruistic. With the current state of the newspaper business, nothing's going to stop him."

"That doesn't change the Center's commitment to having proof beyond any doubt before taking action."

Tannen removed his glasses and rubbed the bridge of his nose. "Then what does all this mean?" he asked, referring to the printouts.

"Not much," Ellen replied. "Most Europeans make their numbers like that. They could've been written by anyone. Probably one of the monsters at Auschwitz."

"That's occurred to us," Tannen said with a look to Stacey. "But Dan Epstein said the writing on the tag could be his father's; and if it does match the numbers on Dr. Epstein's tattoo, one might conclude that he—"

"—that he tattooed himself with the real Jacob Epstein's ID number," Ellen interjected. "I get it; but then why agree to do the ads in the first place? Why take the chance of being exposed? The sight of the suitcase, alone, would have terrified him. Why didn't he get rid of it and everything in it, years ago?"

"We've asked the same questions," Tannen replied. "We came up with: Guilt. A need to wipe the slate clean. To make amends at the end of his life. Sentimentality…"

"It's also possible someone's out to smear him," Ellen said. "Even the finest surgeons are sued for malpractice. It might be a patient who wants to hurt him. Or one of Mr. Steinbach's rivals, for that matter, whose sales will suffer when you run your ads."

"Doesn't compute," Tannen replied with finality. "Stacey found the suitcase on the street. No way anyone could've planted it there and counted on us using it in the campaign, let alone planted evidence in it."

"Yeah," Steinbach grunted. "No competitor of mine would stoop to such tactics. I'm confused. I mean, why are we getting this push-back? Dr. E's deep pockets aside, I'm wondering if there isn't another reason?"

Ellen broke into a little smile. "Ah, you've found out he did my grandmother's hip replacement."

"He did?" Steinbach said, caught unawares.

"Uh-huh. Must be twenty, twenty-five years," Ellen said. "He's done more hips and knees around this place than you can count. I could recuse myself; but nothing would change. If Dr. Epstein is a war criminal, I'll do everything possible to bring him to justice; but I get to play devil's advocate, too. I have to be sure we're on solid ground before committing resources which, as I said, are severely limited."

"Solid ground or not, this has to be resolved and fast," Steinbach declared. "And I don't want to leave it up to a kid reporter. Anything you can do?"

"Well, for the sake of argument, let's say our Dr. Epstein isn't the real Dr. Jacob Epstein. Then, who is he? Well, we know he's a doctor. If he was at Dachau, he'd have been SS—they all were—and we could search data bases for him: The Wiesenthal Center. The European Consortium of Nations. The U.S. Department of Justice. The German Military Archives... If he's wanted for war crimes, chances are he'll turn up; but we can't do a search without a name—an SS Nazi doctor's name."

Stacey, Tannen and Steinbach looked at each other in puzzlement for a moment then, suddenly struck by the same thought, they nodded in unison.

"Maximilian Kleist," Tannen said.

"Where'd that come from?"

"From the man himself," Tannen replied. "According to Dr. Epstein, they were best friends at medical school. He also said, that Max Kleist gave him the suitcase, and that he was in the SS."

"Dr. Maximilian Kleist, SS," Ellen said, mimicking a German accent. "Has a nice Nazi ring, doesn't it?"

CHAPTER THIRTY-TWO

Several days after the incident in the Officers Club, Max was ordered to report to the commandant's office. He found Colonel Weiter staring out the window at the ramp and railroad spur that dead-ended at the Jourhaus. Max stood at attention in front of the desk with growing anxiety. "You wanted to see me, Sir?"

Weiter remained where he stood without replying for a long moment. Finally, he turned, and locked his eyes on to Max's. "You've been accused of disloyalty to the Führer, captain." He let Max live with it, gauging his reaction; then, in a more friendly tone, added, "I can understand why you might show some weakness on your first tour on the ramp. It's not uncommon. One gets used to it over time; and, being a reasonable man, I'm willing to overlook it..." Weiter paused. His lips tightened into a thin line. His eyes burned with intensity. "But mass murder?!" he erupted with seething anger. "You accused the Führer of mass murder and racial extermination?! In front of other officers?!"

Max had been lulled by the commandant's preamble, and shuddered, visibly, at the outburst.

Weiter removed his glasses and blew a speck of dust from one of the lenses, using the time to settle; then almost pleading, said, "Please, Kleist, tell me you didn't make such accusations against the Führer. If you did, you'll soon be facing a firing squad."

"No, Sir, I didn't," Max replied, undaunted by the steely-eyed images of Hitler and Himmler hanging behind the desk. "I did not accuse the Führer of mass murder and racial extermination."

"In other words, Lieutenant Radek is lying," the commandant challenged, slipping his glasses back on as if to assess Max's veracity.

"Yes, Sir. If that's what he told you. Captain Kruger and Major Heiden can testify to what I said."

"Then, why would Radek make such an accusation?"

"I'd attribute it to a personality conflict, Sir. He seems to resent that I don't enjoy this assignment as much as he does; and he shows no respect for—"

"I'm not enjoying it much either as of late," the commandant interrupted, reflectively. "Dachau was originally an indoctrination camp. Many political prisoners were educated here in the National Socialist vision, and released. Now, whether by typhus or pistol shot, it's a death camp. You were about to say?"

"That Lieutenant Radek shows no respect for the protocol of rank, Sir."

Weiter's brows went up. "Oh? And how has this disrespect been manifested?"

"It began during orientation. Not only has he used my given name, but he has also alluded to my having had a Jewish lover; and refers to me in front of other officers as 'the Jew-lover."

Weiter seemed caught off guard. He tilted his head in thought, then wondered, "How could Radek know about that? About your Jewish lover?"

Max looked puzzled. "May I speak freely, Sir?"

Weiter nodded, curiously.

"I assumed he learned it from you, Sir."

"You assumed, incorrectly, captain."

"I apologize, Sir. I meant no offense."

"None taken. Radek is a zealot, a degenerate who has no conscience—" The colonel smiled thinly. "—and he has his uses. On the other hand, as I said when you reported for duty, the officer who used your lapse in judgment against you is a low-class climber unworthy of a commission in the SS let alone his rank."

"I believe you're referring to Major Steig..."

Weiter nodded. "He's a political hack whose zeal to prove your family guilty of harboring Jews is self-serving. I have your best interests at heart, Kleist; and am counting on your performance, here, to undermine Steig's unprincipled ambition."

"And I've been striving to justify your faith in me, Sir," Max said, searching for a way to insure Weiter's support. His eyes darted to a row of file cabinets, taking special notice of the combination lock centered on each drawer front. "I recall you said Major Steig's report of my having a Jewish lover is in my file, sir."

"Yes, and as you can see they're well-secured."

"That's my point, Sir. I can't imagine Lieutenant Radek gained access to it."

"Nor can I. Therefore..."

"Well, the process of elimination suggests some form of collusion between Lieutenant Radek and Major Steig, doesn't it, Sir?"

The commandant's brows arched with intrigue. "Yes, yes it certainly does. You're very astute, captain. Very, very astute."

"Thank you, Sir."

"Leave them to me," the colonel said, his eyes alive with a strategic vision. "Please, be at ease." He circled the desk, joining Max who had taken a more relaxed stance. "I gave you good advice when we first met, captain...as did Major Bruckmann, so I'm told. Take it. Take it to heart. Take it to protect your family."

"I have, and will continue to do so, Sir."

"Good luck, captain. Dismissed."

Max turned on a heel and strode from the office, suppressing a relieved smile. He had been dealt a bad hand and had played it brilliantly. If anyone would be facing disciplinary action, now, it would be Radek and Steig; but the feeling of triumph was tempered by the knowledge that being chastised by the commandant would intensify their zeal to destroy him and his family.

That was almost a month ago.

Today, February 24th, was the first day of Lent. Temperatures had risen above freezing; and the sun was bathing KZ-Dachau in blinding brilliance as Max, in his black greatcoat, crossed the grounds to the ramp where yet another trainload of prisoners was duet to arrive. On any other Ash Wednesday, he'd have been at Mass in the family chapel with his parents and sister, their foreheads marked with an ashen cross. On administering the sign of repentance, the priest would have said, 'Remember man that thou art dust and unto dust thou shalt return. Max was acutely aware they were the same words Lieutenant Radek had used with macabre callousness when pointing out Dachau's crematoria.

Though the trauma of making selections still haunted him, Max had been able to maintain the robotic detachment required to get through them; and had worked his tours without incident; but today would be different. Max knew it the moment he checked the Duty Roster and saw that Radek had been assigned to the same tour. He had a habit of making a grand entrance with an entourage of SS guards and Sonderkommando in tow as the train arrived; and, now, as the locomotive thundered down the gleaming spur that paralleled the platform, Radek emerged from a cloud of steam like a haunting specter. He went to his station in an arrogant stride, tapping his riding crop on his gloved palm in eager anticipation of using it.

As of late, most of the trains carried prisoners being transferred from Auschwitz, Chelmno, Treblinka and other camps in Nazi occupied countries. The advancing Red Army had driven German troops from Warsaw, Budapest and Belgrade, causing Reichführer Himmler to issue an order prohibiting Jews and other prisoners from being liberated by enemy forces. He was so intent on concealing the atrocities that, when faced with a shortage of freight cars, he ordered tens of thousands of prisoners force-marched hundreds of miles through sub-freezing cold. Those unable to walk were executed prior to departure or left to die en route.

Prisoners being transferred didn't erupt in a chaotic surge when the doors to the freight cars were opened. They gasped for air and craved water as they had when first arrested and deported; but, this time, they didn't believe they were being relocated, only to discover upon arrival that many would be executed. No, they knew the ugly truth. Now, weary and emaciated from slave labor, starvation and physical punishment, they were more orderly and subdued, conserving their energy to survive for another minute, another hour, another day.

The announcement from the loudspeakers atop the guard towers was always the same. "There is no need to panic. Follow instructions. Go to the line to which you are assigned. You will be given hot meals, soap and towels for showering, and assigned to heated housing units. If you are a doctor, a nurse, or have other medical training, raise your hand or make this known to your processing officer. There is no need to panic. Follow instructions and go to the line to which..."

The absurdity wasn't lost on the prisoners as they emerged from the first freight car, and were forced to queue at Radek's station by members of the Kommando. They had no luggage, no personal belongings, no valuables to be confiscated, and selections were made swiftly. Many were barely able to walk, let alone work, and were marked for immediate execution by Radek whose cruelty was unrelenting.

One of the prisoners raised his hand in response to the announcement. "I'm a doctor," he said, dragging a suitcase on the ground as he came forward with a group of prisoners, about a half dozen in all. Like him—and unlike the others whose only possessions were the clothes on their backs—they were clutching suitcases and small leather satchels.

Radek eyed the man's bony face, pale skin, shaved head and yellow triangle sewn to his filthy uniform, and recoiled as if accosted by a street beggar. The corner of his mouth curled in disgust. "Liar! You take me for a fool?! You think it will get you special treatment?"

"You asked for doctors, sir," the man replied, cringing at the outburst. "I'm a doctor. So is the woman behind you. We were—"

"Lying Jewish swine!" Radek shrieked, lashing him across the side of his head with his riding crop; then, whip poised to strike, he grasped the woman. "He's a doctor?! You're a doctor?! Everyone's a doctor?!" he shouted with vitriolic sarcasm.

The terrified woman nodded, and managed to whisper, "Yes, yes, I'm a doctor."

Instead of striking her, Radek flinched as if taken by surprise. Despite the terror in her eyes and the hardships she had endured, the woman's face still had an arresting beauty which, along with the yellow triangle on her uniform, had more than gotten Radek's attention. His eyes flickered with intrigue. The riding crop fell to his side. "Your name, fraulein?"

"F-F-Friedman," the terrified woman stammered. "Doctor H-H-Hannah Friedman."

The man, who had identified her and himself as physicians, called out, "Yes, yes, she's a doctor as am I. The others are nurses and medical technicians. We were working in the Hygienic Institute at Auschwitz. It's being relocated here, and—"

Radek silenced him with a slash of his riding crop. It whistled through the air, again and again. The man fell to the ground, raising his suitcase to protect himself as the whip slashed across the personal data painted on it. When finished, Radek turned his attention back to the woman and, with eerie calmness, said, "Ah, Fraulein Friedman, I'm sure we can find something for you to do here." He nodded to the work line which was considerably shorter than the one which led to the courtyard where executions were carried out. The woman hesitated, exchanging a forlorn look with her colleague who had gotten to his feet and was motioning for her to go. Radek glared at him as she shuffled off, and called out, "Get this lying Jew out of my sight!"

An SS sergeant and several guards began pummeling the man and the remaining members of his group with their rifle butts and truncheons, driving them toward the execution line.

Max had been waiting for the occupants of the next car to be released and queued at his station. Sickened by the brutal savagery taking place at Radek's, he realized the prisoner's claims might be the key to saving him and his group. "Lieutenant?!" Max called out, dashing along the platform to where Radek was overseeing the onslaught. "Lieutenant?! I think he's a doctor as he says! And that these people are—"

"He's a lying Jew!" Radek shrieked. "This is my station, Kleist! Mine! It's none of your business!"

"They're a medical team sent here to deal with the typhus!" Max retorted, having no idea, whatsoever, if it was true. "Major Heiden told me about it. Look! They're the only ones with luggage! Some even have doctor bags!" he argued with an angry gesture, referring to the fact that Himmler had given prisoner doctors and skilled medical workers certain privileges because they were vital to dealing with the typhus epidemic raging through the camps. "Now, have these men stand down, lieutenant! That's an order! Have them stand down!"

Radek glared at him, bristling with anger.

"I gave you a direct order, Lieutenant! Have these men stand down! I'm warning you. If you don't, I will."

Radek stood his ground, continuing to stonewall.

"Enough!" Max called-out to the SS guards. "That's enough! Sergeant?! Sergeant, stand down!" He grabbed the back of the man's collar and yanked him aside, then pushed his way between the other guards who were pummeling the cowering prisoners.

The prisoner crouched in their midst had lost hold of his suitcase, and had been protecting his head with his arms and hands. Sensing the onslaught had subsided, he lowered them, slowly, emitting a frightened whimper at the sight of the black-cloaked SS officer looming over him, the hollow eye sockets of the silver skull on his cap staring at him spookily.

Max had glimpsed the man from a distance; but, now, staring at his terrified face, Max's eyes flickered with recognition. It vaguely matched one in his memory; but the damage and pain that had been inflicted on it made the past and the present almost impossible to resolve. Max couldn't process the discord at first; then refused to process it, unwilling to accept the heartbreaking truth that he so desperately wanted to deny: He had barely recognized his closest friend; and, now, almost blurted out, Jake! But he caught himself, staggered by the fact that in a matter of months Jake Epstein had been transformed from a robust man in his early twenties with a zest for life and the practice of medicine into a cowering, sickly human being with a shaved head and a swollen face covered with purple bruises.

Jake was staring at Max with uncertainty, relief and hope. Max sensed he was on the verge of saying or doing something that would reveal their friendship which could be catastrophic if overheard by Radek. Max locked his eyes onto Jake's with penetrating intensity and used several imperceptible shakes of his head to drive the message home. "What's your name, doctor?" he asked sharply, fighting to keep his voice from breaking. "Your name, doctor. I asked you your name."

"Epstein," Jake responded weakly, seeming confused by Max's belligerent indifference. "Doctor Jacob Epstein."

"Where did you study medicine?"

"The University of Munich…"

"As did I. Why don't I remember you?"

"I'm…I'm in my last semester," Jake whispered. "I mean, I was…"

"Ah, that explains it. Captain Maximilian Kleist, SS," Max said, as if introducing himself. He shook Jake's hand, squeezing it in a veiled signal, and prompted, "I understand you and your team were sent here to help deal with the typhus epidemic."

Jake's eyes flickered in confusion.

Max's widened, pleading with him to follow his lead. "It's rampant among the prisoners," he went on, sensing Radek's bristling presence behind him. "Our prisoner doctors have been overwhelmed by it."

To Max's relief, Jake's expression brightened with insight. He seemed to be catching on. "Yes, yes I'm…I'm sure they are," he said, straightening and sounding more engaged. "As I was explaining, we were sent here from the Hygienic Institute at Auschwitz to…to assist them. Epidemiology is our specialty."

"Welcome to Dachau, doctor," Max said, concealing his relief. "You'll have your hands full."

"We'll do our best, Captain…"

"Good. Follow the rules; carry out your duties with competence; and you'll be treated humanely." Max turned to Radek who had been scowling throughout the exchange. "Finish up here, lieutenant," he commanded. "I'm taking these people to the prisoner hospital."

"Why?" Radek challenged with a disapproving sneer.

"So they can be fed, clothed and billeted," Max replied as Jake and his group collected themselves and their belongings.

"That doesn't answer my question, captain."

"I told you, they're here to deal with the typhus epidemic, lieutenant. With luck, they might just save our lives—even yours."

"I don't need Jewish swine to save my life," Radek replied, reacting with a smug grin to the distant crack of a pistol shot that was followed by another and then another as the executions commenced. "I'll be sure the commandant hears of this when I make my report."

"…when I make my report, Sir!" Max corrected as the pistol shots continued in the distance. "I've no doubt it will be as well-received as your last one! When I make mine, I'll be sure to mention your failure to carry out a direct order from a superior officer; and that you ordered the execution of an entire medical team sent here to fight typhus!" Max whirled on a heel, then led Jake and his team from the platform, collecting Dr. Hannah Friedman en route to the entrance gates. Jake trudged along next to him, lugging his suitcase. Shaken by his friend's plight, Max was aching to relieve him of the burden, to carry the suitcase—his suitcase—but didn't dare. "You're safe now, Jake," he whispered.

Jake allowed himself a thin smile, then eyeing the long line of prisoners they were passing, said, sadly, "And they're all going to die…"

Max swallowed hard and nodded, then, through clenched teeth, asked, "What happened?"

"We were at the Mittenwald station," Jake replied in a tense whisper. "I got caught. Eva got away."

"She made it onto the train?"

"I'm not sure. Steig and his thugs went after her; but they came back empty-handed. With luck she's in Venice with her family. I did my best to—"

"Silence! No talking!" Max interrupted with a threatening snap of his riding crop as they approached the entrance gates where two SS guards were posted. Both heel-clicked to attention and greeted Max with Nazi salutes. One of them, his voice ringing with die-hard zeal, exclaimed, "Heil Hitler!"

"Heil Hitler," Max responded smartly, returning the salute. He had purposely maintained his military bearing to keep up the charade; but his Nazi-like demeanor sent a chilling shiver through Jake who found it unnerving in his fragile state.

CHAPTER THIRTY-THREE

Air France 001 from Paris arrived at JFK at 11:25 a.m. Mark Gunther had spent the flight in first-class bliss being feted with champagne and fine cuisine. He really needed a little TLC after this trip. His wife had returned midweek as planned; but the problems with Gunther Global's European operation had forced him to extend his stay. After clearing customs, he handed his bags to a driver who led the way to a Lincoln town car. Gunther settled in the back seat and thumbed a number on his cell phone labeled: Home. It was the first, but not the most pressing, call he would make.

While Gunther was touching base with his family, golden sunlight was streaming through the windows of Bart Tannen's Sag Harbor beach house on this perfect Sunday morning. Celine had spent it giving her whisk and copper mixing bowl a workout; and he was serving-up her fluffy omelets/Pipérade to guests gathered around the table on the screened-in porch.

"So, Sergei…" Tannen said, addressing a grungy-looking fellow who was sipping a mimosa with one hand and toying with the keys to a Ferrari with the other, "…though Celine claims her omelets collapse whenever I talk shop over brunch, I'd be remiss if I didn't give you a brief overview of GG's services…"

"Is why I raise subject in first place," Sergei said, with an amused smile.

"A brief overview," Celine protested with a wink. It happened to coincide with the ring of Tannen's cell phone which prompted her to pout and throw up her hands in the endearing way only French women can.

"Really brief," Tannen quipped when he saw Gunther's name on the screen.

"Sorry, I have to take this. Hey, welcome home," he exclaimed, slipping out the screen door and down a few steps to the beach where gentle waves were lapping at the shoreline. "I hear you were getting beat up pretty good over there."

"Bloodied," Gunther grunted. "We have to talk. Me, you and that quirky little genius of yours who cooked up the Steinbach campaign."

Tannen's brows arched with suspicion. "Sounds like you heard…"

"Damn right I did."

"Well, before we get into that…" Tannen said in a tone that promised something more interesting. "One of Celine's friends shows up for brunch with this guy she's been bedding. Turns out he's Snorkle's C.E.O."

"Snorkle…" Gunther echoed, his eyes widening at the mention of the cutting-edge software company. "Sergei…Sergei Konkoff."

"The one and only. We're on our first round of mimosas when he lets on he's unhappy with his agency, all but begging me to pitch him—which I was on the verge of doing when you called."

"Good. We need all the business we can get; but it's the bird in the hand I'm worried about, now."

"Okay, got it. Give me a few minutes to track Stacey down and I'll conference you in. What about Sol? Should I—"

"No. Just the Three Musketeers," Gunther replied as the Town Car joined the stream of traffic heading north beneath the elevated Airtrain tracks. "I know this is going to be a pain in the ass," Gunther went on, "but I need to go mano-a-mano with you two on this."

"No problem," Tannen said, pleased he wouldn't have to deal with it, now. "We'll do it first thing."

"Not gonna happen. My schedule's jammed: bean-counters, money-lenders and legal-eagles back to back the entire week," Gunther replied in the tone he used when pulling rank. "I'm on the Van Wyck heading into the city. I'll be at the office all afternoon getting caught up. Get your asses over there as soon as you can."

Tannen sent an angry kick into a nearby dune, filling the air with sand, then returned to the house and gave Celine the bad news. A short time later, having made an appointment to pitch Sergei later in the week, he was behind the wheel of his Carrera, heading west on Route 27. The two-lane blacktop that snaked through the Hamptons to the Long Island Expressway was notorious for long stretches of gridlock, especially on summer weekends.

On the Upper West Side, Stacey was on her building's roof deck stretched-out in a bikini across the canvas sling of her newly acquired beach chair, reading the *Sunday Times*. A daily on-line scanner, she preferred the feel of newsprint on weekends, and had *The Book Review* spread across her thighs. The critique of *A Happy Marriage*, a novel by Rafael Yglesias, revealed it to be about a man who comes to appreciate his thirty-year marriage in the face of his wife's terminal illness—not the witty, incisive primer, a la Malcolm Gladwell, Stacey had imagined; and she easily set it aside when her cell phone rang, identifying Tannen as the caller.

Several hours later, having pulled a pair of jeans and a tank top over her bikini, she was camped out in GG's reception area, scanning Facebook pages on her Blackberry to catch-up with what had been going on in the lives of friends and classmates scattered about the country. The office was weekend-quiet save for the distant drone of a vacuum cleaner when Tannen emerged from the elevator, looking frazzled. "Hi, I'm real sorry about this."

"Hey, that's why we get the big bucks," Stacey said with a sarcastic grin as she followed him down the corridor toward Gunther's office.

"Twenty-seven was jammed," Tannen said, sounding exasperated as they entered the sun-washed interior with its bronze-tinted windows and Provence decor. "If the LIE wasn't moving I'd still be in Suffolk County."

Gunther looked up from the spreadsheet he'd been running and, dispensing with his legendary equanimity, erupted with outrage. "When were you planning to tell me about this?! You suspect the key player in a major campaign may be a Nazi war criminal! You know a *Times* reporter is all over it because he dug up the dirt in the first place! You had a meeting at the Wiesenthal Center! And I have to hear about it from my wife! Over the phone! In Paris! In the middle of a fucking meeting!"

"It's…it's complicated," Tannen replied, visibly rattled. "Knowing what you were up against over there, I didn't want to get into it. Especially on the phone."

"So you let Grace do it for you?!"

"Come on, you know better than that," Tannen protested, dropping onto one of the sunflower-patterned sofas. "It could be nothing. It didn't make sense getting you involved until we're sure one way or the other. We're waiting on Wiesenthal, now."

"Tell me about it," Gunther snapped. "Grace touched base with Ellen Rother on Friday afternoon to review her Summer schedule, and—"

"—and Ellen just happened to mention our meeting and the rest is history," Tannen surmised, finishing it.

"She also happened to mention the name Kleist," Gunther continued, leaving his desk. "Which set a little bell in Grace's belfry to ringing. Turns out the name Gisela Kleist appears in the provenance files of some of the Kandinskys she's been busting her ass to borrow. FYI, Frau Kleist was a successful art dealer in Munich in the decades between the wars. Her husband was a wealthy industrialist who produced armor-plating for Nazi tanks. Their son was a doctor in the SS!"

"We know," Tannen said, sounding stung. "But as Ellen explained, not every German was a Nazi. Not every Nazi was a war criminal. And not every Nazi doctor was—"

"The Kleists sure as hell sound like Nazis to me!"

"If they were, according to Dr. Epstein, they were Nazis who saved his life."

"That's assuming he's Dr. Epstein! Which, I hear, is up for grabs! Furthermore, I have no recollection of him saying anything about the Kleists saving his life!"

"You weren't there," Tannen fired back, retaking some ground. "You and Grace had already left with Ellen."

"Whatever. This isn't only a nightmare for us and the client! It's become one for Grace as well!"

Tannen looked confused. "Why? I don't get it."

"During the war, these Nazi bastards confiscated tens of thousands of artworks. Now, thanks to GG, how the Kandinskys that passed through Gisela Kleist's hands were acquired by their sellers is in dispute, endangering their availability! Get it now?!"

Tannen's shoulders sagged with remorse.

Stacey was sitting on the floor against Gunther's desk, keeping a low profile. She got to her feet, and said, "I don't mean to speak out of turn, Mr. Gunther, but we knew this could be dicey from the get-go; from the moment you pointed out the suitcase was from the Holocaust. On the other hand—"

"Yeah, I should've slammed the door on it when I had the chance! This is a fucking catastrophe!"

Stacey stiffened, her sunburned cheeks smarting from Gunther's retort. "As copywriter on this account," she said, undaunted, "I respectfully suggest we revise that to read: This…might turn out to be…a fucking catastrophe. I mean, it's still possible our suspicions are unfounded; that we are mistaken, and—"

"Anything's possible! But we can't wait for the shit to hit the fan before ducking! GG can't afford a P/R disaster let alone a Holocaust scandal! Neither can the client!" Gunther took a moment to settle, then shifted his look to Tannen and indicated his monitor. "No matter how I run the numbers, I'm staring at a negative balance sheet. European revenues are way off. The credit crunch has hit overseas clients even harder than domestic ones. Everyone's hoarding cash. Which means advertising budgets are being slashed; which means GG's financial health's in jeopardy. My father busted his ass to build this company. He kept it afloat in bad times, and got rich when they were good. It's not going south on my watch."

Tannen nodded, digesting it. 'The thrill of victory. The agony of defeat'. Nobody wins 'em all…"

"Stanley Ralph Ross, ABC, Wide World of Sports, 1971," Gunther fired back, referring to the advertising executive who wrote the legendary slogan that had since become a cliché. "One of the best. He and Dad went way back." He settled on the opposite sofa with a reflective sigh. "It was the potential for victory that kept the old man going. I don't see that here. We're looking at a lose-lose scenario. On one side, if Dr. Epstein, or whoever the hell he is, was on the ramp, he's a war criminal in my book, and I want the son-of-a-bitch brought to justice. On the other, from a purely business POV, I want to wake up tomorrow and find out this was all a bad dream."

"What do you want us to do?" Tannen asked.

"Damage control," Gunther replied, going on to tick off the points on his fingers. "Minimize the impact. Work out a plan of action. Do whatever it takes to save our ass. Have you run it past P/R yet?"

"Before running it past you?" Tannen replied. "Not a chance. If push comes to shove, we figure they can spin it so GG and the client get the credit for unmasking a Nazi war criminal."

"Great," Gunther groaned. He laughed at a thought, then giving his sarcasm full rein said, "We could always change the kick-off line to: Not Surviving Harrowing Journeys. We'd be the first agency to build a campaign on endorsements from a family of rich Nazis whose son is a war criminal."

Tannen couldn't help but laugh. "Even Stace would hit the wall writing that copy…"

"Well, now that you mention it—" Stacey said, her eyes coming alive with mischief, "—the Kleist Kandinsky Collection has a sort of catchy rhythm to it. We could spell it KKK and do an interlocking logo…you know, kinda like a swastika?"

Gunther and Tannen stiffened for an instant; then, in obvious need of a light moment, laughed more heartily than Stacey expected.

"Is Sol up to speed on this?" Gunther asked, after they had settled.

Tannen nodded. "He's in the same boat. Itching to bring one of these monsters to justice, but worried the war criminal thing'll kill business. Not to mention he's sitting on a pile of inventory and is terrified of postponing the launch. Makes sense to me."

"Not to me," Gunther snapped. "God help us if it turns out Dr. Epstein's a Nazi monster, and we've already launched. No. No way. We're postponing."

Tannen shot an apprehensive glance at Stacey. "Well, in the spirit of full disclosure, I encouraged Sol to launch, now; to get ahead of the story, build sales momentum, and, if it goes our way, the sky's the limit."

"Not a chance," Gunther declared. "There was a time when that strategy'd fly. Not anymore. I came away from this trip with two words burned into my brain: Risk Management. It's the new global mantra. Nope. Sol'll just have to live with it. No launch until we get the word on Dr. Epstein." He punctuated it with a snap of his head, then glanced to his watch and groaned, propelling himself from the sofa.

"Something I said?" Tannen joked.

"Sunday dinner with Grace and the kids," Gunther replied, picking up his briefcase and heading for the door. "I was late an hour ago. Let me know the instant you hear from Ellen Rother."

Stacey and Tannen stared after him, and then at each other for a long moment.

"Now what?" Stacey prompted.

"Well, if Gunther's right, if it's about to hit the fan…" Tannen said with an engaging grin. "…then, according to your favorite author, we're at a tipping point, no?"

Stacey waggled a hand. "More like a piece'a cake point," she said, a little Texas creeping into her voice. "I mean, from where I'm sittin', we're just gonna have to find a way to have it and eat it too."

Tannen raised a brow in tribute. "The only way to do that is to prove that Dr. Jacob Epstein is really Dr. Jacob Epstein; that all the talk of him being an imposter and a war criminal is bogus."

"You left out defeat terrorism, fix the economy and solve the Middle East crisis," Stacey cracked with an impish grin. "I don't know, boss. I'm afraid this one's a little above my pay grade."

"Mine too."

"Which leaves us with?"

"Ellen Rother…if we're lucky." Tannen paused, contemplating the alternative. "And your boyfriend if we're not."

"I'm not sure he's my boyfriend anymore."

"Hey, it's his loss, kid," Tannen said, giving her spiky hair a comforting pat. "Ever been to the Four Seasons?" he wondered. The legendary. Philip Johnson-designed restaurant on the building's ground floor had an austere, sophisticated interior. Bead chain curtains, hanging in graceful catenaries, rose to the ceiling in shimmering waves across towering windows tinted the color of Seagram's whiskey. This was where the city's power elite had been meeting for more than five decades; where Gunther Global's founder had held court at a corner table feting clients with an endless parade of Beefeater mists. The martini of its day, it was so named because the bartender used a perfume atomizer to spray vermouth into the air above the glass, creating a mist which settled atop the surface of the ice cold gin.

"Cocktails at the bar once," Stacey said in response to Tannen's query.

"Let's make it twice," Tannen said, cheerily, as he got to his feet and led the way from the office.

"I can't afford it."

"Me neither. Gunther's buying. Maybe we'll have dinner too."

"Like this?" Stacy said, indicating her worn jeans and skimpy tank top as she hurried after him.

"Sure. Put on your sunglasses and act like you own the place. They'll think you're a rock star."

CHAPTER THIRTY-FOUR

They were inside Dachau's prison compound now. Separated from the surrounding SS military installation by the high walls, electrified fences, and broad water-filled moats; their every step monitored by vigilant SS guards in the towers with their machineguns.

"Where are we going?" Jake asked wearily as he, Dr. Hannah Friedman and their entourage of technicians and nurses, carrying their suitcases and physician's bags, followed Max down the Lagerstrasse. They were all shivering from the cold and squinting at the sun that was still painfully blinding after their long journey in the darkened railroad car. "We haven't eaten in days, Max. We need food and water…"

"And you'll have them," Max said with the clinical detachment that had become habit. "The typhus is rampant. Delousing comes first." He led the way to a cluster of buildings in the northwest corner of the compound, and opened the door to a vast, windowless hall, where a sign proclaimed: Wirtschaftsgebaude.

The group stiffened in horror at the sight of a communal shower. It was divided into Men's and Women's sections, and could accommodate hundreds. White tile covered the floor and walls. Perfectly aligned shower heads ran to infinity. Frightened looks darted among Jake, Hannah and the others. They had heard of the gas chambers disguised as showers; of how the SS tricked Jews being 'relocated to work camps', to go calmly to their deaths; of how, after being promised soap, towels and hot showers, they were gassed, instead.

"Don't go in there!" Hannah exclaimed with alarm.

"What is this, Max?! What're you doing?!" Jake demanded, his voice trembling at this cruel betrayal.

Max looked puzzled. Having just saved them from Radek's death sentence, he couldn't imagine they would think he was about to carry out his own; and it took a moment for it to dawn on him. "No, no, oh my God, no!" he exclaimed, on realizing they were about to panic and bolt. "No, no wait! Wait, don't run! You'll be shot. Don't. Please, it's okay," he went on, shifting to Yiddish which had become the lingua franca among prisoners, and which he hoped would gain their trust. "It's safe. I promise you," he added, exhorting them to follow as he strode inside, turning on one of the shower spigots and then another and another, first on the men's side, then the women's.

The sight of water gushing from showerheads, of neatly stacked bars of soap and folded towels, of Max inside the shower hall, and his fluent Yiddish, proved reassuring. When Jake, Hannah and their group finally joined him, Max explained that years ago, when only political prisoners were incarcerated at Dachau, inmates were allowed one shower every two weeks. Now, the mass internment of Jews and other groups, and large number of prisoners transferred from camps about to be liberated had increased the population from five thousand to nearly thirty thousand. The unimaginable overcrowding had put an end to even the pretense of hygiene, causing the typhus epidemic. Though delousing had once been routine for all prisoners, the system had broken down and few, if any, were treated. Since Jake and his group had come from Auschwitz, where the disease was also rampant, and would be working with infected inmates at Dachau, Max arranged the delousing for their own safety.

While Jake and the others scrubbed head to toe with antiseptic solutions and disinfectant soap, luxuriating in, what for them was, a rare moment of normalcy, Max had their clothing and belongings treated in an adjacent facility. Germany had no DDT, let alone a vaccine to protect its citizens, and Zyklon-B—the lethal gas used for mass exterminations, was also used on personal items to kill typhus bacteria and the lice that carried it.

After a meal of moldy bread and broth with bits of herring and boiled potato at the prison kitchen—a feast after days of starvation—Max took them to the prison hospital. The Revier was located in the row of housing blocks east of the Lagerstrasse. As Radek had explained, due to the typhus epidemic that was killing hundreds of prisoners a day, the hospital had been expanded, and now occupied Blocks 1 through 15. They were linked by the long, exterior corridor that had been under construction the day of Max's orientation tour.

In the main typhus ward, members of the medical staff were meeting in a windowless administration room as they did at every shift change. Prisoner doctors and nurses going off-duty were briefing those coming on when they heard the clack of jackboots in the corridor. Seated around a crude wooden table, they all stiffened with apprehension as Max came through the door in his black greatcoat and cap with its silver death's head. They couldn't recall the last time a member of the SS—other than Dr. Bruckmann who they referred to as Dr. B—had visited the Revier. Even the guards avoided it out of fear of contracting typhus. Indeed, the camp's Prisoner Committee held their meetings here, in this very room, because it was safe from SS oversight.

Dr. Ezra Cohen, the prisoner doctor in charge of the hospital sat at the head of the table beneath a large poster that proclaimed: Rauchen Verboten. The Führer abhorred smoking, and signs prohibiting it were displayed everywhere. "Have you a death wish captain? Or have you and your Kommando come here in some official capacity?" Cohen asked, making the obvious assumption about the prisoners who had accompanied Max.

"No, I'm a doctor, like you," Max replied, in Yiddish, which seemed to have the same effect on Cohen as it had on Jake's group. "They're here to help you. As am I," he explained and, in an oblique reference to Dr. Bruckmann, added, "along with another SS physician who seems equally committed to his oath as a doctor."

Cohen sat up straighter, taking his measure of Max. "We heard medical personnel from other camps were being sent here to help deal with this—this nightmare. Was that the case with these people?"

"No it wasn't," Jake interjected in a low voice, smiling at what he was about to say. "But thanks to Captain Kleist, it is, now."

"Good. We need all the help we can get," Cohen said, shifting his look to Max. "With all due respect, I haven't been able to bring myself to thank an SS officer for anything, not even Dr. B. whom I believe you referred to earlier."

Max nodded. "I understand."

"So do I," Jake said, his eyes finding Cohen's. "But this SS officer saved our lives. He's my best friend and medical school colleague," Jake added, going on to explain how he, Max and Eva had been working together at the University; and how Max and his family risked their lives to save them from being arrested by Major Steig. "As you can see, Max isn't a typical Nazi doctor."

"No, I guess he isn't," Cohen conceded, his brows arching curiously. "And he just happened to be on the ramp this morning when you arrived from Auschwitz?"

"That's right; and with some quick thinking he kept us from being executed. It was pure luck."

"For all of us," Cohen said, sounding energized. "Get them settled, captain, and we'll put them to work." He stood, then noticed the gash Radek had inflicted on Jake's head. "Better take care of that. Around here, an open wound can be as lethal as a bullet."

Unlike other prisoners, doctors were housed in rooms that had been carved out of the open wards. They also served as examining rooms, and were where the few medical supplies allotted to the prison hospital were kept. The single bed, like the triple-decked ones in housing and hospital blocks, had a simple straw mattress on wooden slats. A small table and chair stood in a corner. There was a sink with a mirrored cabinet above it; but no closet or dresser. A bare bulb hung from the ceiling.

Jake looked about, then set his suitcase on the floor and slid it beneath the bunk. When he got to his feet, he saw Max standing in the doorway, and began to weep. "God Max…" Jake muttered, barely able to speak. "I can't believe I'm standing here…with …with you…"

Max closed the door and embraced him. He could feel Jake's ribs through the coarse denim of his uniform. It was like hugging a sack of barrel staves. The dam of military discipline crumbled on seeing what had become of his friend. "I'm so sorry," Max said, his eyes welling with emotion. "I'm so, so sorry."

"Sorry for what?"

"For all that's happened to you. For the degrading shower, the disgusting food, this pathetic room; but it's all there is, Jake. I just want to keep you alive until the war is over. You're going to get through this. I promise."

Jake pulled a sleeve over his watery eyes. "I want to believe that, Max; but after all I've seen…"

Max grasped Jake's shoulders and stared into his eyes. "You can't give up, now, Jake. You can't."

Jake nodded unconvincingly, then stiffened, struck by the unfathomable absurdity of hugging someone in an SS uniform. In the past, he had compartmentalized the black tunic, jodhpurs, jackboots, and death's head in one box; and had put his friend and fellow physician who, with his family, was helping Jews and others escape the Nazis in another; but after all Jake had endured, Max's ringing 'Heil Hitler!' and Nazi salute at the gate; his clinical detachment as they crossed the grounds; and his initial insensitivity at the shower hall were breaking down the wall between the compartments. Had Max become one of them? Jake wondered. One of the monsters?! So many decent men had. "What are you doing here Max?" he asked in a distraught wail. "How did you end up in this place?"

"Steig," Max replied grimly. "Disciplinary action. My choice was report for duty or sign my family's death warrant. He'll have them in front of a firing squad if he can prove what he suspects."

"I know. He tried to 'convince' me to sign a statement implicating them."

Max gasped. "Please tell me you didn't…"

"My choice was my freedom for my signature."

Max sighed with relief and remorse. "I'm sorry, Jake. I should've known better than to ask."

Jake shrugged and absolved him with a weary smile.

Max returned it, then pointed to Jake's chest where the top buttons of his uniform were undone, revealing a single key that hung from a string around his neck and a few reddened sores. "What are those? I spotted them when you were showering."

"Nazi love pats," Jake replied with a sarcastic smirk, fastening the buttons as he sat on the bed to gather his strength. "I bruise easily."

Max looked unconvinced. "Okay, we'll keep an eye on them," he said, going on to examine the laceration on Jake's head. He was at the medical supply cabinet, fetching some disinfectant and gauze pads when Dr. Hannah Friedman knocked and slipped into the room. "Why don't I do that?" Hannah offered, taking them from Max.

After cleansing the oozing wound, she covered it with a bandage which she affixed with strips of adhesive tape; then, with heartfelt concern, said, "You look so exhausted, Jake. You should get some rest."

"Rest? We have work to do, Hannah," he protested, getting to his feet. "People are sick and dying."

"Yes, and they'll still be sick and dying tonight when you're on duty. I prevailed on Dr. Cohen to assign you to a later shift. Now, get some sleep."

Jake decided the better of arguing and flopped back onto the bed. Hannah leaned over and tucked a ragged blanket around him, lingering for a moment as they exchanged a tender kiss, a lover's kiss; then she joined Max who had drifted into the corridor.

"I've got to get back to the ramp," Max said as Hannah closed the door and they began walking. "I'll check back later."

"Good, Jake will be pleased. By the way, when we were eating, I was teasing him that your Yiddish is better than his. Did you really have a Jewish nanny?"

"Yes, and I still do," Max replied, making her laugh. "Tovah's been with us forever. She runs the household, now. She's like a member of the family."

They had reached the vestibule at the end of the corridor. The exit door was on one side, the door to the now empty meeting room on the other. "Thank you for everything you've done," Hannah said. "Especially for Jake. He's a fine doctor and the sweetest man."

Max nodded emphatically. "How did you manage to find each other in a hellhole like Auschwitz?"

"Happenstance. We were both assigned to work at the Hygienic Institute. A horrible place where horrible things are done to people. We helped each other through it, and became close friends."

"It seemed like more than that back there."

"It is...sometimes," Hannah said with a demure smile. "This is a little awkward, but if you have a moment," she said, leading the way into the meeting room. "I care for Jake, deeply; but, at times, his heart seems elsewhere. He often speaks of a classmate. Eva, the one who was with him when he was arrested? It's almost as if he's smitten with her."

"Not surprising," Max said, keeping the details to himself. "If I were on the run with an attractive and intelligent woman like Eva, I'd be smitten too. Knowing Jake, the more taken he seems with her, the more he's falling in love with you."

"Thanks. I'll keep that in mind if we have the good fortune to survive."

"You will. The war is lost. I'm sure the camp will be liberated, soon."

Hannah's expression darkened. "I just hope Jake is alive to see it."

"What makes you say that?"

"He's developing splotchy sores."

"Yes, I saw them. He claims they're bruises." Max paused and held Hannah's look. "You're concerned it's typhus, aren't you?"

Hannah pursed her lips and nodded.

"So am I. An antibiotic could help."

"Antibiotics? For prisoners?" Hannah prompted with a sarcastic toss of her head. "They're so scarce you probably couldn't even get some for yourself."

"That won't stop me from trying."

"You'll be wasting your time," Hannah said with a despondent sigh. "They'll kill us all before they'll let us be liberated. Every prisoner who dies of typhus is one less they have to execute. They didn't even bother taking names or numbers when we got here." She pushed up her sleeve revealing the number tattooed on her forearm. "No one knows we're here. We're just going to vanish off the face of the earth."

"No you're not," Max said, struck by an idea. "I know you're here. And I'll make an indelible record of it…you, Jake and the others; but I can't do it now."

"The sooner the better," Hannah said grimly.

"Tonight, here, after roll-call and before the shift change meeting."

Roll-call, a twice daily routine, required all prisoners to assemble in the Appelplatz, a large open area south of the barracks, regardless of the weather or the state of their health. Seriously ill prisoners often died where they stood while the lengthy roll was taken. Those too sick to respond were removed from the barracks and executed.

That evening, Jake, Hannah and the others gathered as instructed; but Max never showed up. Almost a week had passed before he finally reappeared. He looked bleary-eyed and gaunt as if he had lost weight. He apologized profusely for the delay and explained: There had been a massive influx of prisoners transferred from other camps. Emaciated, sick and exhausted, they had been arriving by train and on foot day and night by the thousands. He had been doing back-to-back tours with barely a few hours sleep between them; and, as Hannah had predicted he had no luck acquiring antibiotics for Jake; but he had left a prescription for penicillin in his own name at the SS hospital pharmacy, and had gotten Kruger to do the same. Unfortunately, even though the prescriptions had been written by SS doctors, the Nazi obsession for record-keeping and strict adherence to procedures meant it would take days, if not longer, for them to be filled—assuming penicillin was available.

"We've got work to do," Max said, getting down to business as the hour for the shift-change meeting neared. He took his Leica from a pocket, then had Jake roll up his sleeve, and sit at the table, placing his forearm on it. Steadying the camera on the rough surface, Max crouched to the eyepiece, centered Jake's image in the rangefinder and focused on his tattooed ID number in the foreground. The bare bulb overhead provided poor illumination, forcing Max to use a slow shutter speed and wide open aperture. The latter produced a shallow depth of field which, though not visible in the rangefinder, threw everything that wasn't in the same plane as the tattooed numerals, including the subject's features, completely out of focus. Max took several shots; then, as one of the nurses took Jake's place at the table, Max looked about, and asked, "Where's Hannah?"

"Probably still on rounds," Jake replied, seeming more robust and energetic than when he arrived a week ago. "We have many patients in crisis. I'll get her."

About twenty minutes later, Max had just finished photographing the remaining members of the group when Jake returned without Hannah. "I can't find her," he said, riven with anxiety. "She's not anywhere in the Revier. Where the hell could she be?"

"I've no idea, but I'll find her," Max said, taking command. He was crossing to the door when Captain Kruger came hurrying down the corridor into the room.

"There you are, Max," Kruger gasped, sounding out of breath. "Dr. Bruckmann thought you might be here."

"Why? What's going on? What's wrong?"

"We were in the Officer's Club. I overheard Radek sending a couple of his goons to the Revier to fetch Hannah. I thought you'd want to know."

Max looked alarmed. "Fetch her to where?"

"He didn't say."

Dr. Cohen and some members of the staff had begun assembling for the upcoming shift-change meeting. One of the nurses, who was about to go off-duty, overheard them and stuck her head in the door. "I was there when the SS men came. They told Dr. Friedman there was an emergency in Block Thirty-one."

Jake looked puzzled. "Block thirty-one? That's not part of the hospital, is it?"

"No, it's what we call the Puff," the nurse replied, using camp slang.

"The sonderbau," Dr. Cohen said, knowing the word, which meant 'special building,' was nomenclature the prudish Himmler had assigned to the SS and prisoner brothels upon approving them. "But the prisoner brothel would come to us in an emergency. What's Radek got to do with it? Why would he want her brought there?"

"Because he's obsessed with Jewish women," Max said, his worst fears confirmed.

"We've been wondering where he takes them," Kruger said with disgust. "We knew, he'd be a fool to use his quarters or the SS brothel. Too easy to get caught."

"Nazi bastard!" Jake exclaimed, lunging past Max. He darted between Dr. Cohen and the nurse in the doorway, and began running down the long corridor.

"Jake?! Wait!" Max shouted, going after him. "Wait! I'll take care of it!"

CHAPTER THIRTY-FIVE

Moments ago, Ellen Rother typed the name Kleist in a search window on yadvashem.org, the website of Israel's memorial to Jewish Victims of the Holocaust. It was among the databases she had been searching and government agencies she had contacted to determine if Dr. Maximilian Kleist SS might be a Nazi war criminal hiding out as a Holocaust survivor in the guise of Dr. Jacob Epstein. Now, she was staring in astonishment at the data on her screen. It was the one piece of information—of all she had gathered—that had really gotten her attention; and, though the German Military Archives had not yet responded, she decided to meet with Tannen, Stacey and Steinbach whom she knew were anxious to get the situation resolved. They dropped everything and assembled in her office that same afternoon. Tannen went so far as to reschedule the pitch meeting with Sergei Konkoff, Snorkle's CEO. Again.

Ellen had organized the information in a tabbed binder. She knew it would raise as many questions as it answered, and wanted to get it out of the way before dealing with the Yad Vashem data. "Let's start with Jewish-Gen…" Ellen began, using shorthand for Manhattan's Museum of Jewish Heritage. "They've got more than fourteen million Holocaust records on their website…a hundred and fifty thousand from Dachau. They include inmate registers dating to the camp's opening in 1933, and rosters of the SS personnel who staffed it. Captain Maximilian Kleist, M.D. Waffen-SS reported for duty there on Monday, January 9, 1945."

"Dachau?" Stacey echoed with a puzzled frown. "But Dr. Epstein wasn't at Dachau. He was at Auschwitz."

"Yeah," Steinbach chimed-in with a relieved smile. "Both of them being at Auschwitz is the connection."

"And the fact that they weren't blows our problem right out of the water, doesn't it?" Tannen added, brightening. "Not that I'm complaining."

"It does and it doesn't," Ellen cautioned, turning to another section in the binder. "Records found at Auschwitz reveal that Jacob Epstein, prisoner number A198841 was transferred to Dachau on February twenty-fourth of the same year, but there isn't any—"

"That's Dr. Epstein's number. The one tattooed on his arm," Stacey interrupted. "It's also the one in the snapshot with different handwriting."

Ellen nodded evenly. "Right on both counts. Every ID number in the snapshots that were in the suitcase is on the roster of prisoners transferred from Auschwitz with Dr. Epstein."

Steinbach sighed and sagged in disappointment. "So that means Jake and this Nazi Kleist were at Dachau at the same time."

Ellen waggled a hand. "Not necessarily."

"What do you mean by that?" Tannen challenged, his eyes popping with impatience behind his glasses. "They were or they weren't, no?"

"No," Ellen replied, pointedly. "These matters aren't always as clear cut as we'd like. Though Dr. Epstein's name and number are on the transfer roster, there's no record of him ever arriving at Dachau. It was a very chaotic time. Eastern Block camps were being evacuated to keep the prisoners from being liberated. Some trains never arrived at their destinations. Many that did were filled with dead prisoners. Again, from Jewish-Gen—" she flipped back to the first tab. "—Not only wasn't Dr. Epstein listed as having arrived there, neither were all the other prisoners on the Auschwitz transfer roster, including those whose ID numbers were in the snapshots that were in the suitcase."

Tannen groaned in frustration. "I'm confused. If he never got there, why are you telling us there's a good chance he did?"

"Because at the time of the transfer record-keeping at Dachau had ceased. Which—assuming Dr. Epstein actually did get there—supports our theory that the snapshots were taken to make a record."

"At the risk of sounding dumb and dumber," Stacey said, "do we know for a fact there's no record of Jacob Epstein having died there?"

"Not so dumb," Ellen replied. "Prisoner deaths were recorded in separate log books with typical Nazi precision as to the date and time of death right down to the minute; but the last entries were made prior to Dr. Epstein's transfer. One could argue, the man himself is evidence that he didn't die there or anywhere."

Stacey winced. "But...but if there's no proof he ever got to Dachau—or died there—then, it's back to square one."

Steinbach hissed with frustration. "You keep giving us something with one hand and taking it away with the other. We need to know whether our guy is or isn't some Nazi-war-criminal-imposter."

"I know," Ellen said, sounding apologetic. "But as I said, these things aren't always clear cut."

"Why don't we just ask Dr. E," Tannen prompted.

"Ask him what?" Stacey challenged with a facetious smirk. "If he died there?"

"Very funny. No, if he ever got there."

"That only works if Dr. E really is Dr. E, right?" Stacey retorted. "What if he isn't? What if he is this Nazi imposter?"

"Whose side are you on, anyway?" Tannen countered. "I thought you and what's-his-face were over."

"What does that mean?"

"Nothing. Forget I said it."

Stacey took a deep breath and let it out slowly. "You're the guy who said this is too important to take chances, boss. A tipping point. Remember? Now, if—"

"Whoa," Ellen interrupted. "Let's keep our eye on the target: Is Jacob Epstein really Maximilian Kleist? Is he a war criminal masquerading as a Holocaust survivor? Well, his name may have a nice Nazi ring; but all the evidence I've gathered seems to suggest, he isn't."

"Yesss!" Steinbach exclaimed, latching onto it. "Case closed."

"Easy, Sol," Tannen cautioned. "That's just what we want to hear; and that's always dangerous. Stacy's right. We can't risk launching the campaign and have the ugly truth hit the fan after the fact." He shifted his look to Ellen and asked, "What evidence?"

"It's all in here," Ellen replied, referring to the binder. "Maximilian Kleist isn't on the Wiesenthal Center's list of seventy thousand war criminals, or on the one compiled by the European Consortium of Nations, nor does he appear on the United States Department of Justice watch list. I spoke to Eli Rosenbaum at OSI, myself," she went on, referring to the Director of the Office of Special Investigations.

"But the Nazis destroyed many records, right?" Tannen prompted.

Ellen nodded. "Not to mention that vast troves of documents are still scattered in many countries. Much of it poorly indexed or still being processed—which is why the DOJ often acts against Nazis on immigration violations. By the way, there's nothing on Max Kleist in their I.V. files, either."

"But there wouldn't be if he changed his name," Stacey prompted sharply.

"And many Nazis did—along with their appearance. That's why so many war criminals are still on the loose. Of course, many Jews changed their names, too. Some were immigrants who wanted to assimilate; others wanted more traditional Jewish names; a few, like those named on Nazi death warrants, wanted to just...disappear. By the way, records show Dr. Jacob Epstein immigrated with his wife Hannah Friedman on February 19, 1946. Mount Sinai Medical Center sponsored them."

Stacey looked frustrated. "So, the bottom line is, Dr. Max Kleist SS could still be out there somewhere."

Ellen nodded, resignedly. "But there's no evidence he took anyone's identity; is wanted by any nation; or is named by any Holocaust group as a war criminal." She turned to another tab and, playing the card she had been holding, resumed, "All of which is supported by a document I came across on the Yad Vashem website regarding Captain Kleist's family."

"Yad Vashem?" Stacey echoed, sounding puzzled.

"Israel's official Holocaust memorial. It was founded in Jerusalem in the mid-1950s, and has grown into a vast complex comprising archives, a research institute, an educational center, synagogue, library…"

"I've been giving them money for years, too," Steinbach said. "My wife and I were over there when they dedicated the new museum. It was a very special—"

He was interrupted by a knock, "Sorry," a bearded young man, sporting an embroidered yarmulke said as he entered. Ben Hertzberg, Ellen's assistant was a studious fellow with gentle eyes, a degree in Jewish Literature, and an archivist's reverence for things ancient. "Fax from GMA," he said holding up a sheet of paper. "Thought you'd want to see it right away."

"GMA?" Ellen echoed with intrigue. She propelled her tiny frame from the chair and met Ben halfway. Ellen was perusing the fax and drifting back to her desk when her eyes widened at something. "Well, you wanted a clear-cut answer. Now, you have it. According to German Military Archives, Captain Maximilian Kleist, M.D., Waffen-SS was killed in action on April 29, 1945."

Her three visitors stiffened in stunned silence.

"He's dead?" Steinbach finally blurted. "No kidding?"

Ellen nodded and, reading from the fax, said: "Killed in action along with other SS personnel when Dachau was liberated; cause of death multiple gunshot wounds; found in uniform; remains decomposed; military ID and Catholic medal on his person."

"Well, it doesn't get more clear cut than that. Does it?" Tannen enthused, setting his puppy tail to bouncing above his collar.

"Sure as hell doesn't," Steinbach exclaimed, with a little fist pump. "Looks like I'm going to have to double my donation to you guys."

"I have the forms here, somewhere," Ellen said, deadpan, searching beneath papers on her desk.

"I can always drop off a suitcase full of cash," Steinbach joked. "This is fantastic. We're on the verge of scrubbing the launch one minute; and all systems are go the next."

"Yes, sounds like you have lift off," Ellen said with a little smile. "Unless, of course, the name of another Nazi doctor who might be impersonating Dr. Epstein comes to mind."

Steinbach shot a panicked look to Tannen. He cringed and fired a frantic look to Stacey. She shrugged, and said, "No, no, the only thing that comes to mind is the information you found about Captain Kleist's family on that website, Vad..."

"Yad...Yad Vashem..."

Stacey nodded. "I think you said it supported the evidence that he wasn't a war criminal."

Ellen nodded smartly and flipped to a tab in her binder. "In 1995 Maximilian Kleist, his parents Konrad and Gisela Kleist and his sister Anika were posthumously honored by Yad Vashem with the prestigious Righteous Among Nations award. It's been given since the mid-'50s to non-Jews who helped Jews during the Holocaust. The Kleists are among the more than twenty thousand recipients. The citation states: That they were very supportive of White Rose, Red Orchestra and other resistance groups. That they were a devout Catholic family who, at great risk to themselves, sheltered Jews in their home, provided them with false documents, personally transported them to safe houses, and arranged other means of escape."

Steinbach nodded, his eyes moist with emotion. "That's...that's exactly what Jake said happened." He stood and walked to where the photographs of the Nazi war criminals that the Center and its founder had brought to justice were displayed; and stared them down until he had regained his composure. "The Kleists saved Jake's life, and, the lives of many other Jews as well."

"They sure did," Ellen said, equally moved. "And, as you might imagine, the person who nominated them for the award was none other than..." she let it trail off, suggesting they supply the answer.

"Dr. Jacob Epstein," Stacey said rapid fire.

Ellen nodded. "He and his wife Dr. Hannah Friedman Epstein." She closed the binder, suggesting, case closed.

"It doesn't get any better than this," Tannen said a short time later as they left Ellen's office.

"Nope," Stacey chirped. "The story just keeps getting better and better."

"Yeah," Steinbach grunted as they entered the elevator. "Except for our favorite cub reporter. Guess you'll have to give him the bad news, huh?"

"Well," Stacey mused, brightening at a thought. "It's a good news-bad news kind of thing, actually."

"It is?"

"Uh-huh. I mean, the bad news is Adam doesn't have a story about a Nazi war criminal. The good news is he has one about a wealthy and prominent German family who put it all on the line to help Jews survive the Holocaust. I kinda like that one better, anyway."

"Me too," Tannen said with a wily smile. "And, since the suitcase originally belonged to the Kleists, I'm counting on that twisted little mind of yours to work that angle into the campaign."

Stacey swung him a sly, sideways glance and, matching his smile, said, "I knew there was a catch to that dinner at the Four Seasons."

They had exited the elevator and were walking through the building's lobby when Stacey palmed her Blackberry and began scrolling through her emails. She smiled at a message from Adam which read: Breaking news! German Military Archives reports Kleist KIA 4/29/45. Mea culpas in order. Mea maxima culpas! Yes, I was an altar boy! Can I come crawling, later? Will kneel at your feet. Beg for forgiveness. Grovel for sex.

CHAPTER THIRTY-SIX

At about the same time that Jake bolted from the meeting room with Max and Kruger in pursuit, the two SS men were ushering Hannah into the entrance of Block 31, the Prisoner Brothel. A loud, intermittent buzzing was coming from the reception area. Hannah's eyes darted to the desk where the heavily made-up and tattooed Madam sat, wielding a tattoo needle. The intricate, multi-colored images visible on her arms, chest and neck were powerful testimony to her skill. Certain clients paid a premium to see the snake that spiraled up her leg and across her inner thigh, the position of its forked tongue leaving no doubt what she expected of them. Cigarette dangling from her mouth, she was deftly guiding the needle's tip as it danced across the bare shoulder of one of the provocatively attired girls who worked the place.

On the desktop, along with tattooing equipment, a pack of Sturms and a butt-leaden ashtray, was a logbook in which the Madam recorded the name and ID number of each client, and a metal box in which she kept the camp scrip—paper money issued in 1 to 3 Mark denominations —with which they paid her. The staff of professional prostitutes, all Aryans, would service any non-Jewish inmate who could pay the 2 Marks the SS charged per visit. Political dissidents, resistance fighters, former members of the Reichstad, and those with vital skills who were employed in the workshops at the rate of 4 Marks per week made up the clientele. But the breakdown in the camp's administrative systems had kept the workers from being paid regularly, if at all, and business at the brothel had fallen-off sharply.

The Madam set the needle aside, blotting the excess ink from the girl's shoulder as Hannah and her SS escort, one of whom was a sergeant, arrived. "We'll finish this later," she said with a veiled look to the SS men. She had done this many times and Radek paid her well for it. "This way, doctor," she went on, feigning a sense of urgency, as she led Hannah and the SS men down a short corridor to a door with a sign that read: *PROFUNG ZIMMER*. The fully equipped Examining Room was where gynecological tests and procedures were performed on the dozen or so women who worked there. "Hurry! In here!" the Madam exclaimed, opening the door.

Hannah strode through it, clutching her doctor's bag. Neither the madam nor the SS men followed. She came to a sudden stop just inside the room which appeared empty and darkened except for a tall gooseneck lamp on the floor next to an examining table. Its narrow beam imparted an eerie sheen to the table's black leather pad and made the metal stirrups gleam despite their worn plating. Hannah heard the door close behind her, then the decisive clack of the latch. She whirled and turned the knob, frantically, to no avail. "Open this door," she called out, pounding on it with a fist. "There's no one in here. What's going on?"

The Madam slipped her brass key from the lock with a cunning smile. It could open any door in the brothel, and was affixed to a long lanyard that hung around her neck. She went down the corridor in a triumphant stride, leading the two SS men back to the reception area where the young prostitute that the Madam had been tattooing and one of her co-workers were waiting to reward them.

In the Examining Room, Hannah had her back pressed to the door, and was squinting into the sharply angled shadows created by the gooseneck lamp.

"Fraulein Friedman?" a man's voice called out.

The voice which Hannah thought she recognized came from the right and somewhat behind her. She stiffened and turned to see Lieutenant Radek sitting in a shadow-streaked corner with his legs crossed. He had removed his greatcoat and tunic and was wearing boots, jodhpurs, shirt and tie. The tip of a cigarette glowed in the darkness just above the arm of the chair where his wrist draped, casually. He took a deep drag and exhaled, sending a stream of smoke curling toward the ceiling.

"It's Doctor Friedman," Hannah corrected, her voice breaking with anger and trepidation. "I was told there was an emergency, here. What do you want?"

"I want to explore your kosher wetness," Radek replied in a chilling whisper. "Take off your clothes, Hannah, and get on the table. I'm sure you're familiar with the position."

"Don't be ridiculous," Hannah said with a defiant sneer. "You'd be violating the Nuremberg Laws. Unlock this door and let me out of here."

"The Nuremberg Laws prohibit sexual intercourse between Aryans and Jews to insure racial purity," Radek said slyly. He took a final drag of his cigarette which he threw to the floor, crushing it beneath a boot as he stood and came toward her. "I have no intention of impregnating you or catching any of the vile diseases you Jewish whores carry." He eyed her lasciviously and began toying with her hair; then, in a swift and sudden move, he grasped the top of her striped uniform with both hands and ripped it open, exposing her breasts.

Hannah shrieked and slammed a palm into Radek's chest staggering him. She retreated to a corner, clutching her uniform top with one hand and her doctor's bag in the other. A sadistic grin tugged at a corner of Radek's mouth. "Yes, there's something about violent sex, isn't there, Hannah?" he gushed, stimulated by her reaction. "The mere thought of it makes me salivate." He gestured to the examining table and, in an icy whisper added, "See? You even have your own personal Whipping Block."

Hannah cringed, knowing he was referring to the torture rack to which prisoners, singled out for punishment, were strapped and forced to count the lashes aloud while being whipped.

"It's perfect for what I have in mind," Radek went on, his eyes aglow at the prospect. He slipped his riding crop from inside one of his boots and came at her again. Hannah swung the physician's bag at him. It struck the side of his head, raking across his face. One of the metal latches slashed his cheek. Radek yelped and reached to the wound, releasing the riding crop. The sight of his blood-smeared fingers enraged him. "Jewish bitch!" he shouted, backhanding Hannah across the face. The blow sent her spinning into the wall with such force that she slid to the floor and remained there, moaning. Radek retrieved the riding crop, and struck her with it several times, then dragged her to the examining table and lifted her onto it. In a controlled rage, he pulled off her striped bottoms and tossed them aside, placing the riding crop on the table between her thighs before setting her heels in the gleaming stirrups.

Outside, in the frigid darkness, Jake had sprinted the length of the corridor that connected the fifteen blocks of the Revier, and was, now, running on the gravel path between Blocks 15 and 16 on the eastern side of the compound. The narrow alley that separated the three-hundred-foot-long buildings concealed him from the guard towers and their sweeping searchlights. He kept running until he reached the Lagerstrasse that divided the eastern and western rows of barracks. Unlike the alleys, it was ninety feet wide and completely open to surveillance from the guard towers. All Jake had to do to reach Block 31, which housed the brothel, was get across it without being seen. He took a moment to catch his breath and get his bearings, then darted out from between the buildings. A blinding circle of light came sweeping down the middle of the street, driving him back. The crunch of boots on gravel rose behind him as he waited for the searchlight to pass; but he made it across the darkened street well before Max and Kruger, who were in pursuit, could catch up with him.

In the examining room, Radek was standing at the foot of the table on a small platform that enabled patients to climb onto it more easily. In a deranged frenzy he had shed his suspenders and unbuttoned his jodhpurs, letting them fall to the top of his knee-high boots. Now, grasping Hannah's bare hips, he slid her on the black leather surface toward him. She had come out of her stupor, but moaned groggily, pretending to be dazed; then, with a terrifying scream, she lurched upward and attacked, clawing wildly at Radek's face with her fingernails. He screeched in pain, snatched the riding crop from between her legs, and slashed her hard, several times, knocking her back onto the table where she remained, whimpering and barely conscious.

Outside, after crossing the Lagerstrasse, Jake made his way in the darkness to Block 31, next to last in the western row of seventeen barracks. Thanks to the typhus epidemic, SS guards were no longer posted inside the compound, and the entrance was unguarded. Gasping for breath, Jake burst into the brothel's reception area, startling the Madam. He stood there wheezing and looking about frantically, trying to locate Hannah.

"You can't come in here!" the woman screeched, seeing the yellow triangle sewn on the pocket of his uniform.

Jake's eyes were wild with fury. He lunged as she came around the desk, and grabbed a fistful of her hair. "Radek?! Where is he? Where?!"

"Examining room," the frightened Madam replied, hoarsely. "That's where he takes them," she went on, pointing to the corridor.

Jake's eyes darted to the key hanging from her neck. He yanked the lanyard, snapping it, then ran down the corridor. The Madam's eyes were wide with alarm. She hurried down the opposite corridor that was lined with evenly spaced doors in search of the two SS men. She rapped on one sharply, and had just entered the room when Max and Kruger came running into the brothel's reception area.

In the examining room, Radek had Hannah positioned where he wanted her, now: hips pulled down toward the foot of the table, heels firmly in the stirrups, knees bent sharply, pelvis splayed vulnerably. His eyes were fixated with obsessive madness on the lush mound that rose in gentle waves from deep between her thighs and broke across the delicate whiteness of her stomach. Radek drew the tip of a finger along the crimson line that cleaved it; then pursed his lips and slipped it between them with an exuberant smack. He grazed her nipples with his palms, then pinned her shoulders to the table, and prepared to violate her.

"Get off her you bastard!" Jake shouted as he unlocked the door and lunged through it.

All in one motion, Radek whirled and came charging at him. At least, that's what his brain had determined was the most effective course of action; but to Radek's horror and confusion, something entirely different and beyond his control seemed to be happening. Indeed, the unexpected and startling intrusion had caused Radek to lose his bearings—to forget that he was standing on the platform, that his jodhpurs were down around his knees, hobbling him—and when he whirled, instead of charging Jake as planned, Radek pitched headlong off the edge of the platform like a felled tree.

Jake was seized by a massive surge of adrenaline that was fueled by his hatred for the Nazis, for the atrocities they had committed, and for Radek and the monstrous atrocity he was committing, now. He side-stepped and, drawing instinctively on his knowledge of anatomy, drove a fist into his falling adversary's throat. The force of the blow, intensified by Radek's momentum, crushed his larynx and ruptured his windpipe. Simultaneously, Jake grabbed a fistful of his hair and, continuing to use Radek's momentum to advantage, drove him head first into the corner of a steel cabinet. The impact shattered his eye sockets and forehead, driving sharp-edged pieces of bone up into his brain, killing him, instantly.

It was over in a matter of seconds.

Hannah was screaming in horror and crawling off the examining table. She had slid down onto the floor and was retreating to a corner like a wounded animal, when Max and Kruger burst into the room.

"My God," Kruger hissed shaken by the gory scene.

Radek was kneeling on the floor, bent forward at the waist like a praying novitiate. His head had struck the cabinet with such force that the steel corner had remained imbedded deeply in his forehead, leaving his eyes bulging from their sockets, one staring blankly at the front of the cabinet, the other at the side. Blood was flowing down the steel leg to the floor, forming a pool which sent bright red rivulets running in the grout lines between the limestone tiles.

The sight of Hannah cringing half-naked in a fetal position staggered Max and set his mind to reeling with thoughts of Eva: Was she alive?! Safe in Venice?! Or, had she been captured?! And like Hannah, being beaten and raped by deranged thugs?! He removed his greatcoat, and covered Hannah with it; then turned to Jake who was wheezing and staring in shock at Radek's corpse. "Jake? Jake!" Max called out. "Jake, Hannah needs your help!" he went on, almost saying Eva, instead. Jake stared at him blankly for a moment, then his eyes came to life and he hurried to Hannah's side. He was holding her comfortingly when the Madam entered the room followed by the two SS men. Both of them appeared disheveled and were pulling on shirts, buttoning trousers, and fumbling with belt buckles in a frantic effort to get back into uniform.

"Lieutenant? Lieutenant, are you okay?" the Sergeant called out as they came through the door.

"What the hell?!" the other shouted at the sight of Radek's corpse that stopped both of them in their tracks and set the Madam to screaming.

"Silence! Close the door. Now!" Max shouted at the frantic woman, causing her to scurry toward it. "Stand over there!" he ordered, directing the two SS men to the other side of the room. "And stand at attention in the presence of superior officers!" He waited until they had complied then, pacing back and forth in front of them in thought, Max prompted rhetorically, "What happened here, tonight? As I understand it, you were contacted by the Madam because of a medical emergency, involving Lieutenant Radek. You fetched these doctors from the Revier and found him like this on arrival. The doctors examined him, but he was already dead. Am I right so far?"

"Yes, S-S-Sir. Yes, yes you—you are," the sergeant stammered.

"Since you weren't here when this happened, you have no first hand knowledge of what happened," Max went on, like a pedantic schoolmaster. "However, the lieutenant reeked of alcohol, and it was obvious that he was drunk and stumbled head-first into the cabinet. Furthermore, smart SS men that you are, you deduced that all by yourselves because Captain Kruger and I were never here. Do you understand?"

The sergeant nodded. "Sir?" he said, still barely able to speak, "What should we say if...if someone asks what...what the lieutenant was doing here?"

Max raised a brow in tribute, and thought for a moment. "He came here because...because intoxicated and arrogant he didn't want to wait his turn at the SS brothel and...and as a doctor...perhaps with certain proclivities...he preferred to take his pleasures in this room. Do we all have the story straight?"

"Yes, sir," the sergeant replied more strongly.

Max whirled on the Madam. "That goes for you too! One word to the contrary to anyone, anyone, and you'll all be charged with conspiring to break the Nuremberg Laws. Statements signed by two SS captains will be sent directly to Reichsführer Himmler! Have I made myself clear?!" He drove the point home with an angry glare and waited until the Madam had nodded, then asked, "Do you have any scotch or whiskey, here?"

"No, Captain, no it's not allowed," she replied.

Max shifted his look to Kruger. "You think we could get a bottle from the officers club without anyone asking questions?"

"Sure. I buy one every so often to keep in my quarters," Kruger replied, heading for the door. "Be back as soon as I can."

"Now," Max said, returning his attention to the SS men. "It's well after curfew, and I don't want these prisoners shot by the tower guards on their way back to the Revier. So, you will escort Dr. Epstein and Dr. Friedman safely to their quarters. When finished, you will report this—as we discussed—to the Duty Officer as you would any such incident."

"Yes, Sir."

Max turned from the SS men and crossed to Jake and Hannah. He had retrieved Hannah's uniform bottom and helped her into it, and draped Max's greatcoat over her shoulders. Exhausted, emotionally spent, and in pain from the wounds Radek had inflicted, Hannah was leaning against him for support, her head buried in his shoulder. Max wrapped his arms around them and, in trembling Yiddish, whispered, "Comfort her and care for her wounds, Jake; but do it in your quarters, in private. You both know the story. You were summoned here in an emergency and found Radek dead. I know it won't be easy, but try to act as if nothing else happened. Okay?"

Jake nodded, somberly.

Hannah managed to whisper, "Thank you..."

After they had left with their SS escort, Max had the Madam shut down the brothel for the night and confined her to her quarters; then he spent some time checking the examining room for anything that might contradict the cover story he had concocted. Everything seemed to be in order, and he was nodding to himself in satisfaction when he noticed something incongruous about the position of Radek's corpse.

"I've been thinking," Max said when Kruger returned with the bottle of whiskey, "Any doctor responding to this emergency would have checked Radek's life signs and initiated emergency treatment, right?"

"Right..." Kruger replied and, knowing what Max was thinking, added, "...which means they would have moved him off there onto his back."

"Exactly." Max grasped a handful of Radek's hair, and, applying steady upward pressure, began pulling his head free of the cabinet. His flesh and brain matter disengaged from the steel corner with a sickening, slushy thwack. Max continued pulling upward, bending Radek's body at the waist into a kneeling position; then steadying it, he cocked his head back, and nodded to Otto who was holding the bottle. "Down the hatch!"

Kruger unscrewed the cap, worked the neck of the bottle between Radek's teeth and tilted it upright. He left it there until the whiskey spilled out the sides of his mouth and down the front of his shirt. Max grasped Radek beneath his arms and pulled him over onto his back; then took the bottle of whiskey from Kruger and smashed it on the floor as if Radek had dropped it when he stumbled.

"That does it," Kruger said, starting for the door.

"Hold it," Max said, stopped by something that had occurred to him. "We'd better get him back in uniform, or they might think one of the whores was in here with him and saw what happened."

They pulled up Radek's jodhpurs, buttoned the fly, buckled the belt, and set the suspenders on his shoulders. Max noticed the riding crop on the floor and slipped it into the top of Radek's boot. When finished, they stepped back and took one last look around, admiring their handiwork.

"What do you think?" Kruger prompted.

Max tilted his head and smiled. "I think this was the night you stopped blocking it all out. I knew your soul was alive in there, somewhere, Otto."

"You Catholics are all alike," Kruger teased. "Eager to absolve even the most egregious sinner."

"Well," Max said with a sideways glance to Radek's corpse. "There are a few exceptions."

"A few too many, I'm afraid."

Max nodded, ruefully, and studied Kruger's eyes for a moment. "You're worried about this, aren't you?"

"Very," Kruger replied. "The cover story you spun is nothing short of brilliant; but Radek was one of Himmler's fair-haired boys; and, as we know all too well, able to operate without deference to rules or rank." He locked his eyes onto Max's and, sounding threatened, added, "Steig and his little pack of attack dogs in Schellingstrasse aren't going to let this go."

CHAPTER THIRTY-SEVEN

The launch party for the Steinbach advertising campaign was in full swing. Gunther Global's offices in the upper reaches of the Seagram Building were filled with a standing room only crowd. Michael Jackson's death and Sarah Palin's resignation of Alaska's governorship were the default topics of conversation. Banners overhead proclaimed:

TRAVELLING COMPANIONS FOR LIFE.
SURVIVING HARROWING JOURNEYS

Samples of the new line were stacked on brass luggage carts that had once plied the Plaza's corridors. Posters of the kick-off ad featuring Dr. Jake Epstein and Sol Steinbach, and of ads featuring other owners of vintage Steinbachs who had agreed to participate were on display. Among them: A well-travelled diplomat with a distinguished career in the foreign service; a family that had survived the ditching of a jetliner in the Hudson River; a canny businesswoman who had spent decades roaming the globe to bring economic growth to third world countries. Flat screen monitors displayed TV spots and internet ads with travel-themed music tracks that included: Sinatra's version of *Come Fly With Me*, Nat King Cole's version of *Route 66*, Peter Paul and Mary's *Leaving On A Jet Plane*, Elton John's *Rocket Man*, Ray Charles's *Hit the Road Jack*, Madonna's *Holiday*, U2's *The Wanderer*, and Iggy Pop's *Passenger*.

Uniformed servers—balancing trays laden with tinkling flutes of sparkling prosecco and glistening morsels of sushi—slipped silently between groups of marketing mavens, chic buyers, and brown-suited distributors who were engaging cliques of fashion writers, travel journalists, and newspaper reporters.

Adam was among the latter. Stacey had accepted his emailed mea culpas and pleas to crawl, kneel, beg and grovel his way back into her heart; and he had not only apologized for his mean-spirited behavior; but also for allowing his concerns about job security to tempt him to proceed unethically; for pressuring her to be part of it; and, for clinging to the suspicions that had been driving him to write a story similar to one *The Times* had run earlier, exposing the fugitive Nazi doctor whose briefcase had been found in a Cairo basement. Indeed, the person Adam thought might be a Nazi war criminal, impersonating Holocaust survivor Jake Epstein turned out to be long dead. Now, having recommitted to writing a human interest story, Adam intended to approach Jake at the party and arrange an interview.

The high-pitched pinging of flatware on crystal silenced the crowd, calling attention to Mark Gunther who was standing at a podium flanked by Sol Steinbach and Dr. Jacob Epstein. Gunther Global's CEO always managed to project quiet confidence born of success in the cutthroat competition for advertising accounts and the grueling miles of marathons. However, as of late, his confidence had been shaken by the possibility that his company and client would be irreparably damaged by the blunder of featuring a Nazi war criminal in a major campaign. Now, that his fears had been assuaged, Gunther spoke with emotion and eloquence about the themes of the campaign, going on to introduce Jake and Sol as survivors of the most horrific and momentous period in modern history. The room filled with thunderous applause as the three men left the podium and began working the crowd.

Gunther joined a group of partygoers that included his wife Grace, Ellen Rother, Tannen and his companion, Celine. "I don't know how you did it," Gunther said in an aside to Tannen. "But I'd no doubt you and Stace would pull it off."

"You mean me and that 'quirky little genius of mine' who cooked up the Steinbach campaign?" Tannen prompted, echoing the sarcastic wisecrack Gunther had made after his flight from Paris.

Gunther laughed, good naturedly. "Looks like she knows how to work a room, too," he said, eyeing Stacey who was chatting with Hannah Epstein and Steinbach's wife, Bernice, both wearing chic summer dresses. "She's definitely corner office material. Wouldn't surprise me if she ended up in yours one of these days."

"*Mais oui!*" Celine exclaimed, with a sly glance to Tannen. "By then, Bart will be occupying yours! *Non?*"

"*Non,*" Tannen replied with a laugh. "By then Mark will have sold out to S&S and Stacey will be their creative director," he went on, referring to Saatchi & Saatchi, the highly creative British agency with offices in eighty countries.

Like her colleagues, Stacey was aglow with the sense of accomplishment and validation creative people experience when their ideas become reality. "This must be a special moment for you," Hannah Epstein prompted, seeing the look on her face.

"And for your husband," Stacey replied. You have no idea just how special, she thought, concealing the relief she felt at having it all come out right in the end. Indeed, neither Hannah, Jake nor their son Dan knew of Adam's suspicion and the personal destruction it had threatened; nor of how Stacey had been caught in the middle; torn between her innate affection for Jake, her professional loyalty to her client and employer, and her personal commitment to Adam and his career; but all that had been put to rest. Now, she was gazing like a lovesick teenager at Jake, his white mane shimmering in the light as he held court, nearby, in a circle of admiring partygoers. "So, did he capture your heart the first time you saw him?" Stacey asked Hannah, unabashedly. "I mean, the morning he walked into our conference room...God, mine just melted on the spot."

Hannah smiled in reflection. "Oh yes...mine still skips a beat when he enters a room. It's always been that way for me with Jake. There's something about his voice, too. A certain...timbre. I hear it all the time."

"I knew Sol was 'the one' the day I saw him trying to talk Bergdorf's into carrying his line," Bernice offered in her smoker's baritone. "My father was the luggage buyer, and I was working in the stockroom on summer vacation." She winked, mischievously. "Sol spent half the summer 'working' in there too."

Stacey laughed, then emitted a wistful sigh, still gazing at Jake. Refined, educated, culturally engaged, a kind and gentle man, he was all she had ever hoped for in a father figure. The complete opposite of her own, and the men in her family, who were crusty, hard-driving, Westerners. Emotionally distant, they drove pick-ups with crew cabs and winches, and names like Dakota, Frontier, Ridgeline and Sierra, and spent their spare time clearing brush and mending fences in emulation of their favorite ex-Presidents.

"Your husband's a truly special man, isn't he?" Stacey went on. "I mean, the more I learn about him the more amazing he becomes."

Hannah broke into a knowing smile. *"Sie sind lustern,"* she said, feigning she was jealous. *"Sie sind lustern nach meinem Mann, junge Dame."*

Stacey looked baffled.

Bernice was cackling with delight. "She said, you're lusting after my husband, young lady."

"Ooops!" Stacey said with an impish grin. "What can I say? He's a hunk, a hottie, a hottie and a half."

The three women broke into laughter and, collecting Sol Steinbach en route, drifted toward Jake's group that included Dan Epstein and Adam, who had just mentioned the interview.

"Of course," Jake said. "I've been looking forward to it. Anytime this week is fine. Dan?"

His son palmed his Blackberry, checked his schedule and said, "Friday at ten would work. Foundation HQ."

"What's Friday at ten?" Stacey asked as she and Hannah and the Steinbachs joined them.

"I'm interviewing Dr. Epstein," Adam replied, a broad smile dimpling his signature two-day growth.

"Great," Stacey said, plucking a flute of prosecco from a passing tray. "Here's to Dr. Epstein!" She raised her glass and clinked it to his. "I was just telling Mrs. Epstein how we keep finding out he's even more amazing than we thought."

"I've been telling her that for sixty years!" Jake cracked, eliciting laughter from the group.

"No, seriously," Stacey went on. "We didn't know you'd been to hell and back twice. I mean—"

"Twice?" Jake interrupted with a devilish twinkle, his accent thickening when he joked. "I've only been married once!"

"I heard that Jake Epstein," Hannah joked with a fetching pout.

"You've gotten me in trouble with the boss, young lady," Jake teased. "Now, what could you have possibly learned that would make you say that?"

Stacey broke into a chastened smile. "Well, for starters, I learned that you're not only a survivor of Auschwitz but also Dachau."

"Yeah," Steinbach chimed-in. "I'd no idea you were there. All the anti-Nazis in Leipzig who weren't Jews ended up in that place."

Jake nodded, somberly. "Yes, yes there were many political prisoners at Dachau. By the time I arrived the Nazis had lost their obsession for record-keeping and were frantically destroying them. It's a wonder anyone knows anything about who was where. Europe had become lost in the fog of war as someone once said."

"Those snapshots of ID numbers," Stacey went on, energized by Jake's reminiscence. "They were taken to make a record of them as Ellen thought. Weren't they?"

Jake nodded smartly. "My friend, Max, took them. I believe I mentioned him."

"Yes, you did. Max Kleist, right? You sponsored his family for the Yad Vashem award. Another one of those amazing things we learned about you!"

Jake smiled self-consciously and nodded again.

"God, it's so incredible," Stacey gushed, unable to contain her enthusiasm. "I mean, that he was at Dachau when you were transferred."

"Max wasn't just there, he was on the ramp!" Jake exclaimed, getting caught up in Stacey's fervor. "I wouldn't be here now, if he wasn't!" He paused for a moment, trying to recall something, then nodded. "If my memory serves me…" he said, his voice taking on a more hushed timbre, "…it was about a week later that Max took the snapshots. A group of us had gathered in the Revier…that's what we called the prison hospital. Max came with his camera and…and one by one he had us put our arm on the table and photographed the tattoo."

Adam's mind was racing. Hearing Jake tell the story made the puzzling detail that had first caught his eye sparkle with renewed clarity. Regardless of who took the snapshots or why they were taken, he knew, now, beyond any doubt, that the forearm in the snapshot with number A198841 tattooed on it was Jake Epstein's, not an imposter's. He also knew that Jake Epstein, the one right in front of him, had the exact same number tattooed on his arm—but in different handwriting. This wasn't news. It had been identified, investigated and dismissed. Indeed, Maximilian Kleist M.D. Captain, Waffen-SS, the man Adam suspected of being a Nazi war criminal, impersonating the real Jake Epstein, had died long ago. What's more, he had taken the snapshot—the one that had raised Adam's suspicions—to insure that Jake, among others, didn't just vanish without a trace. Like Ellen, Stacey, Tannen, Steinbach and the Gunthers, Adam had accepted the handwriting enigma as one of the many unfathomable mysteries that were part of the fog of war as Jake had just said; but the fog had suddenly lifted, and the glaring incongruity was still there. How could he ignore it? How could he, in good conscience, write Jake's story without asking him about it? "Excuse me, Dr. Epstein," Adam said in a casual tone. "This could wait til Friday; but I was struck by something you just said. Would you mind talking about it, now?"

"Yes, he would," Dan Epstein replied. "My father's already answered enough questions for one day."

Jake sighed, dismissing Dan with a wave of his hand, and nodded to Adam. "Please…"

"Great," Adam said, stealing an anxious glance at Dan as he slipped a hand into his pocket and turned on his recorder; then, he took a deep breath and looked into the old fellow's kindly face. "I know it's been a long time, Dr. Epstein, but over the years, did you ever notice the numbers on your arm are different than the ones in the snapshot taken at Dachau?"

CHAPTER THIRTY-EIGHT

After being escorted by the SS men to the Revier, Jake wasted no time treating the searing bruises and welts Radek had inflicted on Hannah. She spent the night in his quarters soothed by his comforting words and caring embrace. Within weeks, she had healed physically and, despite the shattering emotional trauma, was well on her way to regaining her mental toughness. By the last week of March, she had resumed treating typhus victims. Jake was, now, among them. He had grown weaker and could no longer deny he had contracted it. Though not always able to make it through an entire shift, he continued caring for other victims free from the concern of catching it.

As Major Bruckmann had advised, Max thought about the things that matter in life, like reuniting with Eva, to cope with his tours on the ramp. The influx of prisoners from Eastern Block camps was overwhelming, fueling the typhus epidemic. As Hannah had feared, not only weren't antibiotics available for prisoners, they weren't available for SS officers either. The prescriptions Max and Kruger had left in their own names at the pharmacy hadn't been filled, and never would be. Penicillin was so scarce in Germany, that only the Führer, after being wounded in an assassination attempt in 1944, had been treated with it. Even Major Bruckmann didn't have a source. Nor were other SS doctors, nurses and pharmacists willing to share, or sell, what Max suspected, they had pilfered for personal use.

The SS hospital was running out of basic medical supplies as well. Warehouses were under constant Allied bombardment along with roadways and rail spurs. Expected shipments never arrived; and despite its proximity to the Ruhr Valley and its vaunted mining industry, KZ-Dachau didn't even have coal for heating or cremating the dead.

Everyone had sensed the war was lost. Now, everyone knew it. American troops were across the Rhine, within two hundred miles of Berlin, and sweeping across Bavaria toward Munich and Dachau. Himmler had become obsessed with preventing its prisoners from being liberated. Nothing else mattered, now. Even Radek's bizarre death, which Kruger feared would be rigorously investigated by Major Steig, had been ignored.

On Wednesday, March 27th, Max was dressing for yet another tour on the ramp when Major Bruckmann stopped by his quarters.

"I'm afraid things are going to get worse before they get better," the impeccably groomed major said. "I'll be leaving before the week is out. I wanted to wish you luck."

"Thank you, Sir. I wish you the same."

"I also wanted to give you this," Bruckmann went on, handing Max an envelope.

On opening it, Max's eyes widened in disbelief at the glass vial it contained. "Penicillin?"

Bruckmann nodded. "While packing, I recalled you'd been in search of antibiotics for a friend in the Revier."

"Yes, Sir. My best friend. Jacob Epstein. He's a doctor. An exceptional one. I tried everything short of gunpoint. Where'd you get it?"

Bruckmann's eyes danced with mischief behind his metal-framed lenses. "From Lieutenant Radek."

Max looked astonished. "Radek?"

"The one and only. After his 'accident', Colonel Weiter assigned me to notify his family, and arrange for his remains and personal effects to be sent home. I came across it while going through his quarters," Bruckmann explained. "It seems he'd been requisitioning medicines and supplies for patients and keeping them for himself. Everything from antibiotics and disinfectants like Argyrol and mercurochrome to gauze pads and adhesive tape. It was quite a cache."

"Selling them on the black market, wasn't he?"

Bruckmann smiled, knowingly. "I saw no need to include them with his underwear and socks. I'm afraid it's only one vial. As you know, even several doses are often insufficient when it comes to typhus."

"Better than nothing, Sir." Max wanted to go to the Revier and give Jake the injection, immediately; but had barely enough time to get to the ramp. Before leaving, he took a case that contained a syringe from his physician's bag, and slipped it into a pocket of his greatcoat.

That evening, after finishing his tour, Max went directly to the Revier. Jake, Hannah, Dr. Cohen and some staff members were gathered in the meeting room; but Cohen wasn't chairing a briefing, he was holding a Seder. It was Passover. Some Jewish prisoners had squirreled-away pieces of moldy bread from their rations. Moistened with water, rolled into thin sheets and dried, they had been reconstituted into makeshift matzos that, along with a flickering candle, were in the center of the table.

"Well, we're only short six ingredients," Cohen said, with a facetious chuckle, referring to the seven symbolic foods required at a Seder, matzo being one.

"I beg to differ," Jake said. "By my count, we're short only three." Everyone looked puzzled.

"We have matzo and?" Cohen prompted.

"...the karpas, chazaret and maror," Jake replied, enumerating the bitter-tasting herbs eaten with the matzo as a reminder of the hardships the Hebrews suffered while enslaved by the Egyptians.

Now, everyone looked really puzzled. Everyone except Hannah who, with an amused smile, said, "You pilfered them from the kitchen, didn't you Jake?"

"No need," he replied with a sly grin. "This place is bitter enough to make up for all three."

After the Seder, Hannah began her rounds of the wards, and Max accompanied Jake to his quarters, handing him the envelope the instant the door closed. "A little something for Passover."

"The six missing ingredients?" Jake quipped, dropping onto his bunk exhausted.

"Not exactly," Max replied with a laugh. "Moldy matzos may not a happy Passover make, but green mold does have its uses."

Jake's eyes widened at Max's reference to the process that produces antibiotics. "Penicillin?"

Max nodded, savoring the moment.

"Where'd you get it?"

"You wouldn't believe me if I told you."

Jake shrugged. "It'll be wasted on me, anyway," he said, his eyes brightening despite his gloomy prognosis. "But it might not be too late for Hannah."

Max looked shocked. "Hannah? Hannah has typhus?"

Jake nodded. "Early stages. Abdominal pain, dull rash, fever. Her reward for taking care of me. I tried to stop her: treated her poorly, denied my feelings, talked about Eva incessantly. Didn't do a bit of good."

"Of course not. She's in love with you, Jake. She told me. I assured her you felt the same way."

"I do. I care for her deeply...with all my heart." He emitted a disconsolate sigh. "And I killed her."

"In case you haven't noticed, you're not the only one with typhus around here," Max said, placing a palm on Jake's forehead. "My God, you're burning up."

Jake nodded. "I told you, I'm finished."

"No you're not." Max removed the syringe he'd brought with him from its case, sterilized it with alcohol, and began assembling it. "Hannah has time. The Americans have penicillin. They'll be here soon. We'll save her. I promise. And this..." He took the vial from the envelope. "...is going to save you. And I won't take no for an answer." Before Jake could protest, Max swabbed his bicep and the vial's seal with alcohol, then punctured the latter with the needle, withdrawing the plunger, slowly. The glass cylinder filled with white liquid. He pinched Jake's pasty flesh between his fingers, popped the needle into it, and depressed the plunger. "Happy Passover!"

Later, that evening Max and Kruger were in the Officer's Club celebrating the unexpected turn of events. A depressive pall seemed to hang over the place, which was half empty and had lost its *joie de vivre*. Max was lighting a cigarette when his eyes darted to the entrance. He froze, holding the burning match.

"What is it?" Kruger asked, seeing his reaction.

"My favorite attack dog just walked in." The flame reached Max's fingers making him toss the match aside.

"Steig?"

Max nodded. "And several mongrels from his pack," he added as the Major strode toward their table. "Looks like you were right, Otto."

"Captain Maximilian Kleist," Steig intoned, his greatcoat swirling about him cape-like as he removed it, knowing someone in his entourage would keep it from falling to the floor. "What a pleasant surprise."

Max forced a smile. "Major Steig—Captain Kruger," he said, introducing them.

"Kruger...ah yes, I recognize you from your file," Steig said, sending Kruger's heart rate soaring. "By the way, Kleist," he added, as if it was an afterthought. "Your parents send their regards, as does your sister. A most beautiful young woman. Anika, isn't it?"

Max's heart rate exceeded Kruger's, now. All the unnerving reasons why Steig might have been in contact with his family raced through his mind. He forced a smile and casually lit his cigarette to cover his anxiety. "Thank you, Sir. As you know, communications have broken down. We've been out of touch since I reported here."

Steig dismissed it with a wave of his hand. "All in the line of duty. It seems the Reichsführer learned there was a Jewess in their employ. She's here somewhere, now, I imagine." He sat at the table opposite Max, and frowned with uncertainty. "Or was it Auschwitz? Anyway, the next time I see your parents, I'll let them know you're well."

Max stiffened at the shocking news. He couldn't believe Tovah—sweet, gentle, beloved Tovah—had been taken from his family's home. From *her* home! And sent to a death camp. He exhaled a stream of smoke, fighting to keep his composure. "I'd appreciate that, Sir."

Steig had the advantage, now, and pressed it. "The Reichsführer was quite upset by Lieutenant Radek's accident."

"We all were, Sir. I'm told it was horrible."

Steig's eyes narrowed in. "I'm told you and Lieutenant Radek didn't get along."

"We had our differences," Max said, evenly.

"Yes, but there was one thing you had in common. Wasn't there?"

"I can think of several," Max replied, somehow able to feign aplomb. "We were both physicians, both SS officers, and we both worked the ramp."

"I was referring to your mutual disregard for the Nuremberg Laws," the Major said, eyeing an attractive waitress serving drinks at a table, nearby.

"I wouldn't know, Major," Max said, stealing a look at Kruger whose eyes were blank. "As I said Lieutenant Radek and I weren't close."

"Well, I suspect his appetite for Jewish women was his fatal flaw," Steig said, pointedly. "Speaking of Jews, I'm afraid your friend Epstein was arrested and sent to Auschwitz. I offered him an alternative but he refused to cooperate. It probably cost him his life."

"I'm sorry to hear that," Max said, evenly. If Steig didn't know Jake had survived and been transferred to Dachau, Max certainly wasn't going to tell him. "He was always strongly principled."

"I imagine you'll be pleased to hear your other friend, Fraulein Rosenberg, escaped."

"Well, you can't win them all, Major," Max said, suppressing his elation.

"No, but I will win this one," Steig said with a sly smile. "She's still being hunted. It's just a matter of time. I'll be sure to let you know when I have her in custody." The major got to his feet, and placed a folded sheet of paper on the table in front of Max. "Like your sister, a very beautiful young woman. I'm sure Lieutenant Radek would've found Eva Sarah Rosenberg intriguing."

Max watched as Steig led his entourage from the Club, then lifted the sheet of paper and unfolded it. The heading read: FUGITIVE ALERT. Eva's medical school photo was centered beneath it, her fetching smile beckoning.

CHAPTER THIRTY-NINE

Adam's question had left the group gathered around Jake in stunned silence. They stood unmoving amidst the blaring music and chattering crowd, the launch party swirling around them.

Stacey was rocked. She couldn't believe what she had heard, and winced as if she'd been stabbed. Inside she was screaming, For Chrissakes, Clive! What are you thinking?! Her eyes burned into Adam's like lasers cutting steel.

His eyes were cool and focused.

Steinbach's were panicked.

Dan's were puzzled and pained.

Hannah's were characteristically steady.

Jake's were blinking in confusion. "I'm not sure I understand," he said in his soft accent. "Are you saying the snapshot and tattoo aren't the same number?"

"No, no I'm sorry if I wasn't clear," Adam replied. "The number's the same but the handwriting is different."

"Are you sure?" Jake prompted, looking baffled. "I mean, it doesn't make sense."

"Positive. I don't have a copy of the snapshot with me but there's probably one around here somewhere. Stace?"

Stacey's heart had plummeted along with her spirits. Her enthusiasm had prompted the old fellow to tell a perfectly harmless story, thereby unleashing a demon she, and others, thought had been engaged and forever vanquished. She was dumbstruck by what she had just done, if unintentionally; but now that the glaring incongruity had been resurrected, she, too, saw it with frightening clarity—and it unnerved her. "Somewhere. I guess," she replied, her voice quavering. "I mean, I could try to find one. I could access it on my computer, but--"

"Don't bother," Dan Epstein said with finality, shifting his look to Adam. "Bring one with you on Friday, if you like. Come on, Dad. There are some people here who are anxious to meet you."

"Wait. I want to answer his question," Jake said, standing his ground and engaging Adam's uncertain eyes. "No. No, I can't say I ever noticed the writing was different. Nor can I explain it. There must be some mistake." Jake sipped from his glass and cocked his head in reflection. "As I said, I put my arm on the table and…and Max took a picture of it. Of my arm. This arm!" Jake raised it overhead then, pointing to one of the print ads, exclaimed, "That arm!" He chuckled at a thought and added, "Despite my legendary accomplishments in the field of prosthetics, I assure you it's the same one I had then."

"Well, if anyone should know, it would be you!" Adam said, unable to keep from laughing. "It's just been frustrating. I mean, there aren't any names written on the back…the faces are blurred beyond recognition…you couldn't tell the men from the women if it weren't for the little triangles…"

Jake nodded in empathy and shrugged. "After all these years, I can't even remember how I came to have them. I'm sorry. I guess Max had the film processed and…and you know…sixty years later they turned up in my suitcase." He paused, broke into an impish smile and, said, "…in my vintage Steinbach!" A ripple of relieved laughter ran through the crowd. When it had subsided, Jake shrugged again, and concluded, "I guess we just didn't have the time or, in the end, the need to make notations on them. I mean, once we knew the GIs were coming…" He splayed his hands, suggesting the rest was obvious. "You know, Max promised I'd survive; even after I'd contracted typhus. I refused to admit I had it; but he knew, and, somehow, he got me penicillin even though there was none to be had. I still don't know how he did it. You have to understand, if you were a prisoner, surviving became an obsession. Nothing else mattered. Unfortunately, in the end, it was poor Max who didn't."

Hannah touched his arm, comfortingly, and brushed away a tear that rolled down her cheek.

"A senseless tragedy," Jake whispered, sadly, continuing to reminisce. "At the time, everyone was so excited by the news that the camp was going to be liberated. You can't imagine how it felt when we realized we were going to survive, that we were going to return to our families, to our communities and lives. We had been condemned to death one minute and given a new lease on life the next! Thirty-two thousand sick and starving prisoners crying, cheering, screaming with delight at the prospect of being fed and given medical attention. As for Max, well, he was—" The old fellow paused, overwhelmed by the memory. He took a sip of prosecco and was collecting himself when he sensed the quiet and realized the crowd around him had grown much larger and was hanging on his every word. Evidently, many of the partygoers, Tannen, Celine, Ellen and the Gunthers among them, had sensed something special in the air

193

and gravitated toward him. Jake took a deep breath, then another sip from his glass, and tilted his head as if trying to recall something. "Now, where was I?"

Hannah leaned closer and whispered, "Max."

"Ah yes, Max. Max was so elated," Jake went on, caught up in the reverie. "He kept talking about Eva. Eva Rosenberg. I believe I mentioned her. They were madly in love with each other; and since there was a good chance she had made it safely to Venice...her family lived in the ghetto, there...he kept talking about going to find her. Of course, we talked about being doctors again; about healing the sick, and getting back to our research and working on the prosthetics we'd been developing together. I'll never forget the moment when the Americans marched through the main gate. It was just so...so incredible. I...I can't tell you the feeling that came over us. There we were, me in my ragged striped prison uniform, Max in his black SS uniform with the death head on the cap, crying and hugging each other, and then...then..." Jake began choking up. He paused, barely able to continue. "I'm sorry," he said, his eyes glistening with emotion. He glanced to Hannah who leaned to him supportively, then took a deep breath and said, "And then, a terrible thing happened."

CHAPTER FORTY

A bone-warming sun greeted Catholic Bavaria as it awakened to celebrate the risen Christ. Max's thoughts were of the family chapel where his parents and sister would be attending Mass. He'd have given anything to have spent the day with them. He spent it on the ramp, instead, processing a trainload of Jewish prisoners that had been transferred from Bergen-Belsen. They had suffered the most horrifying of Nazi atrocities, and were the last prisoners Himmler wanted in the hands of the Allies.

About a week later, Max and Kruger were in the Officer's Club numbing their senses after yet another day on the ramp when the wail of sirens and whistle of falling bombs sent everyone running for cover. The camp had been added to the Allies target list and its water main and power house were completely destroyed. Without water for drinking, cooking, showering and toilet flushing, Colonel Weiter was forced to deploy caravans of tanker trucks to fetch and distribute it throughout the camp, daily. In the weeks that followed, Max and Kruger made a habit of commandeering tankers which they drove into the prison compound making certain the Revier was well-supplied.

It was during this time, on Friday, April 13th, the world learned of the death of President Roosevelt. Though cheered by the news, Himmler was shaken by reports that American troops were advancing on Dachau. He panicked and ordered all 32,000 prisoners be evacuated or executed. Colonel Weiter was frantic. There weren't enough trucks or boxcars in all of Bavaria. Besides, every roadway and rail spur had been hit by Allied airstrikes. Death marches? Many prisoners could barely stand let alone walk. Mass executions? Even the vaunted German killing machine wasn't up to the task now.

In desperation, Himmler ordered that the Jewish prisoners who had just come from Bergen-Belsen be evacuated to a subcamp in Austria. Weiter resigned his commission and accompanied them. A previous commandant, Martin Weiss, was put in charge. It took him just two days to see the wisdom of

Weiter's decision; and when a convoy evacuating hundreds of high-profile political prisoners departed, Weiss joined it. Among them: former Chancellor of Austria Kurt von Schuschnigg, former Jewish Premier of France Leon Blum, and Rev. Martin Niemöller, a Protestant minister convicted of treason for anti-Nazi sermons. An inexperienced 2nd Lieutenant was left in charge of the entire SS installation. His name was Henrich Wicker.

The next day, KZ-Dachau was liberated by two combat units of the U.S Seventh Army. Operating independently, they had advanced on their objective from different directions. One came upon the entrance to the SS Garrison, the other upon the entrance to the concentration camp. As a result, their commanders formed two totally different impressions of Dachau, and initiated two totally different courses of action.

Around midday, General Henning Linden, commander of the 42nd Rainbow Division, came down the Avenue of the SS in his jeep to where Lt. Wicker was waiting at the main entrance to the SS Garrison. Its stately houses, picket fences, movie theater, canteen, post office, and barracks with landscaped courtyards sure didn't look like the atrocity-riddled death camp the general had heard about. Indeed, the outstretched wings of the Imperial Eagle above the entrance, seemed to be welcoming its liberator; and with his travelling companion, an attractive blonde who just happened to be an aggressive reporter, at his side, General Linden engaged in the pomp and circumstance of an official surrender ceremony.

However, a few hours earlier, advancing from the opposite direction, Colonel Felix Sparks of the 45th Thunderbird Division, accompanied by troops of I-Company, arrived at the entrance to the Prison Camp, coming face-to-face with its stomach-turning horrors. Sparks had two immediate concerns. First: Contain the typhus epidemic. Though every GI had been vaccinated, he ordered his men not to enter the prison until DDT could be obtained. Second: Contain the 32,000 prisoners---a sick, hungry and angry mix of Jews, anti-Nazi Protestants and Catholics, political prisoners, and resistance fighters---who presented a threat of mass rioting. To that end, Sparks had the entire contents of the SS food warehouse delivered to the prison compound. With luck, the prisoners would remain calm until more troops could be brought in to control them.

But it was the Americans who lost control first. During their advance, Colonel Sparks and the troops of I-Company had come upon, what they named, the Death Train. The long line of flatcars and gondolas had been abandoned on the tracks that led to the prison. Thousands of decomposing, half-naked bodies spilled from the railcars. The stomach-turning sight unnerved the GIs whose outrage was fueled by other atrocities they encountered: The piles of corpses outside the crematoria and burning pits. The twisted bodies of prisoners who had been beaten to death. The skulls of children smashed by rifle butts. The skeleton-like faces of prisoners pressed to the fences, begging for water, food, and medical attention. The moaning typhus victims inside the Revier; and the gagging stench of death that hung in the air.

Gripped by a murderous rage, some GIs from I-Company began to massacre the SS troops defending the prison. Those in bunkers were overrun and given no chance to surrender. Those in guard towers, despite white flags flying from the turrets, were cut down as they emerged from ground level entrances. Many were unarmed and had their hands raised. A few fired weapons. Most were shot on sight.

The news that the Americans had arrived heartened the prisoners. Some became emboldened. Armed with steel pipes and wooden clubs that moments before had been the legs of tables and chairs, they went on a vengeful rampage. SS guards who had brutalized and tortured them were beaten to death; then, armed with weapons confiscated from their victims, the prisoners began executing anyone in a German uniform. Guard dogs were shot in their kennels.

Max and Kruger were inside the prison compound delivering water to the Revier and were unaware of the chaos. After hooking up the tanker's hose to the storage tank, Max went inside to check on his patients. Kruger remained with the truck to monitor the pumping operation. He was checking the tank's water level when a mob of marauding prisoners spotted his SS uniform and came at him with their clubs.

In the meantime, other squads from I-Company, that had maintained military discipline, were rousting SS guards and officers from hiding places. The captured Germans were made to stand along a concrete wall with their hands atop their heads. A sergeant, manning a machinegun on a tripod, was in charge of the squad guarding them. Shocked and angered by the horrors they had seen, the GIs stood glaring at their captives. One of them was a young SS officer with a crisp uniform and a self-assured air which proved contagious and spread down the line of ragtag enlisted men that now numbered several dozen. Their slackened postures became more erect. Their frightened eyes engaged those of their captors. Their downturned mouths rose in cocky smirks. The unnerved GIs began taunting the 'fucking Krauts' who seemed to be enjoying their discomfort. Expletives and threats were exchanged. One of the GIs muttered, "Bastards…we should kill 'em, all." Another overheard, and shouted, "Yeah, kill 'em all!" Others echoed the call that built into a rhythmic chant. "Kill 'em all! Kill 'em all!"

That's when it happened. When the Sergeant manning the tripod-mounted machinegun snapped, and pulled the trigger, unleashing several sustained bursts that killed 'em all; when screams, pieces of flesh and chunks of stucco filled the air; when blood kept spattering the bullet-pocked wall until none of the SS men were left standing. The crazed sergeant was firing at the twitching bodies on the ground when Colonel Sparks, reacting to the gunfire, came running over and kicked him off the weapon.

Inside the Revier, Max had found Jake and Hannah in the meeting room with Dr. Cohen and other staffers. The single dose of penicillin hadn't been sufficient and Jake was still seriously ill. Hannah had lost weight and was looking gaunt but seemed to be holding her own. Aware the camp was being liberated, the group was discussing how to brief and integrate American medical personnel when several prisoners came running down the long corridor into the room. "The Americans aren't taking prisoners!" one of them shouted, excitedly.

"They're killing every German in sight!" another exclaimed with delight.

An almost euphoric reaction came from the group of prisoner doctors and staffers. They knew the war was over; knew they had survived the Nazi atrocities; and there was an undeniable satisfaction in knowing their tormentors were getting all that was coming to them; but the indiscriminate nature of the vengeance, soon, struck them---struck close to home. Concerned looks darted from one to the next and the next. And when they had settled, all eyes were on Captain Maximilian Kleist, Waffen-SS.

"I'm afraid Max is in extreme danger," Jake said, breaking the tense silence.

"Why?" Cohen protested. "We'll tell the Americans he's a doctor. That he's been humane and caring. That he's not one of the monsters. They'll understand. He'll be safe."

Max nodded in agreement. "He's right, Jake. Don't worry. I'll be fine. The Americans play by the rules."

"Not anymore," one of the prisoners said. "They've gone berserk. They're shooting anyone in an SS uniform on sight. No questions asked."

Max winced. "That's hard to believe. Are you sure?"

"Positive," the other prisoner replied. "They lined everyone up in front of a wall and machine-gunned them. Dozens of SS men executed in cold blood."

A gasp of disbelief came from the group.

'It's not just the Americans. Bands of prisoners are roaming the compound beating SS guards to death. I was over by the—"

He was interrupted when a man in an SS uniform, supported by two prisoners, stumbled into the meeting room and fell face down across the table. They turned him over, revealing he had been severely beaten about the head. His scalp was, deeply, slashed, soaking his hair and the front of his uniform with blood.

"Otto!" Max gasped, recognizing Kruger despite the carnage. "What happened? he asked, as Hannah and the medical staff began tending to Kruger's wounds.

"We found him on the ground next to the tanker truck," one of the prisoners who had helped Kruger replied. "He's lucky to be alive."

The other nodded. "If we hadn't seen him with you, we'd have finished him off."

"We have to find a place to hide Max," Hannah said.

"Hide him?" one of the staff members echoed with concern. "What happens to us if the Americans find out we're hiding an SS officer?!"

"He's right," Max said. "I'll just have to take my chances. If I can get back to my quarters...I...I could change into some civvies, and—"

"Forget it, captain," a prisoner interrupted. "The Americans are already searching every nook and cranny of the SS camp. They'll be all over this place, next."

"They're not the problem, yet," Cohen said, taking command. "The Americans have orders to stay out of here. It's the mobs of prisoners I'm worried about."

"Either way Max doesn't stand a chance," Hannah said, clearly alarmed.

"We haven't much time," Cohen said. "We better come up with something."

Jake looked off in thought, then brightened at an idea. "I have it," he said, hurrying from the meeting room. Cohen and Hannah followed, leaving the staffers to care for Kruger. Max paused to check on his friend and winced at his condition. "He's a good man. Do everything you can for him," he said before hurrying after the others who had followed Jake to his quarters.

Max had just entered, and was closing the door when the sound of people running rose in the corridor. Loud voices and more thunderous footsteps erupted. Dr. Cohen guided Max aside and peered out the door to see clusters of frenzied prisoners dashing from block to block at the far end of the corridor. Many were wielding clubs. Some carried guns. "Where's the SS man?!" one shouted on entering one of the blocks.

"We heard one of those SS bastards is in here!" a second yelled, pushing his way into another block.

"We know he's in here somewhere!" the leader of a third group shouted.

Like packs of rabid dogs, the frenzied bands of prisoners were leap-frogging their way down the long corridor from one block in the Revier to the next. In a few minutes they would reach the one where Jake's quarters were located—the one where the SS man they were looking for was now trapped.

CHAPTER FORTY-ONE

If Adam's question had confused Dr. Epstein and stunned those gathered around him at the launch party, the old fellow's answer landed an even more staggering blow. Few, if any, other than Ellen Rother with her in-depth knowledge of the Holocaust, knew of the massacre and execution of SS troops at Dachau by outraged GI's, let alone of the revenge-driven prisoner rampages.

"I've got chills," Stacey whispered to Adam as the crowd, shaken by the terrible thing that happened all those years ago, dispersed into smaller groups.

"Well, according to the GMA, Max Kleist was killed in action," Adam said. "Now, I guess we know how."

Stacey frowned in condemnation. "Executed in action sounds more like it."

"So why do I still have a weird feeling in my gut about this?"

"Come on Clive," Stacey said with an exasperated sigh. "It's over. Don't let it become an obsession. That was Hitler's problem."

"Hitler? Hey, no need to sugarcoat it," Adam said, good-naturedly. "Look, it's more than a feeling. Dr. Epstein said Max took the snapshots of the tattoos—his included. That means the handwriting should match; and it doesn't. How can I ignore it?"

Stacey sighed again. This time in concession. "Fuck. I knew you were going to say that. Every time this thing gets resolved it comes undone."

"Tell me about it."

"But Dr. E seems so honest, so…so convincing. I mean there's nothing mendacious about him. I just can't believe he's been lying all this time."

"Maybe he wasn't…"

Stacey looked baffled.

"…maybe he's been living the lie for so long he actually believes it," Adam concluded.

Stacey tilted her head considering it. "Sixty-five years…Yeah, I suppose it's possible, isn't it?"

Adam nodded. "I can't let this go, Stace. I can't."

"Me neither; but like I said, you can't destroy someone over a feeling. You need proof—beyond any doubt—and you don't have it."

Adam scratched at his two-day growth. "I think it's time to take Paul up on his offer. He edited the Heim piece. He might have an angle on peeling this onion that hasn't occurred to me."

The launch party was winding down. Stacey and Adam slipped away and, twenty minutes later, were getting out of a cab on East 41st Street in front of Motenapo, the chic Italian eatery in the lobby of the *Times* Building. They picked-up a visitor's pass at the security desk and headed for the elevators. The typography tracing across many of the 560 screens read: OBAMA COMMEMORATES 40TH ANNIVERSARY OF STONEWALL UPRISING. MEETS WITH PROMINENT GAYS AND LESBIANS IN WHITE HOUSE. Other screens displayed related stories from the archives: AHMADINEJAD CLAIMS NO HOMOSEXUALS IN IRAN — CONGRESS PASSES MATTHEW SHEPHERD HATE CRIME LEGISLATION — MILITARY'S DON'T ASK DON'T TELL TO BE REEVALUATED.

The next day's edition of *The Times* was being put to bed. The patter of conversation and the muted clack of keyboards filled the well above the newsroom. As they approached Diamond's cubicle, Adam and Stacey were confronted with a disconcerting sight: File boxes were everywhere. On the desk, on the floor, on the chairs; as were documents, books, and toppling stacks of folders. If Adam didn't know better he would have thought the tall, thin fellow with the bald pate in the midst of it all, was—as the saying goes—cleaning out his desk.

"Hi…" Adam said gingerly. "What's going on?"

Diamond tossed some books into one of the boxes then craned his neck around. "What's it look like?"

Adam's eyes crinkled in disbelief. "You've been downsized?"

"Furloughed," Diamond corrected. "It's the newly anointed word. See tomorrow's story on…downsizing."

"You're kidding…"

"Nope. I dodged the first bullet," Diamond said, referring to the merger of the Metro and National desks earlier in the year. "But the next one…right through the heart. Hey, for every one of me they execute, they can hire three of you. They've got to pay all those biz-bloggers, somehow." The latter was a reference to the recent hiring of twelve on-line reporters despite an across the board hiring freeze. The unpopular move had been pushed by executives on the business side who argued that the blogs drew the kind of compulsive readers who were highly prized by advertisers.

"Geezus, Paul," Adam said with a look to Stacey, "I'm…I'm sorry. I don't know what to say, I…"

"Say whatever you came here to say," Diamond said with a glance to his watch. "I mean, they still own me for the next hour and twenty-two minutes. What's up?"

"The suitcase story…"

"Nazis. Holocaust survivor. Ad Campaign…And?"

"Well…we're not sure Dr. Jacob Epstein is who he says he is."

"Oh dear…" Diamond said caught off-guard. "We aren't talking the Heim thing, here, are we?"

Adam waggled a hand. "That's what I'm trying to figure out. It's possible someone stole Dr. E's identity. The evidence points to his med school buddy who was a Captain in the SS. A guy named Max Kleist."

"So what's the problem?"

"According to the records, Max Kleist is dead…"

"How convenient," Diamond said with a knowing smile. "You have recent photos of Dr. Epstein, right?"

"Sure," Stacey chimed-in. "Dozens of 'em."

"You have an old one of Dr. E or this Kleist guy?"

"We might," Adam replied. "Why?"

"Well, when we were developing the Heim piece, we needed to be sure it was really him. We had a shot of young Nazi Heim and one of wrinkled old Heim taken in Cairo years later; and had them computer analyzed."

"Bio-metrics," Stacey said, smartly.

Diamond nodded. "Facial Recognition Technology to be precise. FRT matches dozens of points of coincidence in facial structure; then rates the chance of a match from zero to a hundred percent. We emailed the photos to this company in L.A. Couple of hours later it came back ninety-something percent; so we knew we had him."

"So…" Stacey said, assembling the pieces, "If we can get our hands on a photo of the real Dr. Epstein…like one taken during the war…we do an FRT analysis with the one from the ad campaign. If they match, he's the real deal; if they don't, he's an imposter."

"Exactly," Diamond said. "The technology's highly reliable. It's used routinely in casinos to ID gamblers who've been barred. They're picked-up by surveillance cameras and run against a data base. Soft tissue changes dramatically over time, but bone structure doesn't. Even after decades, FRT can ID one of these sharks in a couple of minutes. Works just as well on war criminals. It identified Mengele, who had plastic surgery and sported a bushy mustache, forty years after the war. Of course he wasn't out to break the bank at the Mirage."

"Well, Dr. E went to Med School at the University of Munich," Adam said with a glance to Stacey. "Didn't he say the Nazis used a photo from his student file on a fugitive alert?"

Stacey nodded. "Yeah, and, with luck, by now, it's all stored in a database…"

"Be my guest," Diamond said indicating his computer.

Within minutes Adam had accessed the University's student database. He typed Jacob Epstein in the name block and 1943-1945 in Years of Attendance, then clicked on Search. Several seconds later, his shoulders slumped in disappointment. "Shit."

"What?" Stacey prompted.

"We struck out," Adam replied, tapping the screen. "The city was heavily bombed in April of '45. Most of the University was leveled. All student records were destroyed. Now what?"

"Well Dr. E's passport and travel documents were in the suitcase," Stacey replied, sounding optimistic. "Every one of them has a photo that was probably taken during the war."

Adam brightened. "Yeah, and they're all on the CD. All we have to do is—"

"Hold it—hold it," Diamond interjected. "This is where it gets tricky. If someone stole Dr. Epstein's ID, chances are they replaced the original photo with one of their own—which FRT would determine a perfect match. Which would give you absolutely nothing."

"Yeah, but if it isn't a match," Adam reasoned, "….we'd know for sure someone's been impersonating him. We just wouldn't know who."

"Point well taken," Diamond conceded, gesturing to his computer again. "One way to find out."

Diamond went back to packing up file boxes, and Adam went back to work on the keyboard. He accessed the computer in his cubicle on the mezzanine above, and searched the data he had downloaded from the Wiesenthal CD for documents with photos of Jacob Epstein. The one on his Austrian passport was the sharpest and least faded. Next, he downloaded the ad campaign photo he had used to compare the handwriting of the ID number tattooed on Dr. Epstein's forearm to the handwriting of the ID number in the snapshot found in the suitcase. "Wow," he said, on seeing the two faces side by side on the screen. "They don't look like the same person at all. Maybe we've got something."

"Maybe," Stacey cautioned.

"What does that mean?"

"Just being realistic. I mean, a couple of months ago, I'm watching this movie on TCM. "The Seventh Cross"? Spencer Tracy, Jessica Tandy? He's on the run from the Gestapo. She and her husband take him in?"

Adam nodded. "Hume Cronyn…her husband in real life too. Where you going with this?"

"Point is, I had no idea it was her. I mean, she looked just like Liv Ullman in her prime. Just like her. You'd never know it was the same actress in "Driving Miss Daisy" forty-what years later. Totally different."

"I second that," Diamond said. "Bill Gallo the sports cartoonist? He's been writing a wartime memoir in his column. Had a couple of photos of him: How he looks now and back then when he was in the Marines. Not the same guy. No way."

"Well, thanks for your support," Adam said with a weary smile and a mouse-click that emailed both photos to the Bio-metric lab in Los Angeles. "It took, what, a couple of hours to hear back on Heim right?"

Diamond nodded and raised a brow. "You have any idea what time it is?"

"Aw shit," Adam groaned, glancing to his watch.

Diamond nodded. "Even with the time difference they've already been shut down for hours out there."

"Then when? Tomorrow? By noon?"

"If you get lucky and they run it first thing."

"And if we don't?"

Diamond shrugged. "What's the difference? You're not on deadline right?"

"Not yet..."

"Well, unless you need the info to stop Al Qaeda from blowing up the Vatican..." Diamond let it trail off; then, reflecting on the Church's weak response to the ongoing pedophile priests scandal, he smiled and added, "Of course, these days, that might be a close call."

"Easier than this one," Adam said, glumly.

"Come on, it's payday," Diamond enthused. "Lighten up and enjoy the fact that you're still employed."

"While I still can, huh?" Adam quipped.

"Hey, Clive may not be on deadline, but I am," Stacey said, her voice taking on an edge. "We just launched a global ad campaign; and if Dr. E turns out to be another Dr. Heim, it's going to blow up right in our faces."

Diamond started to laugh, then stifled it, and held up a hand in apology. "Sorry, I was just picturing all those unsold suitcases with bombs in them."

Stacey's blond spikes were bristling, now. "Just because this isn't in the same league as stopping St. Peter's from being cratered doesn't mean it isn't serious. The sooner I know whether or not I've got a disaster on my hands, the better."

"Spoken like a staunch advocate of truth in advertising," Diamond said with a sarcastic cackle.

"Just doing my job," Stacey said pointedly.

CHAPTER FORTY-TWO

It didn't take long for the groups of prisoners searching the Revier for Max to reach the end of the corridor where Jake's quarters were located. Dr. Cohen was standing in front of the door, now, his face covered by a surgical mask as they rushed toward him.

"There's an SS man in here!" a prisoner, waving a pistol, shouted. "Have you seen him?"

"No, no I haven't," Cohen replied, his eyes darting to the weapon, warily.

"What's in there?" the prisoner asked, gesturing to the door as the others surged around him.

"Doctor's quarters," Cohen replied, holding out a hand to stop them. "You can't go in there."

"Who the fuck are you?"

"Dr. Ezra Cohen, Chief of Staff. I'm in charge of the Revier, and—"

"Not anymore!" the prisoner shouted. He pushed Cohen aside and charged through the door followed by his club-wielding colleagues.

"Wait! Wait! Don't go in there!" Cohen shouted, trying to stop them. "There's a patient in there. He—"

Inside the room, Jake and Hannah were standing on opposite sides of the bunk tending to a patient. They whirled, as if startled by the intrusion, peering above surgical masks as the group of rabid prisoners encircled the bunk where the outline of a figure could be discerned beneath the pile of ragged blankets that concealed it.

The ringleader, brandishing the pistol, grabbed a fistful of the bedding. His eyes darted to an SS collar insignia peeking from beneath it. Instead of firing his weapon or pulling the covers off, he flinched and froze in place at the sight of the SS man's face. The prisoner's eyes were wide in startled recognition. And so were Max's. The prisoner hovering over him was pasty and gaunt now, and his head had been shaved, but Max had no doubt that the man with the pistol, the man who was about to execute him was the farmer he had spared during his first shift on the ramp, along with his robust wife, sickly teenage son, and elderly grandparents—the latter subsequently culled-out and executed by Radek.

The two men's eyes were locked in tense uncertainty when Cohen dashed into the room after the prisoners. "You fools!" he exclaimed, breaking the moment. "That patient has full-blown typhus! It's lethal and highly contagious! I tried to warn you. The sooner you leave, the better!"

"Typhus?!" one of the prisoners exclaimed.

"He's right. Let's get out of here!" the farmer exclaimed, acknowledging Max with a veiled smile as he lowered the pistol and headed for the door. "Check the meeting room," he ordered the others who were already hurrying toward it.

"Wait!" Hannah called out stepping to the supply cabinet. "You must all scrub down." She removed a bottle of disinfectant from the cabinet and handed it to one of the prisoners. "Head to toe, clothing, everything. Go to the shower hall, now! Right now! Or you'll all die!"

Spooked by Hannah's entreaty, the mob of prisoners wasted no time falling over each other to see who could get out the door first. It would have been comical if not for the fact that it had been so threatening.

Hannah closed the door, then removed her mask as did Jake and Cohen. Three sighs of relief greeted Max as he emerged from beneath the bedding in his SS uniform. He sat up and swung his jackboots over the side of the bunk, letting out a long breath. "He recognized me. I thought I was finished."

"Someone you spared, wasn't it?" Cohen said.

Max nodded somberly. "There is a God..."

"Not without Hannah's quick thinking," Cohen said. "If they'd gone into the meeting room and found Captain Kruger, they'd have killed us all. Nothing could've stopped them then. Not even that fellow."

"You stopped them. All of you. You've got more courage than anyone I know," Max said, his eyes welling with gratitude. He got to his feet and, addressing Jake, said, "I don't know what you had in mind, but whatever it is, we better get on with it."

Jake nodded and broke into a wily smile. Within minutes, he had Max out of his SS uniform and seated in a chair in his undershorts. He fetched some scissors from a cabinet and handed them to Hannah. "He needs a haircut."

Max looked puzzled. "A haircut?"

Jake nodded. "One like mine." He pointed to his quarter-inch long bristle and sat on the bunk trying to catch his breath.

"You mean a lice-cut," Hannah quipped, referring to the scalping which had been made mandatory for all prisoners in an effort to combat the spread of typhus.

"We're also going to need some dirt," Jake said as Max's wavy thatches began falling to the floor.

Now, it was Cohen who looked puzzled. "Dirt?"

Jake nodded. "Dirt. You know, soil, from the ground. The stuff we plant things in? A couple of pocketfuls should do it."

Cohen hurried from the room into the corridor and through the nearest exit onto the grounds. The Spring thaw had softened the soil and the pockets of his uniform were easily and swiftly filled. He was on his way back to Jake's quarters when a member of the medical staff got his attention and took him aside.

Moments later, Hannah was putting the finishing touches on Max's scalping when Dr. Cohen, his pockets bulging, returned and said, "I have bad news…"

"The camp is out of dirt?" Jake cracked.

"Captain Kruger…" Cohen said, grimly. "Massive subdural trauma. Nothing my people could do. I'm sorry."

Jake and Hannah sighed in dismay.

Max's posture slackened. He slumped in the chair, collecting himself. "Otto was a good man," he finally said. "And a fine doctor who died upholding his oath."

They took a few moments to regroup, then resumed their work with renewed vigor. At Jake's direction, Hannah and Cohen rubbed the dirt into Max's scalp and onto his face and neck, working it into every pore; then Jake had Max scrub his hands, wrists, feet and ankles with it, and force it beneath his nails, making certain they became chipped and broken in the process. He kept at it until it had been worked into the lines of his palms, knuckles, forehead, lips and teeth.

When Max had acquired the filthy patina typical of long term imprisonment, Jake removed his ragged uniform with the yellow triangle and prisoner ID number stitched above the pocket and handed it to him. "One size fits all," he joked, though they were of similar height and build. "You'll need to get rid of that SS underwear," Jake went on; and, pointing to the religious medal hanging around Max's neck, added, "You won't be needing that any more, either."

Max winced. He'd worn it for more than a decade, since that day at the Vatican with his parents, and was unhappy at the thought of parting with it. With a grudging nod, he slipped the chain over his head and handed the medal to Jake, who gave it a passing glance and put it on. The glittering disc settled against the sores on his chest next to the key that hung from the loop of string. Max's eyes narrowed in confusion. "What are you doing?"

"The penicillin didn't work; maybe Saint whoever-the hell-he-is will," Jake replied with a sarcastic cackle.

"It's Thomas More, Patron Saint of humanists and statesman. He taught by example that government, above all, is an exercise in virtue."

"Well, we all know what happened to him," Jake said, bowing his head as if waiting for the ax. "They say it's painless. Much faster than typhus, too."

"Don't say that," Hannah pleaded. "There's always a chance. Max and I are your doctors, and we both—"

"Enough," Jake interrupted. "No speeches about the dangers of self-diagnosis. I'm finished. We all know it. You're Hannah's doctor, now," he said turning to Max. "You know what she needs. Please make sure she gets it."

"Of course, I will, but you can't just give up. You can't just—" Max paused, glimpsing his reflection in the mirror above the sink, and did a little double take unable to recognize himself. Indeed, in a matter of minutes, the handsome scion of a wealthy and prominent Catholic family, resplendent in the crisp silver and black uniform of an SS officer, had been transformed into a filthy concentration camp prisoner dressed in an ill-fitting uniform of ragged, striped denim with a yellow triangle that designated he was a Jew.

"Mazel tov," Jake said with a cagey grin.

"Thanks, I'll need it," Max replied, wrapping his arms around Jake's bony shoulders. They hugged each other for a long moment, their eyes welling with emotion. When they separated, Max's remained riveted to his image in the mirror—to the prisoner identification number A198841 sewn on the pocket above the yellow triangle. Indeed, despite the convincing transformation and poignant moment, Max's mind was racing to identify potential threats to his survival; and he had just realized that there was one more thing that he had to acquire in order to fully secure his cover; something that would be of vital importance when it came to being processed by the Americans; and thanks to that horrific night when Radek assaulted Hannah in the brothel, Max was certain he knew how to go about getting it.

CHAPTER FORTY-THREE

The morning after he emailed the two photos to the Bio-metrics lab in Los Angeles, Adam returned to Paul Diamond's desk in *The Times* newsroom to wait for a reply. In the event that Facial Recognition Technology determined the photos were not of the same person, thereby proving Dr. Jacob Epstein was an imposter and possibly a war criminal, Adam was using the time to rough out a much-revised version of his story.

It was close to noon when Stacey joined him. It had gotten to the point where she would come dashing into the lobby with her container of coffee, and the security guard would hand her a Visitor's Pass as she hurried past his desk and through the turnstile that controlled access to the elevators without breaking stride. "Hi…Anything?"

Adam shook his head no.

"I just finished briefing Tannen. Needless to say he's ready to jump out the nearest window."

"Makes two of us."

"What're you talking about?"

"Paul. It feels weird sitting here with him gone. Like I'm at a wake or something."

"So? This isn't rocket science, Clive," Stacey said, pausing to drain her latte. "Just have all emails from Bio-Metrics forwarded to your address."

"Why didn't I think of that?" Adam set it up with a few keystrokes and mouse-clicks; and, they were soon bounding up one of the red-sheathed staircases to Adam's work cubicle on the mezzanine above the newsroom where they resumed their vigil.

A short time later, the anxiously-awaited response appeared. "There it is!" Adam exclaimed, his eyes darting to his inbox which read: biometrics@aol.com. The Subject Box read: FRT Report. He opened it with a mouse click. A few seconds passed before the data filled the screen, and Adam groaned. "Shit…"

"It's a match, right?" Stacey prompted.

Adam nodded, glumly. "Ninety-six percent. Paul was right. This was a total waste of time."

Stacey looked uncharacteristically earnest. "So, that means the guy in the old passport photo either is Dr. Jacob Epstein…which would mean the Dr. Jacob Epstein we know and love really is Dr. Jacob Epstein; or, he's an imposter…who switched passport photos with the real Dr. Epstein…which would mean Dr. Epstein really isn't Dr. Epstein. Furthermore, even if he is an imposter…who we suspect might be Max Kleist, he could be somebody else as well; and whoever he is, we still don't have a way to verify either of the scenarios I just laid out."

Adam rolled his eyes. "Well, Stace, it sort of lacks your legendary copywriter's clarity; but it sounds about right." He kicked back in his chair and stared up at the massive skylight. "The only way we'll get a definitive FRT analysis is to get our hands on an old photo of Dr. Epstein—like one taken during the War—that we know, for a fact, is him."

"Or one of Max Kleist," Stacey added.

"Talk about shooting for the moon."

Stacey groaned in agreement. "We've run out of sources, haven't we?"

Adam nodded. "Tell me about it. The question of the day is: Where the hell's it going to come from?"

That same morning, directly across town at the Simon Wiesenthal Center, Ellen Rother, her assistant, Ben Hertzberg, and an archival shipping specialist were in Ellen's office, preparing Dr. Jacob Epstein's vintage Steinbach and its contents for shipment to the Holocaust Museum in Washington D.C. Each item on the table had been tagged or labeled with an identification number at the time Ellen photographed and catalogued it. Now, the shipping specialist was wrapping the suitcase in bubble wrap prior to crating it. Ben was wrapping the individual items in appropriate packing material. Some in layers of bubble wrap, others in sheets of soft cellular foam, and yet others in plastic archival bags which he secured between pieces of stiff cardboard. Ellen was checking each off on a master list as it was wrapped and placed in a shipping container.

After neatly folding and packaging Jake's striped prison uniform, Ben slipped the dog collar into an archival bag, then took the hardcover copy of *All Quiet on the Western Front* from the table. The eighty-year-old volume, in the original German, had intrigued Ben from the moment he first saw the *Mein Kampf* dust jacket. On discovering Remarque's novel within, he quickly reasoned it had been used to camouflage the gray cloth cover because it had been banned by the Nazis. Now, he opened it carefully and turned the pages which, though darkened with age, were of acid-free stock and hadn't become brittle. He ran a fingertip over the soft texture of the paper and took a moment to appreciate the fineness of the printing, then closed it. He was sliding the book into a plastic archival bag when it slipped from his grasp. Despite his efforts to capture it in mid-air, the volume fell to the floor. It landed on the carpet, spine up, with the front and back covers and about half the pages splayed left and right. Ben gasped and stood staring at it in disbelief. "I…I can't believe I did that…" he said under his breath.

Ellen glanced over with concern. "What happened?"

Ben flushed with embarrassment. "The bags… they're…they're kind of slippery…I…"

"Is it all right?"

Ben picked up the book gingerly, and began examining it. His expression brightened. "None of the pages are torn or creased," he reported with relief as he closed it slowly and examined the cover. "Well, one corner's a little bumped; but other than that I think it's okay."

"It's a very old book, Ben. Chances are it's a pre-existing condition," Ellen said, absolving him. She was about to make a notation on her checklist when something about the book caught her eye. "What's that?" she asked pointing to what appeared to be a narrow strip of wax paper sticking out from the spine.

Ben grasped the half-inch-long protrusion and tugged gently, but it wouldn't budge.

"Careful," Ellen cautioned, "Don't tear it."

Ben stood the book on the table as if putting it on a shelf, and, gingerly, opened it—approximately half the pages to the left and half to the right. This relaxed the spine, which he realized was what happened when it fell, allowing the slip of paper to emerge. He grasped it again, and slowly pulled it from the space between the spine and the bound edges of the pages. It turned out to be a glassine sleeve which contained a strip of 35MM black-and-white negatives. The pages of the book were of a high quality stock that had texture and thickness; and the 287 pages of text along with the flyleaves, and title and copyright pages made for a hefty two-inch thick volume. The spine was just wide enough for the long, narrow sleeve to be slipped behind it; and that's exactly what Jake Epstein eventually did with it on that day sixty-five years ago when Anika Kleist came to the cabin at Partnach Gorge with the forged passports and travel documents, and gave him the negatives.

Ben removed the strip of film from the sleeve and, holding it by the edges, raised it to the light to see a row of passport type photos. They appeared to be of two men and two women; but it was impossible to determine what the subjects looked like, let alone identify them. Because these were negatives, everything was reversed. The blacks were clear, the whites were black and the rest, confusing tones of gray. "I guess one of these guys is probably Dr. Epstein."

Ellen shrugged. "In my experience, probably…is the operative word, there. I'll run a routine scan and enter it in the document log." She plucked the strip of film from Ben's fingers, and nodded to the table. "You keep on with that. Oh, and a…do me favor, will you?"

"Sure. Name it."

"Get a grip," Ellen said with, what for her, was a rare flicker of humor.

CHAPTER FORTY-FOUR

Max waited until darkness fell before leaving the Revier and venturing across the grounds in his prisoner guise. American troops had yet to enter the compound; and Max knew he had to move quickly before they did. He hoped the brothel would be quiet, as it was the last time he was there. To his surprise and dismay, the reception area was crowded with prisoners in a festive mood. Some were chatting in small groups; others lounged on the worn sofas that lined the walls; a few hovered about the desk where the heavily made-up and tattooed Madam was working on a client.

The buzz of her needle penetrated the din. She glanced up from the prisoner's arm, on which she was working, and smiled at Max without a flicker of recognition. His ragged prisoner's uniform, shaved head, and dirt-impregnated skin made it easy for Max to cloak his military bearing in subservience; he bore no resemblance whatsoever to the handsome and commanding SS captain who had taken control the night Jake confronted and killed Radek.

"All my girls are busy at the moment," the Madam said with a salacious grin, making the obvious assumption. "There seems to be a celebration going on."

"I don't want a girl," Max said, uncomfortably.

"That thing?" the Madam said, pointing to the yellow triangle on his uniform with a dismissive chortle. "Forget it. They don't matter anymore."

"I know," Max said then, in as casual a tone as he could manage, added, "I…I came to get a tattoo."

"Ah, same as him, I'll bet," she said indicating a number she was tattooing on the man's arm. The glistening ink read 29/4/45, the date the camp was liberated. "It's quite popular all of a sudden."

Max forced a smile. "I've a different number in mind."

"You can have whatever number you like, love. Your mother's birthday, your girlfriend's brassiere size. It's two Marks; and you'll have to wait your turn."

Max suppressed his anxiety, hoping the Madam would care more about the money than what number he wanted tattooed on his arm; and when his turn came she wasted no time collecting her fee in advance; but her brows raised with intrigue as prisoner A198841, KZ-Dachau, indicated the number sewn above the pocket of his uniform was the one he wanted.

"You're a strange one," the Madam said, her tattoo needle poised for action. "Clients have been asking if there's a way to have those removed."

"It's important for processing," Max said, his mind racing to find a way to satisfy her curiosity. "I was transferred from Auschwitz just after I arrived and...and I wasn't fully processed. I don't want any problems with the Americans. I just want to get out of here and find my family..." He pushed up his sleeve, and set his arm on the desk. "...if any of them are still alive."

The Madam sighed in empathy. "Good luck to you," she said, setting to work with her needle.

A short time later, his forearm stinging from her handiwork, Max left the brothel and headed back to the Revier in the darkness, using one of the narrow alleys between the housing blocks to cut across the prison compound. It was littered with the corpses of prisoners that hadn't been transported to the burial pits due to the breakdown in camp routines. Max was just a few steps into the alley when the deathly silence was broken by the sound of fast-moving footsteps behind him. He turned to see a man stumbling down the deeply shadowed Lagerstrasse pursued by a mob of angry prisoners. Many brandished clubs. One had a handgun. Several shots rang out. The bright orange-and-blue muzzle flashes gave Max strobe-like glimpses of an SS officer's uniform and sent circles whirling in front of his eyes. Several rounds struck the fleeing SS man. He lurched and went staggering into one of the darkened alleys between the barracks on the other side of the Lagerstrasse. The mob closed in around their fallen prey and went to work with their clubs and boots. Max shuddered, then, struck by an unnerving thought, he quickened his pace and returned to Jake's quarters in the Revier.

Hannah was alone. She appeared subdued and saddened. Max didn't have to ask why. Her expression said everything.

"He's left, hasn't he." It was a statement, not a question.

Hannah forced a brave smile and nodded. "A short time ago..."

Max sighed, his worst fears confirmed. "And he was wearing...wearing..." Max paused, the words catching in his throat. "...wearing my uniform."

Hannah nodded again. A tear rolled down her cheek.

Max was aching inside. Heartbroken. Unable to speak. He had sensed the man in the SS uniform who had been shot, beaten, kicked, cursed and spit upon by the angry mob was Jake, but didn't want to accept it, and had hurried back to the Revier, hoping beyond hope that he would still be there with Hannah; but there had been no saving Jake from the pack of rabid prisoners he had shrewdly tricked into executing his plan to help Max survive. "He…he saved my life," Max finally said in a hoarse whisper.

"He'd be very pleased," Hannah said, seeming to brighten. "I tried to stop him, but he said as long as he was going to die, he wanted to die doing what doctors do."

"I'm so sorry, Hannah," Max said, hugging her comfortingly. "I'll be here for you. I promise."

"Here?" Hannah echoed as they separated. "You can't stay here, Max. As soon as the Americans take over the prison, they'll quarantine the Revier. If you don't go now, you may never get out."

"I promised Jake I'd care for you, Hannah," Max protested, knowing he'd be prohibited from returning to the Revier once he had left.

"Not every promise can be kept, Max. No matter how well intentioned," Hannah said. "The Americans may have penicillin, but not for me, not for anyone on whom it would be wasted. I can't say I blame them."

"But there must be a way to—"

"No," Hannah interrupted. "I've accepted it, and so must you. Will you promise me something, instead?"

"Of course, Hannah. Anything…"

"Do everything in your power to survive; and live your life in Jake's memory."

Max nodded, deeply moved by her courage.

Hannah smiled weakly, then took a loop of string from a pocket and slipped it over Max's head. While he fingered the key that dangled from it, she reached beneath Jake's bunk and pulled out his suitcase—the gold-monogrammed Steinbach that Max had given him. The pebble-textured leather was scuffed and nicked. The once polished fittings were blackened and scratched. The white, hand painted lettering that spelled out Jake's name, date of birth, and group number was chipped and slashed with whip marks. "Jake asked me to return this," Hannah said setting the suitcase on the floor next to Max. "Now, go," she commanded softly. "They could be deploying guards as we speak. Take that and go while you still can. Remember, you're not out of danger, yet—you may never be."

Max's eyes welled with emotion. "I'll never forget either of you, Hannah. Never…I…" He hugged her, tightly; then turned away and hurried from the room with the suitcase.

CHAPTER FORTY-FIVE

Deep within the warren of cubicles on the mezzanine that overlooked the *Times* newsroom, Adam and Stacey were still coping with the disappointing Bio-metric report when an email appeared in his inbox. The Sender: erother@swcny.com. The Subject: Epstein CD Addendum.

"Something from Ellen," Adam said as he opened it and scanned the text which made his eyes widen. "They found a strip of negatives hidden in the spine of a book that was in Dr. Epstein's suitcase."

"Yeah, look. There's an attachment."

Adam clicked on the link. Another window began to develop on the computer screen. Seconds later the strip of 35mm negatives appeared.

"Intriguing," Stacey murmured.

"Can't make out who the hell they are, though."

"Photoshop has a contact sheet app, doesn't it?"

Adam nodded, downloaded the data, and imported it into his Photoshop program. After a series of keystrokes and mouse-clicks, a strip of positive black and white images appeared beneath the strip of negatives.

"Look at that one," Stacey said, leaning over Adam's shoulder. "Doesn't that guy kinda look like the guy we think is Dr. Epstein, if Dr. Epstein is Dr. Epstein."

Adam's face screwed up in puzzlement. "What I think you just said is, the guy in that photo sort of resembles the guy in Dr. E's old passport photo—the one Bio-metrics determined is a match to the campaign ad shot of Dr. Epstein—which gives us nothing."

"Precisely what I said…" Stacey broke into a fetching grin. "…with my legendary copywriter's clarity, of course; but there's still no way of knowing for certain who those guys are," she went on, referring to the photos of the two men on the screen. "Is there?"

"No, but we can guess," Adam replied. "I mean, Dr. Epstein said Max took the photos they used on the forged documents, right?"

Stacey nodded.

"Maybe Dr. E returned the favor? Maybe we just got our hands on a photo of Jake and a photo of Max."

"Maybe," Stacey muttered, distracted by something on the screen. "What's that?" she said pointing to the one they thought sort of resembled Jake's old passport photo.

"What's what?"

"That," Stacey replied indicating a pale speck visible in the open collar of the subject's shirt.

Adam shrugged. "A freckle, a blemish, a swirl of chest hair. Hard to tell."

"You might want to try enlarging it, Clive."

Adam went into the tools menu and highlighted the indistinguishable speck; then he kept enlarging it in steps until a blurry image filled the screen. "It's some kind of religious medal. Look's like it says St. Thomas More, but...but Jake's Jewish."

"No shit Sherlock."

"So that can't be Jake, can it?"

"Nope," Stacey replied. "The Kleists were Catholics. The GMA archives stated a Catholic medal was found with Max Kleist's remains, remember?"

"Then this photo—the one Bio-metrics determined is a match to Dr. Epstein's campaign ad photo—is a photo of Max Kleist."

"So, what're we saying here, Clive? That Dr. Jacob Epstein is really Maximilian Kleist?"

"Maybe," Adam said, the staggering implications of their discovery, tempering his zeal. "We better have Bio-metrics run an FRT comparison before we go jumping to any conclusions."

"I think we should have an FRT run on both of 'em," Stacey said.

"Good idea," Adam grunted. He emailed both photos to Bio-metrics in Los Angeles, requesting a Facial Recognition Technology comparison of each be made with the campaign ad photo of Dr. Epstein, which he had emailed previously; then he and Stacey headed to the *Times* cafeteria. Its long expanse of circular white tabletops and stackable chairs ran the entire width of the building. They sat in the balcony that was suspended within the double-height space and afforded breathtaking views of the city.

About two hours later, they returned to Adam's work cubicle to find an email from Bio-metrics. It stated the FRT analysis determined that one of the photos was a ten percent match to Dr. Epstein's campaign ad photo; but that the other one matched with a ninety-four percent degree of certainty.

"St. Thomas More's a match," Adam announced.

"My God, Clive, you were right," Stacey exclaimed. "Dr. Epstein is really Max Kleist!"

Adam looked troubled. "Why don't I feel elated?"

"Hey, I don't exactly feel like doing cartwheels, either," Stacey said; then, she winced, struck by an unsettling thought. Her posture slackened. The steam went out of her. "You're not elated because it's still not proof, is it?"

"No, it's not," Adam replied, equally deflated. "Look, you know how bad I want this Stace; but we don't even know if it was Dr. Epstein's book, do we? That photo—if it is the Dr. E we know and love—is just proof that he once wore a St. Thomas More medal, and that's all it is. It's not proof, let alone proof beyond any doubt—as somebody famous once said—that he's Max Kleist or anybody else for that matter."

"It was in his suitcase," Stacey protested.

"Yeah but, like I said, we have no proof it was Dr. Epstein's book or that he was the person who concealed those negatives in the spine."

"Now what?"

"I'm interviewing him tomorrow," Adam replied struck by an idea that seemed to buoy his confidence. "Maybe he can tell us who these people are." A mouse-click brought the Photoshop menu onto the screen. Several more directed the program to make an 8 1/2" X 11" enlargement of each of the four photographs. As the first image came sliding out of the printer, Adam picked up his cell phone and speed-dialed a number at the Simon Wiesenthal Center. "Ellen? Adam Stevens at *The Times*—yeah, yeah just got it. Thanks---Well, actually there is. I need a small favor."

CHAPTER FORTY-SIX

A week after Dachau was liberated, Germany signed the instruments of unconditional surrender. Radio broadcasts and newspaper headlines heralded the end of the war in Europe. One proclaimed: RED ARMY OCCUPIES REICHSTAD. REPORTS HITLER SUICIDE. Another reported: HIMMLER CAPTURED. USES CONCEALED CYANIDE CAPSULE TO TAKE LIFE.

A Displaced Persons Team from the U.S. 7th Army took over administration of Dachau and acted swiftly to contain the typhus epidemic. The thousands of corpses about the grounds and on the Death Train were buried with the forced assistance of local townspeople. DDT dusting teams detoxified the entire camp. All survivors were tested for typhus. Those found to be infected went untreated due to the scarcity of penicillin and were confined to the Revier. Hannah was among them. As she had predicted, quarantine notices and U.S. soldiers were posted at all entrances. Though her health had worsened, she identified herself to American medical personnel and continued caring for patients more seriously ill than she.

Max spent the time living within the compound as a surviving prisoner. As Hannah also predicted, he was still in danger. Though the presence of American troops had deterred survivors from seeking vengeance, some were still quietly hunting down and executing every member of the SS they could find.

The American military administrators quickly realized Dachau's facilities weren't up to processing the more than 32,000 survivors, and set-up a Displaced Persons Center at another Nazi concentration camp that had also just been liberated. KZ-Landsberg, thirty miles west of Dachau, was in a sleepy river town of the same name that had gained notoriety because Adolph Hitler had written *Mein Kampf* there while imprisoned in 1924.

Max soon found himself in a queue of survivors boarding trucks that would take them to Landsberg—where the threat of communal showers and medical examinations awaited him. Like all men, he was born with a physical detail, one he still possessed, which in an instant could reveal he wasn't a Jew. Indeed, the fact that he hadn't been circumcised could easily raise the suspicion of physicians or shower mates. It would be disastrous for a member of the SS to be caught masquerading as a survivor, let alone a Jewish one. For an SS doctor who had worked on the ramp and made selections, had sent people to be executed—it would be a death sentence.

Though it was mid-May, the temperature in Bavaria rarely got above 10 degrees Celsius. Max was shivering in the early-morning chill as an American soldier with a sidearm and a clipboard checked-off each prisoner on a list of names and ID numbers. Several had already been taken aside for further identity verification. The officer looked at the number on Max's uniform, then to his roster. "Epstein, Dr. Jacob?"

Max nodded, indicating the name painted on the suitcase. The officer's pen remained poised above his clipboard with, what Max had every reason to fear was, uncertainty. He pushed up his sleeve, revealing the tattooed number. The officer winced, then checked-off the name next to it, and waved Max aboard the truck.

Just after daybreak, the long convoy of trucks and military support vehicles left the prison, heading west through forested terrain. Half an hour later, it ground to a stop. The roar of engines and rumble of tires gave way to the sound of distant gunfire. Word spread that a platoon of German soldiers, vowing to fight to the last man rather than surrender, had opened fire on the lead vehicles. The pocket of resistance had to be eliminated before the convoy could resume its journey.

Max was fortunate to have gotten out of Dachau's Prison Compound without being discovered; but the threat of processing loomed. He had to escape somehow; had to get out of the truck before the convoy got underway, again. Leap over the tailgate and dash into the woods? Too risky. Too great a chance of being shot or pursued and captured. His mind raced in search of a way that wouldn't raise suspicion, that would keep the Americans from realizing he was missing, at least, until the convoy reached Landsberg. Agonizing minutes, during which he feared it would start rolling, passed before he found the answer, smiling to himself at its obvious simplicity. "I don't know about the rest of you..." Max said in Yiddish to those around him "...but if I don't get out of here right now, I'm going to piss in my pants." Nearly a dozen men piped-up in agreement, and, as Max had hoped, the English speakers among them prevailed upon their military escorts to let them relieve themselves.

Their wretched prison existence had long destroyed any sense of decorum or privacy; and many of them began urinating in the middle of the road upon climbing down from the truck. One aimed his stream at its tires.

"Hey, hey!" an American soldier called out. "Go water some trees, will ya?" He shooed them toward the forest. Noticing Max had the suitcase with him, he said, "I'll keep an eye on that if you want."

Max shook his head no, tightened his grip on the handle, and kept walking toward the tree line. He drifted away from the other prisoners into a thick stand of birches and pretended to be emptying his bladder. Then, making sure he wasn't being watched, he dropped into the underbrush and scurried deeper into the forest. Having grown up in Munich, Max knew the area well. He circled back to the road, emerging from the tree line far behind the convoy. After several miles, the road intersected the railroad tracks that ran from Dachau to Munich, ten miles south. A leisurely half-day's stroll along the right-of-way would take him straight into the heart of the city.

It was just after midday when the smoldering hulk of downtown appeared in the distance. Munich had been heavily bombed prior to the American ground offensive that had taken the city. The sight of the Frauenkirchen, Munich's 15th century Catholic cathedral, took some of the spring out of Max's step. Its massive roof had collapsed and one of its domed towers had fallen. The Hauptbahnhof, where American troops were now posted, had also been hit. Instead of following the tracks into the terminal, Max made his way from the train yard into the adjacent streets, and on through the devastated Altstadt and Lehel Districts to the Isar River. Bogenhausen, where his family's townhouse was located, was on the opposite bank. Max was relieved the Prinzregentenbrucke, that spanned it, was still standing.

Long shadows stretched across the pavement as Max came off the bridge onto the Friedensengel Ellipse and headed north toward Holbstrasse. The once picturesque street that led to Possartplatz was an obstacle course of collapsed buildings and burned-out vehicles. Many townhouses on the tree-filled square had been damaged by airstrikes. The Kleist's among them. The roof had partially collapsed. Many windows had been blown out. And the front door had been torn off its hinges.

A chill went through Max as he stood beneath the park's budding trees, staring at the wreckage. Was his family at home during the airstrike? Had they been killed? Were they buried alive in the debris? Max hurried into the rubble-filled foyer. The scent of explosives and dust hung in the cool air. There was no sign of his parents or sister. He called out several times before proceeding. The walls of the long gallery that led to the chapel, his mother's office, and the library beyond, were bare. Books were strewn about the latter. The large Kandinsky that had hung over the fireplace was gone. A section of the cast iron balcony had fallen, crushing the piano. Every drawer, cabinet and closet had been looted. Not a single piece of artwork remained.

Max assumed his family had fled the city for the relative safety of their lake house. The phones were out. There was no calling them. In need of a passport and money, he went to the chapel in search of the cash and document blanks his father kept in the tabernacle. Debris partly blocked the doorway. Max climbed over it, took a few steps, and then lurched as if he'd been shot. A horrified cry came from deep inside him. His eyes were staring in shock at his sister's body at the base of the altar. Anika's hands were tied behind her back, her skirt thrown up over her torso, her undergarments torn off, her legs splayed widely. There was a bullet hole in the back of her neck. She hadn't suffered the fate Max feared had befallen his family. No, Anika hadn't been killed in the bombing. She had been savagely raped and executed. In the chapel! He was on the verge of retching when he glimpsed the bodies of his parents on the floor nearby. They were fully clothed. Pools of dried blood encircled their heads like mahogany halos. Their hands were tied, and they, too, had been executed. Genickschuss—a bullet in back of the neck, SS style. The way it was done at Dachau.

Max knew who was responsible. It was Major Steig who had accused him of violating the Nuremberg Laws; who had him reassigned to Dachau and coerced him into making Selections by threatening his family's safety; who suspected the Kleists of helping Jews and others escape the SS and Gestapo and tried to force Jake to implicate them. It was Steig who had colluded with Radek and whose smug allusion to Max's parents and lascivious reference to his sister the night he came to the Officers Club left no doubt this was his doing.

Max was still tormented by the way Jake had died. Now, once again, he felt as if he'd been gutted. He took heart in the natural appearance of his family's remains. Indeed, they were in what a physician would identify as the Fresh Stage of decomposition, which meant it wasn't yet visible; but it also meant they had been dead for only a few days and might still be alive had Max gotten there sooner. He was gasping for breath as he lowered his sister's skirt, then knelt between his parents and cradled his mother's head. Tears ran down his cheeks. He was trying to come to grips with all that had happened when he heard the soft crunching of debris, and whirled around, anxiously. His posture slackened as Kunst, the family's German Shepherd, emerged from a pile of broken plaster and roof beams and came loping toward him.

"Hey boy," Max murmured as the animal nuzzled him.

The dog whimpered in reply, then, lowering its head as if in mourning, hovered over the family's remains.

"I know," Max said, faced with the task of burying them. The Kleist family plot was in Ostlicher Freidhof Cemetery where Holy Cross Church was also located. Family members had been interred there since it was built in the 1860s; it was several miles away in the Geising District. He went down to the garage and found the doors wide open and his father's Mercedes and sister's Volkawagon gone. The bicycle that had been left behind by the looters wouldn't be of use. Munich was a paved urban landscape, except for the Englisher Garten, a vast expanse of woods and meadows on the river; but it, too, would require transportation. Possartplatz, just across the street, was the only plot of land logistically feasible; but it was an unsecure and inappropriate resting place, not to mention Max would have to dig three graves with kitchen utensils or his bare hands.

They were his parents, his sister, and the thought of just leaving them there was tearing Max apart. On the other hand, it was more than likely that the convoy had reached Landsberg; and the Americans would soon discover he was missing. He needed to get out of Germany as soon as possible, and had neither the tools nor the time to inter his family properly; but he knew who he might entrust with the task. He fetched some blankets, and wrapped their remains separately, securing each with lengths of cord salvaged from window blinds. When finished, he aligned his mother, father and sister side-by-side at the foot of the altar; then wrote their names and dates of birth on separate cards, affixing them to each. On a fourth, he wrote that the Kleists were decent and courageous people who were executed for helping Jews and others survive the Nazi horrors.

Turning his attention to what had brought him to the chapel in the first place, Max found the vault-like tabernacle door had been opened. The solid gold chalice was gone, the Hosts spilled across the altar and onto the floor. To his dismay, the packets of cash, blank passports and travel passes were also gone, along with the paintings that had graced the walls. This left him with the cash in his wallet and his German passport.

Night had fallen. Max decided to spend it in the townhouse, gathering anything that might prove useful: foodstuffs, clothing, hand tools, medical supplies, and the deed to the cemetery plot which he found in his mother's office. The elevator had been wrecked in the bombing; and with the dog leading the way, Max lugged the suitcase up three bomb-damaged flights to his quarters, which, along with every other room on the upper floors, had also been looted. Some clothing had been left behind, as were the drawings of prosthetic devices he'd been developing with Jake and Eva. He rolled them up and was slipping them into a mailing tube when the edge of a picture frame on the wall next to the luggage closet caught his eye. The door had been swung back in front of it by the looters, concealing the painting from view. To Max's delight, it was Kandinsky's Murnau With Church, one of the artist's smaller works. Once removed from its frame and slipped into a pillowcase for safe-keeping, Max found it fit neatly in the bottom of the suitcase which he had emptied onto the bed.

The luggage closet was empty. Not a Steinbach remained. Ostensibly, they had been filled with booty by the looters. Reflecting on that day four months ago when he had given the suitcase to Jake, Max suddenly realized what Jake had given him. It was more than a way to survive Dachau. Much more. The battered, whip-scarred suitcase with Jake's name and other data painted on it, along with the tattoo and striped prison uniform, would be invaluable in the days to come.

Indeed, the soiled, ragged uniform would not only deter suspicion, but also garner sympathy; and Max had no intention of changing into the civilian clothes he had gathered, though he made immediate use of a pack of Sturms he found in a shirt pocket. The few cigarettes it contained would be stale, and chokingly harsh; but Max hadn't had one in weeks. The smoke soon filled his lungs with its satisfying warmth. He exhaled slowly, savoring it along with the thought of spending one last night in his own bed. He was repacking the suitcase when he noticed the *Mein Kampf* dust jacket amidst the items. Max smiled in wistful appreciation of Jake's witty choice of camouflage on finding Remarque's anti-war novel within. He had read it as a teenager; and, now, settling against the headboard with his cigarette, he began reading the opening lines: *We are at rest five miles behind the front. Yesterday we were relieved, and now our bellies are full of beef and haricot beans. We are satisfied and at peace...*

The next morning, the dog tailing after him, Max went to the chapel and knelt in prayer next to the shrouded bodies of his family; then, bidding them a tearful farewell, he went downstairs to the garage with the suitcase. The front fender of the bicycle easily supported its weight. Max nestled it snugly between the arched handlebars and secured it with a canvas belt. When finished, he coasted down the driveway and, knowing it would be unsettling, resisted the temptation to take one last look at the house in which he'd grown up. The dog had no such compunction and paused, briefly, before bounding after Max who headed for the Prinzregentenbrucke that would take him across the Isar into the heart of Munich where American combat troops were on patrol.

The University District had been heavily bombed. Carcasses of burned-out vehicles lined the streets and University parking areas. Some had been flipped upside- down by exploding bombs, others crushed beneath debris. The Medical school was in ruins. Sections of the staircase to the mezzanine where Professor Gerhard's office was located had fallen into the lobby, filling it with massive chunks of concrete and slabs of jagged marble. Debris blocked the corridors that led to the hospital wing. The building appeared desolate. Not a person, neither student nor teacher was in evidence.

Max was about to leave when Kunst's ears perked up. The animal started climbing the broken staircase, then paused and looked back at Max, as if waiting for him to follow. Max set the bike aside, then made his way up to the mezzanine where he found the Professor picking through the wreckage of his office.

"Professor?" Max called out from the doorway. Several weeks had passed since Hannah had shaved his head, and he now sported a half-inch brushcut; though he still had the gaunt and grimy look of a long-unwashed death camp survivor. "Professor Gerhard?"

The Professor looked up and squinted through his glasses. Though unable to recognize his former pupil, he knew a death camp uniform when he saw one. "Yes?" he said solicitously. "Can I be of help to you, sir?"

"It's me, professor. It's Max. Max Kleist."

Gerhard gasped in astonishment and dropped the books he was cradling, then got to his feet and embraced him. "Max! My God, Max. I knew they'd arrest you. I always knew you were in danger."

"I still am," Max replied and, gesturing to his prison uniform, explained, "It's not wise to be seen in an SS uniform these days. I need your help."

"Gladly. Whatever I can do."

Max handed him an envelope. "The deed to the family plot in Ostlicher Friedhof," he said, going on to explain his horrific discovery and how circumstances prevented him from arranging for his family's burial. "I was hoping you could see to it."

The Professor was visibly shaken and took a moment to compose himself. "As…as you know, the city is in chaos. Nothing is functioning…but of course…as soon as it becomes possible…" Gerhard let it trail-off and tilted his head curiously. "Dare I ask about Eva?"

"With luck, she's safe in Venice with her family."

"Let's hope so. And Jake?"

Max shook his head, no, sadly. "Auschwitz. Dachau. Typhus. I did everything I could to save him." Max indicated his striped prison uniform, again. "He ended up saving me instead."

Gerhard sagged with despair. "And you, Max?"

"I'm going to Venice."

"Getting there won't be easy," Gerhard warned. "You'd best take your sister's car. The Mercedes is much too conspicuous."

"They're gone. Looted along with everything else."

Gerhard groaned. "Train travel is impossible. I can get you to the Austrian border, after that…"

"I've got a bicycle."

"Good, we'll tie it to the roof of my car."

"I'm surprised it wasn't blown to bits."

"I wasn't here. I was making a house call. A favor to a neighbor. I care for his arthritic mother and he keeps my car running. I don't know where he gets the petrol, but he tops up the tank on occasion too. It was pure luck." Gerhard offered Max a cigarette, took one himself, and lit them. "You know…" he went on with a thoughtful exhale, "…after liberating Dachau, the Americans came through Munich en route to Salzburg. It might be smart to cross the border there."

"No, Brenner's much faster," Max said, decisively, referring to the Brenner Pass. Barely thirty-five miles long, it was the shortest route through the Austrian Alps to Italy and, at the lowest altitude, the warmest. "I have to get out of here as fast as possible."

Gerhard grunted in concession. "You have documents?"

"No, I'm taking care of that next."

"Your parents' contacts are still in business?"

Max shrugged. "I've no idea."

"They'd better be," the Professor said. "The Allies wasted no time setting-up checkpoints at every border crossing." He was referring to the fact that as soon as Germany surrendered, the Allies—despite being at odds over just how Germany and the liberated Eastern European nations would be occupied and administered—had swiftly established Prohibited Frontier Zones to prevent Nazi officials, German intelligence personnel, Gestapo agents and members of Himmler's SS from escaping. "You're exactly who they're looking for Max," Gerhard concluded, gravely. "You're not going anywhere without forged papers except a prison cell or worse."

Max left the dog and suitcase with the Professor and headed for the train station on his bicycle. With luck, his mother's contact at the newsstand would still be in business. He was pedaling down Lenblachstrasse on the southern edge of the Museum District when the sound of cheering rose in the distance. It came from a crowd of civilians on a street corner. They were all looking upward, shouting derisively, and shaking their fists at a uniformed SS officer who, to Max's horror, had just been lynched. The young man's lifeless corpse was swaying from the end of a rope that been tossed over the limb of a scorched tree. Its fire-blackened trunk was a perfect match to the color of his greatcoat.

CHAPTER FORTY-SEVEN

Dan Epstein was waiting for Adam when he arrived at the townhouse on East 79th Street to conduct his interview. Slipping a letter from some correspondence on his desk, he led the way to the elevator that took them to the Epstein residence above the Foundation offices. Jake and Hannah were on the sofa in the art-filled library, sipping tea. Wafer-thin slices of Baumkuchen were arranged in a serving dish on a Mies van der Rohe coffee table. All but extinct, the moist, subtly flavored cake had been made in Munich since the mid-1820s by Konditorei Kreutzkamm; and the Epsteins had had a standing order for decades.

The trappings of wealth, professional excellence, cultural depth, New York's Jewish elite, Adam thought as a round of handshakes and pleasantries were exchanged.

"Good to see you again," Jake said, gesturing to the stainless and leather Bauhaus chairs opposite the sofa. "Please, make yourself comfortable."

"Thanks, I'll just put this here," Adam said, setting his recorder, notebook, and several *New York Times* business cards on the table. "For starters, I brought those photos as your son suggested." He took a sheaf of computer-printouts from his briefcase and set two on the table in front of Jake. Both were of the tattooed identification number: A198841. "This one is from the campaign ad. This is the snapshot taken at Dachau. See? Same number. Different handwriting."

Jake set his cup aside, then glanced from one print to the other and nodded.

"Can you explain that, Dr. Epstein?"

Jake shrugged. "No, I'm afraid I can't. As I said, there must be some mistake."

"Well, no need to belabor it," Adam said, deciding to play his next card which he expected would more than trump the first. "I have some other photos I'd like you to take a look at. Would that be okay?"

"Of course," Jake replied, amiably in his soft accent.

Adam showed him the four enlargements he had printed-out from the negatives Ellen Rother had emailed him. "Do you know who these people are, Dr. Epstein?"

Jake leaned forward examining them, then winced and glanced to Hannah who looked troubled.

"Maybe I can jog your memory a little," Adam said, sensing the photos had struck an unsettling chord as he thought they might. "We don't know who these three are, but we know that this man, wearing the religious medal—it's a St. Thomas More by the way—is you, Dr. Epstein."

Jake flinched and stared at the image in silence.

Dan was standing next to Adam, looking confused. "I'm sorry, but what you just said makes no sense."

Adam nodded in agreement. "That was *my* reaction when I saw the FRT analysis. By the way, FRT stands for Facial Recognition Technology. It's a process that—"

"Yes, yes, I'm familiar with it," Dan interrupted, setting aside the letter he'd brought with him, as he took the photograph from Adam. "You're saying this man, wearing a Catholic medal, is my father?"

Adam nodded.

"That's ridiculous. Not only doesn't he resemble him. My father is Jewish."

"I didn't say he wasn't," Adam countered. "The point is, whatever his religious affiliation, we know from the analysis, with ninety-six, percent certainty, that the face in this photo is your father's."

"Don't discount that four percent," Dan retorted, resplendent in his custom-made shirt, power tie, and suspenders. "I spend my day analyzing investment opportunities. Believe me, the anomaly you ignore is the one that comes back to bite you on the ass."

"Where did you get those?" Hannah asked, calmly.

"From the original negatives." Adam reached into his briefcase and removed the copy of *All Quiet on the Western Front* with the *Mein Kampf* dust jacket that he had borrowed from Ellen Rother. "They were hidden in the spine of this book," he went on, offering it to Hannah. "It was one of the items in the suitcase."

Hannah set aside the wafer-thin slice of cake she had been eating and cleaned the tips of her fingers on a napkin; then she took the book, holding it as if it were fragile, and handed it to her husband with an apprehensive glance.

Jake turned the pages, reflectively; then his eyes drifted back to the four photographs on the table as a flood of memories washed over him. A tear rolled down his cheek. He shuddered slightly and began to cry.

Dan wasn't sure what was happening; but, whatever it was, he knew it was serious and meaningful. "What's this about? What…what are you suggesting?"

"That your father isn't who he says he is," Adam replied, evenly. "That he's a man with something to hide; a war criminal who's been impersonating someone named Dr. Jacob Epstein who died in the Holocaust."

Jake stiffened and stifled a gasp.

Hannah grasped his hand, tightly.

Adam noticed and added, "And from your parents' reaction, I'm starting to think I'm right."

Dan's eyes flared with anger behind his rimless lenses. "A war criminal?! That's absurd. That Catholic fellow in your picture may be a war criminal, but he certainly isn't my father. As I said, my father has been an observant Jew all his life. He spoke Yiddish to me when I was a child. We went to temple together. We showered together, went skinny dipping. To put it bluntly, the man is circumcised. I assure you, even in the Roaring Twenties, the Bris wasn't part of the Catholic rite. My father is a Jew."

"He's also a surgeon," Adam countered.

"You're suggesting, what?" Dan said, sounding incredulous. "That he...he circumcised himself?"

Adam shrugged and smiled at what he was about to say. "Not to make a pun, but wouldn't you under the...well...circumstances?"

"What you're suggesting is an outrageous lie! An insult to my father and his family. You said you were writing a human interest story. You've misrepresented yourself and your newspaper; and I promise you—"

"Daniel?" Hannah interrupted forcefully. "Daniel, your father isn't the only surgeon in the family."

Dan looked baffled. "What? What do you mean by that?"

"*I* circumcised him," Hannah replied. "He formally converted to Judaism shortly thereafter."

Dan gasped as if he'd been punched. "I...I don't understand. Are you saying what this...this *reporter* says is true? That dad was some...some Nazi or something?"

"No, I'm not," Hannah replied. "You're father was anything but a Nazi, let alone a war criminal; but this has been going on much too long. It's time you knew your father isn't Jacob Epstein. His real name is Maximilian Kleist."

Dan's posture slackened. The color drained from his face. "Then who...who was Jacob Epstein?"

"He was your father's closest friend and medical school colleague," Hannah replied, going on to explain how Max and the Kleist family had tried to save Jake's life, and those of many others who had been targeted for extermination by the Nazis.

"You see, son..." Jake said, struggling to keep his composure, "...the stories I've told you are all true; and they actually happened to someone named Jacob Epstein. My dear friend, the real Jacob Epstein."

Dan shook his head as if trying to clear it. "So, that man wearing the Catholic medal really is you?"

"Yes," Jake replied, pointing to the photographs with an arthritic finger that seemed to be trembling. "That's me. That's your mother. That's Jake. And that lovely young woman is my sister, Anika." His glistening eyes shifted and captured Adam's. "Have...have you any idea what it's like to..." He paused, his voice breaking with emotion. "...to discover your entire family's been executed?! To come upon their bodies in your own home?! To find your sister lying on the floor dead, half-naked and raped?! All because...because they..." he shuddered, unable to go on, and began to weep. Hannah comforted him. Dan hovered over them, feeling helpless and confused.

Adam had what he wanted, but needed more, needed to confirm it, and gave Jake time to collect himself before proceeding. "I'm very sorry about what happened to your family," he said, his voice quavering. "It makes what I'm about to say all the more awkward; but according to records found at Dachau and in German Military Archives, you were in the SS. You were Captain Maximilian Kleist, M.D., Waffen-SS. Is that true?"

Jake nodded, his eyes pained with anguish. "I had no choice. They threatened to kill my family. Why? Because they were humane and caring; because they helped people to escape from these monsters!"

"Those records suggest you were one of those monsters, Dr. Epstein, or should I call you Dr. Kleist?" Adam said, maintaining his professional demeanor.

"I've been Dr. Epstein for sixty-five years, a lot longer than I was Dr. Kleist," Jake replied, his voice rising, his accent intensifying as it always did when he became angry. "And while we're at it, you've heard the saying, the uniform doesn't make the man?! Well, it doesn't make the monster either!"

"Those records also state that you worked the ramp; you made selections; sent people to their deaths," Adam went on, evenly. "Is that also true?"

Jake flinched, then bit a lip and nodded solemnly.

Dan's eyes narrowed with disturbing insight. "My God, of course...I recall you saying your friend Max Kleist was in the SS; but all along you were talking about yourself. You...*you* were in the SS."

Jake nodded again. "You may also recall I said he took no pride in it; and was disciplined for having a Jewish lover—" He paused, and smiled at Hannah, lovingly, in reflection. "—all of which is also true."

Dan felt helpless, adrift. This wasn't a matter of guiding the Foundation through a financial crisis. He couldn't analyze this catastrophic threat to his family with a spread sheet. There were no algorithms he could use to forecast the outcome or hedge against it.

"I saved as many of those poor souls who'd been sent to Dachau as I could," Jake went on. "It was horrific and gut wrenching. The knowledge that they would've died, if I hadn't been on the ramp, is what got me through it. I told myself I was *saving* lives, doing what doctors are sworn to do."

Adam didn't know whether he felt triumphant or depressed; but he knew the importance of what he had just heard and what his Sony D-50 had just recorded. "Dr. Epstein, do you understand that what you've just said is an admission that you committed war crimes?"

Jake stiffened as if offended. "You're entitled to your opinion; but be advised when Dachau was liberated, my friend Jake, with the help of other Jewish prisoners saved me from angry inmates and outraged Americans who were killing SS men on sight. Would they have risked their lives to save a Nazi monster? A war criminal?" The old fellow took a moment to settle; then in conclusion, said, "You have the power to demean their sacrifice; but, first, ask yourself: Will it be justice? And if so, for whom? What I did, I did to protect my family, and the Nazis executed them anyway. Yes, they've been honored by Yad Vashem; but where is their *justice*? Where is *mine*?"

"I can't answer that," Adam replied, shaken by Jake's challenge. "I mean, it's not for me to decide how justice is best served."

"Perhaps not," Jake conceded. "But you do have a decision to make, don't you? I hope you'll consider that I've lived my life in Jake's memory and in his honor. Whatever I've achieved as a physician, as a philanthropist, as a person, and, yes, as a Jew, I've done in his name." He took a moment to catch his breath; then, his watery eyes engaging Adam's, he added, "You are young and ambitious and determined to find the truth. I've always admired that about journalists. You're the check on society's worst impulses; the ones who give us pause when we think no one is watching; who call us to account when we cross that unethical or illegal line. Considering our current state of affairs, I would think your time could be better spent elsewhere."

"I'd be hard pressed to disagree," Adam conceded. "But I didn't pursue this story. It came to me; and I can't make believe it didn't. I'm sorry."

"Well, I'm old and I'm tired," Jake said with a weary sigh; then he smiled at Hannah, and added, "And I've had a wonderful life. Do with me what you will."

CHAPTER FORTY-EIGHT

Max had been powerfully shaken by the lynching he had witnessed en route to the train station. Now, as he approached the main entrance on his bicycle, the sight of the news dealer in his kiosk, hawking broadsheets that heralded the war's end, raised his spirits. The fact that the fellow was able to put Max in contact with the forger who had worked with his parents, bolstered them.

Milton Glazer's D-K-G studio was in a garret atop a building in the badly damaged Schwabing District. Though Jews were no longer forced to wear yellow stars—making the snap-fasteners the young graphic designer had cleverly used to remove his, unnecessary—the sign on the door still proclaimed Druck-Knopfe-Grafik.

Slight of build with a daring sparkle in his eyes, Glazer had used his talent and guile to survive the Nazis and help other Jews do the same. He took one look at Max and realized a photo of him as he appeared, now, would mark his passport as a forgery. Instead of taking a new one, Glazer expertly removed the one from Max's German passport and touched-out the portion of a seal that circled through the corner; then he made a copy and riveted it to the Austrian passport he'd spent the afternoon forging. A stamped red letter J finished it, nicely. By nightfall, he had also produced a perfect copy of a Displaced Persons Identity Card. Kennecartes, as they were called, were issued to survivors upon their release from processing centers like Landsberg. Each had a photo of the bearer's left ear and a thumbprint. Both documents were in the name Jacob Epstein with the address in Vienna's Leopoldstadt District as his residence.

"With luck, these will get you into Austria," Glazer said with his endearing twinkle, double-checking the details of both documents. "As you know, passports were confiscated by the SS upon arrest. As you probably also know, prisoner doctors had special privileges. That's your answer if anyone asks why you have one. The sweat-stains, creases and grime are no accident. It's been beneath the insole of your shoe for safe keeping during your imprisonment. Are you right-handed or left-handed?

"Right-handed," Max replied.

"So, it would be your left shoe. Border guards find these little details very satisfying. You understand?"

Max nodded. "You're amazing."

"I know," Glazer said with a grin. "By the way, the Jewish Brigade is operating on the Italian side. So that crossing shouldn't be a problem."

Max looked puzzled. "The Jewish Brigade? I don't recall my parents mentioning them. Of course they never mentioned you either—not by name, anyway. Are they with the resistance?"

"No, they're British Army," Glazer replied with an amused chuckle. "All Jews from Palestine. Five thousand strong. They've been in Northern Italy for months. We hear they're working with Bricha."

"Bricha. That's Hebrew for escape, isn't it."

Glazer nodded. "It's also the name of a movement that assists Jews fleeing Germany, Austria and Eastern European nations. It smuggles them into Italy and takes them to seaports so they can book passage to Palestine. Bricha has been extremely helpful to our people."

"I'll keep an eye out for them."

Glazer's expression darkened. "I heard about your family. I'm sorry. They were more than courageous. This is for them, Captain Kleist," he said pointedly.

Max nodded his eyes welling. He wanted to protest, to say I'm not really SS, not one of them; but he had what he needed and thought the better of it.

That evening, Max lashed the bicycle atop the Professor's car, put the dog and the suitcase in the back seat, and settled next to Gerhard. They drove south through Starnberg, Murnau, Garmisch and Mittenwald. In less than two hours, they had covered the sixty miles to Sharnitz, a town on the German-Austrian Border where a Prohibited Frontier Zone had been established. To reach Venice, Max had to clear the checkpoint, traverse the Alps via the thirty-five-mile-long Brenner Pass, clear the checkpoint on the Austro-Italian Border, and bicycle 150 miles through the rugged Italian countryside.

After an emotional farewell with the Professor, Max strapped the suitcase to the handlebars as he had on leaving his family's townhouse, and then pedaled into the darkness, the dog loping down the road after him. Soon, the glare of floodlights at the checkpoint's gated barrier turned night into day. Max shuddered at the sight of a large sign that proclaimed:

IN COMPLIANCE WITH THE TERMS OF SURRENDER
GERMAN MILITARY PERSONNEL
ARE FORBIDDEN TO PASS BEYOND THIS LINE

Bavaria had been taken by American forces; and the squad of U.S. Army soldiers, manning the checkpoint, had strict orders: Only Allied military and civilian personnel with proper travel orders, POWs under escort, liberated civilians, and displaced persons returning home could cross zonal boundaries. A small group of refugees were being processed as Max approached. Those on foot were lugging suitcases and bundles tied with string. Some had knapsacks slung over their shoulders. Several rode motor scooters or drove cars burdened by the weight of their owner's belongings. A few were astride bicycles. Despite the advent of Spring, many wore heavy coats.

Max dismounted and took his place at the end of the line, walking the bike forward. When his turn came he presented his Austrian passport and Displaced Persons kenncarte, the latter, ostensibly, signed and stamped by an official at Landsberg Center upon his release.

The sergeant had a sidearm strapped to his hip. He studied the passport, looking from Max's face to the photo and back. "Vienna's way east of here. Salzburg checkpoint's much closer. Why not cross there?"

"Because I want to get out of Germany as quickly as possible," Max replied, indicating his striped uniform. "I'm sure you understand."

"Dachau," the sergeant said.

Max nodded and pushed up his sleeve to reveal the number tattooed on his arm. "Auschwitz before that."

The sergeant grimaced then, trying to lighten the mood, he nodded to the dog. "Was he there too?"

"No, but he's been tailing after me ever since."

"Good luck, sir." The sergeant returned Max's documents and nodded to the soldier posted at the gate.

Max smiled and began walking the bike toward it.

"Hold on," the sergeant called out, stopping Max in his tracks. A shiver shot up his spine. His heart pounded. Had Landsberg discovered Epstein, Dr. Jacob, number A198841, was missing and put out an alert?! Had it just arrived at the checkpoint?! Max was about to toss the suitcase and bicycle aside and make a run for it when the sergeant asked, "That all you got to wear?" Max looked back and nodded, suppressing his relief. "It's freezing up in that Pass," the sergeant went on. He called out to a soldier, unloading supplies from a truck, "Eddie, you got a spare parka in there?"

A short time later, bundled in official Uncle Sam-winter issue, Max began the steep, twisting climb. The fifteen mile journey to the crest was a grueling challenge on a bicycle; and despite coasting for long stretches on the descent, the exertion, below-freezing temperatures at altitude, and bone-chilling rain in the valleys took their toll—not only on Max but on the dog as well. It was morning when the Prohibited Frontier Zone on the Austro-Italian border came into view.

The Italian military controlled the checkpoint, now. In mid-1943 when Mussolini's Fascist government fell, Italy became occupied by German troops. The new Italian leadership surrendered unconditionally to the Allies and pledged their support. As an offer of proof, they adopted humanitarian policies, and began collaborating with the British Army's Jewish Brigade to support the Bricha movement; and Italian border guards, routinely, turned a blind-eye to such travelers.

As a result Max had no trouble entering Italy. Mud-spattered and exhausted, he shed his parka and lifted his face to the wind, embracing the warmth that rose from the Italian foothills. He pedaled blithely along twisting mountain roads, passing long lines of German POWs being marched north by their captors. The hill towns of Fortezza, Varna and Chiusa were soon behind him, and he was climbing the hills of Ponte Gardena when the drive-chain snapped. The bicycle coasted to a stop. Max dismounted and crouched next to it, examining the damage. Several links had broken and been mangled by the gear sprockets, scattering bits of twisted metal across the roadway. Kunst settled on his haunches next to Max, then laid down as if begging to sleep. The dog was right. They'd been on the move for nearly thirty-six hours and Max decided to nap before attempting to repair the chain. After several hours curled-up on the warm earth with the dog, Max was having little luck reassembling the broken links when the rumble of an approaching vehicle propelled him to his feet.

A military truck came into view. White lettering stenciled on the door read 8th Army. It pulled onto the shoulder and rolled to a stop. The two soldiers in the cab wore British Army uniforms. The driver saw the yellow triangle on Max's striped uniform, and, in Cockney-accented Yiddish, asked, "Need a hand there?"

"The chain snapped," Max replied without missing a beat, his Yiddish polished by regular use at Dachau. "I'm afraid it's beyond repair."

"Well, I've some lovely folks in the back you might like to meet. Where you headed?"

"Venice. I've a close friend there. You?"

"Ancona via Padua. Venice is just a hop and a skip down the road from there." The driver climbed down from the cab and extended a hand. "Marty Goldstein."

"Jake, Jake Epstein," Max said as if he'd been saying it all his life. It was automatic, unthinking, a moment of impromptu social interaction, a transformative moment that convinced Max he could become Jake Epstein whenever the need arose.

Max left the bike on the roadside and climbed into the back of the truck with the suitcase followed by the dog. It was filled with Jewish refugees who had been smuggled into Italy by Bricha and the Jewish Brigade. With any luck they would reach Padua by nightfall.

The old university town—where in 1305 Giotto painted his lyrical frescoes in the Scrovegni family chapel—had been liberated in heavy fighting on April 29th by the New Zealand Division of the British Eighth Army and CNL partisans. Led by General Bernard Freyberg the Division continued on to Venice where resistance was light. It drove the Nazis from their headquarters in Ca' Giustiniani, a 15th Century Palazzo on the Grand Canal; and took up residence in the Hotel Danieli where the General had stayed on his honeymoon years before.

The drive to Padua proved uneventful. Night had fallen by the time Max bid farewell to his rescuers. He spent the evening in a trattoria celebrating the end of the war with gregarious locals, making-up for all the meals he had missed. Barely two weeks had passed since the Germans had been routed. Trains ran intermittently if at all; but the Padana Superiore, the old public road on which the New Zealand Division had marched to Venice was open; and bus service had resumed.

The next morning, Max bought a ticket and boarded with his suitcase. He didn't have to pay for the dog. About an hour later, the enchanting city came into view. Built on pilings more than a thousand years ago, Venice hovered above the water like a fog-shrouded mirage, the domes and spires of its more than sixty churches aglow in the morning light. Max had come here, once, as a child with his family for the Biennale, the world famous art fair where his mother had made many an astute acquisition; but it was a poignant twenty-year-old memory, now; and as the crisp scent of brine came through the open windows of the bus, filling his head, Max was as awestruck as a first-time visitor, and delighted to see the city was completely intact.

Indeed, as President Roosevelt promised after Italy surrendered in the autumn of 1943, nonmilitary objectives had not been attacked by Allied bombers; and Venice's architectural and artistic treasures had been spared. However, mainland industrial areas in Mestre had been bombed as had nearby rail yards. As a result, the Germans began shipping supplies to Venice by sea; and a week before the city was liberated, the Royal Air Force dive-bombed Venice Harbor, destroying the long wharves. The airstrike had been so precise, the city was undamaged but for a few broken windows.

On reaching the end of the Padana Superiore, the bus taking Max to Venice entered a long causeway. The Ponte Littorio swept across the Lagoon in a two-mile-arc, carrying motor vehicles between the mainland and the ancient island city. It terminated at a massive parking garage in Piazzale Roma. Max set-off along the Grand Canal with his suitcase and crossed the steeply arched Scalzi Bridge into Cannaregio, the largest of Venice's six administrative districts and site of the Jewish Ghetto where Eva Rosenberg's family lived. Skittish in the unfamiliar environment, Kunst padded along close on his master's heels.

Small boats, water taxis, ferries and gondolas were plying the network of canals at a leisurely pace, barely disturbing the placid waters. Not a single motor vehicle had ever been driven on the streets of Venice, and never would be, making sidewalks unnecessary; and every Calle, Strada and Via was filled with strolling pedestrians. But for their attire, it was as if Max had stepped back in time to the Middle Ages, to the days of Marco Polo, and the Venetian empire that had conquered Byzantium and ruled the Eastern Mediterranean. The British troops, who were patrolling the bustling city, were the only reminder of the ravages of war Max had left behind.

It was a short walk to Campo Ghetto Vecchio where the city's tallest structures stood. Since all of Venice's Jews had once been forced to live there, and only there, landlords had taken to adding floors to their buildings to house their growing number. Smaller than two side-by-side football fields, it was bounded by canals and connected to adjacent areas by bridges. From the early 1500s when Jews were herded there—in a defiant, if inhumane, response to the Vatican's decree that all Jews be expelled from Western Europe—until the mid-1800s when they were freed, these bridges were gated and manned by Christian guards. A century later, they had been gated, once again, and manned by SS guards who had sent hundreds of the Ghetto's residents to death camps.

There were no guards when Max arrived. He stood beneath the blossoming trees, his heart pounding with anticipation. Locals were swirling about the verre da pozzo as the carved well-heads centered in Venice's campos are called. Animated conversation and carefree laughter echoed throughout the neighborhood as the residents, freed from Nazi oppression, went about their marketing and daily chores. Max collected himself, then crossed the pollen-dusted cobblestones to No. 11.

The red brick building had Juliette balconies and a shop on the corner next to the street level entrance. Simple gold lettering, on the window proclaimed:

MORDECHAI ROSENBERG

GOLD - CUSTOM JEWELRY - COINS

The sight of a swastika painted on the door stopped Max in his tracks. A workman was scraping off the word Juden that had been painted across one of the windows. Peering inside the shop, Max saw that the fixtures had been toppled, merchandise drawers had been thrown to the floor, glass display cases had been smashed, their contents looted. The Rosenberg family lived on the fourth floor. The dog was still skittish and resisted when Max ordered him to "Stay," leaving him in the lobby, but obeyed its master, dutifully. As the condition of the shop suggested, someone else was living in the Rosenberg's apartment, now. They had no information about Eva or her family, and suggested Max speak to the Rabbi at the synagogue on the other side of the campo.

The wizened fellow's eyes brightened at Max's Yiddish and the name Eva Rosenberg; they saddened as he explained her family was taken away by the Nazis. "I recall seeing her one day in winter," the Rabbi went on. "January, early February, perhaps; but not as of late. I vaguely recall overhearing some talk about a hotel. It escapes me. Something with an M, perhaps. Marco e Milano? Marin Pilsen? Metropoli? Yes, I think, maybe, Metropoli...a la laguna. You might try there."

The thought of Eva escaping the Nazis, only to return home to find that her family had been arrested, that their apartment was occupied by strangers, that their belongings had been either confiscated by the SS, or sold-off by the landlord, forcing her to live in a hotel was troubling. But she was alive and in Venice, and Max had no doubt he would, soon, find her. His spirits soared as he made his way through the maze of narrow streets and over quaint bridges to the sun splashed Riva Degli Schiavoni where the Metropoli was located. The baroque, 18th Century hotel fronted on the Lagoon opposite the Island of San Maggiore, the Punta Della Dogana Customs House, and the Santa Maria Della Salute, a magnificent church that presided over the entrance to the Grand Canal. It was an extremely well-to-do neighborhood; the Metropoli was obviously a first class hotel, not the third rate pensione Max had imagined. How could Eva be staying there? he wondered. Had she come into money? Married a wealthy Venetian? Had his gut-wrenching fight to survive and exhausting journey all been for naught?!

CHAPTER FORTY-NINE

Jake and Hannah Epstein's startling admissions and the old fellow's quiet surrender had paralyzed their son with uncertainty. A long moment passed before Dan touched his father's shoulder comfortingly, and then directed Adam aside to a corner of the library. "Well, you have what you came for," he said, in a deflated whisper. "I hope you'll take my father's words to heart. As you can see, this has been emotionally draining for him and my mother, especially at their age...and for me even at mine. We need some time to ourselves. I hope you understand."

Adam nodded, feeling more depressed than triumphant, now. He was gathering his things when Dan reacted to one of the computer-printed enlargements Adam had made from the negatives—the one his father had identified as his mother. "May I see that for a moment?"

"Sure," Adam replied in a respectful murmur. He gave the print to Dan and slipped the others into his briefcase.

Dan studied the photo, then glanced from it to a framed snapshot displayed on a sideboard beneath the windows. Sepia-toned with age, it was of a young couple, their arms around each other's waist, their faces alive with the enchanted glow that belongs to young lovers. Dan pointed to it, and said, "You know, I always wondered about that picture of you and Mom."

"Why?" his father asked. "What do you mean?"

Dan splayed his hands. "There was just something about it. I didn't know what until now." He held up the computer-printed photo Adam had given him. "You said this is Mom, didn't you?"

"Yes," Jake replied, with a loving smile. "And she's as beautiful, now, as she was then, isn't she?"

"She certainly is," Dan replied. "And for as long as I can remember you've been telling this wonderful story of how you and Mom met and fell in love at Auschwitz; but that's not true, is it?"

Jake squeezed Hannah's hand and shook his head no.

"And Mom didn't have her tattoo removed years ago, because she never had one, did she?"

"No, she didn't," Jake replied, softly. "That's not true either. Thank God."

"Because if it was," Dan went on, "There's no way you could've been together when either of these were taken." He paused and pointed to the framed snapshot. "I mean, that one—judging from the background and book bags, and the way you're looking at each other—is of a couple of college kids who are madly in love."

Hannah glanced to her husband and smiled. "Yes, we were college kids and madly in love. Unfortunately, our friend Jake and I were about to be arrested because we were Jews. That snapshot was one of the few things I took with me when I went into hiding."

Dr. Epstein pointed to the photo of Hannah in his son's hand. "I took that one, and the one of Jake, too. People working for your grandparents, Konrad and Gisela Kleist, used them to forge papers for Jake and your mother who we'd taken into our home. She escaped. Jake was captured and sent to Auschwitz."

"That's...that's incredible," Dan said, overwhelmed, his mind jumping from one piece of the story to the next: His mother on the run! His grandparents Konrad and Gisela Kleist! Catholics! Hiding Jews! Working with document forgers! Executed by the Nazis! Honored by Yad Vashem! He was still processing them when his brow furrowed in confusion. "But you said Jake and some other prisoners saved your life at Dachau?"

"If I may," Adam interjected, "There is documentation that suggests Jacob Epstein was transferred there from Auschwitz."

Jake nodded. "But it was at Auschwitz where he, not I, fell in love with a wonderful young woman; and when they came to Dachau, I was able to save them from being executed—but not from typhus." He grimaced at the irony, then resumed, "After the war, they were lynching SS men on sight. So, I became Jacob Epstein, and, soon after..." he paused, and prompted his wife with a look.

Hannah pursed her lips, making a decision, then said, "...and, soon after, also as a matter of survival, I took that wonderful young woman's identity."

"And...and her name was Hannah Friedman?" Dan prompted, barely able to comprehend it.

His mother nodded.

"*Doctor* Hannah Friedman," his father said.

His mother nodded, again. "When those pictures were taken, my name was Eva Rosenberg."

Dan sagged under the weight of it. "But you've been Hannah Friedman all my life," he protested. "You *are* Hannah Friedman. You've been Hannah Friedman to your grandchildren, to your colleagues at the hospital, to all your friends, and the Rabbi at the synagogue. I can't imagine you're anyone else but Hannah Friedman."

"I know, Daniel," Hannah said, gently. "And at the time I couldn't imagine I was anyone else but Eva Rosenberg; but my name was on a Nazi death warrant; and becoming someone else was better than being raped and executed by some vile monster." She gave him a moment to process it, then added, "I'm sorry, but I don't think I'm up to reliving the rest of it right now."

Dan nodded like a puzzled child. "I'm not sure I am either, Mother," he said, his mind racing through the sequence of incomprehensible events with a thousand questions that only led to a thousand more.

Conversely, his parents seemed strangely relieved. They sat side-by-side in sublime repose, shoulders touching, hands lightly clasped, as if a crushing burden had, at long last, been lifted. Like a breakthrough after years of therapy, the unnerving interview seemed to have served as a liberating catharsis.

Adam was both inspired and troubled by all that he had heard and recorded. There were no more questions to be asked, no more mysteries to be probed. He didn't need to know what happened to Hannah next. He had his story. He just wanted to get out of there and write it.

Dan sensed Adam's anxious presence and collected himself. They were about to take their leave when Dan remembered the letter that he'd brought from his office. "I'll be right with you," he said to Adam as he unfolded the sparkling white page and showed it to his parents. "From the Guggenheim. A thank you for loaning them the Kandinsky."

Hannah smiled and glanced to a bare space on a wall across the room where a pale, ghost-like outline was visible on the white paint. She shifted her look to Adam, and said, "Murnau With Church. It's always been my favorite. I miss it already."

Jake was distracted by something in the letter, and responded with a preoccupied nod; then indicating the signature, he looked up at Dan with a curious expression, and prompted, "Grace Gunther. Isn't she…?"

"Yes…married to the head of our favorite ad agency," Dan said, completing the sentence.

"Small world," Jake said with a reflective smile; then, turning to Adam, he added, "A lovely little painting. It's been in our family since I was a child."

CHAPTER FIFTY

Max was staring at the elegant facade of the Metropoli Hotel, trying to fathom how Eva could afford to be living there when an ambulance boat came racing across the Lagoon. It slowed on entering a nearby canal and tied-up at the hotel's dock, calling Max's attention to the Red Cross banner hanging above it. To his profound relief, Max realized that wherever Eva was living, it wasn't in the Metropoli. It had been taken over as a military hospital; and, with luck, what the Rabbi had overheard had something to do with her working there. Several partisans who had been wounded while rooting out recalcitrant German troops in Mestre, the industrial area on the mainland, were unloaded from the ambulance boat and carried on stretchers into the hotel's canal side entrance.

Max hurried along the footpath that bordered the canal to the dock, and followed them inside, the dog tailing after him. The stretcher-bearers strode swiftly down an ornately decorated corridor and through a set of double doors into what had been the hotel's main dining room. Each of the carved wooden doors had a beveled glass window, through which Max could see the richly textured space that had been turned into an Emergency Room. Teams of nurses in pale blue uniforms and doctors in white lab coats converged on the two wounded partisans as they were rolled into curtained cubicles and transferred to examining tables.

Max was on the verge of following them inside, his physician's instincts driving him to get involved, to offer his assistance; but how would the medical staff react to someone who looked like a death camp survivor? That, and his uncertain sense of identity, stopped him. Instead, Max remained where he stood, peering through the glass, anxiously, his eyes darting from one white-coated doctor to the next in search of Eva. His heart leapt at the sight of a long thatch of raven-black hair held in a clasp. It swayed back and forth across Eva's shoulders as she went about assessing one of the men's injuries. Max was aching to burst through the doors and call out her name; but under the circumstances, he didn't dare. Better to wait and reveal his presence to her, and her alone, when he could brief her on recent events. He stepped aside, and dropped with exhaustion into one of the baroque chairs that lined the corridor to wait for her. The dog padded after him and settled on the floor at his feet.

Under normal operations, the corridor would be bustling with guests and bellman pushing luggage carts. Now, it was used to take water-borne casualties to the Emergency Room and saw little other activity, except the occasional delivery. About a half hour later, Max was on the verge of nodding off, when the doors creaked open, propelling him to his feet. A group of nurses emerged from the E.R. and walked down the corridor in the opposite direction. Max caught an enticing glimpse of a physician's white lab coat amongst their pale blue uniforms; but the nurses soon dispersed, revealing the doctor in their midst to be a portly, balding fellow. Max sighed, forlornly, and returned to his chair. Fifteen minutes later, though it seemed as if hours had passed, he had lost patience and was about to go into the E.R. in search of her when the doors opened again, and a woman wearing a white lab coat exited. She went in the same direction as the others, and hadn't seen Max. He hadn't seen her, either; not her face, anyway; but her long thatch of hair, willowy figure and confident stride left no doubt Max's vigil was over. He took several quick steps after her, then called out, "Dr. Rosenberg? Dr. Eva Rosenberg?"

"Max! Max it's you!" Eva exclaimed as she whirled and came running back down the corridor. She rushed into his arms, hugging him as if she would never let go. Her eyes welled and sent tears streaming down her cheeks.

The dog stood watching as if it understood.

A long moment passed before they leaned away from each other, their eyes glistening with joy. "You're amazing," Max finally whispered. "The professor didn't recognize me at all. You did before you saw me."

"Your voice, Max," Eva explained softly, her blue-green eyes affirming the depth of her love for him. "Your voice...I hear it all the time." Then, finally taking note of his brushcut hair, gaunt appearance, and prisoner uniform, she arched a puzzled brow and, only half-teasing said, "You...you look like a refugee from a death camp."

"I am a refugee from a death camp," Max said, brushing at a tear that rolled down his cheek.

A nurse pushed through the double doors and walked down the corridor. Eva sensed Max's uneasiness and, taking his hand, began walking toward the canal side entrance. The dog followed as they went outside onto the dock. "You know," she said, prompting, "I hear Jake's voice once in a while, too."

Max shook his head, no, sadly. "Typhus. At Dachau." He pushed up his sleeve, revealing the number tattooed on his forearm. "I'm Jacob Epstein, now."

Eva's eyes widened in astonishment. She gasped, fighting to collect her thoughts.

"It's a very long story," Max went on. "Can we go someplace? I'm exhausted. I haven't bathed in weeks."

"Of course," Eva replied. "I live nearby." She led the way along the canal to Riva Degli Schiavoni. The broad fondamenta was bustling with fisherman, sailors from naval vessels anchored in the Lagoon, and British soldiers. "I love the Ghetto," Eva went on as she and Max walked to a working class neighborhood in Castello not far from the hospital. "But I couldn't bring myself to stay there. Not after what happened to my parents."

Eva lived on the second floor of a row house on Calle Grimana. The narrow street angled off Via Garibaldi, the area's main thoroughfare, and ended at a canal that ran behind the buildings. Brightly colored laundry fluttered on clotheslines overhead. Eva unlocked the door to a modest flat that had a main room with a kitchen area and a separate sleeping alcove. She dashed inside ahead of Max and the German shepherd, retrieving a small picture frame from a table. It was the snapshot of she and Max in medical school with their arms around each other's waists—the one she had taken when fleeing her apartment in Munich. "Look! Remember those days?"

"Yes, every minute of every one," Max replied, overwhelmed by the flood of memories it unleashed. "It seems so long ago."

Eva nodded sadly; then, her eyes brightening, she pointed to a door and said, "The bathroom's in there. Water's usually ice cold, I'm afraid." She sat on the bed and, with a seductive smile, began unbuttoning her blouse. "I'm sure we'll think of a way to warm you up."

They spent the rest of the afternoon in Eva's bed, embracing, touching, kissing, caressing...satisfying their insatiable hunger for each other. Deliriously happy, barely able to believe they were alive and together, they affirmed it through tender lovemaking that seemed all but impossible only hours before.

That evening, while Eva prepared a dinner of pasta and fresh bronzino, the latter from a local fisherman who sold the day's catch from the stern of his boat, Max briefed her on the events that had taken place at Dachau. She was in tears when he finished.

"I'm sorry," Max said, holding her comfortingly. "I should've known it would upset you."

"I'm not upset, Max. I'm frightened...for you," Eva explained. "The partisans have been lynching informers and shooting German soldiers on sight. You won't stand a chance if they find out you were in the SS. You'd never get to tell them of the people you saved, or of those who saved you."

Max nodded glumly. "Who'd believe me if I did?"

Eva's posture straightened. Her eyes widened. She studied Max as if seeing him for the first time. It was as if she'd had a sudden and powerful insight, a life-changing epiphany; and she had. "You are Jacob Epstein, now, aren't you."

Max nodded, then smiled at a thought. "And you'll be Mrs. Jacob Epstein..."

"Yes," Eva said spiritedly and without the slightest hesitation. "Yes, Jake, I will."

And that was the moment Maximilian Kleist ceased to exist. As the weeks passed, his hair grew longer, his face filled out, his color returned, and he began looking more and more like the photograph on his passport; the one, Milton Glazer, the clever young graphic designer had transferred from his German passport to the Austrian one he had forged in the name Jacob Epstein. Eva called him Jake, spoke about him as Jake, introduced him as Jake; and soon, the neighbors, and the local vendors, and the waiters in the trattoria and the corner coffee bar were all calling him Jake, along with everyone on the medical staff at the Metropoli who came to know him as Dr. Jacob Epstein. Indeed, the hospital was overwhelmed and understaffed and, having already traded his striped prison uniform for civilian clothes, Jake donned a white lab coat and began working there with Eva; setting broken limbs, reassembling shattered people, and saving lives.

When not on duty, Eva and Jake spent time outdoors, went to the islands, bicycled along the Lido, swam in the Adriatic. And overcome with joy at having survived, at having found each other, and at the prospect of spending their lives together, they began to believe they just might be able to have that life in la bella Venezia.

One evening, they attended an outdoor concert in the Giardini Publicci, a broad expanse of trees and gardens in the heart of the Castello District. La Fenice, the city's legendary opera house, which had been shut down throughout the First World War, had been kept open during this one by the German staff who prided themselves on being cultured; but their largesse hadn't been extended to the Jewish musicians who, having been expelled from the orchestra, resorted to these public performances to earn a living; and they were still doing so despite the War's end. When the concert was over, Eva and Jake walked home along the Laguna Veneta, the dog tailing after them in the darkness. They had just turned into Garibaldi, and were still humming the opening of Vivaldi's Four Seasons, when Eva stopped suddenly and emitted a loud, horrified shriek.

Jake had every reason to think she was either in cardiac arrest or had been shot. "Eva?! Eva, what is it? What's wrong?!"

Eva was trembling, paralyzed with fear. A long moment passed before she pointed to a nearby building.

Jake gasped at the sight of a flyer taped to the wall. Large block letters proclaimed: FUGITIVE JEW. The name Eva Sarah Rosenberg was beneath her picture. It was a copy of the same Fugitive Alert that Major Steig had issued all those months ago in Munich. The same death warrant that he had left on the table in the Officer's Club at Dachau the night he slyly informed Max that Jake had been arrested; that his 'other Jewish friend' was still at large and being hunted; and that her capture was just a matter of time.

CHAPTER FIFTY-ONE

The poster-sized enlargements of the print ads featuring Jake and Steinbach along with other visuals related to the campaign were still in evidence throughout Gunther Global's headquarters; but the sense of accomplishment and excitement of the launch party had given way to a sense of impending doom as Adam briefed Stacey, Tannen, Steinbach and Gunther on his interview with Dr. Jacob Epstein. "He admitted everything," Adam concluded. "Right down to working on the ramp."

Tannen looked baffled. "Why? Why would he do that?"

Adam shrugged. "He was raised a Catholic. Maybe he needed to go to Confession."

"So, you're saying," Tannen went on, barely able to repeat it. "Dr. Jacob Epstein really is Maximilian Kleist, M.D. Captain, Waffen-SS..."

Adam nodded. "He's a Nazi war criminal."

Steinbach stiffened, then his shoulders slackened. He looked crushed. "Jesus H. Christ..." he muttered.

"You're sure?" Gunther prompted.

"Absolutely. I just wanted to give you guys a heads-up, and a chance to comment on the record."

Gunther splayed his hands. "I don't know, I've...I've got questions, not comments. I mean, he's lived such an exemplary life. Chairman Emeritus of Beth Israel, museum trustee, generous philanthropist. What did he say? How did he explain it?"

"He claims he was coerced, that the SS threatened to kill his family if he didn't do their bidding."

"He's always come across as so credible," Gunther said. "Did you believe him?"

Adam shrugged. "No, not really. He can say whatever he wants, knowing there's no way to—"

"Why should we believe you?!" Steinbach erupted, feeling stung. "You think this is going to make up for what your fucking newspaper didn't do when it had the chance? When it would have mattered!"

Adam looked puzzled. "I'm sorry Mr. Steinbach, I've no idea what you're talking about."

"Not surprising," Steinbach said, his tone laden with contempt. "If you're going to write about this, get the facts. All the facts." He leaned forward in his chair, jabbing a forefinger at Adam as he went on. "From the mid-thirties to the mid-forties, *The New York Times*—owned and operated by a Jewish family—ran damn near twenty-five thousand front page stories on World War Two. Only twenty-six of them—twenty-six—had anything to do with the Nazis killing Jews."

"I'm sorry, it's the first time I've heard that," Adam said, sounding chastised. "But I'm writing one, now—with all the facts—as I found them. As I said, I've no way of knowing if Dr. Epstein's telling the truth."

"You're saying, he's lying about being coerced?" Tannen prompted, his voice taking on an edge.

"No, I said I have no way of knowing if he's—"

"Then maybe you ought to back off until you do!" Tannen snapped.

"Hey—hey, come on," Stacey interrupted, once again caught in the triangulated conflict that had become her life: torn between her feelings for Adam, her adoring affection for Jake, and her loyalty to her company—not always in that order. "For what it's worth, Adam said something about this the other day that seemed to make sense: Maybe Dr. Epstein's been living a lie for so long he's come to believe it."

Tannen seemed to soften. "Hadn't thought of that."

"I wasn't offering it up as an excuse," Adam said. "What he believes doesn't change a thing. By his own admission, he was an SS officer. A Nazi doctor at a concentration camp—who made selections."

Stacey frowned. "Ellen Rother said not all of them were monsters. Remember that book...*The Nazi...Nazi Doctors...*"

Tannen nodded. "As I recall, it condemned these bastards, while acknowledging some were conflicted and coerced."

Stacey nodded smartly. "They were pained at violating their Hippocratic Oath. They drank heavily. They suffered post traumatic stress..."

"They decided who lived and who died. They sent people to be executed," Adam added, using Stacey's rhythm. "And Dr. Epstein was one of them."

Stacey could barely contain herself. "But he said they threatened to kill his family. The fact that they did proves he's not lying, doesn't it?"

"Good point," Gunther chimed in. "This is different—if it's true. The trouble is, as Adam has so astutely observed, it's hard to prove one way or the other."

Tannen nodded in agreement. "Which is why as Ellen also said, the DOJ uses immigration violations to get these guys. I mean, there's no doubt the good doctor lied about his past when he immigrated."

"They both lied about it," Adam said. "Mrs. Epstein is not Hannah Friedman, a Holocaust victim who, as it turns out, was in love with the real Jacob Epstein. Her real name is Eva Rosenberg."

"What?!" Stacey blurted.

Adam nodded.

Incredulous looks darted from Steinbach to Gunther to Tannen who said, "That alone could cost them their citizenship and get them deported."

"Adam nodded again. "In Dr. E's case, it's basically the Al Capone thing: He's into murder and extortion, but he destroyed the evidence and killed all the witnesses, so we can't prove it; but we can nail him on tax evasion. The bottom line is, Nazis were prosecuted at Nuremberg for what he did."

"And still are," Steinbach added with an angry growl. "Regardless of age or accomplishments. Demjanjuk just had his ninetieth birthday in a Munich prison where he's finally standing trial. That snake Waldheim had been the head of the U.N. and was President of Austria when they finally nailed his ass. I could go on. The point is, justice was finally served."

"And should be," Adam said. "Though as I told the Epsteins, I'm not in the business of dispensing it. I deal in facts, and the fact is, he's a war criminal."

"But there were mitigating circumstances," Stacey retorted. "Not only was he coerced, he and his family saved many lives. Jake's, Eva Rosenberg's, and others in Munich and Dachau. We know he's not lying about that."

"True," Steinbach conceded, his tone softening. "Yad Vashem wouldn't have honored them without having corroborating witnesses and evidence. Come to think of it, he's not lying about the suitcase either. The Kleists purchased it years before the real Jake Epstein was sent to Auschwitz. It's his name and DOB painted on it. How else could he have gotten it? And how else could Max Kleist have gotten it back?"

Gunther nodded thoughtfully and locked his eyes onto Adam's. "You've just been put on notice. Should you proceed with your story, you're more than obligated to mention the Kleist's Yad Vashem award—which they paid for with their lives—as well as all of Dr. Epstein's good works as a physician and philanthropist."

"Of course. I'll also be obligated to mention that after the war, the Allies declared that the SS was an illegal criminal organization; and that SS doctors were war criminals. Did you know that? People were hung for what Dr. Epstein did."

"You want to see him hung?" Stacey asked, forlornly.

"My job is to get the story."

"They lived it, and you get to judge it."

"No, Stace. *Society* gets to judge it. We do it all the time. It's called the criminal justice system. Evidence is uncovered, witnesses come forward, trials are held, verdicts are rendered..."

"Convictions and acquittals," Stacey retorted.

"The man was in the SS. He made selections."

"Come on, Clive! He was protecting his fucking family!" Stacey erupted, pushing up out of her chair."

"Yeah," Tannen chimed in. "Unlike those weasels at Nuremberg, he isn't claiming I was just following orders."

"Hey, I'm the guy who lived it," Steinbach said. "Half of me would like nothing better than to see that Nazi son-of-a-bitch destroyed. The other half..."

"You'd be feeding your revenge fantasies, Sol," Gunther cautioned.

"Bet your ass I would," Steinbach cracked. "And I love every damn one of 'em!"

"We all do," Gunther conceded in quiet reflection. "Grace spent years learning not to entertain them. It wasn't easy. It's a constant tug of war between the emotional craving for vengeance or, what we've come to call, closure; and the cerebral counterweights of patience and reason, of taking the moral high ground."

"It comes down to 'An eye for an eye,' versus, 'Do unto others'," Tannen said. "Even the Bible equivocates...not that I'm an expert."

"Yes, we live in a painfully polarized society," Gunther went on. "Things are either black or white, red or blue, my way or the highway. No gray areas allowed. We think in extremes and demand simple answers to complex problems; but, whether it be the Middle East, health care reform, financial institutions, or the one we're wrestling with, they're far and few between, if any."

"Well, I've been accused of taking the moral high ground on occasion," Steinbach said with a self-deprecating cackle. "Which is why the other half of me is thinking we probably ought to let the good doctor off the hook."

Adam looked puzzled. "The facts are clear and compelling. Why am I the only one who's not ambivalent about this?"

"Because you're young and ambitious and see this as your chance to make your mark as a journalist," Tannen replied. "And you're probably right."

"Not to mention scared shitless about being laid-off," Stacey sniped, dropping into her chair and swiveling around, coming face-to-face with Adam. "Not that there's anything wrong with that."

"What's your excuse?" Adam challenged, rhetorically. "That he's a mensch who's spent his life caring for his fellow man. And you Mr. Steinbach. You're a survivor of Auschwitz. You have a number tattooed on your arm. Your family was gassed by these monsters. My readers will be really interested to know why you don't want this guy exposed and punished."

Steinbach nodded, appearing to be deep in thought. "The bottom line is, I don't see the good that comes from destroying the man and his family. Why trash everything he's done as a doctor, as a philanthropist and, despite the Catholic thing, as a Jew? It doesn't compute. As Mark said, I'd just be feeding my revenge fantasies."

"But I'm not out to destroy him," Adam said, matter-of-factly. "That's not my goal. Never has been. I'm just searching for the truth. I mean—"

"Which will destroy him!" Steinbach interrupted. "Along with the name Dr. Jacob Epstein—the name of a Holocaust victim. It'll be forever linked to this ugliness...forever soiled and sullied. The headlines will read *Dr. Jacob Epstein Revealed As War Criminal*," Steinbach went on, his face reddening, his voice rising, his pace quickening. "*Dr. Jacob Epstein Nazi Fugitive! Dr. Jacob Epstein Murderer! Imposter! Fake!* The fucking *Post*'ll have a field day with it! *Jewish Surgeon Exposed As Nazi Slicer-Dicer!* The fact that his name is really Maximilian Kleist will get buried in paragraph ten, the Catholic thing even further down. And you know it! It bothers the hell out of me."

"Makes two of us," Gunther said, contemplatively. "As you know, Adam, I'm very close to this because of my wife; and I'm just as conflicted as Sol. We all have the luxury of time, distance, perspective; of sitting back in comfort and evaluating decisions people made under duress and the threat of death before most of us were even born. We don't know what it was like to be tested, to live every moment in fear, in a nation ruled by a psychopath. On the other hand, we all have genuine emotional outrage that cries-out for justice, and we have every right to demand it; and have demanded it. In most cases—whether it be Mengele, Eichmann, Klaus Barbie, or one of the hundreds of lower echelon monsters—there's been no reason to equivocate; but this one...this one's not an easy call."

Adam bit a lip, seeming to be moved by Gunther's impassioned appeal. Indeed, he had become keenly aware that Gunther and Steinbach, the two people with a personal connection to the Holocaust, were counseling restraint. "Look, I didn't come here to be talked out of writing this story," Adam said, sounding more defensive than he planned. "And I'm not saying I have; but..." he winced and emitted an ambivalent sigh. "...you're right, it isn't an easy call."

"Well, it's your story, Adam. You're the only one who can make it," Gunther said with finality. "The sooner the better for all concerned."

"If I walk away from it, you'll run the campaign as planned, right?"

Gunther winced. "Frankly, that remains to be seen. Either way, we have a lot of work to do. So, let's hop to it." He punctuated it with a little fist-pump and strode from the room followed by Tannen and Steinbach.

Adam remained seated, head down, arms crossed, deep in thought.

Stacey started after the others, then hesitated, torn between her professional responsibilities and her concern for Adam. "Hey," she called out, hurrying to catch-up with the three men who were striding out the door. "Just give me a minute, okay?"

"Take two, take ten," Tannen replied. "Take the rest of the day if you think it'll do any good."

"Yeah, kid," Steinbach chirped. "You're our last hope. Knock yourself out."

"No pressure," Gunther said with a little smile.

CHAPTER FIFTY-TWO

The fugitive alert had been taped to the facade of a shop on the corner of Grimana. Eva's apartment was at the end of the street close to the canal that ran along the rear of the buildings. Jake ripped the alert from the wall in disgust. "Steig… He's found us, he's toying with us."

The dog sensed the tension and looked about warily.

Eva looked traumatized. "Maybe…maybe we should go to the Carabinieri…"

"The police?" Jake said, aghast, as he went about tearing down several other alerts that been posted. "No thanks. I've had my fill of document-checks and tense moments with men in uniform. I've also had some luck, and I don't want to push it."

"We have to do something, Jake. It's obvious Steig knows where we live, and probably where we work."

Jake nodded, his eyes clouded with concern. "I don't think he'll chance showing up at the hospital; but the apartment's not safe. We better put together a few things and get out of there."

"I can't believe I'm on the run, again," Eva said with a distraught sigh as they hurried toward her building. "What about the partisans? They'd love to get their hands on him."

"They'd love to get their hands on me!" Jake retorted. "Besides, Steig won't be easy to find. He isn't strutting about Venice in his greatcoat and jodhpurs, believe me." He tossed the alerts he had collected in a trash bin in front of the building. "We should think this through before doing anything."

Eva reached into the bin and retrieved one of them. "If anyone contacts the partisans, it's going to be me," she said with steely resolve, brandishing the alert. "They'll need little convincing to hunt down Steig once they see this."

"If anyone contacts them," Jake cautioned as they entered the building. He left the door open and waited for the dog that had remained outside to do its business. "Kunst, stay," he commanded when the animal appeared, posting it in the vestibule in the event Steig showed-up. Though the dog had become less skittish, it growled in protest, pawing at the staircase. Jake repeated the command and stared him down. He waited until Kunst had settled on his haunches, then hurried upstairs after Eva who had gone on ahead. Jake had just reached the landing when he heard her shriek, exactly as she had outside on seeing the fugitive alert. He dashed into the apartment after her, and froze in place.

Major Steig was in a chair opposite the door, aiming a pistol at Eva who stood in front of him, trembling. As Jake had just predicted, the Major was wearing civilian clothes. His SS uniform was gone but the malevolence in his eyes was still there. "Vivaldi..." he said with a cagey smile. "A little too sublime for my taste but perfect on such a beautiful night. Close the door."

Jake nodded, and did as instructed.

"I promised I'd let you know when your other Jewish friend had been captured," Steig said in his sly way. "Little did I know it would be so easy."

Jake's eyes flared with anger. "The war's over, Steig. The Führer's dead. Himmler's dead. You and your kind are finished."

"I beg to differ," Steig snapped, as he got to his feet, holding the pistol on them. "You think you're the only one with an escape plan, Hauptman Kleist? Please, let's not be naive. No SS man worth his salt is just waiting around to be arrested and strung up like a common criminal. Jews aren't the only ones fleeing from Italian ports!"

"Then flee! What the hell are you doing here?!"

"My sworn duty to carry out the Führer's vision," Steig replied as if it were obvious. "We are his acolytes. His holy instruments. His warrior-priests. Centuries after his death, the SS will still carry his banner as the Jesuits still carry Loyola's. You of all people should know that. It's what Catholics, doctors and SS men—men who have taken oaths—do, isn't it?" Steig stepped toward Eva and cocked the pistol. "It's called God's work."

Eva stiffened, her eyes darting to Jake's.

"Eva Sarah Rosenberg, you will turn and kneel," Steig commanded and, in an aside to Jake, whispered, "It will be quick and painless as it was for your family."

"As it was for my sister? You bastard!"

"The spoils of war," Steig said with an icy sneer. "Both of mine were turned to cinders when your refined British friends firebombed Dresden!"

"That doesn't make us even," Jake said, coldly.

A reptilian smile turned the corners of Steig's mouth. "I must admit there is something strangely exhilarating about fucking a woman before you execute her. An exquisite flower like your sister takes it to a level you can only imagine; as would this one, I'm sure," the Major said, lasciviously, his eyes drifting to Eva. "But unlike you, I have respect, not disdain, for the Nuremberg Laws." He aimed the pistol at Eva's head, and commanded, "Kneel! Kneel at my feet Jewess as you will kneel at the Führer's in the afterlife!"

Eva raised her chin in defiance and glared at him.

Jake was seething at Steig's repugnant diatribe. The man was a deranged fanatic well-beyond the reach of any appeal to reason or common decency; and, despite his anger, Jake had kept his eyes focused on the pistol. At the last instant, when Steig's finger seemed to tighten on the trigger, Jake lunged for the weapon, knocking it off line just as it fired. Eva screamed in fright as the bullet whistled past her and tore into the sofa. The surprising move knocked Steig off balance. He stumbled backwards, tripping over the rug. Jake went after him, grabbing hold of the weapon. The two men were rolling across the floor struggling to gain control of it when Steig drove a fist into the side of Jake's head, staggering him. The major clambered to his feet, clutching the Luger. Jake shook-off the blow and came at him. Steig whirled and drove the muzzle into his chest, stopping him. Instead of pulling the trigger, he grinned, savoring his triumph. "Step back," the major ordered, evenly. "I said step back and watch as your Jewess—"

He was interrupted by a ferocious growl as the door burst open, and Kunst came charging through it. The latch hadn't engaged when Max closed it, earlier, because Steig had jimmied the lock to gain entry, and it had remained retracted. The snarling animal was in mid-leap when Steig fired. The dog yelped as the bullet tore into its chest. The powerful animal's momentum carried it through the air into the Major, knocking him to the floor. The gun skittered across the carpet. With another ferocious growl, the animal locked its jaws onto Steig's throat. Its glistening canines ripped a gaping hole in the soft flesh from which shredded viscera erupted. Blood came in crimson spurts. It spattered the dying animal's coat and formed a widening pool around its victim's head. Steig thrashed about on the floor as if struck by a seizure, his hands clutching at the carnage that had been his throat, then emitted a chorus of sickening gurgles as the life went out of him.

Paralyzed with fear, staggered by the sudden violence, and stunned by massive surges of adrenalin Jake and Eva stood unmoving for what seemed like an eternity. She was still trembling when Jake wrapped his arms around her and took her aside. They held each other, tightly, ignoring the bloody aftermath. After they had settled and Jake had collected his thoughts, he noticed the fugitive alert still clutched in Eva's fist. "You won't be needing that…"

"No. No partisans necessary," Eva said, staring numbly at her image on the flyer.

Jake lit a cigarette, then touched the match to one of the corners. "And no police."

"No police," Eva echoed.

"Unless someone heard the shots and notified them."

"I doubt it," Eva said as the flame crept across the paper, turning her image to particles of fiery ash that rose into the air. "Gunfire's become part of life. Nobody pays attention to it, anymore." She took a few steps and dropped what was left of the flaming page into the sink.

Jake nodded in relief, exhaling a stream of smoke. His expression saddened as he crouched to the dog and removed its collar, then went about wrapping the animal in a large towel Eva had fetched from the bathroom. When finished, he went through Steig's pockets, took the cash from his wallet and, with Eva's help, rolled him up in the carpet on which he'd fallen. Several hours had passed by the time they had cleaned the place up, and it was well after midnight when Jake, shouldering Steig's rug-entombed corpse, carried it from the apartment and down the stairs to the darkened street.

Though gregarious by day, Venetians turned into privacy-obsessed cave-dwellers at night. Just after sundown, regardless of the forecast, they battened their storm shutters as if expecting one of the Adriatic's violent squalls to come raging across the Laguna Veneta at any moment. This peculiar habit plunged the streets into impenetrable darkness, giving them an air of medieval mystery that lasted until morning. Indeed, those sequestered behind the shutters could hear, but could not see, what was going on just outside their windows; and vice-versa for those on the street, adding to the city's nocturnal intrigue.

Jake was approaching the canal at the end of the street when the soft throb of an engine rose in the darkness. Bent beneath Steig's weight, he took cover in a doorway as the prow of a small boat emerged from behind the buildings. The weathered skiff motored slowly past the opening between them, its dim running light sending shadows stretching across the cracked stucco. Jake waited until the sound had faded before proceeding to the narrow fondamenta that bordered the canal. He lowered his cargo to the pavement and wasted no time rolling it into the placid waters. It sank quickly beneath the brackish surface, emitting a stream of bubbles. Jake tossed the pistol in after it and returned to the apartment for the dog.

The thought of disposing of the animal as they had Steig brought both Jake and Eva to tears. It was a short walk through the desolate, darkened streets to the Public Gardens where they had attended the concert earlier. Jake concealed the towel-shrouded animal in an out of the way thicket of boxwoods, concealing it with stones that he and Eva gathered. He remained on one knee for a long moment, reflecting on his parents and sister. He had done for the dog what he hadn't been able to do for them; and hoped the Professor had been able to arrange for their proper internment.

The following morning after a few hours of fitful sleep, Jake and Eva walked to the Lagoon and sat on the seawall, looking across to San Giorgio Maggiore, the Lido and the Venetian Gulf beyond. Seagulls soared overhead in sweeping arcs, piercing the misty silence with their plaintive screaks. Jake took a deep breath of the sea air, and let it out slowly, savoring its briny freshness, then lit a cigarette and watched the smoke taken off in long thin streams by the wind.

"You know," Eva said, more chilled by a thought than the dampness and rolling fog. "Steig was right. Just because the Nazis are on the run; doesn't mean they'll all be caught, let alone cured of this madness."

"Not in a million years," Jake said, shaken by her insight. "It was insane to equate the SS with Jesuits and doctors. Steig was so deranged, he couldn't see that neither we, nor the priests, are sworn to evil as he was; but he was right about blindly obedient men, blindly loyal to an oath, being driven to fulfill the Führer's vision long after his death."

"Yes," Eva said, shuddering. "His prediction is so chilling because it's so eerily astute. There must be thousands of those death warrants with my name on them; and a month from now, or a year, or even twenty years for that matter, one of these obsessed monsters will find one, and come looking for me."

"For Eva Sarah Rosenberg," Jake said, pointedly.

Eva's eyes narrowed in uncertainty. "What are you suggesting?"

"Well, I have a new identity; maybe you should have one too. Do you still have the papers? The ones my parents got for you?"

Eva shook her head no. "Lisl Hausmann is long gone. The Gestapo was after one of the Jewish nurses at the hospital. The partisans were hiding her. I gave them my papers. They changed the picture, bleached out the signature...I don't know what happened to her."

"Do you know who altered them?"

"I've no idea; but I could find out. Why?"

"Well, our dear Jake fell in love with a woman he met at Auschwitz. I was thinking..."

"Really?" Eva said, her expression brightening. "How wonderful for him. If even for a short time."

"And for her as well," Jake added. "She was quite lovely, intelligent and courageous. A fine physician, too. Reminded me of someone I know," he concluded with a sideways glance.

"I see..." Eva said, playing along.

"The camp was overrun with typhus," Jake went on. "It was inevitable she caught it." He paused and took a thoughtful drag on his cigarette. "I promised her if I survived, I'd live my life in Jake's memory. All things considered, I was thinking, it might be appropriate for you to..." He let it trail off, implying the rest was obvious.

"...to live my life in hers," Eva said, slowly, taking a moment to contemplate the idea. "Yes, all things considered, I suppose it would, wouldn't it?"

Jake nodded, solemnly.

"So...So, then, who am I?"

"Her name was Hannah. Hannah Friedman."

"Hannah Friedman," Eva echoed, trying it out. "I never thought of myself as a Hannah, but it's a nice enough name. I guess I could get used to it."

"Me too," Jake said with an endearing smile. "And as soon as we can get papers forged, it will be yours."

"And then what? Everyone knows me as Eva Rosenberg. It might be possible to stay here with a new identity; but it would be complicated..."

"...and dangerous," Jake added, his eyes narrowing in concern. "We can't go back to Munich. I don't dare come forward and announce I'm Max Kleist, heir to the metal works fortune."

"No you don't dare," Eva said with a spirited toss of her head. "Both our families are gone. There's nothing holding us here. I've heard about a hospital in New York. A Jewish hospital. Since the mid-'30s they've had a special program to hire doctors fleeing the Nazis."

"Yes, I've heard of it, too. Mount Sinai as I recall."

Eva nodded. "I was thinking maybe they could use a top-notch team of orthopedic surgeons." She grinned, and added, "Jewish orthopedic surgeons."

"And if they can't, I have a way to convince them they should."

Eva looked puzzled.

"The prosthetics. The ones we were developing at school. I have all the drawings with me."

Eva's eyes filled with hope. "Well, they'd convince me," she said, smiling at a thought. "Though if you're going to be working in a Jewish hospital, Dr. Epstein, there is one thing you might not want to have with you any longer; one little detail that could reveal you aren't Jewish."

"I've noticed it," Jake said with a little wince. "I came within a hare's breath of compulsory showers and physicals at a Displaced Persons Camp."

"Well, as you may recall, I'm pretty good with a scalpel," Eva said with a mischievous grin. "I might even reduce my fee; after all, I have a vested interest in seeing the procedure done properly."

Later that day, after fetching a few items from the hospital, Eva employed the most basic of her vaunted surgical skills, and removed the last bit of evidence that could reveal Jacob Epstein wasn't a Jew. That evening, while Jake was recovering on the sofa, Eva settled next to him with her sewing box and went about mending the bullet-torn bolster.

"Now, all we have to do is get to New York City," Jake said, squirming in discomfort.

Eva paused in mid-stitch and raised a concerned brow. "Easier said than done. Everyone wants to go to America now. Berths have become quite expensive. It'll be a while before we can save enough to replace that rug, let alone buy passage to New York."

Jake looked off in thought. "Maybe not." He walked across the room, gingerly, fetched the suitcase from a closet, and set it on the rug in the sleeping alcove.

"Ah, the proverbial suitcase full of money…"

"Not exactly." Jake slipped the key from around his neck and showed it to Eva. "Traded my St. Thomas More medal for it," he said with a wistful smile; then he unlocked the suitcase and raised the lid. The striped uniform had been thrown atop the other contents. Eva watched curiously as Jake reached beneath them, found what he wanted, and with a magician's flourish, removed the protective pillowcase, revealing the Kandinsky. "Murnau With Church," he announced holding it up. "It should fetch enough for a couple of tickets."

"And a rug," Eva said with a laugh, her eyes brightening at the sight of it. "It's beautiful. I remember it from your room."

Jake nodded, almost sadly.

"It's my favorite, Jake. Don't you even think of selling it. I'll…I'll…I'll sell my body first."

"You'll have no shortage of buyers," Jake said, pulling her into an embrace and nuzzling her.

Eva wiggled her brows, fetchingly, and slipped from his grasp, her hair sweeping across her shoulders as she spun away from him. "As your surgeon," she said with a giggle, "I don't think your little buddy there is up to what you're contemplating."

Jake winced. "How could I forget?"

"…and stop trying to change the subject," Eva went on. "The painting goes back in the suitcase. I mean it. Put it back in there. Now."

Jake nodded like a chastised child. He slipped the Kandinsky back into the pillowcase and did as instructed.

"Take good care of that," Eva cautioned as Jake closed it and snapped the latches.

"I know, Eva, I know, it's your favorite."

Eva smiled, charmed by his naïveté. "I was referring to the suitcase. It's your Jewish passport, Jake. That, and the number on your arm, are irrefutable, empirical, historical proof of who you are."

Jake nodded, taken with her prescience." I know, they've already served me well."

"You might want to do something about that," Eva said, pointing to the double-K monogram near the handle.

Jake nodded again, then fetched a kitchen knife and began scraping-off the tiny letters. The bits of hot-stamped gold fell onto the rug making the pile sparkle. When finished, Jake stared at the battered, whip-scarred suitcase for a long moment then, with a gentle touch of reassurance, ran his fingertips over the thickly-painted lettering that spelled out Jacob Epstein. "In your memory," he said softly.

CHAPTER FIFTY-THREE

After getting her marching orders from Tannen, Steinbach and Gunther, Stacey closed the door and crossed the office to where Adam was sitting. She came up behind his chair, wrapped her arms around his shoulders and, in a soft voice, said, "Between a rock and a hard place, aren't you, Clive?"

Adam swiveled around to face her and nodded glumly.

"Well, welcome to the club." There was nothing sassy in Stacey's tone, now, just heartfelt empathy. "What are you going to do?"

Adam shrugged, then pushed up out of the chair and crossed to one of the tall, bronze-tinted windows that looked out across the city. The late afternoon sun was sitting above the Palisades, sending magenta rays streaming down the crosstown streets and across the avenues where vehicles were crawling in Manhattan's rush hour gridlock. Thousands of workers were hurrying from office buildings and shops in the direction of Grand Central, streaming into subway entrances, hailing taxis, and heading for local watering holes while thumbing their cell phones and Blackberrys. Adam was watching them dragging long shadows across the pavement, their minds focused on their families, their lives, their friendships and love affairs, their newspapers and novels, the coming weekend, the state of the economy, of the Yankees and the Mets, when Stacey appeared beside him. She stood in silence for a moment, looking down at the street.

"Well?"

Adam turned to face her, and let out an uncertain breath. "I don't know, Stace. Do me a favor, will you?"

"If I can…"

"Put your feelings for the old guy on hold, forget what's at stake for your company and client, make believe I'm a stranger and, for a moment, just a moment, become one of them down there, okay?"

Stacey nodded dutifully.

"Now, knowing all that you know," Adam said, softly, holding her eyes with his, "What would you do?"

EPILOGUE

As Adam requested, Stacey made a conscious effort to set aside her first hand knowledge and feelings, and make an objective assessment of the dilemma he faced. "Not an easy one," she said after spending some time looking out the window to the street, wrestling with it. "But human nature being what it is, I figure half the folks down there would say, 'Blow the whistle on that miserable Nazi. Write your story and let the chips fall where they may.' The other half, like Sol and Gunther, would say, 'Why destroy an obviously decent man? Spike it. And let the good doctor off the hook...'"

"And you?"

"Me? Come on, Clive, you know where I'm at on this," Stacey replied with a wince. "For openers, I'd forget I ever noticed the same prisoner ID number was tattooed in different handwriting..."

Adam raised a brow and cocked his head evaluating it. "It sounds like you're suggesting I dispense with my legendary certainty and professional detachment..."

"Sure am," Stacey said, brightening at his compliant tone. "Then I'd delete all your computer files, erase the data chip in your recorder, and make a beeline for the nearest shredder with your notebook."

Adam nodded, thoughtfully, digesting it; then he slipped the spiral bound pad from a pocket and handed it to her. "Here you go..."

Stacey took the notebook and studied Adam's eyes. "You sure about that, Clive?"

Adam held her look unblinkingly and nodded.

Despite Adam's decision to bury the story, Gunther, Tannen and Stacey subsequently determined it would be unethical, indeed unconscionable and professionally dangerous for the agency and for their client to proceed with the campaign as planned.

Sol Steinbach had little choice but to agree when they advised that the kick-off ads featuring him and Dr. Jacob Epstein be withdrawn; but he was heartbroken over losing the opportunity it had presented to keep the memory of the Holocaust alive. "Well kid," he said to Stacey, half-heartedly. "You saved my ass more than once. I can't imagine there's anything left in that bag of tricks; but if there is, now's the time."

Stacey shrugged at the obvious impossibility of it, and then tilted her head in thought. A few moments passed before her eyes flashed with a mischievous twinkle at an idea that occurred to her. Tannen, Gunther, and Steinbach exchanged puzzled looks as she dashed across the office and fetched one of the discarded kick-off posters of Steinbach standing next to Dr. Jacob Epstein seated on his vintage suitcase. The three men became further mystified when Stacey tore it in half top to bottom and handed one of the pieces to Steinbach. It was the half that depicted him in his warrior-like pose with arms crossed against his chest, displaying his Auschwitz tattoo. "Roll up your sleeves Mr. S!" Stacey exclaimed with a grin. "Be a tough, proud Holocaust survivor. Roll up your sleeves and stick it to those Nazi bastards!"

The following week, full page ads with the copy line SURVIVING HARROWING JOURNEYS centered above a gritty black and white image of Steinbach with his own vintage suitcase ran in magazines and newspapers the world over.

Concurrently, *The New York Times* published a human interest story, under Adam's byline, about a Holocaust survivor who was five years old when Auschwitz was liberated, escaped from Communist East Germany with his uncle, and came to America; and about how, more than sixty years after surviving that harrowing journey, and rebuilding the family business into an extremely successful manufacturer of high quality luggage, Solomon Steinbach had become not only the company's CEO but also its advertising spokesman. He was especially proud that each advertisement carried the following secondary copy line:

A PORTION OF THE PROFITS WILL BE CONTRIBUTED BY STEINBACH & COMPANY TO THE SIMON WIESENTHAL CENTER TO EXPLORE ISSUES OF PREJUDICE, TEACH TOLERANCE, AND FIGHT ANTI-SEMITISM.

CPSIA information can be obtained at www.ICGtesting.com
Printed in the USA
BVOW020440050313

314742BV00010B/263/P